THE WATCHER IN THE WALL

< Owen Laukkanen >

THE WATCHER
IN THE WALL

A Stevens and Windermere Novel

G. P. Putnam's Sons   >   New York

PUTNAM

G. P. PUTNAM'S SONS
Publishers Since 1838
An imprint of Penguin Random House LLC
375 Hudson Street
New York, New York 10014

Library of Congress Cataloging-in-Publication Data

Laukkanen, Owen.
  The watcher in the wall : a Stevens and Windermere novel / Owen Laukkanen.
    p.   cm.
  ISBN 978-0-399-17454-4
  I. Title.
  PR9199.4.L384W38   2016   2015026298
  813'.6—dc23

Printed in the United States of America
10 9 8 7 6 5 4 3 2 1

Book design by Meighan Cavanaugh

For Shannon

THE WATCHER IN THE WALL

< **1** >

It was time.

Adrian Miller had planned to wait, a few more days, another week, maybe. Hell, when he woke up for school that morning, before school, he wasn't even sure he would do it anymore. He'd thought about his mom and dad and sister, about Lucas, and wondered what kind of monster would want to hurt them the way he was planning. He'd hugged his parents good-bye and walked out the front door, and it was a beautiful fall morning, crisp and bracing and clear, and he'd decided, *Not yet*. Maybe not ever.

But then he showed up at school, and it all started again.

Lucas wouldn't talk to him. Lucas *never* talked to him, not in public, anyway. Lucas avoided his eyes in the hallway, wouldn't eat lunch with him, made him wait until the final bell rang and they could go to the park, or to Lucas's dad's basement, somewhere far away from school and Lucas's real friends.

Today, though, Lucas acted even more distant. Wouldn't even answer Adrian's texts. Laughed along with his friends when they mocked Adrian in math class, when someone poured water on his seat, so that when he sat down it seemed like he'd pissed himself. He'd glared over at the jocks in the corner, Lucas among them, all of them pointing and laughing and losing their minds, snapping pictures to upload to Facebook. Lucas was laughing with them. Lucas didn't even have the courtesy to look away, even when Adrian caught his eye, like, *What the hell, man?*

Like, *I thought you were my friend.*

The pictures showed up online by lunchtime. Followed him around for the rest of the day. By the time the final bell rang, he'd forgotten how happy he'd felt that morning. He'd remembered why he wanted to do it.

And now it was time.

He was alone in the house. His parents wouldn't be home for another couple of hours at least. His little sister was off with her friends. He set his backpack on the bed and opened up his laptop, heard the chime from a hundred and one Facebook notifications.

Fag.

Loser.

Fucking skid.

He opened a new window in his browser. Logged on to the website he visited most. Found Ambriel98 and opened a chat window.

I think I'm ready. I think I'm going to do it today.

A long pause. He pictured Ambriel on the other side of the screen, staring into her own laptop somewhere in Pennsylvania. Wondered if she'd try and stop him.

She didn't.

It's the right decision, she typed. *U'll be in a better place.*

At least I won't be in this place, he replied.

I wish I had your balls.

He kind of laughed, despite himself. *Take them.*

Turn your webcam on if you're doing it, she typed. *Your microphone, too, like we talked about. You'll inspire me. You'll inspire so many people like us.*

He surveyed his room. Wondered if he was really ready to do this. Heard the chime from Facebook again, another asshole he couldn't avoid, even in his own bedroom. Pictured going through another year of this shit, graduating, and then what?

More shit, probably.

More assholes.

Never any escape.

He dug into the bottom drawer of his desk. Pulled out the bottle he'd stolen from his dad, uncapped it, and took a drink. Grimaced at the burn. Then he turned back to his laptop. Screw it. He was ready.

Get ready for the show, he told Ambriel as he switched on his webcam. *See you on the other side.*

< 2 >

The phone wouldn't stop ringing.

Carla Windermere looked up from her computer, irritated. Looked across the small office to her partner's empty workstation, then out into the hall and the Criminal Investigative Division beyond. Kirk Stevens had disappeared somewhere, and he'd left his dinky old cell phone behind.

Windermere pushed herself out of her chair, crossed to Stevens's desk, where the cell phone kept bleating its tinny electronic ringtone. She snatched up the phone, walked to the doorway, and scanned CID, fully intending to give her partner a lecture on the merits of his handset's "silent" feature. But there was no sign of Stevens anywhere.

Windermere was still getting used to the whole partner thing. She'd worked with Stevens, a special agent with Minnesota's Bureau of Criminal Apprehension, on a number of high-profile cases during her four years at the FBI's Minneapolis office. She liked the man, a twenty-year cop with sharp instincts and a steady aim, figured they worked well together—and history proved it. But when their bosses had decided to put them together on a joint FBI-BCA violent crimes task force, they'd shunted Stevens into the FBI building, given him an office with Windermere. And Windermere still wasn't sure how she felt about sharing.

Still clutching Stevens's phone, Windermere walked deeper into the CID bullpen, splitting the rows of cubicles until she came to Derek Mathers's desk. "Seen Stevens?"

Mathers grinned up from his computer when he saw her. He was a junior agent, a boyish, good-looking Wisconsin farm boy. He'd also managed to thaw Windermere's heart enough that lately she'd been calling him her boyfriend, despite how much the lovey-dovey stuff nauseated her.

"Stevens? No idea," Mathers said. "You try the kitchen?"

The phone shut off. Stayed silent a moment. Then it started back up again. Around CID, people poked their heads up from their cubicles.

"I swear, the bastard's doing this to piss me off," Windermere said.

Stevens was just replacing the coffeepot when she walked into the break room. "Carla," he said. "You want coffee? Fresh pot."

"I swear to God, Stevens, if this thing keeps ringing, I'm going to answer it myself," she said, brandishing the phone. "And I can't be held responsible for what happens next."

Stevens made his eyes wide. Put down the pot and his coffee mug, crossed the break room to the door. "Give it here," he said. "The last thing I need is you swapping more stories with my wife."

He took the phone, flipped it open. "Agent Stevens," he said, ducking out into the hallway.

Windermere savored the silence for a moment. Regarded the coffeepot. *As long as I'm here.* She poured herself a cup. Replaced the pot. Left the break room and found Stevens standing in the hall, staring at his phone, pale.

"You okay?" she asked.

"That was Andrea," Stevens told her. "There was an incident at her school. I have to go get her. One of her classmates, uh, well, I guess he killed himself."

Windermere felt something twinge inside her, something small and tucked away and long forgotten. "Shit," she said. "Stevens, that's awful."

"Yeah," Stevens said, still staring at the phone. "Andrea's a mess. I should—"

"Go, definitely. Get out of here."

Stevens nodded. Walked off down the hall like he was in a kind of daze. Windermere watched him go, all the way back through CID to the bank of elevators on the far wall. Watched him until he'd disappeared, and wondered why she wasn't moving.

< 3 >

"His name was Adrian Miller," Kirk Stevens told his wife. "His parents found him in the bedroom when they got home from work yesterday. They figure he did it about as soon as he came home from school."

Across the dining room table, Andrea Stevens wiped her eyes with a Kleenex. "He was in my math class," she told her parents. "Some asshole jocks from the football team poured water on his chair yesterday and took pictures of it when he sat down. It was all over Facebook."

She blew her nose. Glanced at her mom. "Sorry for swearing," she said quietly.

Nancy Stevens waved her off. Dabbed at her own eyes. "Kids can be so mean."

Stevens nodded. Had nothing to say. He'd driven to the school as soon as Andrea called, found her with her boyfriend and the rest of her classmates, along with the principal and a couple of grief counselors besides. Three weeks into senior year, everybody was still wearing the last of their summer tans, nobody prepared for this.

He'd called his wife at the law office, and she picked up JJ, their eleven-year-old son, brought him back home for a family day.

"He was just a quiet kid," Andrea said. "He dressed kind of funny, and he didn't have any friends, but he was a nice guy, anyway. There was nothing *wrong* with him."

"Why didn't he have any friends?" JJ asked.

"I don't know," Andrea said. "People were always picking on him, that's all." Her face seemed to crumple. "It's all just so *stupid*."

You got that right, Stevens thought. He'd dealt with plenty of different kinds of cruelty during his career as a BCA investigator, but the ways kids had of tormenting each other still made his stomach turn. Andrea, smart and athletic and popular, had managed to avoid the worst of the bullying, thank God. But JJ would be starting high school soon enough, and who could say how his classmates would treat him?

Andrea looked up. "You have to do something, Dad. You have to make it so the people who did this to Adrian have to pay."

Stevens swapped glances with his wife. "I don't know if there's anything I *can* do, Ange. This kind of thing, it's probably too late to solve anything. There's not really any point in mucking people around."

"You're a cop. Adrian's *dead*. Aren't you supposed to punish the responsible parties?"

Nancy rubbed Andrea's back. "He can't just arrest all those jocks, honey," she said. "It wouldn't solve anything, anyway. It's not going to bring Adrian back, no matter who gets arrested."

"You have to do *something*, Dad. You can't just let people get away with this."

Stevens studied his daughter across the table, her fierce eyes. *She has her mom's sense of justice,* he thought. *Always fighting for the underdog.* It was the quality he admired most in his wife, a brilliant law mind who'd turned her back on a comfortable salary to work Legal Aid for the city's downtrodden. It warmed Stevens's heart to know his daughter had inherited the same passion.

"Let me see what I can do," he told Andrea. "I can't promise it'll make you feel any better, but maybe I can make a few calls."

< **4** >

Windermere had tried to get back to work after Stevens left. She'd had a whole pile of paperwork to process, the last hoops to jump through on a sex-trafficking case she and Stevens closed during the summer. Had all afternoon to work on it, her office blissfully free of any distractions, any annoying ringtones, but somehow the work didn't get done.

"It's nothing," she told Mathers at dinner that night. "I'm fine, Derek. No big deal."

They'd gone back to her condo in downtown Minneapolis, as usual. Were supposed to do some cooking, had all the ingredients for a kick-ass ceviche. Windermere had started her career in Miami; she was slowly weaning Mathers off of his meat-and-potatoes dependency. But tonight they ate take-out Chinese, fried rice and egg rolls. And conversation was minimal.

She'd done some searching after Stevens had left that morning, dug through yesterday's police reports until she found the right file: Adrian

Miller, seventeen years old, a senior at Kennedy High School. Found hanging in his bedroom, a clear suicide. There wasn't much more in the file, not much more to say, but she'd stared at the screen all afternoon, anyway.

She couldn't say why, exactly. Windermere prided herself on being the tough cop, the no-nonsense hard-ass who brought the bad guys to justice without dragging any emotional baggage behind her. She was strong, independent, barely needed Mathers in her life, much less any friends and family. And kids? Forget it. So why did some poor teenager's suicide have her rattled?

Big Bird, that's why, she thought. *Wanda Rose and Rene Duclair. Things you thought you'd managed to forget.*

She drank another beer while Mathers cleared the table. Knew he was watching her, waiting for her to say something, ignored him. Just sat at the table and drank her beer, thought about Adrian Miller and Wanda and Rene, tried to chase those long-ago voices from her ears.

"You know you can talk to me, right?" Mathers said, tucking the leftovers in the fridge. "I mean, something's bugging you, Carla. I'm your boyfriend. I can help if you let me."

She drained her bottle, set it down on the table. "Bring me another one, Derek," she said. "Seeing as you're so keen to help."

< 5 >

Windermere had been a junior when Rene Duclair moved to Southaven. She came from somewhere across the Mississippi River, some backwater town in Arkansas, as far as Windermere could figure. She was quiet, kind of homely, wore the same three outfits in constant rotation, the colors fading from all the washing, the fabric thinning to nothing.

"Poor," Wanda Rose would whisper, watching Rene pass. "Her dang clothes don't even fit right. Must have been wearing them since she was normal-sized."

Rene was tall, had inches on most of the boys in the grade, let alone the girls. Plus, she was clumsy. Awkward and ungainly as a baby giraffe, the kind of girl who'd set fire to her chemistry experiment, cause an evacuation. She was always knocking things over, tripping over her feet and falling on her face, spilling her lunch, sending her homework flying. Rene was an easy target to pick on. And Wanda Rose did.

Thing is, for all that, Rene was a decent girl. Windermere had a couple classes with her, senior year, walked a similar route home, till they'd covered about a half mile from school. Sometimes they walked together. Sometimes when they walked, they talked.

Turned out Rene had been all over the place before she came to Mississippi. Her dad had worked barges on the river, from the Gulf Coast all the way up to Saint Louis, and he'd taken Rene with him.

"My mom wandered off when I was little," Rene told Windermere.

"So I had to go along when my dad found a new job. We lived in just about every state within fifty miles of the river."

But her dad had hurt himself, fallen hard off an oil barge onto the dock, and so he'd moved her in with her aunt and uncle in Southaven, which was pretty well Memphis, inland from the river and far from what few friends she'd accumulated, miles away from her dad.

"He kinda gave me up," she told Windermere. "Said he couldn't raise a daughter while he was laid up in recovery."

"You think you'll go back when he's better?" Windermere asked her.

Rene scuffed her toe on the sidewalk. "Dunno," she said. "It's been almost a year. I get the feeling he's enjoying the break."

So that was Rene. Quiet, downcast, and lonely, rarely with a smile on her face. Taller than every girl in senior class, and meek as a mouse. But a decent person, a nice girl. Windermere found she didn't mind walking home with Rene, kind of enjoyed the company, at least when they'd made it far enough from school that Wanda and her friends couldn't see.

Wanda Rose was the queen of Martin Luther King High, the most popular girl in the school. She set the fashion trends, made the social rules, determined who mattered. She'd decided pretty quick that Rene Duclair didn't matter, and the rest of the school followed her lead, even Windermere, who was kind of too-tall herself, kind of embarrassingly bookish, who was secretly grateful that it was Rene Duclair who'd captured Wanda's attention, and not her.

Windermere had always been too smart to really fit in. She'd always been brash and competitive, an overachiever. She pulled top-of-the-class grades, and she ate lunch alone. She was lonely. She envied Wanda Rose and her circle of friends, ached to be included.

So Windermere didn't stand up for Rene when Wanda and her friends picked on her. When the girls' locker room echoed with Wanda's laughing, mocking singsong. "Big Bird, Big Bird, go fly away."

Windermere didn't set Wanda straight, not even as Rene was breaking down, fleeing in tears, even as she knew that Rene could really use the friendship. Windermere did nothing. She stood on the sidelines and watched as Wanda's taunts got louder and the chorus grew behind her, watched as Rene withdrew, more and more.

And then one day Rene walked out of school and didn't come back, not ever, and Wanda Rose and her friends just kept on laughing, as if they didn't know, as if they hadn't played a part in driving Rene to do what she'd done.

They graduated without Rene. Wanda Rose was the prom queen. She married a dentist, moved on to another chapter of her charmed, lovely life, and if she ever gave another thought to Rene Duclair, she didn't show it.

But Windermere did. Windermere thought about Rene Duclair, couldn't escape her. Windermere hated Wanda Rose for what she'd done to Rene. Hated herself even more for the part she'd played in it. She'd gone off to college mired in guilt, unable to shake Rene Duclair from her mind.

She graduated, got her law degree. Knew pretty quick that she was headed for police work. The Bureau. Took a post in Miami, hit the streets, went to work, and it turned out she was a damn good cop. She'd done good in the world, more than her share, and gradually Rene Duclair faded from her mind.

But now she was back, and Wanda, too, fueled by Adrian Miller, this latest tragedy. All that guilt and self-loathing had come flooding back, everything, and Windermere didn't have the first clue how to deal with it.

< 6 >

The next day, Windermere was waiting when Stevens came into the office. Knew from the look on his face that he'd had the same kind of night she'd had.

"The poor kid," he told her, easing into his chair. "Had people posting pictures of him all over Facebook, doctored up so it seemed like he'd wet his pants."

He laughed a little. "Andrea's all out for justice. Wants the bullies tarred and feathered, I guess, and who can blame her? I told her I'd see what I could do."

Windermere sipped her coffee. Felt that twinge again, deep in her gut. Couldn't see that there was any justice to be had, not here, not in her experience. But she knew Andrea Stevens wouldn't see it that way. "What are you thinking?" she asked her partner.

Stevens shrugged. "I made a few calls to the Saint Paul PD, told them what Andrea had told me about the jocks and the pictures on Facebook. Maybe they bring a few kids in on bullying charges, but so what? Doesn't bring Adrian Miller back, does it?"

"No," Windermere said. "It damn well doesn't."

Stevens caught her tone. "You okay?"

She nodded, reached for her coffee mug again. "Of course I'm okay," she said. "Didn't sleep well, is all. Mathers hogging all the blankets, you know?"

Stevens laughed again. Then his smile faded. "Andrea wants answers," he said. "I don't exactly know how to tell her there's some things you just can't make sense of in this world."

Windermere took another sip of coffee. Saw Rene again, Wanda. Wanda the prom queen, Rene just gone.

"You got that right," she said. "Shit."

Life went on, though.

Kirk Stevens pushed Adrian Miller from his mind, tried to focus on the job. Went back to chucking paperwork, tidying up the last scraps of that sex-trafficking ring. Mostly busywork at this point, a few low-level thugs and a couple perverts with money, the organized crime units in New Jersey handling most of the actual legwork. The blockbuster stuff, the shootouts and car chases, was long over.

Then Derek Mathers knocked on the door to the office, poked his head inside. "Agent Stevens—Kirk," he said, still waffling a little on the familiarity side of things. Still getting used to seeing Stevens in CID every day, a colleague, where he once might have been a rival for Windermere's affection. "Got a couple visitors down at the front door. Your, ah, daughter and her boyfriend."

Stevens put down the warrant he was scanning. "Andrea?"

"Said she needed to talk to you," Mathers said. "Something about the Adrian Miller case."

Across the office, Windermere was watching Stevens. "Uh . . ." Mathers said. "What exactly *is* the Adrian Miller case, you guys?"

"Guess we're about to find out," Windermere said, standing.

Stevens blinked, surprised. "You're coming with?"

"This paperwork is boring the crap out of me, partner. Let's go see what Andrea has to say."

She was out the door before Stevens could argue, and he swapped shrugs with Mathers instead, stood, and followed Windermere across CID to the elevators.

< 7 >

The FBI building was a fortress, a brand-new structure designed to withstand a terrorist attack. Located in Brooklyn Center, northwest of the Twin Cities, it had replaced the Bureau's previous regional office, whose location in a skyscraper in downtown Minneapolis made it vulnerable to the kinds of threats the FBI tended to fixate on these days, the homeland security stuff, whether from al-Qaeda operatives or the Timothy McVeigh types. Security in the new headquarters was tight, and that meant Andrea Stevens had to wait for her father outside the metal detectors and checkpoints that guarded the building's inner reaches.

Stevens followed Windermere out past the guards and scanned the lobby, wondering what had spurred his partner's interest in this Adrian Miller thing. The boy's death was a tragedy, to be sure, and Andrea no doubt felt she was doing good by coming all the way out here, but Stevens figured he was on deck to spend an hour or so placating his daughter's concerns before driving her back to school, nothing more. Adrian Miller was dead, an obvious suicide. It sounded harsh, but what else was there to say?

Andrea was sitting in an easy chair by the bank of windows near the front door, slouched in her seat like your typical bored seventeen-year-old, her blond hair lit gold by the light. She perked up when she saw Stevens and Windermere, and nudged the kid beside her—Calvin, her boyfriend, a thin, lanky boy with a couple of acne patches and an endearingly goofy smile. Both kids stood from their seats as the agents approached.

"Andrea," Stevens said. "You should be in school, kiddo. What are you doing here?"

Calvin raised his hand, sheepish. "I drove," he said. "My mom lets me take the car to school sometimes."

"I have a spare," Andrea said, glancing at Windermere. "As long as we're back after lunch, I'm okay."

"And Calvin?"

Calvin blushed a little bit. "It's only history, Mr. S.," he said. "I can just look it all up on Wikipedia when we get back."

Stevens opened his mouth to argue. Didn't get the words out before Windermere spoke.

"So what's up?" she asked the teenagers. "What brought you all the way out here, anyway?"

"It's about Adrian," Andrea said. "The kid at my school who died." She looked at Stevens again. "I know it's weird that we showed up here, but this stuff—we didn't want to wait until after school. We couldn't."

"Saint Paul PD promised me they'd send someone to talk to those jocks you were telling me about. They—"

"This isn't about the jocks, Dad," Andrea said. "This is about the real reason Adrian died. We figured it out."

"Heck," Stevens said, feeling his heart break a little. His daughter looked so earnest, like her mom working a case, trying to do good in the world.

She's from a cop family. Still figures every injustice can be solved with solid police work and a decent attorney.

Windermere seemed to read his expression. "Let's hear them out, Kirk," she said. "This doesn't sound like some misguided crusade."

"No," Andrea said, "it's not like that. It's . . . Adrian had a friend, this guy Lucas. I think you should hear what he has to say."

She gestured behind her, down the bank of windows to the far wall, where another teenager stood in the shadows, staring out at the parking lot. He was tall, wore a varsity jacket. But he carried himself with a hunch to his shoulders, like he was trying to shrink or disappear. It had pretty much worked; Stevens hadn't noticed him until now.

"This is big, Mr. S.," Calvin said. "It's really, really big."

Stevens studied the kid across the lobby. Considered it. He'd been hoping to tie up the last of the sex-trafficking case today. Put a nice bow on it for Drew Harris, Special Agent in Charge of CID, and start casting around for a new bad guy to chase. But Windermere was looking at him, too.

"Whatever it is," she told him, "it was important enough that they brought this kid out here, partner. We should probably pay attention."

Stevens looked across the lobby again. Lucas stuck to the shadows, practically a ghost, and Stevens realized he was actually kind of curious.

What could this kid have to tell them that would make a difference in the grand scheme of things? He supposed he was going to find out.

"Okay, sure," he said. "Bring him on over, then."

< 8 >

His name was Lucas Horst. He was a tall, good-looking kid, athletic. Probably played receiver on the Kennedy varsity team—didn't have the bulk to play tight end, didn't carry himself with the easy confidence of a quarterback. He sat in the little office and sipped a Coca-Cola and ignored Andrea and Calvin, studied the carpet instead.

"We weren't friends, me and Adrian," he told Windermere and Stevens. "Like, not exactly. We didn't, like, eat lunch together or anything. We hardly ever even hung out."

"Sure," Stevens said. "But you knew him."

Lucas hesitated. Looked over at Andrea and Calvin again. Turned a little bit red, but didn't say anything.

Windermere studied him. She'd been watching the way he acted around Andrea and Calvin, kind of distant, almost shy. He was keeping a secret, something important.

"Why don't you kids run off with your dad for a little while," she told Andrea. "Hit the cafeteria, grab some lunch, okay?"

Andrea balked. Made to argue, but caught the look on Lucas's face and, bless her, figured it out.

"Come on," she told Calvin, taking his hand and fairly dragging him from the room. "This is a police station, right? Let's see if they have any donuts."

Stevens watched his daughter walk out, then turned back to Windermere. "Everything okay?"

"Go," Windermere told him. "Everything's fine. It's just, we don't need the peanut gallery hanging around."

Windermere waited until Stevens had followed Andrea and Calvin from the room. She closed the door behind them and sat down again, across from Lucas.

"Just you and me," she said. "You're all right. Nothing you say leaves this room, if you don't want."

Lucas nodded, but he didn't say anything. Just stared down at the carpet beneath Windermere's desk. Then he sniffled. Spoke without looking up.

"I didn't actually think he would do it," he said. "Like, he talked about it a lot, how miserable he was at school, but everybody's freaking miserable, you know?"

"Yeah," Windermere said. "I doubt it's changed much since I was your age."

"I wasn't really being truthful, what I said to Andrea's dad," Lucas told her. "Me and Adrian hung out a little bit. After school, mostly, in the park. Sometimes at my place, before my dad got home." He met Windermere's eyes. "I'm not, like, *gay*. We were just . . . I didn't want anyone to know. I would have been so screwed if anybody found out."

His eyes were bright, tears welling. "I made sure nobody suspected anything. I didn't talk to him in the hall, didn't hang out with him. I made him meet me a few blocks from school whenever we went to the

19

park. I didn't, like, *defend* him when people made fun of him. I knew he was miserable, and I didn't do anything." He started to cry. "I just didn't think he would actually *do* it. But he did. And I could have done something to stop it."

Windermere pushed a box of Kleenex across the desk. Felt it in her heart for the kid. Figured she could pretty well pinpoint exactly how he was hurting.

"I'm sorry, honey," she told him, wishing she was more like Stevens, a people person, instead of a blunt instrument, wishing she knew the words to offer comfort. "I'm really, really sorry."

Lucas blew his nose. Took a moment. "He told me all about how he was going to do it," he said. "He told me all about it. How he'd rig the noose, where he'd get the rope. He said he had some friend on the Internet, some girl who knew all the best ways."

"A friend." Windermere sat forward. "What kind of friend?"

"I don't really know much. It was this girl in Pennsylvania, some depressed chick. They were supposed to have a suicide pact, or whatever. She gave Adrian the idea of hanging himself. Told him to do it on a webcam so she could watch. She told him all this crazy shit—" He caught himself. "*Stuff,* like how it was never going to get better for them and they were really saving themselves a lot of misery by doing it. She said if he filmed it, he would inspire her."

Lucas's eyes welled up again. He hid his face in his hands. "And I didn't do *anything*. I let him fucking *die*."

Windermere barely heard him. Her mind was racing. A suicide pact. Another girl. *Shit.*

This might not be violent crimes material, she thought, reaching for her phone. *But I'll be damned if I'm going to get hung up on a technicality.*

‹ 9 ›

Adrian Miller had lived with his family in the Lexington-Hamline neighborhood in Saint Paul, west of the downtown core and just north of the bluffs overlooking the Mississippi River. It was a quiet, older neighborhood, plenty of families and leafy, tree-lined streets. Stevens and his own family lived barely half a mile away.

There was a newish minivan parked in the driveway when Stevens and Windermere pulled up to the Miller house, and an old sedan at the curb. Stevens had called ahead from CID, told Windermere he'd talked to a Brenda Miller, Adrian's mother. She was home, she'd told Stevens. She had no plans to leave anytime soon.

Stevens pulled his Cherokee over, and Windermere stepped out onto the sidewalk, looked around. Caught Stevens watching her over the roof of the Jeep, a funny expression on his face.

"What?" she said.

"You all right?" he asked her.

"Never better," she said. "Doing great, partner. Why?"

She'd called him back in after her interview with Lucas Horst. Explained about the suicide pact, didn't tell him about the rest of what the kid had told her. Insisted on coming along when Stevens wanted to take a drive to the Miller place.

"No reason," Stevens said, still watching her from the other side of his truck. "Just, this isn't even our case, really. I'm just doing this as a favor for my daughter, you know?"

"There's a girl in a suicide pact," Windermere said, staring up at the house. "Her partner's already dead, Stevens. I'm supposed to sit back and do nothing?"

Adrian Miller's father greeted them at the door. Nick Miller, his name was. He'd probably been an imposing man a couple days ago, tall and broad-shouldered. He seemed shrunken now, stooped over, his eyes weary. He wore a rumpled suit; there was a stain on his tie. Windermere looked at him and saw Rene Duclair's dad when he'd come to the school to collect Rene's belongings. She'd passed him in the hallway, a wrecked man. Nick Miller looked just as shattered.

"Sorry about the mess," he told Stevens and Windermere, leading them into the living room. There were flowers everywhere—bouquets and arrangements. Sympathy cards. Casserole dishes. "People seem to just come out of the woodwork with this stuff when, you know . . ."

He gave them a forced smile, gestured to the couch. "We're still coming to terms with it all, I guess. Everything just seems so surreal."

Before Stevens or Windermere could respond, Brenda Miller appeared from the kitchen, holding a tray of coffee mugs, some cream and sugar. She, too, wore a smile, like she was desperately trying to maintain the illusion that this visit was a social call, that this whole thing was just a bad dream. Behind her, in the kitchen, a little girl of about six colored at a high table.

"So nice of you to come," Brenda Miller said, setting the tray down on the coffee table. "I made coffee. I hope that's okay."

"More than okay," Windermere said, reaching for a mug. "Thanks very much for seeing us. This can't be easy, we know."

"What can we do for you agents, anyway?" Brenda Miller still wore the smile, but there was an edge to her voice, as if any further conversation would knock the whole house of cards over. "What does the FBI want with our situation?"

Stevens cleared his throat. "One of Adrian's friends paid us a visit this morning," he said. "My daughter, Andrea, had math class with your boy. She's been distraught about what happened, trying to find ways to help out with the case."

"What case?" Brenda Miller asked. "Saint Paul PD says it's just teenagers being bullies. Something Adrian took a little too personally, they say. And that even if they could prosecute the kids who drove him to this, there's not much they could charge them with, anyway. It's not like they made him do what he did, right?"

Her voice wavered, and Nick Miller reached over, took her hand. "We're not out for revenge," he told Stevens and Windermere. "We know there's no way to bring Adrian back. We figure those kids who bullied Adrian probably learned a lesson they'll carry with them for as long as they live, and as angry as we are, that's pretty much the best we can hope for."

"I'm not so sure about that," Windermere said. "We talked to a friend of Adrian's today, Lucas Horst. Does that name sound familiar?"

"Oh, yes, Lucas," Brenda said. "He came over once or twice. He was a nice boy." She paused, and the hint of a smile played on her lips. "I think Adrian had a little bit of a crush on him."

"It sounds like he may have," Windermere said. "Enough that he was willing to confide in Lucas with secrets he kept from everyone else." She outlined what Lucas had told her back in CID, the suicide forum, Adrian's secret friend. "According to Lucas, this girl encouraged Adrian to buy a webcam, told him how to tie the rope the right way," Windermere said. "She coached him to do what he did."

Neither Miller responded right away. Brenda Miller had gripped her husband's hand tight with both of her own.

"He asked us to buy him that webcam," she said. "He told us it was for Internet gaming."

"We think he recorded it so this online friend could watch," Stevens said. "As far as the why, we're afraid this girl wanted to replicate what Adrian did."

"We want to borrow your son's laptop," Windermere said. "We need to track down this Internet friend of his. And if Adrian was part of some suicide pact, we want to put a stop to it before anyone else dies."

Brenda Miller dabbed at her eyes with a napkin. Held tight to her husband with her other hand. Nick Miller squeezed her hand for a moment. Then he straightened, squared his shoulders.

"Adrian's room is upstairs," he told Stevens and Windermere. "Take whatever you need."

< 10 >

An hour later, Stevens and Windermere had Adrian Miller's laptop open on Windermere's desk, Mathers bent over around back, fiddling with a couple of cords.

Lucas Horst was long gone, back at Kennedy with Andrea and Calvin, one of Windermere's business cards in his pocket. Windermere figured she'd be calling the school a little while later, asking the grief counselor to have a chat with the kid, as discreet as possible.

She wondered if Lucas would find a way past this, if he'd figure out a way to move on. Thought about Rene Duclair, heard Wanda's voice again, that old mocking singsong. The laughter as it echoed down the hall, the way Rene slunk past. The hurt on her face when her eyes found Windermere's, the betrayal. She'd turned her back, sold out her friend, just as Lucas had.

Forget it. Everything came secondary to Adrian Miller right now. Miller's parents had handed over the laptop without complaint, the webcam, too, a brand-new, high-def model purchased for one purpose. The thought made Windermere's stomach churn.

Nick Miller had walked them out.

"Find that girl, and anyone else in the pact," he'd told Stevens and Windermere. "If there's any way you can save them, agents, you do it. No parent should have to go through what we're going through."

Windermere had looked back into the house: Brenda Miller tidying up the coffee mugs in the cluttered living room, her cheeks tracked with fresh tears. Nick Miller with his tired eyes and dirty suit, the little sister coloring away in the kitchen, the whole place looking like a bomb had gone off, imploded a family, while outside, on the rest of the block, families came home, walked dogs, ate dinner. The leaves overhead starting to turn. Life went on.

Windermere tucked the laptop under her arm. "If we can save this girl," she'd told Nick Miller, "we will."

. . .

Now Stevens and Windermere waited and watched as Mathers hooked up the laptop to a power source and a hardwired Internet connection.

"Let's hope this thing isn't too hard to hack," Mathers said, turning the laptop around to study the screen. "If this kid was some kind of computer genius, we'll have to call the tech guys in. Could take hours."

"We don't have hours, Derek," Windermere said. "For all we know, this girl's already dead. We need to find her, and fast."

She'd already put out feelers to law enforcement agencies in Pennsylvania, local cops in the major cities, state police, the Bureau. Asked them to check for reports of teenage suicides from Wednesday night to now. So far, they'd heard nothing to suggest that Adrian Miller's online friend had gone through with her end of the bargain.

Pennsylvania was big, though, and the search criteria were flimsy. At this point, Windermere had no idea if she and Stevens were still in the race or in last place by a mile.

Mathers tapped a couple of keystrokes. "Got it," he said. "I'm in."

Windermere and Stevens crowded around behind him. Studied the laptop's screen. A browser window. A black background. "'Death Wish,'" Stevens read. "'For those ready to make the transition.'"

It was a pretty low-rent website, to Windermere's eyes. A bunch of forum postings arranged newest to oldest down the page, topics like GUN PILLS OR KNIFE PLZ ADVISE and GARAGE EXHAUST PROS/CONS. The first page had fifty postings, a button to push to navigate backward. Had to be hundreds and hundreds of topics, some of them with a thousand replies. Suicide fetishists, sitting around all day debating the best ways to kill themselves. It would have been pathetic if Windermere hadn't just come from Adrian Miller's ground zero. Instead she felt only a mounting urgency.

There was a link to Adrian's profile at the top of the page. Windermere clicked through, read the details. His profile. "'Seventeen years old, sick of the bullshit,'" she read aloud. "'Nothing could be worse than this.'"

"Check the chat history," Stevens told her. "He was probably talking to this Pennsylvania girl before he died."

Windermere scrolled down, found a page for private chats. Waited as the browser loaded, then leaned in to study the screen. Found what they were looking for at the top of the page.

"Ambriel98," she read. "Harrisburg, Pennsylvania. 'Seeking a friend for the big good-bye.'"

The chat log was dated Wednesday afternoon. Hours before Adrian Miller's parents found his body. Windermere clicked through and forced herself to read, fighting the sudden wave of nausea that washed over her, feeling like she was watching a plane crash in slow motion.

AM: *I think I'm ready. I think I'm going to do it today.*

Ambriel98: *It's the right decision. U'll be in a better place.*

AM: *At least I won't be in this place.*

A: *I wish I had your balls.*

AM: *Take them.*

A: *Turn on your webcam if you're doing it. Like we talked about. You'll inspire me. You'll inspire so many people like us.*

AM: *Get ready for the show. See you on the other side.*

AM: *Here goes nothing.*

A: *Do it. Do it for me.*

That's where the chat log ended. There was no response from Adrian Miller. Nothing more.

That was it.

"The girl talked Adrian into it," Stevens said, stepping back from the computer. "Goddamn it all, Carla."

Windermere was already reaching for the phone, pushing the bad feelings away, the adrenaline taking over. "I know, partner," she said. "So let's find her."

< **11** >

"Her name's Ashley Frey," Mathers told Stevens and Windermere. "That profile on the Death Wish forum links to a free Outlook account registered in her name. But there's no real-world address linked to either the email account or the Death Wish profile, so we can't trace her."

"The IP address," Stevens said. "That'll find her, right?"

"It damn well better," Windermere said. "Mathers, run a trace on her IP address. I'll get on the phone with Harrisburg PD, tell them to run down any and every Ashley Frey they can find."

"On it." Mathers turned back to the computer, started typing again. Windermere picked up the handset, picturing this Ashley Frey girl somewhere, a length of rope in her hands. Got someone on the line from the Bureau's Harrisburg resident agency, filled him in and told him to start canvassing for people named Frey. Slammed down the phone just as Mathers came back frowning.

"Weird," he told them. "Really weird. I can't get a trace on her location. This IP address is blocked."

"Blocked?" Windermere leaned forward and studied the screen. "No, forget that. Unblock it, Derek. There's no time."

"Too complicated for me," Mathers told her. "I think we need to call tech."

The tech was a young guy named Nenad. Close-cropped haircut, a Superman tattoo on his forearm. He couldn't do much more than Mathers could.

"Whatever this girl's up to, she knows what she's doing," he told Stevens and Windermere. "She has this IP address bouncing all over the freaking globe. *Really* doesn't want to get found."

Windermere stared at the laptop. Felt that roiling, churning starting up in her stomach again.

"She's using something called an anonymizer," Nenad told them. "Basically, it's a proxy server that you can use to shield your Internet usage. Hide out from prying eyes, that kind of thing."

"We need a location, Nenad," Windermere said. "This girl's life is in danger."

Nenad nodded. "Yeah," he said. "The thing is, this program she's using is *really* freaking good. Like, it's the same shit that Snowden guy used when he was whistle-blowing on the NSA. They couldn't find him, and believe me, they tried."

"I don't know much about modern technology," Stevens said. "But what the heck does a teenager need with that kind of encryption? This sounds like a little more than a lock on her diary."

Nenad scratched his forearm absently, the Superman tattoo. "Oh, it's much bigger than that," he replied. "This kind of program, I'd say the only way you'll find this girl is if she decides she wants to be found."

"So the question remains," Stevens asked Windermere, "why the heck is Ashley Frey so intent on staying hidden?"

Windermere didn't answer. Didn't have an answer. Figured, whoever Ashley Frey was, her clock was ticking.

< 12 >

Windermere watched Nenad walk back out through CID to the elevators. Felt empty inside, nauseous. Felt like she'd just let Ashley Frey die.

The phone was ringing behind her. Windermere turned, watched Stevens pick it up. Watched him answer, nod, do more listening than talking. When he hung up the phone, he went to where she stood in the doorway.

"Harrisburg PD," he told her. "Turns out there's more than a handful of Freys in the phone book. Even a couple of Ashleys, they said, but they're older, grown-ups, not our person. The PD is hitting every Frey household, looking for underagers named Ashley, asking around."

He shook his head. "Thing is, none of the schools in Harrisburg have any record of an Ashley Frey in their registers. High schools, middle schools, private schools, none of them."

Windermere watched the elevator doors close behind Nenad, knew Stevens was waiting for her to come up with something good.

"They try outside the city?" she asked her partner. "Surrounding districts? Heck, maybe she lied on her profile. Maybe she's not in Harrisburg to begin with."

Stevens followed her gaze out across the office. "Yeah, I mean, maybe. That girl's using some pretty heavy-duty concealment technology, Carla. She could be anywhere on the planet, for all we know."

She looked at him. "And?"

Stevens made a face. "I'm just saying," he said. "This is starting to look a lot like one of those needle-in-a-haystack gigs we tend to attract. Only this time, there's no FBI-slash-BCA-sanctioned investigation attached."

"You're saying we're wasting our time. You want to drop this thing?"

"I'm saying . . ." he started. She could feel his eyes on her again. Refused to turn his way. "Sooner or later, the Special Agent in Charge is going to want to know why we commandeered his best tech guy— and Mathers—on a wild-goose chase, when we still have a case left to close on our desks."

Windermere turned. Studied Stevens until he looked away. "The sex traffickers are dead or in jail, Stevens," she said. "We're just tying up loose ends, and you know it. There's a girl out there who needs our help, and you—"

"It's been two days, Carla," he said, and she could tell he was trying to be gentle about it. Kid gloves. "For all we know, she's dead already."

"But we *don't* know, Kirk," she said. "I'm not going to let this girl off herself while I stand around and file paperwork. We could still find her if we—"

"How?" Stevens asked. "You heard what Nenad said. If this girl wants to stay hidden, we're never tracking her down."

"Bull-*shit*." She was aware that heads were turning across CID, people staring at them over the top of their cubicles. She ignored them. "I'm freaking finding her, partner. If the SAC wants to tell me otherwise, he can come and tell me himself."

She walked away. Didn't look back, didn't know where she was going. Felt Stevens's eyes on her from the doorway, the rest of CID.

Windermere walked fast. Tried not to let on she was hurrying away. Kept going until she knew they couldn't see her anymore.

< 13 >

It started with the hole in the wall.

Randall Gruber was fifteen years old when his mom took up with Earl and his daughter, moved them out of town into that shitty doublewide, the place nothing more than a few flimsy particleboard walls and some aluminum siding. Sarah would have been sixteen, just a few months older than he was.

He'd noticed the hole within an hour of moving in, after his mom shoved him into the little bedroom and Earl chucked his battered suitcase in behind him. He'd lain on his bed, drawing pictures in his sketch pad, stifling hot and bored out of his mind already, and he'd looked across the room and noticed the hole.

It was about the size of a dime, belt-high, kind of ragged around the edges. He'd put down his sketch pad and climbed off the bed, crossed the little room and knelt at the hole, peered through, blinking a couple times to focus. And there she was, like his own private movie.

Sarah was brushing her hair on the other side of that hole, primping and preening in a little mirror above her dresser, the sides of the frame all tacked over with pictures of teen idols and movie stars, the New Kids on the Block, Tom Cruise and Luke Perry. Sarah was wearing a pretty dress; she was singing to herself, singing along with the radio. The dress was light blue; her hair was honey blond.

She was getting ready to go out. Gruber watched her brush her hair, watched her dance around her little bedroom. Watched her pause while fixing her makeup to stick another poster on the wall.

He knelt at the hole, hardly daring to breathe. The hot, late-summer air suffocating, his shirt sticking to his skin, his whole body tense as he watched her. He was sure Sarah would notice him. Still, he couldn't turn away.

He'd been afraid to move out there. He'd been afraid of the meanness he'd seen in Earl's eyes, when he'd come to call on Gruber's mother. Gruber suspected that Earl would have left him behind if he could have. That he'd only agreed to move them both so that he could be closer to Gruber's mom.

But his new stepsister seemed *happy*. She looked radiant through that peephole, far too good for her bedroom, for that crummy trailer. And watching her, Gruber felt better. Maybe life with Earl wouldn't be quite as bad as he'd imagined. Maybe he could survive there.

He watched Sarah bop around her little room. Watched her put the finishing touches on her makeup and wondered where she was going. If she had friends in this dump of a trailer park—a "motor court," they called it, as if a fancy name could hide the sorry state of the place. He wondered if they would share the same friends. They weren't so far apart in age after all.

The thought buoyed him. He hadn't had many friends back in the city. The kids who'd known him in school had made fun of his soda-bottle glasses, the way he lisped when he talked. They'd left him alone, on his good days. On the bad days, they hadn't. But maybe here would be different. Maybe everything would finally be all right.

All too quickly, the illusion shattered. Gruber was watching Sarah buckle her shoes when, behind him, Earl pushed open the door. Barged into the little bedroom; didn't bother to knock. Just walked in and waited for Gruber to notice.

Gruber scrambled up from the floor. Prayed Earl hadn't seen the hole. Prayed he wouldn't think to ask why his new stepson was kneeling at the wall. But Earl didn't notice. He fixed Gruber with a hard stare, didn't bother to hide his distaste.

"Live in my house, you've got to earn your keep," he said, and there was a menace to his tone. "There's a pile of junk and old scrap out back. Get on out there and move it."

The whole trailer seemed to still, waiting on Gruber's response. He couldn't even hear Sarah in the next room, or her music anymore. Earl's eyes narrowed, and his fists clenched. "Don't make me ask you twice," he said.

Gruber glanced back at that hole in the wall. Knew Earl was waiting, itching for an excuse. And as he followed his new stepfather out through the shitty double-wide to the gravel-patch yard, the stench of cheap bourbon lingering in the warm air, Gruber knew he'd been wrong to put faith in what he'd seen through the wall, foolish to believe it had any bearing whatsoever on his own life in Earl's trailer.

< **14** >

Windermere stayed up late. Sat in her living room and drank beer in near darkness, thinking about Ashley Frey, in the dim light from the kitchen and the glow of the streetlights outside. The condo was quiet. Mathers had long ago gone to bed. She'd pretty much pushed him away.

"So crazy about that Frey girl," he'd said over dinner. "If Nenad can't track her down, believe me, nobody in the world can find her."

Windermere hadn't said anything. She'd picked at the Greek salad he'd made them, tried not to think about the girl, how lonely she must feel, how desperate. Tried not to think about the people who must have driven her to that stupid, shitty end.

Big Bird, Big Bird. Go fly away.

Mathers scraped his plate. Studied her across the table. "You okay?"

he said. "I don't think I've ever seen you get so caught up in a case." He laughed. "And it isn't really even a case."

She didn't answer. Speared a piece of lettuce with her fork and examined it, couldn't find the energy to take the process further. She knew she should talk to Mathers, tell him what she was feeling. Knew a good girlfriend would communicate with her partner, tell him what was on her mind. Couldn't bring herself to do it.

You sold your friend out for a stab at popularity. You let her walk away, and you laughed with the rest of them, even when you knew she was hurting. What's Mathers going to say when you tell him? What's he going to think of his girlfriend?

"You know you can talk to me, right?" Mathers asked her. "Anything you're thinking about, that's what I'm here for."

She cracked open a beer. "Nothing to talk about, Mathers. Don't go getting all soft and sappy on me. I'm not that kind of girl."

He gave it a moment. "Yeah," he said. "Yeah, I know."

A couple minutes passed. Mathers stood, took his plate to the sink, came back to her, leaned down and wrapped her in his arms. Windermere stared out the window at the dark, stayed rigid, drank her beer.

"Carla," Mathers said. "Whatever you're fighting yourself over, you can tell me. I can help."

"I just want to freaking know this girl's all right," she said, pushing the chair back, breaking free of his arms. "Can you figure that out for me, or no?"

Mathers sighed. "Carla—"

"Didn't think so," she said. Then she stood. "It's fine, Derek. I just need to be alone."

Now it was late. She'd killed a couple more beers, chased her tail think-ing about Ashley Frey and that goddamn anonymizer, or whatever the hell it was called. Realized with some surprise she was craving a cigarette.

She'd smoked only briefly in her life, a year at law school in Florida, when the stress threatened to overwhelm her, derail her career and send her spiraling back to Mississippi. To Wanda and Rene. She'd hated smoking, how dirty and weak and damn *needy* it made her feel, quit after that first year and hadn't really looked back. She'd smoked a ciga-rette, once, when Stevens's daughter had gone missing during the Carter Tomlin bank robbery case. Half a cigarette; she couldn't make herself finish it.

Now, though, she wanted one. More than one. A pack. She wanted to smoke and drink and feel self-destructive and miserable. And, screw it, that's what she was going to do.

Windermere dug out a pair of running shoes, pulled on her coat. Rode the elevator down to street level and stepped out into the night, the streets mostly empty and the air cold and raw. She wrapped her coat tighter and hurried down the block to the corner store, bought a pack of Marlboros and a little plastic lighter. Had to fiddle with the lighter a little bit to get it working—she was out of practice—but she made a flame. Lit the cigarette and inhaled, closed her eyes and held the smoke in her lungs. Wondered what Mathers would say if he saw her. What Stevens would say.

She'd expected that the cigarette would make her feel better. It didn't. She'd figured she could coast on those latent, long-ago feelings of worthlessness and self-loathing as she smoked a couple, three cigarettes, go back upstairs and drink and smoke some more—in the condo, yeah, because, screw it, why not?—and forget about Ashley Frey and go to bed foggy.

But Ashley Frey wasn't going away. Neither was Adrian Miller. At least one kid was dead, and another was still out there. Fuck Stevens and Mathers; there had to be a way to find her.

Windermere finished her cigarette. Flicked it to the curb and started back toward her building. Made the lobby and called the elevator, hit the down button, the parking garage. Figured if she was going to be up all night being self-destructive, she might as well be getting some work done.

< 15 >

Earl never found the hole in the wall. Gruber made sure of it.

He found a framed painting sitting in a trash pile a few lots down from the double-wide. A sailing ship in a storm. The glass was broken, but the painting was all right. The frame was decent, too.

He brought the painting home. Propped it up against the hole so that Sarah wouldn't notice the light leaking in from his room to hers. Wouldn't catch a glimpse of any movement.

He wondered what he would do if Sarah found out he was spying on her. How he would explain it if she found the hole. He needn't have worried. Sarah was too focused on boring, teenage girl stuff to even look in Gruber's direction.

She talked on the phone, at least while Earl wasn't around. She lay on her bed and wrote in her journal and listened to those boy bands she liked. Practiced her makeup in the mirror. Sometimes she snuck a cigarette from the pack she stashed in the broken vent in the floor, slid open her window and smoked.

She never smoked when Earl was home. She never drank from the bottle of peach schnapps she kept hidden under the bed. She stuck to her best behavior, kept the music turned low, even though it didn't matter so much what she did. She was Earl's daughter after all. She was never going to get it half as bad as Gruber did.

It didn't take much to set Earl off. Just a bottle of something strong and a perceived injustice, serious or otherwise. Then it was duck and cover. Run and hide. Listen to Earl's heavy boots in the hallway and pray they didn't stop at his door.

Most of the time, however, Gruber was shit out of luck. Earl seemed to reserve a special hate in his heart for his stepson. He'd kick open the flimsy door, come through piss-drunk and armed with some kind of blunt object. Take swings at Gruber for any reason he could think of— the dishes weren't done, or Gruber watched too much TV, or he'd flunked his social studies quiz, or whatever.

"Runt," he'd say. "Pip-squeak little shit-heel runt." He'd punctuate his words with his weapon of choice, bear down on Gruber, belts and backhanded slaps, Gruber hunched over and trying not to cry, because crying only made Earl worse.

"Men don't cry," he'd tell Gruber. "You a man, son? Or are you just a pussy?"

. . .

There wasn't much escape from the misery, even when Gruber got free of the double-wide. The local high school was small, mostly farm kids from the county. They didn't like kids from the trailer park. They laughed when Gruber tried to call it a motor court.

"It's a garbage dump," someone told him. "Nothing but white trash and four-eyed hillbillies."

Sarah didn't have many friends, herself. Those she did have, she guarded. Wouldn't introduce them to Gruber, wouldn't let him talk to them. She hurried off to school before he could catch up, before he knew she'd gone. Gruber didn't make friends. He stuck to himself. And it wouldn't have been so bad—he'd done it before, back in town, lots of times—except now there was Earl, too, waiting at home. And Gruber was still young. He was small and afraid. He wasn't strong enough to stand up to Earl, not yet.

Oh, but he ached to. He ached to do *something*, show the world he was more than just some dumb runt. The weeks passed, months, and nothing got any better. Earl kept bursting in, the drink on his breath. Kept beating Gruber. Nothing Gruber could do about it but dream of the day he could stand up for himself, the day he found an outlet for the frustration and hatred Earl was creating inside of him.

It was past midnight when Windermere piloted her daddy's old Chevelle out of the parking garage. Saturday morning, early, the last of the Friday-night partiers still straggling their way home. She drove across downtown, aiming for the interstate, ran into a roadside checkpoint just before the on-ramp. A handful of patrol cars were pulled over with their flashers on, cops with flashlights and reflective vests funneling cars into a long, single line.

Windermere examined her reflection in the rearview mirror. Checked her breath. She'd had, what, three beers? Felt fine, not even tipsy, but knew she shouldn't be driving. Screw it. Too late to turn around.

She rolled down the window for the young cop who approached the Chevy. "Had anything to drink?" the cop asked her.

"One beer with dinner," she lied, handing over her license and her FBI badge.

The cop studied the badge. "Working tonight?"

"Headed up to the office," she told him. "Couldn't sleep, so I figured I'd kick around some casework instead, you know?"

"No rest for the wicked, huh?" The cop handed the badge back, Windermere's driver's license. "Stay safe out there, anyway. Lots of crazies out tonight, especially this neck of the woods."

"Don't I know it." Windermere rolled up the window, pulled ahead. Pointed the Chevelle north, trying not to think about what Stevens and Mathers would have thought if the young cop had pulled her over for a breath test.

CID was quiet when Windermere walked off the elevator. Dark, just a handful of emergency lights, and the hum of the computers in the rows of cubicles. Windermere walked past a motion detector and the lights came on around her. She navigated through the department to the office she shared with Stevens.

She'd angled for her own office for three years before Drew Harris, her SAC, finally relented and made good on the promise he'd given her when he recruited her from the Miami field office. "Your own office. Plenty of room. Plenty of autonomy."

Well, she had her own office, anyway. Had to share it with Stevens, though—and Windermere was pretty sure she'd still be working a cubicle if her BCA colleague hadn't joined the violent crimes task force.

Adrian Miller's laptop was where they'd left it, on Windermere's desk, still connected to the Bureau's network but otherwise forgotten. Come Monday, Windermere knew she and Stevens would be back tidying up the last of the sex-trafficking case, no more time to spend on Ashley Frey, wherever and whoever she was.

But that left Saturday and Sunday. And Windermere wasn't ready to give up on the girl yet, not after seeing Adrian Miller's parents, after talking to Lucas Horst. She pulled up her chair and flipped open the laptop, squinted at the screen, the bright electronic light. Brought up the chat logs Adrian had cached from the Death Wish forum. His conversations with Ambriel98.

Adrian had talked to Ashley Frey for four months before he hanged

42

himself. Windermere scrolled to the top of the logs, the very first conversation. Scanned the office, Stevens's desk, the pictures of his wife and kids, looked out through the door to the empty cubicles beyond. Felt the pull of fatigue and craved a cigarette, wondered what she was doing here, middle of the night and a weekend besides.

Giving up already, Supercop?

She turned back to the computer. Settled in and started to read, the chat logs and Adrian Miller's profile, Ashley Frey's, anything that would help her get a fix on the girl.

Around dawn or so, she figured she'd found it.

< 17 >

Even Sarah couldn't dodge Earl's reign of terror forever. She lost her family immunity about the time Earl figured out she had a boyfriend.

The boyfriend's name was Todd McGee. He was a skinny kid with red hair, in Sarah's grade at school. Drove a pickup truck, an old F-100. Todd would come by after Earl had gone out for the night. Honk his horn from the road, and Sarah would spring up from her bed, check the window, fix her hair in the mirror, and dash out the door before Gruber's mother could stop her. Not that Gruber's mother really cared.

Sarah timed her escapes just fine for the first month or so. She waited until Earl'd gone out with his buddies, until Gruber's mother was more or less catatonic on the couch, the shopping network blaring. Then she'd sneak out to Todd and they'd peel away in his truck. Show up back home around midnight or so, a little later. She'd creep down the hall and into her bedroom, like she was never gone at all.

Gruber never hated her more than when she came home from those dates. She would dance around the bedroom, humming to herself, smiling some secret smile. She would write in her journal, scribbling the words out fast, as if she were afraid she'd lose them if she didn't write quickly. She would study herself in the mirror, fluff her hair, a normal girl, a happy girl. As if she never had to worry about Earl breaking her door down. As if she never had to wait as Earl reached for his belt.

Gruber hated her then, for being so normal. He resented that she was so *happy*, that her life was so different from his own, even as they shared space in the same shitty trailer.

But he never looked away. He watched her until she turned off the light, until she climbed into her bed in the darkness, and he would watch for longer still, listening to the rustling of the sheets as they clung to her body, wondering what it would feel like to slip between those sheets with her. When he was sure she was asleep, he would—reluctantly—move away, replace the painting against the wall, and retreat to his own bed, where he'd lie awake, replaying the images in his head.

< **18** >

"I don't think Ashley Frey killed herself," Windermere told Stevens. "I don't think she ever intended to kill herself at all."

On the other end of the line, Stevens stifled a yawn. "It's seven in the morning, partner," he said. "How come you're so awake?"

"Couldn't sleep," Windermere replied. "Went home last night and couldn't stop thinking about Ashley Frey and this little problem we were having tracking her down. So I went back to the office and did a little research. Stayed up all night on this suicide forum."

Nancy Stevens must have been nearby, because Stevens was talking to someone else, his voice muffled. Windermere waited, heard Nancy reply. Couldn't make out the details, but she figured it didn't matter.

"Sorry," Stevens said, coming back on the phone. "So, sure. You stayed up all night. What did you figure out?"

"I was reading through the logs for some kind of clue," Windermere told him. "Something that would help us place this girl. I got nothing. All Ashley Frey would tell Adrian is that she's from Pennsylvania and she's unhappy about the way her stepfather mistreats her."

"Sure." Stevens yawned again. "So?"

"So it's not the chat logs," Windermere said. "It's the anonymizer thingy. That's our key."

Stevens paused, and she could tell he was struggling to follow. "I thought that thing was for hiding your identity."

"It is," Windermere said. "But Ashley Frey isn't the only Death Wish member trying to stay incognito. I was trying to figure out if maybe Ashley Frey had another username, a different account, some other way to find her, so I got a list of about sixty other profiles that exhibited the same cloaking patterns."

"*You* got this list?" Stevens said. "You figured this out yourself?"

"Nenad helped," Windermere told him. "He came in about an hour ago, had some homework to catch up on. I prevailed on him to help me out instead."

"I bet you did."

Windermere hunkered down in front of Adrian Miller's laptop, her own desktop beside it, the file Nenad had opened with the list of usernames. "Check this out," she told Stevens. "Ambriel98, that username Ashley Frey was using, it's religious. It's the name of an angel. There's like eight other usernames that match the same profile."

"What?" Stevens said. "Angels? Carla, I get that you're trying to help this poor girl, but this is some mighty weak—"

"Yeah," Windermere said. "See, that's what I thought, too. But then I did some poking around."

She brought up the list of usernames: Muriel94, Penemue96, Seraphiel97. Opened the Death Wish forum and brought up the first profile, Muriel94. *Sixteen-year-old with a death wish, Orlando, Florida.* An old username, opened three years ago last January. Real name: Ashley Frey.

"It's not just angels, partner," Windermere told Stevens. "These are Ashley Frey's accounts. All of them."

Stevens was quiet for a long moment. Windermere could hear a coffeemaker in the background. "I was going to drag the kids down to the river today, get some fresh air," he said. "Guess I'll give them a reprieve."

. . .

Stevens showed up at CID about an hour later, eyes bleary and shirt rumpled, his thinning hair mussed. He handed coffees to Windermere and Nenad, looked over the tech's shoulder at the laptop screen. The Death Wish forum.

"'Muriel94,'" he read aloud. "'Enter password.' What the heck is this girl doing with all these accounts? Why make more than one?"

"The hell if I know," Windermere told him. "But I figure maybe these other accounts could give us a way to track this girl down."

Stevens nodded. "You sure we don't need a warrant for this?"

Nenad glanced at him. "I mean, technically," he said. "But considering this is more of a humanitarian mission, we can probably get away with it."

Stevens looked at Windermere. Studied her for some sign, some reason why she'd taken up this crusade, of all the misery in the world. "Sure," he said. "Just don't let the SAC hear about this. I'm still kind of on Bureau probation around here, you know?" He leaned forward. "How are we doing, anyway?"

"Doing just fine." Nenad typed something into the password box and sat back with a flourish. "I'm in."

< **19** >

It was bound to happen. One night, Sarah misjudged. Screwed up her timing. One night, Earl came home first.

Gruber was lying in bed, waiting, as usual. Heard a vehicle approaching, the pitch of the engine sounding a little off. The lights swept across the bedroom wall, the tires kicked up the gravel, too bright, too fast, all of it wrong. The screen door slammed open, no pretense of secrecy. The footsteps in the hall were too heavy—boots, not the heels she kept under the bed by the bottle.

Earl was home, and he was drunk. Gruber could hear him through the double-wide's thin walls. Heard glass breaking in the kitchen, heard the TV switch on, the shopping channel, then sports, too loud. Heard Earl swear at his mother, heard another glass break. Then the boots were coming down the hall.

Gruber pulled the covers up, pretended to be asleep. Hid his eyes as Earl shoved open the door, waited without breathing as Earl looked him over. Heard the chuff of Earl's breath, a muttered insult. Gruber could feel it coming in the worst possible way. Like when a kid told you he was going to fight you after school and all you could do was watch the clock tick toward the last bell.

Then Earl was at his bedside, shaking him, rough, rousing him awake. Cuffing him by the collar and dragging him to the floor, that awful, cheap-liquor breath in his face, demanding answers to some question Gruber didn't even know he'd been asked. He rolled away, fought to get free, caught a glimpse of the far wall, the little painting of the ship in the storm. Made a flash decision to save his own skin. Turn the tables, let Sarah get in trouble for a change.

"Sarah snuck out," he told Earl, arms up to ward off the inevitable blow. "She's gone with her boyfriend. You can check her room."

Gruber braced himself. But Earl didn't hit him, and when Gruber opened his eyes, Earl was gone.

He heard Earl's boots in the hall again. Heard him open Sarah's bedroom door, heard the grunt as he took in the empty bed. Heard the boot steps, the snarl as he searched the room, searched for Sarah, discovered her gone.

Then Earl was back. *"Where did she go, that little slut?"*

Gruber didn't know where Sarah was, but he didn't let that stop him. He told Earl everything he could think of, the way Sarah'd been sneaking out for weeks, that she was probably kissing Todd somewhere. Making out, petting, all the things Gruber ached to do with her. Was midway through his spiel when Earl stiffened and straightened. Looked up from the bed to the window.

An engine outside, the familiar pitch this time. lights on the bedroom wall. Gravel under the tires.

"There she is," Gruber told Earl. *"See?* I told you she was gone."

< **20** >

Gruber heard it all.

Earl waited until Sarah had climbed out of Todd's truck. Until she was halfway up the path to the screen door, turning back to wave good night. From his bedroom, Gruber heard the screen door squeal open. Heard Earl go out of the trailer.

He went for Sarah first. Gruber watched from the window, how Earl cuffed Sarah around the neck, wrenched her toward the house. Heard Earl tell her, *"Get in the goddamn house."* Watched Sarah stumble and fall onto the gravel as Earl steamrolled past her.

Earl was going for the truck, Todd's truck, Todd sitting in the driver's seat, going pale like he didn't know whether to stand on the gas pedal or get out and fight. He did neither, just froze up. Let Earl come around to the driver's side of the truck and drag him out and start whaling on him.

"Piece-of-shit goddamn dog," Earl was saying, punctuating every syllable with a fist or a boot. *"Teach you to lay hands on my daughter."*

Todd wasn't answering. He didn't have time to answer. Gruber couldn't see him from the window, could only see the Ford and the shadows and Earl aiming his punches downward, straightening up now and then to come in for a kick. Sarah picked herself up from the gravel, made a run at Earl, crying. Circled around the front of the Ford and launched herself; it didn't help. Earl swatted her away like a nuisance fly, sent her sprawling again. Returned his attention to Todd.

Lights were coming on up and down the lane. The neighbors. Earl was yelling and Sarah was crying, and Todd was hollering something, too, from the ground beside the pickup, begging Earl to stop. A lot of noise, too late at night. People were starting to appear in their windows and doorways, just watching for now, but Gruber knew they'd have to step in sooner or later.

Apparently, Earl knew it, too. He stood up from where he'd been beating on Todd, caught his breath, huffed and puffed for a second or two. Told Todd if he knew what was good for him, he wouldn't come around anymore. Then he grabbed Sarah where she lay crying on the gravel, pulled her to her feet, and dragged her, stumbling, back to the double-wide. The screen door squealed open. Slammed shut. Gruber hurried back to his bed.

He heard the rest of it, though. Earl in the living room, breaking things. Glass, naturally, and heavier stuff, too. The thudding and crashing sounding like the end of the world, and through it all, Sarah sobbing. Pleading with Earl. Crying out when Earl would slap her. This went on for a while. Gruber listened, rooted to his bed. Knew he should feel guilty about selling out his stepsister. Didn't. Felt giddy, instead.

You did this, he thought. *You caused this chaos. Maybe you're not such a little shit stain after all.*

< 21 >

"Ashley Frey's original profile says she's from Harrisburg," Stevens said, "but as Muriel94, she claims to be from Orlando. Is that right?"

"Correct," Windermere said. "And she told Adrian Miller she was sixteen. But Muriel94 was sixteen nearly four years ago."

"So maybe it isn't the same girl," Stevens said. "Maybe there's some kind of mix-up with the IPs or something, some kind of coincidence. Maybe there's a couple different Ashley Freys on this forum."

"Nope." This was Mathers, lodged in a corner with his own laptop, scrolling through Muriel94's chat logs. "This Muriel girl sends a picture of herself in this conversation I'm reading. Looks more than a little familiar."

Stevens and Windermere abandoned their own computers. Crossed the room to where Mathers was holding up his laptop, a picture of a pretty teenage girl about Adrian Miller's age, dark brown hair past her shoulders, a bright smile. A school picture. Windermere recognized it instantly.

"Ambriel98 sent that same picture to Adrian Miller," she said, feeling that churning in her stomach switch to something more electric, her cop instincts taking over. "Three years after Muriel94 sent hers."

"So either Ashley Frey found the fountain of youth," Stevens said, "or she's lying about her age. Who's she talking to in that chat you're reading, Derek?"

"Some kid in Texas," Mathers told him. "Loco459. He tells her his name is R. J. Ramirez. Says he's . . ." Mathers scanned the page. "Sick of life and everything about it, ready to join his brother in the next world. Seems like Muriel94 is trying to convince him to do it. 'Do it for me,' she says."

"'Do it for me.'" Stevens looked at Windermere, and his eyes were dark and concerned. "That's exactly what Ashley Frey told Adrian Miller before he—"

"Yeah." Windermere felt that tingling in her nerves turn into a buzz, a serious misgiving. She hurried back to her computer, punched R. J. Ramirez's name into a Google search. The first result gave her what she was afraid she would find: "El Paso Teen Found Dead by Suicide."

"*Stevens,*" she said, clicking through. "Come here."

Stevens caught her expression, came over fast. Read the news report on the screen. "'Authorities say sixteen-year-old R. J. Ramirez leapt from a railway bridge to his death early Monday morning. Foul play is not suspected.'"

He looked up. "What the heck, Carla?"

"What the heck is right," Windermere said, feeling her stomach start to churn. "What else can you give us on Ramirez, Mathers?"

"Muriel94 was trying to convince Ramirez to hang himself," Mathers said, his nose still in his laptop. "Asked him if his computer had a camera, she could watch him do it. Ramirez was noncommittal, told her he wasn't sure about the hanging part. Didn't want his mother to find him." He met her eyes. "That's the last conversation they ever had."

"And a month later, the next angel shows up." Stevens was reading through Nenad's username database. "Penemue96."

"Penemue96 had an online relationship with a fourteen-year-old from Sacramento, California, Shelley Clark," Mathers said, eyes on his own screen. "Sent the same picture, same details. Only, this time, Ashley Frey claimed to be from Detroit, Michigan."

"Shelley Clark committed suicide in November of that year," Windermere said. "Hanged herself in her bedroom, according to this article."

"At Ashley Frey's urging, apparently," Mathers said. "Again with the webcam, with the rope. 'Do it for me' all over again, just like with Adrian Miller. Shit, Carla, who the hell is this girl?"

Windermere didn't answer for a moment, staggered by the implications. This wasn't about finding some suicidal mystery girl, not any longer. There was something going on here, something deeper than a couple of kids with a death wish.

"Who the hell is she?" she replied. "The hell if I know, Mathers. But she isn't a victim, I'll tell you that much." She looked at Stevens. "This girl is a goddamn predator."

< **22** >

Sarah was different after that night with Earl.

Todd didn't come around anymore. No longer did Sarah hum and dance around her bedroom, checking her makeup in the mirror, batting her eyelashes, fixing her hair. She didn't smile at her secret thoughts, or giggle as she wrote in her journal. When Earl went out for the night, she stayed home. Sat in her room or watched TV, listless. Made sure she was in bed, lights off, by the time Earl's tires ground over the gravel again.

"Me and Todd broke up," she told Gruber as they walked home from school one day. Her lip quivered a little, and she bit it, looked away into the distance. "He said he couldn't deal with our family's drama. It creeped him right out, he said."

Our family. Meaning Earl.

Gruber knew she was fishing for sympathy. Wasn't ready to give it. Told her she shouldn't have been running around with Todd like that, anyway. Told her she was acting like a tramp and that she got what was coming.

Sarah turned on him, her eyes fierce. Drew back like she was fixing to slap him. He stood tall, dared her to do it. He was nearly as tall as she was, and just as strong.

But Sarah blinked first. Looked away, her shoulders slumping. Spent the rest of the walk home in silence.

Gruber watched her, knew he'd broken her. Realized he kind of liked the sensation. For the first time in a long time, he actually felt strong. He felt like he'd regained something, something Earl had taken from him.

He felt like a man, not some runty boy.

From then on, Gruber made Sarah his project. Every time Earl hit him, every mean word, he found his outlet in Sarah.

"Why are you so mean to me?" Sarah asked him after he'd broken into her bedroom, stolen her journal. Left it by the lunch tables in the school cafeteria, watched as someone found it, read it aloud, an audience gathering. "What did I ever do to you?"

She'd come home in tears. Knew it was he who'd done it; who else could it have been? Gruber hadn't hidden from her. Hadn't denied it. He'd stood up to her, dared her to do something. Hit him, fight him, tell Earl or his mother. He knew she wouldn't.

"Don't you dare tattle on me," he told her. "I'll tell Earl about the bottle under the bed. The cigarettes. He'll whup your ass worse than he whups mine, and you know it."

She stared at him, tears in her eyes, fists clenched, totally powerless, and he knew the frustration was driving her crazy. Knew the anger was worse when there was no kind of outlet, nothing she could do. Knew it because Earl had made him feel the same way.

"Now the whole school knows about me and Todd," Sarah said. "Todd won't even look at me, he's so embarrassed. He told his friends I'm nothing but a cheap slut."

"You are," Gruber told her. "You're a tramp for doing those things with Todd. You shouldn't have carried on with him like that."

Sarah didn't say anything. Ran off to her room, slammed the door shut, and through the hole, Gruber watched her collapse on the bed, watched the tears come down freely, watched and almost felt decent again.

< **23** >

"So here's the bad news," Stevens told SAC Harris. "Not only is there no record of an Ashley Frey anywhere in our systems, but the picture she sends out to her victims—we're calling them victims, because it seems to make sense—isn't even of our subject. It belongs to a young lady named Chantal Sarault. She lives in upstate New York, happily married, a couple of kids. She was shocked when we told her about Ashley Frey."

Drew Harris tented his fingers. Leaned forward and studied Stevens and Windermere across the desk. "Well, damn," he said. "Any good news?"

They'd brought the case to Harris first thing Monday morning. Explained the situation—Andrea Stevens's classmate, the suicide forums, Ashley Frey, R. J. Ramirez, Shelley Clark. Frey's other accounts, at least two, maybe more. The Special Agent in Charge had been a little miffed at first, at his violent crimes task force's use of Bureau resources on an unauthorized investigation, but Windermere watched him perk up as she outlined the details of the case, until he was nodding along with her, eyes alert, jotting little notes on his blotter as she talked.

"The good news?" Windermere shrugged. "I mean, at this stage, there really isn't much good news. We have a handle on Frey's MO, for starters, and she doesn't know we're on to her. Or *him*. Or whoever the hell this freak turns out to be."

"Regardless," Harris said. "You can essentially camp out on the forum and wait for the process to repeat itself."

"While we comb through the rest of the subject's online personas for clues as to her real-world location," Stevens added. "She's cultivated relationships with these victims lasting months, in some cases, so she's bound to have left some kind of lead behind." He paused. "I suggest we operate under the assumption that our subject is female until proven otherwise. But Carla's right. We can't even be sure Ashley Frey is a woman at this point. She's been that careful about hiding her true identity."

Windermere nodded along as her partner briefed the SAC. Tried to project the cool, rational Carla Windermere, the kickass special agent. Inside, she was all nerves and turbulence.

These leads are weak sauce, she thought. *There are how many other forums out there, and Ashley Frey could be lurking on any of them. We need to track her down fast.*

Harris said nothing for a beat. He leaned back in his chair. "You know," he said, "the legal side of this is kind of murky. According to the Supreme Court, people are within their First Amendment rights to encourage other people to commit suicide. There are state laws that say otherwise, but it's anyone's guess whether they'll hold up in court as constitutional."

"This is an online predator advising teenagers to kill themselves, sir," Windermere said. "The subject is giving them the methods and the means, down to the proper diameter of rope they're best using. Are you saying Ashley Frey isn't worth our resources?"

"I'm saying it's a gray area in the eyes of the law, Agent Windermere," Harris replied. "You track this person down, bring her up on charges, you might watch your whole case disintegrate on a free-speech argument. You really want to build a whole investigation just to see the courts let her off?"

"You're goddamn right we do." The words came out louder than Windermere had planned. Harris raised an eyebrow, but said nothing.

"This is *kids*," Windermere said. "This is some pervert on the Internet taking advantage of vulnerable children. You're saying you want us to sit back and let her keep doing this?"

"You don't have a legal reason to pursue this subject, Agent Windermere," Harris said. "She's not breaking any federal laws." He gestured to Stevens. "The state of Minnesota may want to look into whether any of their laws have been broken, but this isn't a federal matter."

"*Bullshit.*" She was standing now, leaning over Harris's desk. Knew Stevens was watching her, making eyes at her, telepathically screaming at her to calm down. She didn't. She wouldn't. "That's bullshit, Harris, and you know it," she said. "We shunt this off to the BCA, they're going to tell us they can't do shit because Frey's operating out of state, and they don't have a clue how to find her. They'll kick it back to us in a month, anyway, after they're through spinning their freaking wheels, and by that time Frey's got herself another victim, or maybe she's gone to ground."

Harris lifted a finger. *Caution.* "I hear you, Carla, but legally—"

"My ass, *legally*," she said. "Those laws were written before the Internet was invented. This is the first time anyone's ever seen a case like this. And if I'm the only one in this room with the balls to pursue it . . ." She pushed her chair out. Stood. "Then screw it. I'll see y'all at the Supreme Court."

She kicked her chair back in, turned on her heel, and stalked to the door. Shoved it open, caught it with the same motion, slammed it back so hard that heads popped up like prairie gophers all throughout CID.

"*Mind your freaking business,*" she told them, still running hot, breathing hard. "God *damn* it."

< **24** >

Windermere leaned against the wall outside Harris's office, catching her breath. Calming down, best she could. Trying to pretend like she hadn't just blown her stack in front of Harris, Stevens, heck, the whole CID.

Trying to pretend like the Supercop wasn't losing her cool.

Time passed. Five, ten minutes. Harris's door clicked open; Stevens stepped out. Scanned the hall and saw her, closed the door behind him. Took a couple steps toward her, rocked back on his feet and let out a long breath.

"Harris is okaying the investigation," he said. "Says he has our backs if we want to pursue this, says he'll go to bat for us with the ADA if it comes to it. Says you're right about the Internet thing, the interstate angle. It's probably up to the courts to decide, but that doesn't mean we can't track down this girl. That's what Harris says, anyway."

Windermere kept her eyes on the carpet. "Great," she said. "Guess I'm not going rogue, then, huh?"

Stevens didn't laugh. She looked up at him, and he was studying her, his eyes concerned. "You want to talk about what just happened in there, Carla?" he said.

"What just happened?" Windermere said. "What do you want to know, Stevens? You think I'm acting out of line or something?"

Cripes, she was thinking. *First Mathers, now Stevens. Word's going to get around I'm losing my cool.*

Stevens seemed to be choosing his words. "This is a screwed-up case," he said. "That Adrian Miller kid, the others. This isn't like anything else we've ever worked before. I get it."

She didn't say anything. Figured she'd let him talk until he ran out of steam. Then, maybe, they could get back to the freaking job.

"I'm just saying," Stevens said, "I can see how this stuff could affect you. And I want you to know I'm here for you, as your partner. If you ever want to talk about it, you know?"

Windermere pushed herself off the wall. Straightened up. "Yeah," she said, "I get it. I appreciate the gesture. But whatever you think you're seeing, it's not there. Nothing's up. I'm just fine, okay?"

Stevens shifted his weight. Windermere held his gaze.

"Can we *please* get back to work?" she said. "Maybe solve this case, instead of standing around wasting time talking about feelings?"

"Fine," Stevens said. "Sure, of course. But if you do want to talk—"

"I'll find you, I promise," she said, turning away from him. "Meet you back in the office, okay? I need a little fresh air."

She left him before he could answer. Crossed CID to the fire doors and hurried down the stairs to ground level, across the lobby to the front doors, the parking lot. Didn't slow down until she was outside in the chill air, the sky a flat, joyless gray above her.

She wanted another cigarette. She'd left her Marlboros at home, the pack hidden under the bathroom sink, behind her blow-dryer and curling iron and a couple boxes of tampons, squirreled away like contraband in the last place Mathers would dare poke his nose. Still, she craved a smoke now.

There were a couple of young women, admin people, smoking in a little huddle a few feet away. Windermere walked over, pasted a smile on her face, bummed a Virginia Slim and a light, hating herself for the need in her voice as she asked for the cigarette, for the way that first drag calmed her down.

She thanked the women for the cigarette, walked far enough away so she could smoke alone. Caught sight of her reflection in the Bureau building's massive black façade, stopped and examined herself, tall and angular and unpretty, her mouth too big, her neck thin and veiny.

You're losing it, Windermere, she thought. *These freaking kids and that Ashley Frey creep, they're pushing you over the edge.*

She took a last drag off the cigarette and immediately wished for another. *Keep it together. Just keep it together until you track Ashley Frey down. Don't let them all know what a head case you are.*

Windermere flicked the butt to the curb. Turned back to the front doors and caught her reflection again. *Yeah,* she thought. *Right. As if they can't tell already.*

< 25 >

Gruber focused all his anger on his stepsister. She'd ignored him at school, and now he didn't have any friends—but neither did Sarah, not after the journal incident. She spent her school hours alone, chased through the halls by laughter, by jeers, Todd's friends' knowing eyes.

Gruber set about making her home life just as unhappy. He put dish soap in her lemonade, scrubbed the bathroom floor with her toothbrush, put it back dirty. Poured bleach on her favorite blue dress the night of the school dance. Hurt her in every way he could think of, big and small, until she wasn't the same Sarah anymore, happy and carefree and dancing in her room. No, she was more like a lion in the zoo when he watched her, dragging herself around her bedroom all listless and defeated, her will to live gone.

Somehow, Earl's belt didn't hurt as much, now that Gruber had found his own outlet. He didn't spend his waking hours in fear, didn't tremble at the sound of Earl's boots in the hallway.

One day, he thought as Earl hit him again. *One day, I'll be bigger than you. And then you'll regret every second of this.*

The thought kept him warm. Kept him going. He was growing every day. Soon enough, he'd be a man. Just ask Sarah how tough he could be.

And then one day, maybe a month after the Todd incident, Gruber knelt down at the hole and saw that Sarah had found herself a razor blade.

She was sitting in the corner, her back against the door. She'd taken off her shirt, wore only a bra, and Gruber felt a tingle of excitement when he saw her pale stomach, the flimsy white fabric. Sarah was staring at her forearm, at a thin line of red.

He was confused at first, until he saw the razor in her other hand. Flat metal, the glint of the blade. He didn't know where she'd found it. Didn't understand what she was doing.

She stared down at the trickle of blood for a long time. Watched as it oozed from the cut and dripped down her pale skin. He watched, too, mesmerized. It made a beautiful contrast, the deep red and her near-translucent white. It had to hurt, but she didn't seem upset about it. She looked enthralled, captivated, *relieved*.

He watched Sarah with the razor for days before he found the courage to ask her about it.

They were in the living room, watching TV. A weekend. Earl and Gruber's mother were out buying groceries and liquor, and Sarah kept eyeing the door. Gruber wanted to say something to her, something about the cutting, but he couldn't think of anything that wouldn't give away the hole in the wall. So he kept his mouth shut, kept searching his brain. Then she twisted in her seat and the sleeve of her T-shirt rode up, exposing the scars on her arm, long and red and ruler-straight.

He stared. Sarah caught him, followed his eyes. Stiffened and turned away. She didn't say anything for a long time.

He waited.

"It feels good," she said finally. "I don't expect you to understand. You wouldn't *get it*. You don't know how hard it is to grow up in this awful place."

"Are you kidding?" Gruber replied. "Of course I know. I didn't ask to move out here. Your dad fricking hates me. This place is *hell*."

"You got that right. Even more so when you're around."

Sarah looked at him, hard, challenging him, defiant. New life in her eyes, like she'd found something in that razor blade the same as what he'd found when he hurt her.

"These scars are mine," Sarah told him. "And no matter how much he or you or anyone else tries to fuck up my life, this is something that will never be yours. The way the blood comes, that's mine, and mine alone."

Gruber watched her study the scars, run her fingertips over those ragged lines. "Cool story," he said. "Maybe someday you'll have the guts to actually do it right."

< 26 >

Even with Drew Harris's blessing, Ashley Frey wasn't easy to find.

Stevens and Windermere combed the NCIC—National Crime Information Center—database for records of anyone named Ashley Frey. For cases with a similar profile. Found nothing.

"It's like Harris said," Stevens told Windermere. "This is a legal gray area. People kill themselves. It's not like anyone's putting in too much legwork tracking down the buddy who told them how."

Windermere had been searching for suicide cases that fit the description. Came up just as empty. "Thirty-five thousand people commit suicide in this country every year," she said. "Four thousand teenagers. It's impossible to track down the details on every single case."

They had Mathers reading through Ashley Frey's old chat logs, dating back nearly four years. Hundreds and hundreds of pages, the victims mostly complaining about their parents, their classmates, how much they hated their lives.

"It would be tedious if I didn't know how these stories ended," Mathers told them when they gathered for coffee and a status report. "Instead, it's just chilling. This Ashley Frey person plays along with the whole thing. In one version, she's the only child of an absentee father. In the next, her stepfather's molesting her. In another, she's just a rich kid who's depressed. It's like she tailors her profiles to fit the situation, like she waits to see what kind of personality the victim will like best."

Windermere drank her coffee, imagined Adrian Miller online, trolling the forums. Imagined this Ashley Frey girl befriending him, playing him, guiding him to his death. Shook her head clear and tried to focus.

"But you're not finding anything that points us to Frey," she said. "She's not giving you any clues?"

"Nothing concrete," Mathers said. "She uses a lot of the same arguments to coerce her victims, though. That's a constant."

"What kind of arguments?" Stevens said.

"Like when she was telling Adrian Miller to do it for her," Mathers told them. "She did the same with Ramirez and Clark and the others. Like, she talks about how she's too scared to do it by herself, how she needs someone to do it with her, to show her how it's done."

"She's worked out a formula," Windermere said. "Figures this is the best way to get kids to kill themselves for her. Like it's a freaking science."

"There's something else," Mathers said. "Frey has all these made-up stories, like I was saying. Her backstory is never the same, from victim to victim, but there are common elements. The biggest one is this Earl thing."

"What's the Earl thing?" Windermere said. "Like, she talks about knowing someone named Earl? Please tell me it's more solid than that."

Mathers put down his coffee mug. Picked up a sheaf of printouts, Ashley Frey's chat logs, and she could see he'd highlighted passages. "In the absentee-father scenario, Earl's the dad," he said. "Ditto the step-father who's molesting her. A couple of times, with Shelley Clark and Adam DeLong, the third victim, Frey talks about how she just wants to prove to Earl that she'll go ahead and actually do it."

Windermere eyed him over the printouts. "So who the heck is Earl?"

"No idea," Mathers said. "But whoever he is, it sure sounds like he and Frey have some unresolved issues."

< 27 >

In the end, it wasn't the blade that Sarah chose, when she decided to do it right.

Gruber was watching her through the hole again, after dinner, a weeknight. She'd been quiet on the walk home from school, even quieter than usual. She'd picked at her dinner, excused herself fast, disappeared down the hall.

Gruber did the dishes and went to his room, pushed the painting aside, eager to watch her some more. It had been five or six months that he'd been peering at her through that hole, a half year's worth of secret glimpses. It felt good, an addiction, the only thing that really mattered. Gruber lived for these moments, for the stirrings they built inside him, the electric urges.

Sarah was kind of boring tonight. She lay on her bed for a long time, staring up at the ceiling. Sometimes she stood and paced around the bedroom. Dug under her bed for a magazine and flipped through the pages, her face a blank mask.

He grew frustrated, then bored. Left her alone and went to watch TV in the living room for a while, game shows with his mother, *Jeopardy!* and *Wheel of Fortune*. Sarah stayed in her room. He didn't know how she could stand to be in there for so long.

When he checked on her, it was dark, and Earl had disappeared for the night. Their mother had retreated to her bedroom, closed her door. Gruber's homework was finished. He had nothing to do. He hoped Sarah would be more interesting this time around.

She had the bottle out, was the first thing he noticed. It wasn't the same bottle obviously; she'd been sneaking them in with an increasing frequency as the months wore on. This bottle was filled with brown liquid, Jim Beam, like Earl drank. She was about halfway through it, and it was the first time Gruber had seen it.

It was the first time he'd seen the rope, too. Yellow rope, like the kind the guy across the trailer park used to tie up his poor dog. Rough, plasticky stuff, the kind that burned through your skin if you held on too tight while playing tug-of-war, or whatever. The rope was about an inch thick. Sarah was fiddling with it, tying some kind of complicated knot.

She wasn't crying, but she didn't exactly seem happy, either. Her face was still blank, her eyes almost lifeless. Like she was through being the lion at the zoo. Like she was a robot carrying out some mechanical task. She finished the knot and held it up to examine it. Gruber recognized it. He'd seen it in Western movies, cowboys and Indians. A hangman's noose.

Holding the other end of the rope, she brought it to her closet. Shoved her clothes to the side, the blouses and dresses and sweaters, until there was only a bare stretch of dull metal dowel. She examined it for a moment. Then she started to loop the rope around its length.

He watched her, the thrill starting deep in his belly and radiating outward. This was serious, he knew. This was something far more dangerous than the game with the razor. He wondered if she would really do it, how far she would go.

But he could see from her face that she was finished playing games. She was beyond that point; she was determined. He had convinced her. The only question was whether he would let her go ahead with it.

Gruber was breathing heavy, feverish, sweat blearing his glasses. He knew his stepsister would die if he didn't do something. Knew it was wrong to watch and do nothing. Couldn't turn away. Couldn't move.

She was in the closet now. She was almost ready. He watched her take a deep breath, survey the little bedroom. Her eyes scanned the window, the mirror, the bed. And then they landed on the hole in the wall.

Gruber froze. Held his breath as long as he could, until he couldn't stand another second and he had to inhale, a loud, sucking gasp that *must* have given away his position, must have betrayed to Sarah that he was watching her.

But if she knew he was watching, she didn't seem to care. She looked away from the hole, leveled her chin, her shoulders squared, her eyes defiant. She took another breath, tested the rope. Closed her eyes.

Gruber watched. He watched until it was over, and Sarah was gone.

< 28 >

Madison Mackenzie was sick of it.

Another city. Another crummy neighborhood to bum around in, another shitty house. Family dinners with her mother and her sisters, her mom's forced cheerfulness doing nothing to hide the stress in her eyes, the fatigue. Another move. Still no work. Still no money.

Another high school. Classes full of kids wearing designer clothes, talking on expensive cell phones, driving cars their parents had bought them. Eating lunch at McDonald's every day of the week, while Madison filled her brown bags with last night's leftovers, with tomato sandwiches, celery sticks. Cheapness.

She ate those brown-bag lunches alone. Not that this was anything new, either. She was sick of having to smile and be pretty and fight to fit in all over again, when, if history was any precedent, her mom would just pick up the family and skip town like usual in a few months, a year.

She was sick of having to dress the way everyone else dressed, hit the right parties, date the right people. Sick of having to put forth all that effort.

She'd put forth the effort the first, like, dozen times. She'd pooled her meager savings and splurged on a few outfits that resembled what the popular kids were wearing. Tried to make friends with the people who everyone liked, hung out at the trendy spots after school. She tried her freaking hardest to fit in, make friends, be cool. But something always went wrong. Somebody always noticed that the clothes she was wearing were off-brand. The gap between her front teeth was a little too wide. Her accent was funny. She walked goofy.

There was always a reason they turned on her.

It took maybe two weeks for Tampa to go sour.

Madison looked in the mirror on a Monday morning and found the biggest, reddest zit in the world staring back at her from the end of her nose. Like a supersized growth, all angry and huge. Like no makeup in the world was going to cover it up; the zit was probably visible from space.

Lena Jane Poole saw it first. Within five minutes of Madison walking through the school doors.

"Holy *zit*." Lena Jane pointed, giggling, her friends crowding around. "New girl, you're Rudolph the Red-Nosed *Loser*."

And that was that. Rudolph. Nobody in the whole school could remember Madison's name, but they sure remembered "Rudolph." The name chased her down the hall, through every class, in stereo. Even after the zit disappeared, the nickname stuck.

Rudolph with your nose so bright . . .

Not that the details really mattered. There was always a reason they turned on her, always something she did wrong. She cut out of class and smoked cigarettes by herself down the block, far away from the school and Lena Jane and her friends. Screw them. She was sick of busting her ass to be normal when, no matter what she did, someone always came around and pushed life's giant reset button, and everything wiped away and she had to do it again.

She was sick of it.

She'd started lurking around online suicide forums a week or so after her mom moved them to Florida. She'd read a little about Sylvia Plath, about Virginia Woolf, figured if it was good enough for those women, why not for her?

You say you want to do something, don't talk about it. Do it. But most of the people on the forums were weirdos. There were the obvious fetishists. Goths, or whatever. The people fascinated by death, but not so much enamored of the idea to experience it firsthand. People for whom suicide was a fantastic idea in theory, but not so much in the gritty reality. After all, how could you continue to obsess over your own personal melodrama if you weren't around to enjoy it?

As far as Madison could figure, most people who were actually serious about ending their lives were out doing exactly that. They weren't online moaning about their situations, or batting around theories and conjecture. They were dead already, or in the process of becoming. Maybe going on the forums was nothing but a stupid waste of time.

But then she found something. Someone. Not on any of the major forums, the ones that attracted the bulk of the posers and death freaks. A smaller site that showed up at the bottom of her Google search, a place simply called The End.

Here, wandering through the personals section of the forum, she found Gabriel98.

According to his profile, Gabriel98 was an eighteen-year-old boy from Iowa. He had a cute picture, was handsome in a midwestern, unpretentious way. He was smiling, but there was something behind the smile, a pain in his eyes that made Madison immediately want to reach out and hug him.

Seeking like-minded spirits who are fed up with the struggle, his profile read. *Fellow quitters, apply within.*

He'd been online for four months, Madison noticed. A slightly concerning amount of time. If he'd really been serious about quitting, wouldn't he have gone ahead and, you know, done it already?

Still, he seemed interesting. Cute and kind of mysterious. Madison opened a chat box.

So why haven't you done it yet? she typed.

‹ 29 ›

Randall Gruber was creating a new persona on the Death Wish forum when he heard the chime from another open tab on his browser. He'd been riding the high all week, seeing Adrian Miller every time he closed his eyes: the boy rigging the noose, downing the last of the whiskey. Felt an electric thrill when he thought about what came after.

Adrian Miller. The ninth teenager he'd watched die, six of those recorded on webcam, not only for Gruber's viewing pleasure but for those of his acolytes, too. He'd packaged Adrian's footage, sent it off yesterday. The response from his contact was almost instantaneous.

Outstanding! Great picture quality. Awesome sound. We're going to make a lot of money with this.

Good news, though Gruber didn't care so much about the money. The real magic was in the footage itself, in the images burned into Gruber's mind.

Nine dead now. The first two, those awkward fumbling efforts—the breakthrough in Texas and the second, Sacramento, soon after. He'd been too caught up in the thrill of victory to care that the footage didn't cut it—the prospect had spurned the webcam in Texas; in Sacramento, the footage was grainy and off-center—but later on, replaying the kill, he'd realized he needed clarity. A better picture, and sound. If he couldn't be in the room with the victim, Gruber wanted the next best thing.

Adrian Miller had given him that clarity. But the killing was addictive, and Gruber wanted to watch again. The high never lasted long enough.

The notification hadn't come from any of the big forums, Gruber saw, but from one of the minor sites.

The End, it was called. Catered to the no-nonsense crowd, high turnover rates. The users weren't there to buy webcams or learn about rope. They had their plans. They were looking for tips, troubleshooting, one last affirmation, but they generally killed themselves without needing Gruber's help. Which would have been fine, except they wouldn't let him watch.

Gruber wasn't "Ashley" on this site. He was Brandon, a clean-cut farm kid, his profile designed to cater to lonely girls mostly, and to the kind of teen boys whose uncertain sexuality had driven them to the forums in the first place. He'd found one prospect here, a fifteen-year-old from Baltimore named Dylan, but it wasn't Dylan who'd messaged him today. The user was a young girl, a teenager, "DarlingMadison." Gruber clicked on her profile picture. Stared.

The resemblance was uncanny.

She was Sarah, this person. Give her lighter hair, just a little. Maybe put a smile on her face instead of that tough-girl glare. She *was* Sarah, though, the same bone structure. The same way her bangs curled down over her eyes. She looked like Sarah had, years ago, in her bedroom in that double-wide.

Gruber stared at her picture and felt his heart pounding. Felt as if he could reach through the screen and touch her.

He'd gone online to talk to Dylan. To cultivate his next prospect. He hadn't intended to make more friends; he had a rule about these accounts, one prospect per persona. Plus, he'd just opened a new Death Wish account no more than five minutes ago. But this girl, this DarlingMadison—if ever there was a sign from above, this was it.

Gruber clicked through to her message. *So why haven't you done it yet?* she'd asked.

He hesitated, his mind searching for just the right words. Draw her in slowly. Don't scare her off.

Guess I'm just waiting for the right partner, he wrote. Hovered his hand over the mouse for a long time.

Then pressed send.

< **30** >

"Here it is," Mathers said, looking up from his computer. "Someone behind that anonymizer software just opened up a new account on the Death Wish site. Links back to that same Ashley Frey Outlook account."

Stevens and Windermere hurried over. "'Azrael99,'" Windermere read. "'Sixteen years old. Vancouver, Canada.'"

"Guess she's broadening her range," Stevens said. "Trying to get a piece of that Canadian market?"

"Whatever she's doing, she literally just did it," Mathers said. "This account wasn't here fifteen minutes ago."

Windermere studied the profile. As with Ashley Frey's previous personas, there wasn't much information. A username. A profile picture—poor Chantal Sarault, standing in yet again. A location, and a tagline—LIFE IS FOR THE DYING—that could have belonged to anyone on the forum. Nothing to give away Ashley Frey's real identity. Nothing but a blank slate onto which the next unhappy teenager could project his desires.

"It sure didn't take her long to get over Adrian Miller," Windermere said. "This chick is picking up speed."

"She's found a model and she's using it," Stevens said. "Refining her MO, streamlining it. Just like we figured."

"So how do we stop her?" Mathers asked.

THE WATCHER IN THE WALL

Stevens and Windermere looked at each other, and Windermere knew Stevens was having the same thoughts as she was.

"We create a fake profile," she said. "Lure Ashley Frey to us. String her along as a potential victim, and hope like hell we can pry something out of her to reveal her location. Best-case scenario, we catch her. Worst-case, she spends her time with us instead of some other poor teen."

"Works for me," Stevens said. "So let's do it."

< 31 >

Madison hadn't really expected a response from Gabriel98. She'd logged off as soon as she sent the message, ashamed that she'd even bothered. But then she'd logged on again, just a few hours later.

Maybe just to see, she thought. *Just to see, what if he actually answered.*

He had.

Guess I'm just waiting for the right partner, he'd written. Kind of a cheesy line, like something he'd practiced. Or maybe he'd used it before.

Slow down, tiger, she typed. *You on here to get laid, or do you really want to die?*

Then she waited. Regarded Gabriel98's profile picture again, those haunted, piercing eyes. Felt something, and it wasn't necessarily the urge to die. *Write back,* she thought, and immediately hated herself for thinking it.

Then her computer chimed. His reply. *Oh, I'm going for it,* he wrote. *One hundred percent. I'm just searching for someone who's actually serious about doing it with me.*

There are so many posers on these sites, Madison wrote back. *Most of these assholes are going to die warm in their beds in the nursing home sixty years from now. There's nobody real.*

Totally agree, Gabriel replied. *Too many time wasters. And you?*

Madison blinked. *And me what?*

Are you real?

Madison looked at Gabriel's picture again. *Hell yes,* she wrote. *I'm as real as it gets.*

< **32** >

They worked on the profile for a solid hour. Chose a username—XXBlackDaysXX—and raided Mathers's laptop for an old school picture.

"Why me?" Mathers asked Windermere.

"You're barely out of grade school," Windermere told him. "Plus, you're not famous yet. Stevens is too old to be playing a moody teen, and I've had my picture in the paper too much to stay incognito."

Mathers grinned. "The curse of the Supercop."

"Anyway, if we want to attract this girl's attention, it's better if we're a guy."

"That's assuming she's a girl at all."

"She's playing a girl on the Internet, Derek. We're playing the guy who thinks she's cute in her profile picture. That's all that matters, at this point."

"Fair enough," Mathers said, uploading the picture. "But we need some kind of backstory. What's our boy doing on this forum, besides scoping out the hotties?"

Stevens and Windermere didn't say anything for a moment. Then Stevens shifted his weight. "Sure," he said. "What if we're being bullied in school? That seems pretty common."

"Okay," Mathers said. "Why, though?"

"Because we're clumsy and awkward," Windermere said. "Because we're constantly doing silly shit like falling on our faces in front of the whole school, or wearing our shirts inside out. Or wearing the same clothes over and over because our dad's in the hospital and our relatives don't have enough money to buy us a new wardrobe every month—or year, for that matter. Or maybe we don't have any friends because we're too tall and funny-looking, and we don't go to school dances, because if we do, we just stand against the wall because nobody would ever be caught dead dancing with us.

"We're lonely," Windermere continued. "We see everyone else in the whole goddamn school walking around with friends and, like, girl-friends or whatever, but we go home alone. We go home and wash our shitty clothes until they're threadbare so we can wear them tomorrow without smelling bad, and we don't go to parties or out to the movies, and even the friends we *do* think we have would sell us out at a moment's notice, just for a chance to be more popular." She exhaled. "How's that?"

Stevens and Mathers were staring at her. Mathers's eyes were wide, like she'd just told him she'd emigrated from Neptune. Stevens was studying her with that concerned-dad expression of his, like he knew there was something the matter and he didn't want to let it go until he'd sorted out the problem.

Windermere took a step back, feeling flushed. "Or, whatever," she said. "Those are just, you know, suggestions."

"That's a backstory, all right," Mathers said, turning back to his laptop. "Should I just type that out and send Ashley Frey a message, then?"

"Heck, no," Stevens replied. "We send her a message so quick, she's going to smell something funny. We need to draw her to us."

"Okay. How?"

"We wait," Windermere said. The men turned to her, as though they hadn't expected her to speak up again. As though they figured her little rant had been her exit speech. She pressed on. "We bat our eyes and try to look pretty, and hope that she sees us. Maybe we post something on one of the forum threads, something she's bound to see. Something that'll make her take notice."

"I like it," Stevens said. "Some kind of forum post. She likes lonely teenagers. Let's play up Carla's angle."

"But we're not lonely teenagers," Mathers said. "What if she sees through us, smells a rat?"

"We'll take that chance," Stevens said. "I'd say we have a pretty authentic, ah, backstory to work with."

"Fine." Mathers studied the screen, his picture in the profile XXBlack-DaysXX. "But if this comes back to bite me, I'm going to be pissed, you guys."

Windermere hit him. "What are you going to do, Mathers?" she said. "Tell the principal?"

< 33 >

Gruber friended DarlingMadison on "Brandon's" Facebook page. Printed out her profile picture and brought it to work with him, taped it up in his locker in the break room.

He couldn't see her picture without thinking about Sarah. Without flashing back to that last night in the double-wide, to the thrill he'd felt as he watched her, that high-voltage intensity, the power. Earl hadn't killed Sarah; *he* had. And he would do it to this girl, as he'd done with all the others.

He typed her a message on his phone. *So what brought you here? Why do you want to kill yourself?*

She answered. *I'm just sick of living,* she said. *You know? Sick of putting out the effort all the time just so a bunch of assholes at school can push me around. My mom keeps moving us to new cities and I keep having to change schools and I never fit in. I hate feeling like an outsider, but it's never going to change. I figure I might as well get on with it.*

Yeah, Gruber wrote. *I know what you mean. Why do you move around so much?*

Mom's broke, DarlingMadison replied. *Dad ran away. Dog died. It's like a country song. Wah-wah.*

Gabriel98: *Do you like country music?*

DM: *Hell no. Sure made it awkward when we were living in Texas.*

DM: *Do you?*

G: *Not really. Some of it's okay.*

DM: *What music do you like?*

Gruber opened a new Internet window on his phone, brought up a music website, trendy hipster stuff. One of his prospects had sent him the link when he'd made the mistake of telling her he liked Justin Bieber.

G: *M83. Kanye. Arcade Fire. I like a bit of everything.*

G: *You?*

DM: *Yeah, pretty much. I really like classic rock, but nobody else does. One more reason I'm an outcast.*

G: *What kind of classic rock?*

DM: *Zeppelin. Rush. The Who. Frank Zappa. I dunno. Shit my dad used to play when he drove me to school in the morning.*

Gruber almost wrote back, telling her he hated that stuff. Remembering Earl playing it in the kitchen of that little double-wide, volume cranked, singing along, loud. Realized he was forgetting himself, getting careless. Too caught up in the whole Sarah connection.

Right, he wrote back instead. *I know a little bit of that stuff. It's cool.*

DM: *Hah. You don't have to patronize me. I know I have weird tastes.*

Was she mad? Gruber wished he could see her face. He could always tell if Sarah was mad, just the way she looked at him. The way she said his name, *Ran-dy,* the syllables clipped and distinct. He always knew.

He couldn't know with this one, but he wanted to know. He didn't want to lose her. He couldn't.

Then she wrote back. *Anyway, whatever. Why are you doing it?*

The door to the break room opened before Gruber could think up an answer. Adam Osing, Gruber's acne-scarred punk boss, poked his head inside.

"Gruber," he said, frowning. "What are you doing in here? Your shift started twenty minutes ago."

Gruber held up his phone. "Important phone call. Family emergency."

Osing's expression didn't change. "Yeah, well," he said. "Do it on your own time. We need you in ladies' fashions. Cleanup in the maternity aisle."

Osing waited, watched as Gruber made a show of turning off his cell phone, tucking it away in his locker. Turned on his heel and walked back out of the break room as Gruber closed the locker door. Quickly, in case Osing returned, Gruber fished the phone out of his locker. Opened the chat box.

DarlingMadison had written, *Hello?*

Gruber stared at the screen, Earl fresh in his mind, Sarah. He could see Sarah dancing around her little bedroom in that pretty blue dress. He could hear Earl's music cranked out in the kitchen, Jim Morrison singing "Five to One" at high volume. Could remember the way his body tensed up when Earl's boots stopped outside his bedroom door, the way his whole being would freeze up from the fear.

The break-room door opened. Osing again, his cheeks flushed and getting redder. "Move it, Gruber," he said. "I catch you on that phone again during work hours, I'll shit-can you, I swear."

Gruber turned away. "Yeah. One second."

Why am I doing this? he wrote. *Because fuck my stepfather, that's why.*

< 34 >

Fuck my stepfather, that's why.

It was Earl who'd found Sarah's body. Gruber watched him push open Sarah's door, watched his bleary, drunken eyes scan the room. Watched the way those eyes seemed to come into focus when he found Sarah in the closet. Watched how Earl didn't do anything, didn't run to her, try and save her. Just took a pull from the bottle in his hand and spit and looked at her.

"Well," he said. "Shit."

The police showed up pretty soon after that. Gruber replaced the painting and climbed into bed and pretended he didn't know, pretended to be surprised and sad and scared. The police investigated Sarah's room and took her body away, and then an officer in plainclothes came into Gruber's room and sat down on the bed and started asking questions. Gruber didn't tell him about the hole in the wall, and the man never knew.

But the police found out about Earl. It took a few days, but then they came back to the motor court again and parked in front of the trailer, three patrol cars, and they came into the house and stood in the living room with Earl and Gruber's mom, and they talked about the autopsy and the bruises they'd found, and the cuts and the other things, too.

And then Earl was shouting and swearing and fighting with the cops, and a couple big officers put him in handcuffs and took him out of the trailer and locked him up in the back of their cruiser and drove away, and then it was just Gruber and his mom in that double-wide, and even that didn't last very long, a day or two, maybe, and then the doctors came for Gruber, he'd gone with them, and that was the last he ever saw of that shitty double-wide.

But he dreamed of going back. Finding Earl—it wouldn't be that hard. Showing him how he'd grown up. What he'd become. Showing Earl what it felt like to be the weak one for a change.

He'd traced the route home many times in his head, imagined himself surprising Earl with a visit. Turning the tables on the bastard, bashing his head in. Showing him just what a powerful, hateful being he'd created.

But he hadn't done it, not yet. He didn't know where Earl was living, for starters. And anyway, he knew he'd go to jail if he murdered his stepfather, might even wind up on death row. And Gruber didn't want to die, no matter how much he hated Earl. He was too addicted to the watching.

It had taken a long time to develop his method, a lot of trial and error, a few narrow escapes. People didn't take kindly to men with Gruber's tastes. They called the police, or sometimes they came after Gruber themselves, with baseball bats, knives, a pistol once or twice. He'd learned to steer clear. Picked up a snuff habit, underground videos. Death and dismemberment from the comfort of his home. Knew there had to be a way he could get his own fix.

The epiphany came unexpected and was long awaited, more than a decade after Sarah. He was working the next state over, some dead-end job pumping gas for cash a quarter mile from the local high school.

Three kids came into the gas station, burnouts, all of them, black clothes and heavy makeup, the strong odor of pot.

"That's not how the guy on the forum said to do it," the tallest one was saying, his voice a dull, disinterested monotone. "He said you need to run a hose from the tailpipe to the window, if you really want it to work. Otherwise it'll take, like, forever."

The only girl in the group shook her head. "Whatever," she said. "It's not like I have a car, anyway."

"Besides, who says you can trust a guy on a suicide forum?" the third one said. "By the very nature of his still being alive, he's untrustworthy."

The kids brought their purchases to the counter—bags of chips, Snickers bars, a bag of beef jerky. Gruber studied them as he began to ring it up.

"What forum?" he asked.

The kids looked at one another, suspicious, surprised that he'd spoken. Looked around the tiny store.

"The forum you're talking about," Gruber said. "What is it?"

Another long pause. "Never mind," the girl said. "Just ring up our lunches, *please*. We're late for class."

"You said a suicide forum," Gruber told her. "What does that mean?"

"Duh," the girl said. "It's a forum for people to talk about suicide. Like, methods and stuff. And if you're not sure and want someone to talk to."

Gruber felt an electric thrill course through his body. "A forum," he said. "On the Internet?"

The kids didn't even bother to answer. Just looked at him the way the kids at his school used to, like he was slow. Simple.

"What's it called?"

The kids hesitated again. "Death Wish," they said finally. "You're not, like, going to tell anyone, are you?"

Gruber finished ringing up their purchases. Took their money, bagged their junk food. The girl asked for a box of Marlboros, almost as an afterthought. Gruber rang those up, too. Didn't even bother to card her.

He had bigger things to think about.

< 35 >

Windermere stayed late at the office, worked into the night, scouring the Death Wish forum and Ashley Frey's history for a way into the subject's head. The Criminal Investigative Division was deserted, dead quiet, perfect working conditions. But Windermere wasn't making any progress. Frey was a cipher; she didn't leave clues.

The elevator dinged across the long rows of cubicles. Windermere ignored it, forgot the sound as soon as the echo died away. Stared at her computer screen and searched for an answer. Then someone knocked at her office door.

Mathers. He smiled in at her, sheepish, held up a bag of Thai takeout. "Date night," he said. "Teach Mathers to Cook Day, remember? Did we reschedule again, and I missed the memo?"

Windermere stared at him until she got it. The freaking ceviche they were supposed to make together. They'd rain-checked the last time. Apparently, tonight was the night.

She looked back at her computer. "Give me a couple minutes, Derek," she said. "I'm still working this Frey deal. Let me just finish up."

"Take your time." Mathers came into the office, sat in Stevens's chair. Set the bag down in front of her, grease and glorious smells. "I figured you'd probably want to postpone our little cooking class, even if you didn't tell me," he said. "I brought nourishment."

"Thanks." She kept her eyes on her computer. Only, this time she wasn't sure what she was looking for. Mainly, she was just hoping Mathers would leave.

But Mathers wasn't getting the telepathic hint. He rooted in the bag, pulled out a paper carton, a pair of chopsticks. Chicken pad thai, panang beef. Windermere's stomach grumbled despite herself. The bastard knew the way to her heart.

"I've been thinking about this case," he said, chewing. "I know it has its hooks in you, more than most cases we've worked. I've been trying to figure out why."

He paused, apparently to allow her to respond. Windermere ignored the opportunity. After a moment, Mathers continued.

"It's about the kids, isn't it?" he asked her. "That's what's different about this case. That's why it's affecting you. It's that they're kids, right? That's what's getting to you."

She exhaled, closed her eyes. Pictured her old high school, the days after Rene Duclair, the way the halls were so quiet. Hushed voices, muffled sobs. Wanda Rose dabbing at her eyes like she and Rene had been best friends.

And then, a week later, the big game against Olive Branch. A pep rally, Wanda leading the cheer squad. No mention of Rene, as if she'd never existed.

Windermere remembered. She'd cheered as loud as the rest.

"Yeah, Derek," she said. "It's the kids."

"I knew it." Mathers was smiling a little, couldn't meet her eyes. "It's a tragedy, that's for sure, but I have to say, Carla, it's kind of cool that you actually *care* about these people."

She frowned. "What are you talking about?"

He kind of blushed. Hemmed and hawed, like he'd jumped into the deep end and realized he couldn't swim.

"I know we haven't been together that long," he said. "I guess I always wondered how you'd feel about starting a family someday. Like, I always thought you'd be against it, no debate, and maybe you are, but it's still nice to see you caring about these kids."

She stared at him. "That's what you think this is?" she said slowly. "You think I'm freaking out because my maternal instinct suddenly decided to kick into gear?"

"I guess I don't know what to think," Mathers replied. "You won't talk to me, Carla. I'm stuck throwing darts in the dark over here."

"Did you forget who you're talking to?" she asked him. "Do you know who I am, Derek? You're asking me to bring more people into this world? To *raise* them?"

"Why not?" Mathers said. "You're not as bad a person as you try to pretend. I think I know you pretty well by now, and I think you'd be a pretty good mother, if you wanted."

Windermere laughed in his face. "Well, you're wrong," she said. "You don't know me at all. I'm a piece of shit, Derek. You just don't know it yet."

Mathers leaned forward. Reached for her hand. She pulled it back.

"What on earth makes you say that?" he asked her. "How can you feel that way? You're the freaking Supercop, Carla. How many lives have you saved? How can you sit there and try and tell me that trash?"

Because I'm a monster, Windermere thought. *Because there's a girl who's been dead, what, nearly twenty years, and she might still be alive if I was just a fraction of a decent human being, but I'm not.*

She'd never told Mathers. Couldn't do it, knew he'd leave her if he knew. Knew he'd tell everyone—Stevens, Harris, the whole goddamn Bureau. She couldn't have that. Couldn't deal with it. Especially not in the middle of this case.

She turned back to her computer instead. "I gotta get back to work, Derek. That means you have to go."

He started to argue. Windermere cut him off.

"This case isn't going to solve itself," she told him. "Ashley Frey isn't going to just show up in the lobby and reveal her true identity. That means I have to find her. That means you have to leave. I'll see you back at home later, and we'll forget this ever happened, okay?"

Mathers met her gaze, held it, seemed to be weighing his options. Finally, he deflated. "I'm worried about you, Carla," he said.

"Don't be," she told him. "I'm the freaking Supercop, remember?" She eyed the cartons of food on the desk, felt her stomach growl again. "You want to do something nice for me?" she asked him. "Leave the pad thai when you go."

< 36 >

Even with Windermere pulling all-nighters at the office, the Ashley Frey case had stalled out.

"It's been a week," Windermere said when Stevens came into CID the next Monday. "I have Mathers scouring Urban Dictionary for the hottest new slang every day, and we still can't get Frey to notice our profile."

They'd played it cool, like they planned. Focused on building a presence in the forum, building their avatar—XXBlackDaysXX—into a fully realized personality. Mathers spent a couple hours a day trolling the forums, posting in current threads, making his own posts, juicy stuff, bait for Frey. *I'm sick of everything. Want to die. Help.*

But Ashley Frey wasn't biting.

"Says here she hasn't even been online more than fifteen minutes, total, this past week," Mathers told Stevens and Windermere. "Whatever our subject is doing, wherever and *whoever* she might be, she's not focused on this site."

"Keep trying," Windermere told him. "She's built a new profile because she wants a new victim. We damn well better be that victim, or another kid is going to die."

In the meantime, Stevens and Windermere worked through the last remnants of their sex-trafficking case, closed the doors on the degenerate brothel owners and strip-club bosses who'd bought the young women their prime target had imported. Closed the case, more or less, dropped the file on Harris's desk and waited as he flipped through it.

"Good stuff," he told them once he'd scanned the report. "Really good. Guess we're just about ready to put that nasty business to bed, huh?"

"Done and done," Stevens told the SAC. "At this point, we're pretty confident we nailed every scumbag who even thought about buying a woman from those bastards."

Harris slid the file aside. "And what about the current case? Any progress?"

"Nothing concrete," Stevens said. "Our subject opened a new account on the Death Wish forum last week. Same Ashley Frey alias. We've been trying to attract her attention, but she's been offline more than she's been on. When she comes back, we'll be ready."

Harris thought it over. "How many of these forums do you think there could be?"

"Tons," Windermere said. "The Death Wish site is the biggest, but there are others of comparable size. And smaller ones, too, more special-ized. Newsgroups and the like."

"But you've only traced this Frey person through the one big site," Harris said. "You think there's a chance he or she could be trolling the other sites, too?"

Stevens and Windermere looked at each other. "It's a definite possi-bility, sir," Windermere told Harris. "We only have a lock on the Death Wish account. No way to trace her to the other forums."

"So she could be working her next victim as we speak," Harris said. "On one of the other forums. And we might never know about it."

"That's correct, sir," Windermere said.

"We need to change that," Harris told them. He stood. "You closed your big case. Did a fine job of it, too. Let's focus our resources on this one right away. Get your subject's attention back, and hurry."

< 37 >

Gruber had logged on to The End to cultivate Dylan Price. More and more, it was DarlingMadison who commanded his real attention.

They'd spent a week together now. Madison still believed he was Brandon, some disenfranchised musician type from the Midwest. Gruber played up the Jim Morrison vibe, the aimless, nihilistic artist angle. Told Madison he just didn't *care* enough to keep living, wanted to go out in a blaze of glory.

People act like they're going to wake up one day and their lives will suddenly be awesome, he'd written her. *It's just a lie they tell themselves to get through the torture. Fact: Your teenage years are the best years of your life. It doesn't get any better. So if it's not awesome now, you're pretty much fucked.*

I never thought about it like that, Madison replied. *But I guess it makes sense. I don't want to be miserable for another sixty years.*

Of course not, Gruber wrote. *It's always better to go out with a bang than fade away with a whimper, right? Why not be remembered for something?*

So, what? Madison wrote. *What are you going to be remembered for?*

I just want to show them the truth, Gruber told her. *I want to show them it's better to get out of this life on your own terms. Free yourself from this unhappiness.*

I see, Madison wrote. And then she typed the sentence that proved she was hooked. *Well, if you need a copilot on this deadly little misadventure, I might know somebody who's free.*

Gruber's breath had caught when he'd read the message. He read it again, twice over, to make sure he was seeing it right.

Oh yeah? he wrote. *You might, huh?*

I might, Madison replied. ☺

Madison lingered in Gruber's mind, morning and night, kept him awake, restless in his tiny bed, thinking of ways to keep her attention, push her toward the end. She came to work with him, stored safe on his phone; he stole away at quiet moments to chat with her some more.

Today, though, when Gruber ducked into the break room to check his phone for messages, he found nothing new from DarlingMadison in his inbox. Nothing from Dylan. But there was an email notification from the Death Wish forum about a new private message. Some user named XXBlackDaysXX.

Hey. I've seen you around the site. Sounds like you know a little bit about getting things done. Do you have any tips for someone who's ready to go?

Gruber read the message a couple of times. Studied the attached profile—the requisite moody description, a bland profile picture, nothing unique or special at all. Gruber had seen this boy around the site, read some of his posts and pegged him immediately for a poser. A time waster.

Adam Osing's voice over the loudspeaker, jarring Gruber from his thoughts: "Randall, we need you in children's wear. Bring a mop."

Gruber ignored his boss. Reread the message. Normally, he might indulge this kid. Take a chance, try and draw him out, search for some latent weakness the user never knew he had, an absentee father or an unrequited crush, some secret shame. Find the kid's buttons and press them until the poor bastard was made aware of life's profound unfairness and misery, of the opportunity death had to erase pain. Gruber had never struck gold with any of these dilettantes, but he liked to imagine that one or two of them had wandered off and killed themselves anyway, after they'd logged off.

But Gruber already had Dylan and Madison. He wasn't lacking for prospects. And frankly, this kid with his by-the-numbers profile description, his goofy, corn-fed picture, this kid annoyed Gruber. As if anyone would believe an asshole like this would ever do anything more than lurk in a suicide chat room. As if the kid believed his fanboy questions were worth a minute of Gruber's time.

Osing's voice on the loudspeaker again. "Randall Gruber, children's wear. Mop and bucket. Now."

Osing sounded tired. Frustrated. Fed up. Well, forget him. Gruber would deal with the situation in children's wear in good time.

Gruber opened a reply. Typed fast.

You're wasting my time. You'll never do it.

Sent the message.

And that's when the break-room door opened, and Osing was there. He stood in the doorway, took in the phone in Gruber's hand, the open locker with DarlingMadison's picture inside.

"Gruber," he said, his voice granite-hard. "What did I tell you?"

< 38 >

A thousand miles away, Mathers's computer chimed.

"Got a response," he told Stevens and Windermere. He read it aloud. "'You're wasting my time. You'll never do it.' Not exactly promising."

Stevens and Windermere looked at each other.

"She doesn't believe you," Stevens said.

"Yeah," Mathers said. "So what the heck do I do about it?"

Windermere smacked his shoulder. "What do you do?" she said. "You *make* her believe, you big dummy."

< 39 >

Gruber was almost home when he realized he'd left DarlingMadison's picture taped up in his locker. He'd been in such a hurry to get out of there that he'd forgotten it.

Well, it was lost. True to his word, Osing had fired him. Kicked him out with a barely disguised satisfaction.

"I told you what I'd do if you kept playing on that phone," he told Gruber as he escorted him to the front doors. "You had to test me, Randall, and now you're out on your ass."

Gruber hadn't argued. He was sick of the job, anyway. They'd walked past children's wear on the way to the exit, passed a screaming child and a harried mother and a puddle of puke on the dirty floor. Any other day, Gruber knew he'd be mopping it up. Today, he was free.

He rode the bus away from Osing and that shitty store, zoned out, thought about Dylan and Madison. Climbed off the bus and walked up the front steps of his tiny house, unlocked the door, and surveyed the place, dark and dingy, a kitchen and a cramped living room and a bedroom, light filtering in through greasy windows, sodden take-out containers and candy bar wrappers everywhere. It was a shithole. Even so, it was more than he could afford.

He would need money, fast. The snuff films he sold, Adrian Miller and the rest of the victims, they made a decent profit, sure, a tidy monthly stipend. Combined with his earnings from the store, Gruber could afford to pay rent and buy groceries each month, as long as he was careful. But now he'd been fired, and Osing hadn't even paid him severance.

Gruber kicked off his shoes, shrugged off his coat. Crossed to the dark living room, the walls plastered with pictures of Sarah, of Madison, of the rest of the victims. With Earl's picture, too, a couple of news articles. From when Earl went in, and when Earl came out.

Gruber turned on his computer and brought up his email account, began to compose a message.

I need an advance, he wrote. *Two solid prospects. Good-looking kids, great video potential. Just need a little $$$ to keep me going until they're ready to do it.*

He sent the message. Wondered what his contact would think.

Gruber had never asked for an advance before; he'd never needed one. But his product was top-of-the-line. He'd made them both plenty of money. Surely, the guy would see the value in keeping his best producer solvent.

Gruber's contact didn't write back right away. Gruber found a half-eaten bag of Cheetos, rummaged inside. Scanned the rest of his emails.

A reply from XXBlackDaysXX on the Death Wish forum: *I'm dead serious about this. Just need a little help. Maybe a partner, if the timing is right.*

Gruber rolled his eyes. Licked orange from his fingers and wiped them clean. *What do you need a partner for?* he wrote. *This isn't a team sport. Find a tall bridge and take a flying leap.*

He pressed send. Sat back to wait. Checked his watch, his email inbox again. Nothing yet from his contact. But an answer from XXBlackDaysXX came back almost immediately.

I'm scared. I want to do it. I just don't want to screw it up, you know?

Gruber leaned forward. *You don't want it,* he wrote. *If you wanted it, you'd be dead. Good-bye.*

> > >

"Shit," Windermere said. "You're losing her, Derek. You can't just throw yourself at her like a sacrificial lamb."

"So, what?" Mathers said. "What do you want me to say?"

Windermere thought for a minute. "Give me the keyboard," she said.

<<<

Gruber's computer chimed. Another email. He opened his account, expecting a reply from his contact. A money transfer, best-case scenario.

But it wasn't his contact. It was XXBlackDaysXX again. *You're scared, too,* the message read. *It's obvious. You act like you're some kind of big shot, but you're still here, aren't you? The only real measure of success on this site is a headstone and a six-foot hole in the ground. And you're still breathing. So what's up?*

Gruber opened a reply. *I'm working on something,* he typed fast, punching the keys. *I wouldn't expect a poser like you to get it. Soon as I get my shit in order, I'm out of here.*

Bull, XXBlackDaysXX replied. *What kind of shit do you have to get in order? This isn't complicated. Find a tall bridge and take a flying leap, remember?*

<<<

"Bam." Windermere sat back from the keyboard. "Let's see how the little freak likes them apples."

She watched the computer screen as she waited for her answer. Wondered if she was reading Ashley Frey right, if the subject would rise to the bait. Beside her, Stevens and Mathers hovered. She knew the men were wondering the same.

"Come on," she muttered, refreshing the inbox. "Come on, come on, come *on.*"

>>>

Gruber's fingers hovered over the keyboard as he plotted a response. He'd had enough of this kid, was trying to figure out the perfect way to tell him to screw off, when his computer chimed again. Another email.

Gruber switched back to his inbox, found what he'd been waiting for. An email from SevenBot, his contact. Gruber clicked it open, eager. Read the contents and felt like he'd run into a brick wall.

No can do, buddy. No advances. Pay to play, you know it. Get me something good, and I'll transfer the $$$ ASAP.

End of message.

No money.

Gruber stared at his screen. Calculating. Running the numbers and feeling a pit in his stomach. The profits from the Adrian Miller tape weren't nearly enough to pay the rent, put food in the fridge. To say nothing about the Internet and the power.

Another chime. Another message. XXBlackDaysXX: *Cat got your tongue?*

Shit.

Gruber stared at the screen, an idea forming in his head. His contact wanted new product. Gruber needed money, the faster the better.

Well, okay, he thought, studying XXBlackDaysXX's profile. *Let's see if this punk is for real.*

He opened a reply. Typed. *I'll do it if you do it. Tomorrow night, no pussying out. And you have to let me watch you on webcam.*

< 40 >

"Tomorrow night," Windermere said. "That give us enough time to pin down an ID and a location?"

Stevens thought about it. "Shoot," he said. "A day? We're really going to have to run the full-court press here, Carla."

"Oh, we'll bring the pain," Windermere said. "I have Frey's number now. Won't take but six hours before the freak's calling me Mama."

Stevens grinned, and she knew that he'd bought it. Inside, though, Windermere didn't feel half as confident.

Twenty-four hours, she thought. *Clock is ticking. And once it hits zero and Ashley Frey calls your bluff, then what?*

Your predator disappears into a puff of smoke, is what. Gone forever. You'll never find her again.

And another five, ten, twenty kids are going to die.

< 41 >

As weird as it was to admit, life was kind of looking up in Madison Mackenzie's world.

She still hated school. Crept through the halls, actively trying to avoid Lena Jane Poole and her gang of sycophants, hiding out at lunchtime and at the back of the classrooms, keeping her head down and trying to avoid speaking to anyone, learning anything, interacting with the outside world at all.

She followed pretty much the same strategy at home, too, steered clear of her mom and her sisters and spent most of the time in her bedroom, on her computer, talking to Gabriel98 on the forum.

It was strange. They were supposed to be figuring out how they wanted to die, plotting their particular blaze of glory. Superficially, anyway, that's what they did. Brandon—that was his name, Gabriel98, *Brandon*—had always wanted to rent a Ferrari from one of those high-end car rental places, talked about getting really stoned and driving it off a cliff.

There weren't any Ferraris for rent in Iowa, Brandon said. *Anyway, I'm way underage. No way they'd let me take one.*

There's a Ferrari dealership in Tampa, Madison told him. *We could steal one and go out together, Thelma and Louise–style.*

Which one of us is Thelma? Brandon responded.

LOL, Madison wrote back. *Dunno. I haven't actually seen the movie.*

It was fun to talk about. It was *cool,* even if it was only fantasy. Brandon was so nihilistic, so detached from the world. He was sensitive and thoughtful and—if the pictures on his Facebook page were any indication—really cute, too. Madison felt giddy when she talked to him, naive and silly and not at all worthy of his attention. She looked forward to their conversations every day.

I don't even know why you're wasting your time with me, she told him. *You're so much more advanced. You have this whole death thing figured out. I'm still trying to decide what I'm doing here.*

That's why I'm here, he wrote back. *To help you realize your potential. To guide you along on your journey.*

But why me? she wrote. *I'm just some girl on the Internet. I'm nobody.*

Brandon's response was fast. *You're not nobody. You're more special than you could ever know.*

"What are you smiling about over there?"

Madison looked up from her phone. At the front of the classroom, Mr. Rhodes was droning on about the Louisiana Purchase. Madison wasn't taking notes. Why bother?

"You'd better be careful," the same voice said from beside her. "If Rhodes catches you with that thing, he'll chuck it out the window."

Madison slid her phone away. The source of the voice was some sandy-haired guy with a goofy *Caught you in the act* smile on his face. Paul, she thought his name was. Paul Dayton. He'd been sitting beside her for, what, a month already? Kept trying to catch her eye, like he was angling for a way to make conversation and couldn't quite find the opening.

Madison ignored him. Pretended like she was making notes, doodled pictures in the margins of her notebook instead. A sports car. A cliff. Two people inside, speed lines behind. Nothing but the abyss ahead.

"It was the smile that did it," Paul said. "Gave you away, I mean. You want to text people in class, you can't be smiling like that. Believe me, *nobody* finds Robert Livingston that exciting."

"Thanks," Madison said. Drew more speed lines under the sports car. Stared straight ahead. She could feel Paul's eyes on her, avoided his gaze until he turned away.

Just leave me alone, she thought. *In a month or two, you won't remember me, anyway.*

< **42** >

Ashley Frey sent XXBlackDaysXX a message the next morning.

You still want to go through with this?

Windermere set down her coffee mug, settled in at the computer. Called Stevens over to watch. *Damn right,* she wrote. *Why? You backing out already?*

Just making sure. Don't want to waste time.

So stop it, then, she wrote. *What do I need to do?*

Get a webcam, Frey replied. *Preferably something high-def. Mount it somewhere where I can see what you're doing.*

"The voyeur stuff again," Windermere told Stevens. "Just like with Adrian Miller and the others."

You like to watch, huh? she wrote. *What's that all about?*

Want to make sure you're doing it right, Frey replied. *What's the point of doing this together if you screw up and fail?*

"Gee, I dunno," Windermere said aloud. "I guess you'd die alone?"

As soon as I've seen that you've done it, Frey continued, *I'll follow you. We'll see each other on the other side.*

Why do I have to go first? Windermere typed.

The response was instantaneous. *You came to me, remember? No debate.*

. . .

"We have to figure out a way to pin this girl down," Stevens said, pacing the office. "If all the high-tech tracing stuff isn't working, we're going to have to go old-school."

Windermere was busy staring at her computer screen. "Old-school?"

"You know, real policing?" Stevens said. "Interrogation. Probing conversations with the subject. Looking for weaknesses and exploiting them."

"Is that how they used to do it?" Windermere said.

"How they still do it, where I come from," Stevens told her. "You gotta be careful, though. You're a sixteen-year-old boy, remember? Try not to sound like an FBI agent."

Windermere gave him a look. "Do I sound like any other FBI agent you ever met in your life?"

She brought up the chat box and typed again. *So why are you doing this, anyway?*

Ashley Frey (as Azrael99) replied, *What? Killing myself?*

XXBlackDaysXX: *Or whatever.*

"Let's see if she'll rise to the bait," Windermere told Stevens. "Sometimes all these assholes really want is to brag about all the sick shit they're doing."

Azrael: *No reason to live anymore. Life sucks. The usual. Don't reduce me to a pile of clichés.*

BD: *You're reducing yourself. Why the forums? What brought you here?*

A: *Who cares? Why are you asking?*

"Careful," Stevens said. "You don't want to rattle the cage too much."

"Who's rattling cages?" Windermere replied. "This freak's trying to get people to kill themselves. She should damn well have a convincing argument."

BD: *I'm curious. We're about to do something pretty intimate together. Here: I'll go first. I'm doing this because I'm sick of being picked on at school. I have no friends and everyone makes fun of me for being clumsy and ugly and poor. I figure whatever's in the afterlife has to be better than here, right? I'm better off dead.*

Windermere pressed send. Knew Stevens was reading over her shoulder. Wondered if he could sense Rene Duclair in what she'd written, the cesspool of guilt from which she'd dredged that stuff.

Azrael99 wrote back. *You are better off dead.*

BD: *I guess I'm going to find out.*

Ashley Frey didn't respond, not for a few minutes. Five, maybe ten. Windermere stared at the computer screen, hit the refresh button. Stevens paced the tiny office, muttering about how she'd scared the subject away. Windermere ignored him. Kept hitting refresh, wondering if she should write something else.

The computer chimed.

Azrael99: *I'm here because of my stepfather. He's a piece of shit and I hate him.*

Windermere snapped her fingers. "Stepfathers again," she said. "If Mathers is right, there's some truth here."

XXBlackDaysXX: *Why do you hate him so much?*

Another long pause.

Azrael99: *He's just a dick. Alcoholic. He gets drunk and whales on me, tells me I'm worthless. He used to do shit to his daughter, too, my stepsister. Sick shit.*

"My God," Stevens said.

WTF, Windermere typed. *Scumbag. Can't you just call the police?*

Too late for that, Frey responded. *She's already gone. She got sick of him messing around with her and she already took the leap. I'm just following in her footsteps, I guess.*

Windermere turned to tell Stevens to write this stuff down, found he was already scribbling in his notebook.

XXBlackDaysXX: *What was her name?*

Azrael99: *My sister?*

BD: *Ya.*

Another pause. A couple minutes. Then:

Azrael99: *I don't want to talk about this anymore.*

Azrael99: *GTG.*

Azrael99: *C ya.*

< 43 >

They put Mathers on the grunt work.

"We want suicide victims," Windermere told him. "Dating back, what, four years? That's when Frey first showed up on the forum."

Stevens tapped his pen against his notebook. "Sure," he said. "Except we have no idea how long it took Frey to come up with this idea."

"Ten years, then," Windermere told Mathers. "Bring us everything. Bonus points if there's an Earl involved somewhere."

. . .

Mathers came back a couple hours later, clutching a rain forest's worth of printouts.

"Got about twenty thousand dead girls dating back the last ten years," he said. "I tried controlling for family members named Earl, but all these cases are reported differently. Sometimes they list the family, sometimes they don't, so I figured better safe than sorry, give you the whole stack."

Windermere took the stack of pages, flipped through them. "We don't have time to go through every one of these cases," she said. "Not by the end of the day, anyway."

"What about a stepsister?" Stevens said. "Can we pare this down to cases where Ashley Frey had a stepsister?"

"Or a stepbrother," Windermere said. "Given that Ashley Frey could be the Prime Minister of Canada, for all we know."

Mathers scratched his head. "Most of these cases don't specify," he said. "Like I said, suicide reporting tends to be pretty bare-bones."

Windermere dropped the printouts on the desk beside her. The stack landed with a resounding thud. "We need more information," she said. "We're not moving fast enough, guys. We have to do better."

She sat back down at her computer and reviewed what they knew. Thought about Ashley Frey on the other end of that chat room connection, reeling in her victims and watching their deaths on her computer screen, playing the unhappy teenager. An idea began to form in her head.

"It's risky," Stevens said when she explained her thinking. "It's an all-in bluff, and we don't have the cards to back it up."

"Risky pays the bills, partner," she replied. "We're bluffing anyway, and sooner or later Ashley Frey is going to call us. We can flail around until the last possible moment and do things on her terms, or we can bring the fight ourselves."

Stevens nodded. "It's ballsy, that's for sure," he said. "If anyone can pull it off, Carla, it's you. Just be careful."

"Always, Stevens," she said. "Who do you think you're talking to?"

<<<

Gruber was coming out of the bathroom when his computer chimed. He dried his hands on his pants, sat down, and hit the space bar, blinked in the dim light as the screen flashed to life.

A message from XXBlackDaysXX: *You still there?*

Counting the minutes, Gruber replied. *You getting cold feet?*

Nah, came the response. *I've just been thinking about you. About your stepfather.*

Gruber's eyes shifted involuntarily to the lineup of taped pictures behind his computer. Sarah's yearbook picture. DarlingMadison and Adrian Miller and Dylan Price, too. And Earl, watching him, always. *Oh yeah?* he typed.

There was a pause.

Do you have a webcam? XXBlackDaysXX wrote. *Would be cool to see your face before we do this.*

That wasn't the agreement, Gruber replied. *I never promised a webcam.*

I just want to see your face, is all, XXBlackDaysXX wrote. *Would be nice to hear your voice. This typing is so impersonal.*

Sorry, Gruber wrote. *Impossible. You want to add me on Facebook, knock yourself out, but why bother?*

Skype? FaceTime? You're asking me to kill myself on webcam for you. I don't think it's crazy to want to see your face first.

You came to me, Gruber typed. *I didn't ask for any of this. I don't have to prove anything to you.*

There was another pause, a long pause. *I don't think you are who you say you are,* XXBlackDaysXX finally replied. *I don't think you want to kill yourself at all. I think you're one of those suicide freaks who gets off on watching other people die.*

Gruber stared at the screen, felt something oily and viscous start to slither around his intestines. Before he could type a response, his computer chimed again.

I bet that's why you want me to go first, the prospect wrote. *You'll wait until I'm dead and then you'll use the webcam footage to get yourself off. I bet you've done this before, haven't you?*

The snake in Gruber's bowels lurched a little. Rumbled, threatening. He realized his heart was pounding.

Earl glared down from his mug shot photo. Gruber could hear his words without trying.

Shit stain.

Pip-squeak.

Runt.

Pussy.

I bet your stepdad's not real, XXBlackDaysXX wrote. *I bet you made up that whole story about your stepdad so I would feel sorry for you and believe you were legit.*

He's real, Gruber replied. *Earl is too real. I never lied.*

I bet there is no Earl. I bet you lied about him like you lie about everything else.

The room narrowed into a tunnel, the computer screen tiny at the end of it. Gruber heard his pulse in his ears, his heavy breathing. Felt his temperature rising. Just who did this asshole think he was?

There's no Earl, XXBlackDaysXX wrote. *You don't have a stepdad and you probably don't have a dead sister, either. It's all just a big lie so you can get people to do what you want.*

Stop trying to act like you know me, Gruber wrote. *You'd never understand. I'm so far above your level it's not funny.*

Uh-huh. Just admit there's no Earl. Admit you don't have a stepsister.

Gruber inhaled sharply. Pounded the keyboard. *OF COURSE I DON'T HAVE A STEPSISTER. SHE'S FUCKING DEAD. SHE KILLED HERSELF BECAUSE OF ME.*

How'd she do it?

Gruber didn't reply.

Did she hang herself, Ashley? Did you watch? Did you like what you saw?

Gruber was aware he was gasping for breath, his eyes watering, the lenses of his glasses fingerprint smudged. He was aware he was hyperventilating, felt like he was rocketing downward into some dark abyss.

You liked watching your stepsister die. Admit it.

YEAH, I FUCKING LIKED IT. SARAH WAS A STUPID LITTLE TRAMP. SHE DESERVED TO FUCKING DIE AND I'M THE ONE WHO MADE HER DO IT.

I'M AN ANGEL OF DEATH, YOU STUPID LITTLE SHIT STAIN. YOU DON'T EVEN KNOW WHAT I'M CAPABLE OF.

A long pause. Gruber stared at the screen, breathing hard, furious. Then: *I do now.*

< **44** >

Stevens sat back from the computer. Wiped his brow and exhaled. "Well, hell," he said. "I'd say we broke her, Carla."

Windermere paced the small office, trying to burn off the adrenaline. The online conversation with Ashley Frey had revved her up about as much as any in-person interrogation she could remember—maybe more so, given the stakes at play.

She'd wondered what the predator would do when she and Stevens called her bluff. Wondered if Frey would fight back or disappear, hoped it would knock her off-kilter enough that she'd give them something concrete to work on, some kind of new lead.

Figured it was the only shot they really had.

"You think she's gone?" Stevens asked Windermere. It had been fifteen minutes since that last message, and even though Windermere had thrown out a few more salvos, Frey hadn't replied.

"She's gone," Windermere said. "She's either hurling her computer through her bedroom window, or she's realizing she said too much. And meanwhile . . ." She scrolled up the page. "We have a few more scraps of information to plug into the machine."

Stevens read over her shoulder. "'Sarah,'" he said. "I guess that's his stepsister."

"Gotta be," Windermere said. She copied the chat log, hit the print button. Shivered a little—the last residual adrenaline, and something else, too, something spookier.

"So let's see if we can't work with this," she said, reaching for the printout. "Between Earl and Sarah, we must have a lead somewhere."

< 45 >

Gruber woke up to darkness outside, his head pounding, saliva dried and crusted on his lips. A train whistled down the block, the rumbling of a switch engine. He sat up, rubbing his face, found his glasses where he'd knocked them to the floor, and surveyed his living room.

There wasn't much to see. The curtains were drawn, blocking most of the yellow glow from the sodium streetlight outside. What light did penetrate came in sharp lines, illuminating the table piled high with dishes, empty take-out containers, photographs torn from newspapers. It shone on the computer desk, too, the now dormant computer and the secondhand desk chair, and it shone on the pictures he'd taped to the wall.

It shone on Earl. His dark eyes, his sallow skin. His anger.

Shit stain. Pip-squeak.

Runt.

Gruber pulled himself to his feet. Pressed a button on the computer's keyboard, and the screen came to life. The Death Wish forum was still running in his Internet browser, the chat box with XXBlackDaysXX. The sight of the message history was enough to make Gruber's intestines churn all over again.

He'd messed up bad. BlackDays, whoever he was, had pushed him into dangerous territory. He'd revealed too much of himself.

Gruber knew he couldn't go back to the Death Wish forums. Black-Days would tell the administrators, report him to whomever would listen. Gruber's IP address was blocked, untraceable, but the site wasn't safe anymore. He would have to sign off for good.

Well, fine. There were other forums. He had other accounts. This wasn't the first time a project had gone wrong, and Gruber figured it wouldn't be the last. But he'd been planning to sell the XXBlackDaysXX footage. He desperately needed money, and he needed it fast.

Gruber paced the little house, listening to the trains rumble and shift outside. This was not an easy question. He'd sloughed off his old identity years ago, preferred to live under the radar as much as he could. Osing had paid him in cash, when he'd paid at all. The owner of the little house took cash the same, no questions asked. But arrangements like those were hard to find; they were risky. They didn't just show up in the classified ads.

Anyway, Gruber was sick of working. Sick of cleaning up baby puke for less than minimum wage. He'd found his passion in life, and he wanted to pursue it. He was sick of the distractions.

He stopped in front of his computer. Studied the machine. On the hard drive, tucked away and encrypted, was footage of six deaths, all of it clear and of reasonable quality. Those files were assets, Gruber realized. He'd sold them once already, to SevenBot, reached a few hundred buyers. Surely there was a bigger market out there.

Gruber picked up his phone. Dialed a number he'd memorized a long time ago, a number he'd figured he would never call again. Tapped his feet on the floor as he waited, tried to tell himself it wasn't nerves.

A man picked up on the third ring. "Yeah?"

Gruber paused. Let out his breath. "Let me talk to Rico," he told the man. "Tell him it's Randall Gruber on the phone. Tell him I have something he wants to see."

< 46 >

Mathers was good.

"Earl Sanderson," he told Stevens and Windermere. "Brought up on child abuse charges, some place called Elizabeth, Indiana, February 1993. An autopsy on his daughter revealed injuries consistent with blunt trauma and sexual assault. The girl, one Sarah Ashley Sanderson, had been found hanged to death in her bedroom closet in what was ultimately ruled a suicide."

He was holding more printouts—the police report from the arrest, whatever clippings he could find. He handed the file to Windermere, who started paging through it.

"Here's the interesting part," Mathers said before she could get very far. "Sarah Sanderson didn't have any stepsisters."

"Ashley Frey's pretty fixated on her sister, Derek," Windermere said. "What makes you so sure this is our case?"

Mathers held up a hand. "She didn't have any stepsisters," he said, "but she *did* have a stepbrother, Randall Allan Gruber. He was fifteen at the time, and it was his testimony that ultimately put Sanderson away." He gestured to the file. "Seems this guy liked to get liquored up and beat on his nearest and dearest. Liked to do a little more to his daughter, apparently."

Windermere flipped through reports from the police and the ME, a bunch of photographs: close-ups of bruises, black eyes, battered ribs. The autopsy photos from Sarah Sanderson's inquest. Pictures of Randall Allan Gruber, too, his injuries similar to his sister's.

"Cripes," Windermere said. "Tell me this fucker burned, Mathers."

"Served three years in the state pen," Mathers told her. "Walked out and moved back to southern Indiana, not far from Louisville. Periodically gets himself busted for petty crimes, nothing major."

"If karma was worth anything, he'd be in a shallow grave somewhere," Stevens said, scanning, flipping pages. "Where the hell was Mom for all this?"

"Mom was Tammy Gruber, a former cocktail waitress," Mathers said. "Guess she caught her share of Sanderson's bad moods herself. Told the court she was pretty well terrified old Earl was going to kill them all."

"Sounds like she had a valid case." Windermere flipped until she found a picture of Randall Gruber. Some psychiatric assessor had taken it, when they'd brought the kid in after the murder. Gruber was small, gaunt, and hollow-eyed, Coke-bottle glasses and a shock of plain brown hair sweeping over his forehead. He gazed into the camera with a flat, empty expression.

"Says here Randall Gruber spent some time in psychiatric evaluation in Louisville," Stevens read. "A period of years, not that you could blame him. The things he would have lived through in that trailer . . ."

"Sick," Windermere said. "Sick and twisted. Where is this guy now?"

"Nowhere that I could find," Mathers told her. "Mom, either. I'll keep looking, but it seems like they skipped town about the same time Randall hit the age of majority."

"People don't just disappear in this country," Windermere said. "They've got to be out there."

"Roger," Mathers replied. "You want to run this down in the meantime? Sort out whether this is really our guy-slash-girl?"

She studied the picture of young Gruber again. The vacant stare. The expressionless eyes behind those thick glasses. Really, the picture didn't tell her very much. More than a few domestic abuse victims had suffered the same as Randall Gruber and his stepsister. More than a handful of victims had met ends like Sarah's. As far as Windermere could tell, none of the victims had gone on to build successful careers luring teenagers to their deaths via suicide forums.

She put down the picture. "It's a better lead than anything else we've got," she told the men. "Let's wander down to Indiana, see if we can track this guy down."

‹ 47 ›

They booked tickets on a Delta regional flight to Louisville, left Mathers behind to continue the search for Randall Gruber from his cubicle.

"Good luck," Stevens told Mathers as they walked out of CID. "If this guy's Ashley Frey, he's been vigilant about protecting his identity. Probably not going to show up in the phone book."

Mathers grinned. "That's why they pay me the big bucks, isn't it?"

"They pay you the big bucks?" Stevens said. "Cripes. I gotta talk to Harris."

Mathers put a hand on Windermere's shoulder as they reached the elevators, nudged her back into the cubicles a ways. Studied her with those blue eyes, his brow furrowed. *Like a worried dog,* she thought. *Solid and dependable and loyal. And completely oblivious to any complicated human emotion.*

"I just wanted to make sure we're okay," he told her, glancing over her shoulder to where Stevens stood, waiting for the elevators. "I hate the thought of you skipping town without me knowing you're all right."

Windermere looked over her shoulder at Stevens, the elevator doors still closed, the damn car taking its time. "What is it with you two?" she said. "Every time I turn around, you're asking me to *talk.* You have something you want to say to me, Derek?"

Mathers looked at Stevens, too. "We're just worried," he said. "This case—it's messed up. I think it's messing with all of us."

The elevator doors dinged at last. Mercifully. "This is me you're talking to," Windermere told him. "I don't get messed up."

She turned for the doors. "I gotta go, buddy. Try not to miss me too much."

She walked away, joined Stevens in the elevator, stared at the bank of buttons until the doors slid closed, until the car was dropping toward street level. Rode down to the lobby in silence. Rode out to the airport more or less the same way.

< **48** >

You haven't told anyone about us, have you?

Madison laughed to herself as she reread the message. *Who would I tell?* she typed. *My sisters? My mom? You think I'm going to tell them I'm talking to some dude on a suicide website? How crazy do you think I am?*

LOL, Brandon replied. *Just making sure. What about your friends?*

Friends? LOL, Madison wrote. *Dude, I don't have any friends. You're my friend. Why so paranoid?*

Don't want anything screwing this up, Brandon wrote. *What we're going to do, it's too important to mess up by being careless.*

I promise, Madison told him. *I haven't told anyone. I'm not as dumb as you clearly think I am.*

Don't think you're dumb.

Whatever, Madison wrote. *I GTG. Class is in session.*

Do you really think I'm just some dude on a suicide website? Brandon asked.

Madison glanced up at the blackboard, where Rhodes was blabbering on about Lewis and Clark.

Of course not, she started typing. *I really like—*

"*Miss Mackenzie.*" This was Rhodes, finished with Lewis and Clark and fixing a thousand-watt death stare in her direction. "Would you care to share what you're texting with the class?"

Madison felt eyes turning to stare at her. Heard Lena Jane Poole giggle from three rows over, felt herself blushing. Felt an undercurrent of panic, too, as her mind flashed ahead to what would happen if Rhodes took her phone, if he read what she was typing, and to whom.

"No, sir," she told the teacher. "Just inputting the date of the midterm into my calendar. I was listening, I swear."

Rhodes glared at her. "You swear," he said. "Well, since you were obviously listening, you'll have no problem telling me the name of the member of the expedition who died first."

Madison closed her eyes. Blew out a sigh. Of course she didn't know the dude's name. She wished she could run away to Brandon right now, find that Ferrari and that cliff and just be done with it.

"Miss Mackenzie?" Rhodes had his eyebrow arched, milking the moment, getting his money's worth. Madison could tell from the smirks on the faces of the kids around her that everyone else was enjoying it, too. Lena Jane Poole had her iPhone raised, probably shooting video. Something to post online later, something for everyone to laugh at.

What else was new?

Rhodes waited. Madison didn't answer. Just stared at her teacher as her teacher stared back, a standoff. Then someone whispered nearby.

"Floyd." It was Paul, the goofy guy who sat next to her. *"Charles Floyd."*

Madison hesitated. Paul had his head in his textbook, his whisper barely louder than a breath.

"Uh, Charles Floyd?" she said.

"Very good." Rhodes took a couple steps closer. "And how did he die?"

Madison stifled the urge to look at Paul. Waited, strained her ears for Paul's answer. *"Appendicitis."*

"Appendicitis," she repeated.

Rhodes nodded. "Very good," he said. "Very good answers, Mr. Dayton."

Paul's head snapped up. He went red. "Pardon?"

"I'm not so deaf as to be unable to hear a whispered answer, Mr. Dayton," Rhodes said. "It's very kind of you to want to assist Miss Mackenzie, but she is going to have to learn to sink or swim on her own." He turned back toward the blackboard. "For texting in class, Miss Mackenzie, I'm awarding you two days in detention. For helping her, Mr. Dayton . . ." Rhodes paused, gave it a dramatic flourish. "I award you the same. See you this afternoon."

Ugh, Madison messaged Brandon. *Sorry about the delay. History class. I just got a detention for texting in class.*

Class was over. Rhodes had, mercifully, avoided picking on her for the rest of the period, but the damage was done. Detention, first off, and the embarrassment that came with looking like a fool in front of Lena Jane Poole and the rest of the class.

Not that it mattered.

I have to get out of this place, she wrote Brandon. *Soon. I'm dying here, and not in the good way.*

She pressed send and carried on down the hall, waiting for Brandon's reply. Didn't hear Paul coming up behind her until he was tapping her on the shoulder, saying her name.

"Hey," he said, a sheepish expression on his face. "Sorry about what happened back there. I didn't think Rhodes could hear me."

"Never mind," Madison said. "It is what it is. I was going to get a detention either way, I guess."

"Yeah. Now at least you have company, right?"

"Right," Madison said. *"Exactly."*

If Paul could sense the sarcasm, he wasn't letting on. "Who are you texting, anyway?" he said. "You always have your nose in that phone."

Madison tried to project a *Don't bother me* vibe. "Why do you care?" she asked him. "What's it matter to you?"

"You're just always so, I dunno, antisocial," Paul said. "Like you never talk to anyone or even smile or make eye contact. But you're always smiling when you're on your phone."

"I'm talking to my boyfriend," Madison said. "All right? Not that it's any of your business, but there you go."

Paul's smile faded a little. His cockiness dissipated. "Ah," he said. "Okay. I see how it is."

"Yeah," Madison said. "That's how it is."

She left Paul standing in the hallway, eating her dust. Pulled out her phone again and saw that Brandon had answered.

So you really don't think I'm just some dude on a website, right? he'd written.

Madison frowned. Boys were so needy. Still, it was kind of cute that he cared this much.

Of course not, she replied. *You're special to me. Thelma and Louise, remember?*

The answer came fast. *LOL. I'm Thelma.*

I still haven't seen the movie, Madison wrote. Realized she was smiling again, looked around to make sure Paul wasn't watching. *I reserve the right to choose until I do.*

< 49 >

Mathers had a location for Tammy Gruber by the time Stevens and Windermere touched down in Louisville. But what he'd found wasn't promising.

"Mom's in Cincinnati," he told Windermere. "But she hasn't seen her son in more than fifteen years. Says he cut out on her shortly after they left Louisville, hasn't shown his face since."

"No phone calls?" Windermere said. "No letters?"

"Not even a postcard. Didn't sound like old Tammy was too broken up about it. I got the feeling she was happy to be rid of her little boy. Said he was always a bit of a weird kid, kind of gave her the creeps."

"Imagine what she'd think of him now," Windermere said. She thanked Mathers and told him good-bye, ended the call before he could get all wishy-washy again, that *Carla, we need to talk* crap.

"Tammy Gruber's in Cincinnati," she told Stevens as they walked out of the terminal. "But she can't point us to her boy."

"So what do we do?" Stevens asked her.

Windermere scanned the parking lot, found the rental car. "I have some ideas," she told him. "Toss me those keys, would you? I'm driving."

They picked up Randall Gruber's trail at a psychiatric hospital in southeast Louisville, a pleasant, five-story brick facility set amid a campus of rolling lawns and the odd copse of trees. Windermere parked the rental car in the visitors' lot, and they rode the elevator to the residential ward, where a doctor named McCarthy met them at a security station in front of a pair of locked double doors.

"Call me Rosemary, please," she said as she led them through the doors and into a cluttered office. "We try to keep things informal in this part of the hospital. Try to keep the whole situation as humanizing as possible."

"Sure," Stevens said. "I imagine the kids you're dealing with here have it rough enough as it is."

"Very true," McCarthy agreed. "And if you're here about Randall Gruber, you already know all about it."

"So you remember Randall," Windermere said. "That would have been, what, twenty, twenty-five years ago?"

"I remember," McCarthy told her. "I was younger then, just starting out, and Randall . . . What happened in that trailer out there is one of the saddest situations I've ever come across, professionally or otherwise."

She picked up a file folder from her desk, opened it, scanned the contents. Stevens and Windermere watched her.

"You treated Randall here because of what happened to his stepsister, correct?" Stevens said. "And because of what his stepfather—Earl Sanderson—had been doing before Sarah died. I assume that's standard procedure in child abuse cases?"

"It is," McCarthy replied, "though not to the extent that we treated Randall. This was something more than simple child abuse."

"I don't understand," Windermere said. "How do you mean?"

McCarthy put down the file. Slid it across the table. Photocopies of drawings, an unsteady hand. A girl or a woman with hair the same color as the rope around her neck.

"I began treating Randall under the assumption that he'd played a bystander's role in everything that went on," McCarthy told them as they studied the drawings. "I assumed he'd been a victim of his stepfather, and nothing more. But that was before Randall told me about the hole in the wall."

Stevens felt a bolt of electricity, his cop instincts perking up. "The hole in the wall," he said. "Can you explain?"

"Randall watched her," McCarthy told them. "From the day they moved into that trailer, five or six months before Sarah's death, he watched her through the wall. He told me it was sometimes the only thing that kept him going, knowing that he could watch her, like his own private movie."

"Did she know?" Stevens asked. "Was this some secret game of theirs?"

McCarthy shook her head. "Not until the end, Randall said. Not until the moment before she died. He said he tried to hold his breath, but he couldn't, and she saw him as she was setting up the rope. She saw him, he said, but she did it anyway. That's how he knew it was okay."

Stevens and Windermere looked at each other again. "So he watched her," Windermere said. "Just like Ashley Frey."

Stevens nodded. "Only, Ashley Frey has a webcam."

"Is there a connection here?" McCarthy asked, frowning. "You mentioned this pertained to a case you're investigating. Is Randall involved in some way?"

"That's what we're trying to figure out," Windermere said. "We're dealing with a predator who finds depressed teenagers online and encourages them to hang themselves while she watches. So far, we count five victims, and the similarities are striking. Right down to the color of the rope."

"You treated Randall Gruber," Stevens told McCarthy. "We don't want to ask you to make a leap that you can't, but does this sound like something in Randall's ballpark?"

McCarthy didn't answer for a moment. She'd paled, Stevens thought, unless it was just a trick of the light. She exhaled heavily and sat forward.

"It's in his ballpark, yes," she said quietly. "To be perfectly honest, I've often wondered just when I would have to have this conversation. We couldn't keep treating Randall after he turned eighteen. We just don't have the resources, or the legal right. His mother took him away, and I think they moved out of town. But—"

"But you would have kept him here, if you could have," Windermere said.

McCarthy nodded. "What happened in that trailer, it changed Randall," she said. "He came to me troubled, and I wasn't able to reverse it. His stepfather had reached him in a place where I couldn't, no matter how hard I tried."

She looked down at the file folder. Flipped through the drawings. Stevens and Windermere waited, the doctor's words hanging in the air.

"He told me he enjoyed it," McCarthy continued, and her words still bore scars. "He hated his stepsister, thought her father gave her special treatment. He told me he made it his mission to push her to the edge. He told me it made him feel powerful."

She shuddered. "He told me it felt like a game."

< **50** >

"So Ashley Frey's a *he* after all," Windermere said as they drove away from the hospital. "Leave it to a man to come up with a scheme like this."

In the passenger seat, Stevens shivered. "He watched her hang herself" he said. "He pushed his sister to do it."

"A *game*," Windermere said. She'd scanned Randall Gruber's file in Rosemary McCarthy's office. Figured she'd picked up a little bit on the kid. "He didn't have many friends, apparently. Nobody to really relate to. Even his stepsister wanted nothing to do with him."

"Alone in that trailer with his stepfather running rampant." Stevens looked out the window. "Maybe it was his way of asserting himself. Being heard."

"We're sure hearing him now," Windermere said. She signaled, turned onto the interstate on-ramp. Pressed down on the gas, the rental car's engine straining under her heavy foot. "Let's go talk to the stepfather, huh?"

Earl Sanderson lived across the river in New Albany, Indiana, a crummy brick apartment building in the shadow of the Sherman Minton, the big interstate bridge running over the Ohio River and back into Louisville.

They found his place pretty easily. But Earl wasn't home. And the woman who answered his door wasn't exactly bursting with clues.

"Went out," she told them, scratching under her worn robe. "Dunno where, exactly. You try downstairs yet?"

Stevens and Windermere exchanged glances. There was a bar built into the first floor of the place, not the most reputable-looking establishment.

"If Earl's not there, I don't know what to tell you," the woman continued. "My satellite surveillance camera's kind of acting up lately."

She was an older woman, mid-fifties, a couple fading bruises on her arms, a split lip. Wouldn't look them in the eye, either of them.

"He's not in any trouble, is he?"

"Not so far," Windermere replied. "But maybe he should be."

They checked out the bar, the Rusty Nail, a flat painted door and boarded-up windows on the outside, a pockmarked bar and a sticky floor and dim lighting on the inside, the pervasive odor of mildew, cigarettes, and stale beer. But no sign of Earl Sanderson.

"Just missed him," the bartender told Stevens and Windermere. "He shoved off with old Joan about a half hour ago, sounded like they were aiming to party."

"Old Joan," Windermere said. "That lady in his apartment doesn't mind?"

"Couldn't tell you," the bartender said. "Don't think she knows about Earl and Joan, and I suspect Earl'd like to keep it that way."

He reached under the bar, pulled out a bowl of mixed nuts that must have dated back to the Nixon administration.

"Listen, if it's Earl you're after, you're just as well staying in one place," he said. "Try and follow that man, you'll be chasing him around all night. Hard to pin down, what I'm saying."

"So where would you suggest we stay?" Windermere asked. "If we were aiming to pin him."

"Tomorrow's what, Wednesday? He usually comes around Wednesdays. Happy hour, three o'clock. Buck-fifty Budweisers, three-dollar highballs. He'll be here."

Windermere surveyed the joint, the scarred tabletops, the hunchbacked regulars. Figured the last thing she wanted was to spend another two or three hours scouring places like this.

"Three o'clock," she said. "Guess we'll see you tomorrow."

< 51 >

It was dark when Stevens and Windermere pulled into the little town of Elizabeth, twenty miles down the Ohio River from Louisville and New Albany, on the Indiana side of the water. The place was quiet, sleepy, little more than a single main road and a couple ramshackle storefronts, a decrepit mechanic's shop and a general store with greasy windows and a hand-painted sign.

Windermere peered out the windshield, idled the rental slow down main street. Took one lap of the town, then another.

"Place is a ghost town," she muttered. "Or a horror-movie set."

She sent Stevens into the general store for directions, watched ragged trees claw at the wind in the shadows as she waited. Stevens came out a couple minutes later, scratching his head. "About a mile out of town," he said, sliding into the seat. "Back toward the river. The guy in there said it's been abandoned for years."

"Even better," Windermere said, shifting into drive, her free hand checking her shoulder holster for the familiar weight of her service pistol. Might have been silly, but the place was kind of spooky. And the thought of Randall Gruber out here, somewhere, gave her the creeps.

The guy in the general store hadn't been lying. The Shady Acres Motor Court came off like more of a junkyard than any kind of neighborhood. The sign over the front gate was pitted with shot, the gate itself rusted and sagging off its hinges. Someone had dragged a log across the driveway, spray-painted a warning on its side for trespassers to KEEP OUT.

In the light from the rental car's headlights, Windermere could see the rusted hulks of old trailers lined up like cemetery headstones beyond the gate, their sides covered with graffiti, their windows smashed. There were no lights on, anywhere. No signs of life.

She pulled the car in close to the log at the gate. Shifted into park and killed the engine. Stevens frowned. "We're going in there?"

"Might as well check it out," Windermere said. "Bring a flashlight."

She climbed from the car before he could come up with a better idea. Circled around to the trunk and dug in her gear for a tactical flashlight. Beside her, Stevens found a light of his own, slammed the trunk down. The noise echoed among the trees, the old trailers. Seemed to echo forever.

Windermere had her Glock out. Caught Stevens eyeing it. "I don't like surprises," she told him. "Whether it's Gruber in here or meth heads or a rabid raccoon, I aim to be ready."

"Sure," Stevens said. "Words to live by."

He drew his pistol, too, she noticed, as they stepped over the log and into the park itself. Shined his light up the main road, the beam dying on the rusted body of somebody's old speedboat, a hole the size of a fist in the hull.

"Which one of these places is Gruber's?" Stevens asked. He was whispering, barely audible over the wind in the trees, the blowing leaves on the asphalt, the cracked patch of road.

"Dunno," Windermere said. "Mathers didn't have an address, just the name of the park."

She peered through the darkness, trying to get a sense of the size of the place. Figured there must have been four or five rows of trailers, each ten trailers deep. Fifty homes, give or take, and beyond them nothing but black forest and scrub, a tangle of branches and dense underbrush.

Fifty homes. All of them filled by families at one time, mothers and fathers and brothers and sisters, lovers and neighbors and friends. And Randall Gruber and his stepsister. And Earl Sanderson.

The wind sent a chill through Windermere's thin jacket. Or maybe it was the history of the place that was doing it, the knowledge that young Randall Gruber had watched his sister in one of these run-down double-wides, kneeling at his little hole in the wall as she slept, dressed for school, wrote in her journal. As she died.

Windermere kept her flashlight moving, aimed it at each trailer as they made their way down the row, studying the empty doorways and windows for any signs of habitation, anything that might point them to Randall Gruber. Wondered what she'd do if she found him, if she'd be able to suppress the anger that burned inside her at the thought of the little bastard.

Shady history or no, the guy was preying on kids, vulnerable kids. And he wasn't even man enough to show his face when he did it. Windermere figured she'd have something to say to the guy once she and Stevens found him.

Assuming you do find him.

Windermere pushed forward, into the darkness, the jagged, looming trees, searching the trailers for any sign of the predator.

But Gruber wasn't hiding at the Shady Acres Motor Court. She and Stevens searched the grounds for a solid hour, paced up and down each row of trailers, shined lights into every open doorway. Found nothing more than a few piles of empty beer cans, a ton of graffiti. The remnants of a few campfires and three or four rusted beaters.

"No sign of him," Stevens said, holstering his pistol as they reached the front gate again. "I don't know whether to be relieved or disappointed."

Windermere dug in her pocket, came up with the pack of Marlboros, a lighter. Figured she'd gone all day without one, she deserved to light up. She lit the cigarette, inhaled. Realized Stevens was staring at her, at the cigarette, looking like she'd just showed him her third arm or something.

"What?" she said. "You've never seen a girl smoke before, Stevens?"

Stevens held up his hands, didn't push it. "I didn't know you smoked," he said. "Just surprised, is all."

"Yeah, well." She took another quick drag, felt dirty inside and wondered why she'd bothered. Flicked the butt away half-smoked. "Sometimes I do, and sometimes I don't. Let's get out of here."

< **52** >

"So where's your boyfriend live?"

Wednesday afternoon. Second—and final—day of detention. Paul Dayton had spent Tuesday's prison sentence casting looks Madison's way, trying to catch her eye. She'd kept her face in her history textbook and ignored him, counted the minutes until Rhodes freed them and she could text Brandon again.

Wednesday, though, and Rhodes had disappeared about ten minutes into the sentence, left Paul and Madison alone in the classroom together. They could hear Rhodes in the hall, talking Rays baseball with some other teacher. He wasn't really bothering to check on them.

Madison had pulled her cell phone from her purse the moment Rhodes disappeared. Logged on to The End and opened a message to Brandon.

Stuck in detention, she wrote. *Blah. You around?*

But Brandon hadn't answered. She wondered where he was—was school over in Iowa yet? It wasn't like he had a job. He swore he didn't have friends but Madison knew that wasn't true. She'd seen his Facebook page, and he had almost a hundred friends. He was cute and pretty funny, and he was charming, too, the way he actually paid attention to her when they talked. So why couldn't he see himself the way the rest of the world did?

"Hello?" Paul leaned over and rapped on her desk. "Earth to Madison. You're, like, zoning out."

Madison blinked back to reality. Glared at Paul. "Please don't interrupt me while I'm thinking," she said. "In fact, it would be great if you could just leave me alone."

"Was that your boyfriend you were texting?" Paul asked. "You guys must really be in love, huh?"

In love. A month ago, the thought would have been nauseating. Now Madison kind of liked how it sounded.

"We care about each other a lot," she said. "Duh. That's what boyfriends and girlfriends do."

"Does he live in Tampa? Or back in your old town, wherever you came from?"

Madison rolled her eyes. "I came from Houston. But no, Brandon's not from there. He lives in Iowa."

"Iowa." Paul whistled. "Wow. That's, like, a long way away."

"Fact."

"So you guys just text all the time? What, do you, like, spend all night on the phone together, too?"

"We mostly just text," Madison told him. "Not that it's any of your business."

In fact, she had been trying to convince Brandon to call her. So far, he was resisting.

What's the matter? she'd asked. *Aren't you sick of just texting and emailing all the time? Don't you want to, like, talk to each other?*

I'm not good on the phone, Brandon replied. *It's better if we just text.*

What, like you're awkward? Madison wrote. *Big deal, dude. Everyone's awkward. I'm just sick of getting carpal tunnel every time we talk.*

Brandon had hesitated. A long, awful pause. *I just hate phone calls. My voice is weird. I have this lisp. You'll know I'm a loser as soon as you hear it.*

I won't, she wrote. *I don't care about stuff like that. I just want to talk to you.*

But Brandon hadn't given in. *I can't,* he said after another long pause. *I'm just not ready yet.*

"So you haven't actually *talked* to him?" Paul said. "What the hell, dude? How do you know this guy's not just one of those Internet freak shows?"

"He's not a freak show," Madison said. "He's real, a lot more real than anyone at this school, that's for sure."

But she'd considered the possibility that Paul was right. She'd logged on to Facebook while she was chatting with Brandon, brought up his profile page. Studied it, the familiar picture, those arresting, deep blue eyes. He'd posted a new status that afternoon, a selfie. He was smiling at the camera, a river behind him, a beautiful blue sky above. He had a beautiful smile.

This is a gorgeous picture, she wrote. *Did you go out walking today?*

Another pause. *What?*

On your Facebook, Madison wrote. *That selfie you posted. It's really pretty.*

Oh, Brandon wrote. *Yeah. That's the Missouri River. I just had to get away from people for a while.*

It looks like a beautiful day there.

I guess so, Brandon replied. *It's cold here. I'm freezing in that picture.*

You look cute, Madison told him. She scrolled down his page. Wall posts from friends, some girl named Ashley Frey in a couple of them, a boy named Dylan Price. Brandon had ninety-four friends in total; not a huge number by any means, but he'd told her he wasn't a people person. And that still meant nearly a hundred people knew he was real.

Paul held up his hands.

"All right, all right," he said, grinning. "But how do you guys, like, hook up, if he's all the way in Iowa? Don't tell me you're one of those cybersex freaks, are you?"

"Gross." Madison turned away. Ended the conversation. She could feel herself blushing, couldn't help it, couldn't stop imagining what it would be like to kiss Brandon, to make out with him. To pull him close and feel his hands. She wondered if he was a good kisser. If he—

Enough, she told herself. *You're supposed to be plotting to kill yourselves together, not falling in love and getting married.*

Still, it would be nice to make out with him, just once, before they drove the car off the cliff. Was that so much to ask?

‹ 53 ›

Earl Sanderson showed up at the Rusty Nail at a quarter past three the next afternoon. The bartender caught Windermere's eye, jerked his head toward the door as Sanderson walked in.

He was a rough-looking man. Shorter than Windermere had imagined, thin, almost gaunt, his skin yellowed with age. Was probably in his late fifties, but alcohol and hard living and who knows what else had added at least a decade to his face. He wore a mustard coat and a bad, careless haircut. Stevens and Windermere watched him order a Jack and Coke, find a booth.

"Guess you don't want to handle this one yourself, huh?" Windermere asked Stevens. "Let me hit up that Holiday Inn hot tub one more time?"

Stevens was already on his feet. "Come on," he told her. "You want, I'll play bad cop this time."

Windermere snorted. "Fat chance." She followed him across the bar.

Sanderson looked up as they approached. Didn't look surprised, scared, or wary. Just watched, half-interested, like it was all happening to someone else. Didn't even flinch when the badges came out.

"FBI," he said. His voice was raspy, chain-smoker rough. "Shit, I'm moving up in the world."

"We're here about Randall Gruber," Stevens said. "Anywhere you want to go we can talk?"

Sanderson chuckled. Looked around the bar, gestured across the booth. "Here's as good as any," he said. "If you come to talk about Randy, it should be a short conversation."

"When's the last time you saw him?" Windermere asked, sliding into the booth, not liking the way the vinyl stuck to her pantsuit. "You talk to him lately?"

"Lately, nah." Sanderson drank. "Haven't seen him in twenty years. Wouldn't want to. Far as I'm concerned, that little punk died the same day as my daughter. Wish he'd gone ahead and died earlier, you want my opinion."

"Certainly would have done you a favor if he did," Stevens said, nodding. "Was his testimony that put you away, wasn't it?"

Sanderson narrowed his eyes, didn't answer, and Windermere moved her hand down to her holster, just in case. But Sanderson stayed put. Spat something unhealthy onto the floor, narrowly missed Stevens's shoe.

"Far as I'm concerned, they should have locked him up along with me," he said. "The boy's about as screwed up as I was, maybe more." He looked Stevens in the eye. "Didn't neither of us kill that girl, though."

He reached for his drink again. Sipped it, cool. Replaced the glass. "Now, do you have any more questions? Or did you just come here to break my balls about the shit I already did my time for?"

"We're trying to find your stepson," Stevens told Sanderson. "That's all we care about. Do you have any idea where he is?"

"Short answer? No," Sanderson said. "We weren't exactly the kind to hold family reunions. Though I did get a visit from a guy a few years back, said he was a film producer or something. Some outfit out of Cleveland. He said Randall owed him money. Guess I'd done time with a guy he used to know, and he tracked me down thataway, not that I had the means or the inclination to make the loan good. He was persistent, at least until I showed him my .45."

"Cleveland," Stevens said. "A few years back?"

"Call it five," Sanderson said. "I thought it was Randall's idea of a practical joke. His way of saying, 'Wish you were here,' 'Happy Father's Day,' that kind of thing." He sipped again. "Or maybe he was saying, 'Fuck off.'"

‹ 54 ›

According to Earl Sanderson, the film producer who'd paid him a visit wasn't exactly the reputable kind.

"More of an underground guy, you understand?" Sanderson said. "Wasn't about to win an Oscar for his flicks, nothing like that. I don't know how old Randall got involved with him, but I suspect he saw the baseball bats coming, figured he'd better wash his hands of the whole mess. He was always a coward, that kid."

"Guess he learned from the best," Windermere replied. Sanderson said nothing, lifted his middle finger.

"That's all you know," Stevens asked. "An underground film producer out of Cleveland, five years ago?"

"That, and, well, let's see," Sanderson said slowly. "I had a dream about Randall once, maybe a year ago. Dreamed he was dead."

Stevens and Windermere looked at each other. "That right?"

"Sure is," Sanderson said. "Then I woke up. Turned out it was just indigestion. Ate some bad chicken, had the shits for days."

Windermere slapped her hand on the table, stood up. "Cleveland," she said. "Guess that's all we're going to get, partner. Let's let this old-timer enjoy his long decline in peace."

Sanderson watched them stand, file out from the booth. Waited until they'd taken a few steps before speaking again.

"The film producer," he said. "Big burly guy named, let's see, Rico. Kind of an asshole, to be perfectly honest." He spat. "Anyway, he told me Randall wasn't going by Randall anymore, not as far as Rico could figure."

Windermere turned around, slow. "Oh no?"

"Rico mentioned something about Randall hanging around outside the local high schools," Sanderson said. "Creeping on the kids coming and going. Said he'd heard Randall had a real thing for girls with honey-blond hair, green eyes."

"Same as Sarah," Stevens said.

"Same as Sarah. Anyway, the local law enforcement caught wind, figured to bring Randall in. Rico said that's why he'd skipped town. Why he stopped using his given name." He finished his drink. "Guess he forgot to pay his late fees before he left."

He rattled the ice in his empty glass. Waved it in the direction of the bar. "You FBI guys have expense accounts, right?" he said. "Figure I've given you enough intelligence you can put a dent in my tab?"

< 55 >

"Rico Jordan," Mathers said over the phone. "You said big and burly, right?"

"That's what the father of the year told us," Windermere replied. "Why? You found the guy?"

"Think so," Mathers said. "Kind of a despicable character, if we're talking the same person."

"Sanderson said film producer, underground stuff."

"Underground like snuff," Mathers said. "Car crashes, executions, suicides: buy, sell, and trade. Throw a little bit of amateur porn in there, to boot. I got a hold of his rap sheet, Carla. It's as long as something really long."

"Sweet," Windermere said. "Got an address? We'll drive up tonight."

"Save it. This guy died in a prison riot like six months ago. Unless you want to check out his headstone, you're better off staying put."

"Dead. Well, shit."

"You get anything else out of the old man?"

"Our boy liked to lurk around high schools," Windermere said. "Searching for the second coming of his sister, apparently. And," she said, "some people weren't cut out for fatherhood."

< **56** >

The drive up from Cleveland took a shade over three hours. Curtis Donovan did the speed limit, to the decimal point, just like Rodney had said. Didn't need any headaches from the law, not with what he had tucked away in the glove box—or stashed in the trunk, for that matter.

Donovan had never met Randall Gruber, the man he was driving to meet, but from what Rodney was saying, he had to be the dumbest human being alive, coming back out of hiding after all this time.

"Rico gave up on that dude a long time ago," Rodney told Donovan, before Donovan left. "We ran down his old man, his mother, got nothing, no trace. Figured that money was gone, wrote it off. You know, the cost of doing business."

But then Gruber called the studio a couple days back, Rico's old place. It was Rodney's business now, mostly legit after Rico got pinched. A holdover from the old era, Rodney making the bulk of his money elsewhere. But this guy asked for Rico anyway, didn't realize the dude was six-months dead. The guy claimed he was Randall Gruber. Claimed he had product to sell, on top of settling his debts.

Rodney wanted to put Marcus Smart on the job, the crew's usual hitter, experienced muscle. But Marcus had to meet his parole officer, wasn't supposed to leave the state. So Rodney had scanned across the studio to where Donovan was sweeping out the back room. He'd studied Donovan awhile. Donovan kept sweeping, tried to make out like he wasn't hanging on Rodney's next words.

"You want to make a quick five bills, rookie?" Rodney called over, and Donovan looked up, set the broom down, nonchalant.

"Go talk to this asshole," Rodney continued. "Get loud if you have to. Just bring back our money, or leave this dude in the ground. You think you can do that?"

Across the table from Rodney, Marcus snorted. "You're really sending this kid, huh?" he said. "You really think the fucking *janitor* has what it takes?"

Rodney stared over at Donovan again. Donovan stood tall, tried to make like he fit in. Tried to make like he was good for the job, like he wasn't scared shitless. Like this wasn't what he'd been waiting for since he'd signed on with the crew.

"What about the product?" he asked Rodney. "You want me to bring that back, too?"

Rodney made the jack-off motion. "This isn't Rico Jordan's crew," he said. "That creepy shit ain't our business anymore. But outstanding debts *will* be paid. You think you can handle this?" He gestured to the broom. "Or you want to be the guy who pushes brooms in the clubhouse instead?"

Donovan told Rodney he would do it. Loaded up his old Lincoln, hit the I-90 and drove. Did the speed limit, kept his eye on the shoulder for cops, the rearview mirror. Couldn't stop his gaze drifting to the glove box, his uncle's borrowed Smith & Wesson, his hunting shotgun in the trunk. Couldn't help feeling nervous, feeling like maybe he wasn't cut out for this shit after all. Feeling like maybe he really was meant to sweep up after guys like Rodney and Marcus his whole life.

Just get this money, he told himself, drumming his hands on the steering wheel. *Make this cornball pay up, and you're part of the crew. You can do this.*

< 57 >

Dylan Price was ready.

I bought the webcam, like you said, he told Gruber. *Swiped a bunch of cash out of my dad's wallet to pay for it. Kind of poetic, right?*

Excellent, Gruber wrote back. *The bastard deserves it. What about the rest of the supplies? Did you get the rope like I told you?*

The rope, yeah, Dylan wrote. *The yellow kind, right? What else do I need?*

G: *Just a place to set everything up.*

D: *Why with the hanging, though? I mean, wouldn't it be just as easy to slit our wrists? Why do we have to hang ourselves?*

G: *We just have to. It's important. Hanging is REALLY important.*

D: *LOL. Okay, whatever. I'll find a place.*

D: *Maybe I can try the attic or something.*

G: *When will you be ready?*

D: *I'm ready today, LOL. I would jump in front of a freight train in five minutes if I lived near the tracks.*

G: *Don't do it. Wait for me. I need to watch you or I won't have the guts to do it myself.*

D: *I'm JK, don't worry.*

D: *I don't want to wait long. My fucking dad is going to find out I stole that money, and then he'll probably kick my ass or something. I want to be out of here before that, if possible.*

G: *Okay. So when?*

A long pause. Gruber imagined Dylan sitting at his computer, calculating how much longer he wanted to stay on this earth.

D: *How about Friday? My mom and dad are going out of town to some conference in D.C.*

Gruber smiled to himself. *Friday is excellent.*

He sent the message. Leaned back in his chair, felt a pang in his stomach, hunger gnawing away. Was about to wander into the kitchen, scrounge up what was left of the groceries, wondered when the hell Rico's guy would be here with the money. He'd told Gruber he needed a day or two to move some cash around. Rico was dead, but sure, they could do business. Just the little matter of those outstanding payments.

"The product will more than cover it," Gruber had told him. "Give me a little something to live on up front and you can have the footage, sell it how you like, pocket the proceeds. Cover my debts and keep whatever you earn. It's quality footage. You're guaranteed to make money."

The guy—Rodney was his name—had insisted on doing business in person. "Guess you can understand how trust ain't exactly forthcoming around here," he'd told Gruber. "Your word's worth about as much as the paper it's printed on, after you did Rico so dirty."

Gruber tried to explain. Told Rodney he'd been running for his life, the cops on his ass. Anyway, it was just as easy to send the footage online. Send the payment the same way.

But Rodney was unmoved. "Nah, we don't play that way," he'd told

Gruber. "We deal in cash and hard product. Tangible shit. I'll send my boy up tomorrow. Be ready."

That was yesterday. Tonight, Gruber was hungry. The fridge was just about empty, the cupboards the same. If Rodney's guy didn't get here soon, Gruber figured he might starve to death.

He found half of a frozen burrito, a plastic cup of guacamole gone brown. Was just fiddling with the oven when the headlights flashed through the kitchen, tires on wet pavement outside.

Gruber went to the window, pulled open the curtains. A white boat of a car was parked at the curb, a Cadillac or a Lincoln or something, something big and American and near prehistoric. Gruber watched the door open, couldn't see much of the driver as he climbed from the car, started up the walk toward the house.

Rico's guy. Rodney. Had to be.

Gruber pushed the burrito away. Turned off the oven, seeing better meals in his future already. Went to the front door, unlocked it. Swung it open as the guy reached the stoop.

"Rodney, right?" Gruber said, smiling, thinking, *Maybe a steak.*

The guy didn't smile back. He was young, Gruber saw, might have still been a teenager. Tall and lean, wore his bravado like a mask, his face hard everywhere but his eyes. He scowled, spat on the concrete.

"Nah, I ain't Rodney," he said. "But I *am* here for that money."

< 58 >

Windermere called up the Cleveland PD, asked around. Connected with a detective named Balint who said he was the guy who'd put Rico Jordan away.

"Sure, I remember Rico," he told Windermere. "How could I not? Guy was built like a lineman, a solid two-fifty pounds. We made sure we brought numbers when we came to haul him in, I'll tell you."

"We heard Rico was into some dirt," Windermere said. "Amateur video hour, snuff stuff."

"*King* of the snuff films," Balint said. "Obtained and distributed. There were rumors he produced the shit, too, but we could never pin that on him. Fortunately, the kiddie porn was enough to put him away, and I guess his fellow inmates did the rest."

"You remember Rico hanging out with a guy named Gruber?" Windermere asked. "Probably a bit of a loner, used to lurk around high schools. Might even have drawn some complaints?"

Balint grunted, mulled it over. "Kind of a portly guy?" he said. "Ungainly, bad haircut? Worked at the gas station, down by Riverside High?"

"Your guess is as good as mine. Last picture I saw, the guy was fifteen. He'd be about twenty-six, twenty-seven when you met him."

"Coke-bottle glasses. Real thick and greasy, made his eyes look way big, like a bug?"

"That's the guy," Windermere said. "You know anything about him, anybody who could tell us where he might have gone?"

Balint gave it another moment's consideration. "If it's the same guy we're talking about, he was a minor player at best. There was the high school situation, yeah, and we pegged him buying some video off of Rico, some suicide stuff. People jumping off bridges and the like, the sicker the better. We nabbed a few of those guys, but most of them slipped through the net. I guess this guy was one of them."

"What about the high school angle? Anybody who'd remember him?"

"Nah," Balint said. "You get perverts like that three deep around the school yard. They all blur together, you know? Lonely white men with bad social skills. Who can tell them apart?"

"Tell me about it," Windermere said.

"Anyway, why the sudden interest? This guy haul off and do something crazy? Like I said, he was minor when we heard about him."

"He's major now," Windermere said. "Rico have any friends? Anyone who might have followed up on my guy?"

"If they followed up, your boy wouldn't be breathing," Balint told her. "Rico Jordan's crew wasn't exactly the type to forgive and forget, you know?"

"Yeah, I figured." Windermere thanked Balint, ended the call. Climbed back in the rental car and gave Stevens the head shake and the frown.

"No dice," she said. "Cleveland PD knows Rico, sure, but they didn't think enough of Randall Gruber to pay him much notice. As far as they're aware, he's long gone."

Stevens pursed his lips. "So that dries up that lead."

"If only we had an alias on the guy, a location," Windermere said. "We've got nothing, partner."

"So how do we find him?" Stevens said. "This is a pretty cold trail we're running."

Windermere nodded. "And while we're chasing our tails, Gruber's out there somewhere, trolling for another victim."

"Exactly," Stevens said, and the conversation died there. Windermere stared out the windshield of the rental car, the night beyond, bare trees and blowing wind, pale streetlights and shadows.

He's out there, she thought. *Somewhere in all that darkness. He's out there, and he's going to kill another kid.*

She fumbled in her pocket. Found another cigarette.

< 59 >

The cornball didn't have the money. As far as Donovan could tell, the guy didn't have shit but the videos he was peddling. And Rodney had already made it clear he didn't want those.

"I'm here for the money," Donovan told Gruber. Tried to keep his voice deep, flat, hard, like Rodney's. Like Marcus. "Twenty-five hundred dollars, plus interest. Call it four. You pay what you owe, and I get out of your face, get it?"

Randall Gruber was an ugly motherfucker. Short, chubby, going bald, the hint of a pervert's mustache and a pair of greasy glasses. He stood in the middle of his filthy living room and laughed and gestured at the mess.

"Do you see four thousand dollars lying around?" he asked Donovan. "I can't even afford breakfast tomorrow. Why the hell do you think I called you people in the first place?"

Donovan followed Gruber's eyes, surveyed the house. The tiny living room, empty junk-food wrappers everywhere, a grimy carpet, no light. The kitchen was more of the same, an ancient, stained stove, a pile of dishes in the sink. Somebody's half-eaten burrito. *Filthy, man. Savage.*

"Guess you should have thought of that," Donovan told him. "Man, you were stone-clear of us, dude. Rico checked in on your moms, your stepfather, didn't nobody know where you were. The way Rodney figured it, that money you owed was a lost fucking cause. But you—"

"Hold up." Gruber lifted a hand. "What did you say about my stepfather? You said Rico found Earl?"

Donovan glared at him. "So? Who cares, B? I'm here about that money."

Gruber was silent for a long moment. "It doesn't matter. I'm flat broke. The only way I can pay you is with this."

He dug in his pocket, came out with a portable hard drive, about the size of a wallet. Donovan knew there were movies on there, the kind of movies Rico Jordan used to make, the sick shit that had landed him in jail and then in the grave. Back when Rico ran the crew, those movies were relevant. But Rico was gone, and Rodney didn't fuck with that kind of depravity. For what it was worth, neither did Curtis Donovan.

He hesitated. Heard Marcus laughing at him. Saw Rodney handing back the broom. Fuck that. He ignored the hard drive. Reached for his uncle's Smith & Wesson instead.

"I guess that's where you're wrong," he told Gruber. "That little hard drive right there isn't the only way out."

<<<

The kid wasn't used to the gun; Gruber could see that. The way he fumbled, pulling it from his waistband, the nervous way his hand shook, the doubt in his eyes. Gruber wasn't afraid of this kid, of the threat. He was angry.

"What the hell do you think you're going to do with that?" he said. "How is that going to get your money back, shit stain?"

The kid flinched a little. Drew himself up. "They told me, come back with the money," he said. "Said if you didn't *have* the money, I should leave you to rot."

"I'm giving you the goddamn money." Gruber held out the hard drive again. "You take this footage, sell it, you'll make a hell of a lot more than four grand, I'm telling you. Just leave me a cut so I can pay my fucking bills, and you can walk out of here and leave me alone."

The kid hesitated. Worked his mouth like he was thinking it over. "They don't do that shit anymore," he said finally. "Those little movies you're into, that's not really their style. Sorry, dude."

He raised the revolver. Leveled it direct at Gruber's face, left him staring down the barrel. Gruber felt the frustration surging through him like magma, something awful. Figured, young as he was, scared as he was, the kid still might just talk himself into pulling the trigger. Proving himself. Might just stay blind to this mint fucking deal.

Shit.

Gruber's gaze drifted. Fell on Earl's picture on the wall, Sarah's. DarlingMadison and Dylan Price. He had an idea.

"Look," he said. "Put the gun down. You want the money, right?"

The kid didn't answer. Didn't lower the gun.

"I have these two projects," Gruber told him. "Kids I'm working on. They're almost ready to go. You get what I'm saying?"

The kid still didn't reply, but the revolver wavered.

"So, listen," Gruber told him. "I do my thing, tape it, sell it to my guy. He sends me the money, we settle up. I do the first kid on Friday, that's half your money right there. A couple more days, maybe, for the second kid, then my debt's repaid, you go home happy. Sound good?"

The thug stayed quiet. Still hadn't lowered his big-ass gun. Seemed to be mulling it over, disgust and impatience written all over his face.

"It's a good freaking deal," Gruber told him. "Do you want your money, or no?"

> > >

Donovan stared at Gruber. Felt the weight of the Smith & Wesson in his hand and ached to pull the trigger. Kids, he was talking about. Projects. Footage. Call it what you want, he was talking about sending two kids to their grave, selling the tapes. The thought made Donovan's stomach recoil.

Bring back our money, or leave this dude in the ground.

Rodney had been clear: no coming home until the job was done. *Not unless you want to sweep floors your whole life.*

This was a solution, messed-up as it was. It would mean babysitting this freak until Friday, at the bare minimum, but it would settle the debt, and that's what Rodney had sent him to do.

Settle the debt.

Donovan straightened. He lowered the gun. "Friday," he said. "But if you fuck with me, dude, you'll be dead by the weekend." He surveyed the mess. "Y'all got anything to eat in here, or what?"

< **60** >

Something was itching in the back of Kirk Stevens's mind.

Stevens and Windermere had returned to Louisville. Traded the rental car for a couple of desks at the regional office on the east side of town. They'd connected with a local agent named Wheeler, a fair-skinned, middle-aged guy who didn't say much, but who'd hooked them up with computers and a secure link back to Mathers in Minneapolis. They'd settled into their new digs, pored over what they knew. Racked their brains for another lead on Randall Gruber.

They hadn't made much progress yet. But there was something bothering Stevens, some kind of clue he was missing.

He'd combed through the Death Wish forums when Andrea had first brought him the case, figured he should get a read on just what kind of people frequented the site. Realized pretty quick that most of the users weren't in any obvious danger—more hobbyists than bona fide suicide risks. Some of them had been active for four or five years on the boards, had written tens of thousands of posts on the subject. They were experts, sure, but in a field where the only true experts were dead.

But some of the users clearly needed help. Stevens had read through a handful of sad stories—*Wife left me and I have nothing left*, or *The bank's coming to foreclose in the morning*, or *Just got the test results; the doctor couldn't look me in the eye*—and felt a growing numbness in his chest.

He'd read a post by a paraplegic, a young man in Tallahassee who'd paralyzed himself diving into the shallow end of a swimming pool. The man wrote that he'd had enough of being useless. He was sick of watching able-bodied people do the things he used to do, the things he couldn't anymore.

I'll go insane if I keep on like this, he wrote. *I can't come to grips with my injury, and it's eating me up inside.*

Stevens had reached for the phone, ready to call Tallahassee, the local law enforcement, get this kid on their radar. Happened to scroll down the page as he was dialing, realized the guy had already gone and done it. Too late.

He'd stopped reading the forums pretty quick after that. Figured, there were thirty-five thousand suicide victims in the country every year; he'd drive himself crazy trying to save them all. Figured this was triage, and at that moment, saving Ashley Frey was about the only thing that mattered.

Of course, that was when Ashley Frey was a person of interest, another potential suicide victim. Not a predator.

Stevens fired up the Death Wish forums again. He wasn't looking for victims this time, or hobbyists. He was looking for a third brand of user he'd discovered in his reading, the creeps who filled the comment boxes underneath the sad stories, urging the miserable to go ahead and kill themselves already. They were the fetishists who lurked around the forums in hopes that they could witness death like spectators, and it was here, Stevens hoped, that he would pick up the trail to Randall Gruber.

The breakthrough came in an older post, dated a few months previous. A middle-aged man, a drug addict. *Lonely and tired of failing at life,* he wrote. The fetishists jumped all over him.

Stevens followed the thread, read thirty or forty responses, from fetishists and sympathizers alike. Felt his Spidey sense start to tingle as he kept reading, knew he was on the right path, even if he didn't know yet what he was aiming to find.

Just go ahead and do it, one of the fetishists had written. *Head on the train tracks. Don't forget to bring a GoPro.*

That malignant brand of human was nicknamed DeathAngel, and seemed to be a fixture on the site. Stevens made a note of his profile and kept reading down the thread.

The original poster—a man named N33dlep0int—had stayed tuned in to the thread for about a week. Then, abruptly, and in the middle of an argument about technique by a couple of spectators, he'd cut in:

I'm going to do it. Enough bullshit. Chicagoland, watch the news tonight. And sorry about your commute.

There was a slew of replies underneath, either words of encouragement or pleas to reconsider. But N33dlep0int hadn't replied, not to anyone. On page four of the thread, DeathAngel posted a link.

I think this was our boy, he wrote. *Click through. Some news footage, but nothing juicy.*

It was a link to a news article, some Chicago-area site. "Commuters Delayed by Suicide on the BNSF Line." Details were sketchy, just a video clip of a reporter in front of a Metra train.

"Witnesses say the man threw himself in front of the five forty-five out of Union Station," the reporter said. "Commuter trains were halted as much as an hour, causing no shortage of headaches to those trying to get home."

Trying to find something better, DeathAngel wrote. *Hoping for amateur footage or, if not, a security camera.*

Keep us posted, someone else replied. *Would love to see a better angle of this.*

But the thread petered out about a month after the original post, three weeks after N33dlep0int's real-life identity, one Roger Graham, had jumped in front of the train.

No luck, DeathAngel wrote. *I've contacted all my sources, and nobody has anything. Guess we're going to have to make do with our imaginations, kiddos.*

Thank God, Stevens thought. He clicked through to DeathAngel's profile, found a history of all the posts he'd made on the site. At the top of the page, he found what he was looking for. Another thread with a tragic end: TEEN SUICIDE IN MINNESOTA.

Got the hookup on some sweet webcam footage, DeathAngel wrote. *Subscription required, but well worth the price.*

He'd attached a link. Stevens clicked it, waited as his browser loaded up the page, feeling his stomach start to churn, knowing this was Adrian Miller, knowing he couldn't unsee what he was about to watch.

But the link only brought Stevens to a password-protect screen. No decoration, no website name, just a black background and a couple of white boxes, USERNAME and PASSWORD.

Stevens stared at the screen. Felt his cop instincts humming like a live wire, knew this was the right track. Someone was selling footage of Adrian Miller's death. Somewhere through this portal, Stevens knew, there was a way to find Randall Gruber.

All he needed was to know how to crack it.

< 61 >

Madison's phone buzzed just as first period ended. A text message from Brandon. *Hey. You around?*

Just got out of class, she wrote back, dodging people in the hall as she typed. *What's up?*

She was almost at her locker when her phone buzzed again. Only, this time it kept buzzing. Was he actually *calling* her?

She ducked into an alcove. Composed herself as the phone kept vibrating in her hand, tried to calm down, get a grip. She accepted the call. "Hello?"

A pause that seemed to stretch forever. Then: "Madison?"

It was *him.* Madison felt an electric current jolt through her body. "Hey," she said. "Hi. You actually *called.* Is it as bad as you thought it would be?"

Brandon laughed, a fast, nervous laugh. "It's pretty bad," he said. "I'm kind of freaking out right now. I told you I speak pretty funny."

"You don't have to be scared," she told him. "I don't care. It's just nice to hear that you're, like, a real person."

His voice *was* kind of funny. A little hint of a lisp, just something a bit off. Of course he didn't want to call her. People probably gave him all kinds of shit every time he opened his mouth.

"I just wanted to hear your voice," he said. "I feel like we really have a connection. Like we're really ready to do something huge together."

Madison held the phone to her ear, surveyed the hallway. Kids at their lockers, laughing, texting, shooting mean looks her way. Nudging each other and whispering, giggling.

That's the girl. That's Rudolph. What a loser.

Screw you, she thought. *Screw all of you. I'm talking to my boyfriend and he's a real person and he's cute and awesome, and we're going to leave you all in this shithole and do amazing things together, just watch.*

"So let's do it," she said. "Let's run away, just the two of us, Thelma and Louise, or whatever."

She waited for Brandon to reply. He didn't. "We could move to California or something," she said. "Or, hell, Canada. Or Europe, or Thailand, or wherever you want. We can leave our shitty lives and be together forever, just the two of us."

There was another pause, long enough that Madison wondered if the call had dropped. Realized, no, that Brandon just wasn't answering.

"Or, you know, whatever," she said, hating how desperate and lonely and lame she sounded. "It was just a suggestion, you know? What were *you* thinking?"

She heard him inhale. "I was thinking about the plan," he told her. "What we always talk about doing. I'm thinking that now is the time."

"I thought we talked about being together," she said. "I just feel like everything would be okay if we could just hang out together."

"We will be together," Brandon told her. "After we're dead, we'll be immortal. They'll never say my name without saying yours, too."

"Well, yeah," Madison said. "But who says we have to be dead? I just want to get out of here. And don't you want to see what it's like to be face-to-face? To, like, actually have a conversation together?

"Come on," she said. "What do you say? Who cares about suicide? Let's just freaking bail."

Another agonizing silence. Then: "I can't do it," Brandon said. "I can't see you. I'm sorry."

"Why not?"

"I'm just . . . I'm afraid I'll lose my nerve," he said, and the lisp was back, a stutter. "I'm afraid I'll see you and I won't want to go through with it anymore."

Madison felt a little thrill. The hint of a smile. "And what's so bad about that?"

"I don't want to live," Brandon said. "I just want to die, Madison. I thought you were coming with me. I thought we were in this together."

The smile faded, fast. "We are," Madison told him. "You and me, together, nobody else. I just . . . thought it would be nice to spend some time with you first, is all."

"We'll have all the time in the world," Brandon said. "Once we're both dead, Madison, we'll have nothing but time."

Kids were dispersing from the hall headed for second period. Madison stood in the alcove and watched them go, imagined Brandon's face in the pictures he'd sent her, those sad, lonely eyes. Wondered why he couldn't just want to live with her, just run away together.

Wondered why she wasn't good enough to convince him life didn't have to be so bad.

"I need you, Madison," he said. "I can't do this much longer. Are you with me, or not?"

The bell rang. She was officially late, but who cared? This call was more important. And if she answered wrong, Madison knew that Brandon would hang up the phone and disappear from her life and probably go off and do something awful. She couldn't have that.

So she lied. "I'm with you," she told him. "You and me, forever."

‹ 62 ›

Gruber turned off the voice distorter and put down the phone, satisfied with himself. Madison was invested, her escape fantasies deflected. She would follow him to the grave and believe it was romance. All things considered, Gruber figured he'd done pretty well, especially when he factored in the sketched-out kid with a *Dirty Harry* revolver listening in to the whole spiel from the couch.

"You have to develop a rapport with them," Gruber told the kid. "It's a fine line. They have to get to know you, trust you, but there's gotta be a reason they can't be *with* you, you know? Otherwise . . ." He laughed, gestured to himself. "Well, I mean, the gig would be up pretty quickly, right?"

The kid looked at the burger he was holding. Grimaced, and put it back in the bag. "Yeah," he said. "I get it, man."

The kid's name was Donovan. Whether that was a first name or a last, Gruber couldn't be sure, but he'd listened in on the guy's phone call last night, to his boss or whoever. Made sure he was explaining the situation properly, the two prospects. Gruber figured he would have to put the screws to SevenBot a little bit, hold out for more money up front, but he knew the Dylan Price footage would be worth the investment. And DarlingMadison would be even better.

Heck, a part of Gruber wished he really *could* see the girl in the flesh. She looked so much like Sarah; it would be a treat to meet her in person, cook up something special for her, for the both of them.

But, alas, Gruber figured this Donovan character wouldn't go along with that kind of excursion. The kid was disgusted enough by the whole procedure as it was.

He was sitting on Gruber's little couch, the big revolver in one hand, a sack of White Castle sliders in the other. He'd been watching Gruber, listening in, his face all screwed up, as if Gruber were performing a home birth on the dirty carpet.

"It's an art form, what I'm doing," Gruber told him. "Not everyone could do what I do."

"Yeah, I guess you got that right."

Gruber studied the pictures of the victims he'd taped to the wall.

161

R. J. Ramirez. Shelley Clark. All the rest. Felt a little rush of adrenaline just seeing their faces.

"I would say I'm pretty well an angel of death," he said. "Shepherding people across to the other side, right? It's a hell of a rush, if you want to know the truth."

"I don't." Donovan pushed the sack away. Wiped off his hands on a napkin, then picked up the revolver. "Do me a favor, though?"

Gruber met his eyes. "Yeah?"

"Stop talking," Donovan told him. "That fucked-up shit you're saying, it's making me lose my appetite."

Gruber stared at him, momentarily deflated. Then he shrugged. "Not everyone can do what I'm doing," he said again. "Not everyone has what it takes."

< 63 >

"It's an underground website," the agent told Stevens and Windermere. "Kind of a clearinghouse for snuff films. Password-protected, access by referral, the whole bit. As you can imagine, the people who watch this stuff are pretty careful about their privacy."

The cyber crimes agent was a guy named Spinarski, probably around Stevens's age, sensible shoes and a mustache going to gray. Agent Wheeler had brought him up from the basement to see if he couldn't help.

Turned out he could.

"There's footage on this site that could impact an investigation we're working," Stevens told him. "So how do we get in?"

Spinarski smiled. "Easy." He reached for the keyboard, typed in a username and password, pressed enter. Stepped back in triumph as the page loaded.

"We've known about this site for a while," he said. "They don't know it yet, but we managed to finagle a referral. It's been mighty helpful when it comes to tracking these guys down."

As if to punctuate his remarks, the screen came to life behind him, a video player, a black background, none of the theatrics that came with the suicide sites.

"Just be careful while you're on here," Spinarski told them. "My agents worked long and hard for this referral. Anyone figures out who you are, you're blowing months of hard work, get it?"

"Look, but don't touch," Windermere said. "We got it."

Spinarski lingered, an anxious parent handing over the car keys. "Okay," he said at last. "Happy hunting." With one more look at the computer screen, he made his exit. Left Stevens and Windermere to their work.

"So what are we doing here?" Windermere said. "Take me through your thought process, Stevens. Why the snuff films?"

Stevens outlined his theory. Rico Jordan and the snuff films in Cleveland. Gruber's webcam fascination. "I figured there might be a connection," he told Windermere. "Found a guy who peddled snuff on the Death Wish site, followed a hunch."

"And?" Windermere said.

"And—" Stevens reached for the keyboard, "I think I'm on to something."

. . .

The file had been uploaded a few days after Adrian Miller's suicide. It had accrued a couple hundred views, lodged in the snuff site's archives between footage of executions and brutal car accidents.

TEENAGE BOY SUICIDE BY HANGING, the file description read, and when Windermere clicked through and the video began to play, she recognized Adrian Miller's face instantly.

The image was haunting. Adrian stared at his computer, fiddled with the webcam a bit, his eyes sunken and distant, his jaw set in an expression of resolve. Windermere watched him, her stomach knotting and unknotting, every one of her muscles drawn taut. Adrian was a slender kid, his features delicate. It was not hard to imagine the crueler kids at Andrea Stevens's high school finding ways to make his life hell.

Satisfied with the webcam, Adrian stood up, walked away. Crossed his bedroom to the closet. Windermere could see the yellow rope on the floor behind him, the noose already fashioned, crooked and amateurish but instantly recognizable. As Windermere watched, Adrian picked up the rope. Fastened it to the crossbar in his closet. Took the other end and—

Windermere reached for the stop button. Stevens stayed her hand. She looked at him, sharp, ready to cuss him out, but he pointed at the screen.

The image of Adrian had paused. Faded dark behind bright white lettering. PURCHASE REQUIRED FOR FULL VIDEO, the title card read.

"He's *selling* these things," Windermere said. "He's not just a voyeur, he's a freaking marketplace."

"Sure," Stevens said. "So how does one make a purchase?"

"I'm guessing you get in touch with the guy who uploaded this file," Windermere said. She was studying the screen again. "Which means we're about to get really friendly with . . ." She clicked on a link, the uploader's name. "Someone who calls himself SevenBot."

SevenBot's real name was Frank Abrams.

"Scottsdale, Arizona," Spinarski said, reading from his screen. "Address is 3875 North Pueblo Way."

"We fell for this before," Windermere said. "Guy's using an anonymizer or something, sending us off on a goose chase. No way he leaves a trail this obvious."

Spinarski smirked. "Oh, he *thinks* he's hiding his identity," he said. "Has his IP address blocked, probably thinks that's enough. Only thing is, he's using a fairly simple program to do it, and we"—he waved his hand at the computer like a magician's assistant—"can bypass it quite easily. Don't forget to tip your tech guy."

"Frank Abrams." Windermere studied the screen. "You sure this address is legit?"

Spinarski tugged on his mustache. "Guarantee it," he said. "You hit this guy's house, you'll find that machine. Or your money back."

"Good enough for me," Windermere said, straightening. "Come on, Stevens. Either this Abrams cat is Gruber's new alias, or he's close enough to our boy to know how to find him. Whichever is true, I want to talk to him." She was halfway to the door already. "Don't you?"

< **64** >

Stevens and Windermere landed in Phoenix just as darkness fell. They were met in the terminal by a local FBI agent named Schwartz. Windermere had talked to him on the phone before boarding the flight.

"We have eyes on Abrams's house as we speak," Schwartz told them, leading them through the crowded maze of baggage carousels to the parking garage. "Your man's at home, we suspect alone. Last report I got, he was watching TV." Schwartz grinned. "The Food Network, in case you were wondering."

"He going to have dinner waiting?" Windermere asked.

Schwartz led them through the parking garage to his ride, a black GMC Yukon. "Doubtful," he said. "Abrams had KFC tonight, one of those party buckets. I guess you could ask if he has any leftovers."

He climbed into the truck, and Stevens and Windermere followed. Buckled themselves in as Schwartz drove away from the airport.

"Got a tactical team on standby, as you requested," Schwartz told them. "This guy Abrams doesn't appear dangerous, no criminal record, but they'll be there if you need them."

"Whether we need them or not," Windermere said, "this guy's posting snuff videos online, teenagers killing themselves. He could be an actual, real-life Care Bear. I still want his door busted down and his ass dragged out in cuffs."

"What my partner is saying," Stevens told Schwartz, "is that we want to take every precaution on this one."

Schwartz kept driving, a sly smile on his face. "Well, all right then," he said, reaching for his radio. "I'll tell the tactical guys to be ready."

The visit played out as per Windermere's instructions. Frank Abrams had a little one-story house, Southwestern style, adobe and red tile and cacti in the front yard, a quiet little street in either direction. Stevens and Windermere hung back in Schwartz's Yukon as the tactical guys swarmed the place, assault rifles and battering rams and a bullhorn to wake up the neighborhood.

Lights came on up and down the block. Shadows appeared in doorways, living room windows, watching and listening as the tactical guys broke down Abrams's door. Stevens and Windermere followed them in, found the tactical team in the living room, rifles pointed at the floor, where Frank Abrams lay facedown in handcuffs and boxer shorts, struggling against the boot at his back. On the TV, a guy with frosted spiky hair was eating what looked like deep-fried Jell-O.

Abrams was shouting something about his constitutional rights, how he wanted a lawyer. Windermere hunkered down in front of him, showed him her badge.

"You'll get your lawyer," she told him. "Get your trial, too. Judge, jury, the whole bit. And I promise you, that all will go a hell of a lot smoother for you if you decide to cooperate."

Abrams stopped shouting, panted his breath back. Regarded her from the rug. "What's this all about?" he asked her. "I never did anything. What are you trying to pull here?"

Windermere nodded. Pursed her lips. "You never did anything," she said. "Okay. You ever hear of somebody named . . . what was it, partner?"

"SevenBot," Stevens told her.

"SevenBot," Windermere repeated. "That name sound familiar?"

Abrams's eyes went wide. "Never heard it before in my life," he said. "I don't know what you guys are talking about, but I want a lawyer right now."

"Fine," Windermere said, standing. "Could be you're right, and this is all just a misunderstanding." She gestured across the living room to the doorway, where Schwartz was supervising the tactical guys as they carried out a desktop computer, a few external hard drives, some serious computing power. "I guess we'll find out soon enough."

Abrams went limp, dropped his head to the rug. Watched as the tactical agents walked out with his gear. "Aw," he said. "Aw, shoot."

"'Aw, shoot' sounds good," Windermere said. "So how about you pick yourself up off the floor and we have ourselves a conversation?"

< 65 >

They brought Abrams to an interview room in the FBI building on the north side of Phoenix. Found him a T-shirt, told him if he played nice, they might be able to dig up some pants.

"We're not here for you in particular," Windermere told him, settling down across the table. "I mean, we don't like you, or your creepy-ass hobby, but we have bigger targets in mind."

"Basically, help us catch our subject, and we'll make sure the ADA who pulls your case knows you were cooperative," Stevens said. "Might not be enough to keep you out of jail, but you never know, right?"

Abrams stared down at the table, the fight all but gone. He'd stopped screaming for a lawyer about the time the FBI agents had pulled him out of his house in plain view of the neighbors, had spent the ride to the FBI office in silence. He looked defeated now, and scared, and Windermere knew he would tell them whatever he knew if he thought it would save his own ass.

Sure enough, he seemed to gather himself. "So, okay," he said. "What can I do?"

"Two weeks ago, you posted a video online of a teenage boy hanging himself," Windermere said. "Do you know the file I'm talking about?"

Abrams looked away. "Yeah, I do."

"Did you create the footage?"

"No," Abrams said. "Hell, no. I just, you know, acquired it. I posted it for interested parties. I don't actually *make* the stuff."

"Sure," Stevens said. "Because making it would be sick and twisted. So where did you get it?"

Abrams didn't answer for a moment. "It's him, isn't it?" he said. "That's your target, the guy who's making this stuff. That's who you're after, right?"

"You know him?" Windermere said. "You give us something workable, it'll go a long way toward getting you back home to that bucket of extra crispy."

Abrams sighed. It was not the sigh of someone who'd just been shown a way out of his predicament.

"I *don't* know him," he said. "I mean, nobody knows him, not that I can tell. We're kind of a small community on there, and he—he's kind of a ghost." He shook his head. "If you're hoping I'll draw you a map to this guy, believe me, I wish I could, but I got nothing."

"That's a lie," Stevens said. "You have something. You got hold of the video somehow. That's a start."

"I only know the guy through a dummy email account," Abrams said. "Swear to God, that's it."

Windermere pulled out a notebook. "The email account," she said. "Write it down."

Abrams did as he was told. Slid the notebook back across the table, and seemed to anticipate the next question coming. "The guy just chose me," he said. "It's not like I went searching for him. But you guys have been on the forum. You've seen my profile. I'm kind of a big deal. Any snuff you're trying to buy or sell, I'm the guy."

"Congratulations," Windermere said. "I bet that looks real good on your résumé."

"What was I going to do, turn him in? Call the police and tell them a guy on my snuff forum is taping kids killing themselves?" He shook his head again. "Anyway, I looked it up. It's not illegal, what he's doing."

"That's up for debate," Stevens said, "but it's still a shitty thing to do."

Abrams gave him a look like he'd been out of class the day they were teaching morality. Kind of shrugged, his face blank.

"So he found you," Windermere said. "And then?"

"And then he asked if I wanted to help him sell a video of a kid killing himself," Abrams said. "Clear footage, perfect angle—he was pretty proud of his work. And rightfully so, I guess. I mean, you have to realize, this guy's stuff is golden. It's top-notch, the way he gets these kids to do it. He's an artist, for sure. I was happy to buy the first clip, and the ones that came after. They've made us both a ton of money."

"How do you pay him?"

"Western Union, money transfer," Abrams said. "Through that same dummy email address. I send it to someone named Earl Ashley, but if you're talking to me, you probably already know that's a fake name."

"His stepfather's name was Earl. His stepsister's middle name was Ashley," Stevens said. "She died twenty years ago. Hanged herself while he watched."

"Unfortunately, there's no footage," Windermere said.

Abrams made a face. "Funny," he said. "I see what you did there."

"So, this last file you posted," Windermere said. "Kid named Adrian Miller, a high school student in Minnesota. Killed himself because kids were bullying him at school."

Abrams stared at her, like he knew this was supposed to make him feel contrite, and he just wasn't feeling it. Windermere inhaled a long breath, willed herself to stay calm, to resist the urge to reach across and smash this guy's head into the table.

"Anyway," she said, exhaling. "Adrian Miller. That the last time you heard from this Ashley guy?"

She was hoping she knew the answer, hoping Adrian Miller was the last of Gruber's victims. It had only been two weeks after all, and they'd had Gruber distracted for some of it. But that didn't mean squat.

"That's the last time he sent me any footage," Abrams said, "but it sounds like he's gearing up. He tried to hit me up for an advance a couple days ago, said he had something big in the works. Two more kids—prospects, he calls them. Sounded like a couple mint scores."

Windermere twisted in her seat, met Stevens's eyes. "Two more prospects, partner," she said. "I knew he'd keep going."

171

"Clock is ticking," Stevens said. "But where is he operating? He hasn't been back on Death Wish since we made him."

"Oh, he has more accounts," Abrams said. "This guy's everywhere. Like a dragnet for hopeless cases. Sweeps them up, grooms them, tells them how to end it all." He paused. "And films it, hopefully."

"These new prospects he's grooming," Windermere said. "Where did he find them? Which of these forums is he working now?"

Abrams shifted in his seat, didn't answer. Avoided eye contact.

"If you know something, share it with the class," Windermere told him. "Otherwise, not only will I make sure you're prosecuted to the full extent for this shit, but I'll see to it that everybody on your little forum knows you're the guy who got them all arrested, locked up, and publicly outed, to boot. Get it?"

"Shoot." Abrams looked up, a shade paler. "Okay, yeah, I get it," he said. "Like I said, I don't really know much. But I think he's grooming his next, you know, *prospect* on a site called The End."

< **66** >

"Why so glum, homey?"

Madison spun, found Paul standing a few feet from her locker, leaning against the wall and looking smug. She tucked her phone into her backpack, picked up her history textbook. Slammed her locker closed.

"You don't have to follow me," she told him. "We have class together. You'll be right beside me for the next, like, hour and a half."

"Figured I could maybe walk you to class," Paul said. "Like, we could walk and tell jokes and, I dunno, *gossip*. Like, you know, *friends*."

"We're not friends," Madison said, before she could stop herself. Paul laughed, smiled wider.

"Well, not with that attitude," he said. "Anyway, come on. The bell's about to ring."

He turned and started down the hall, stopped after a few steps and waited for her to catch up. Madison hesitated. Sighed and walked after him.

"So how come you're so miserable?" Paul asked her. "This have something to do with that Internet boyfriend of yours?"

"That's none of your business," Madison said. "But yes, it kind of does."

"Ooh. Well, go on. What did lover boy have to say? Did he flunk a test? Pollute a river? What terrible stories did this guy have to tell you?"

"It's nothing like that," Madison said. "Don't worry about it, dude. It wasn't anything, really."

But it was; it was everything. She'd been thinking about Brandon all day, about that phone call, how miserable he'd sounded, defeated. Like he was ready to find a cliff and drive off it without her, like he didn't even care that he'd already changed her life.

She didn't want to die. She knew this. She didn't want Brandon to die, either. She wanted to meet up with Brandon and drive off somewhere—Los Angeles, maybe, if that wasn't too cliché, or Mexico— and live badass lives together and be the envy of everyone and never miss anything about their homes or their old towns or their crummy families. Madison would take that. She could accept it. She didn't need to die.

"So he told you he was sad," Paul said. "And you've been worrying about him ever since. How cute."

"He's not just *sad*, moron," Madison told him. "He's really depressed. Like, he's talking about wanting to kill himself. I don't know what to do about it."

"Wow." Paul dodged an army of jocks coming down the hall in the opposite direction. "This is the guy you've never actually met, right? The one who might be, like, a forty-six-year-old sex pervert?"

"He's not a sex pervert," Madison said. "We talked on the phone and he's an amazing guy. We're going to run away together, and you'll never see me again."

"Until they dig up your body."

"Screw off." Madison gave him the finger. Pushed ahead of him into Mr. Rhodes's class. Left Paul standing in her wake, but couldn't stop thinking about Brandon.

I have to do something, she thought. *There has to be a way to save him. If he freaking dies on me, I actually* will *kill myself.*

< **67** >

Windermere put Mathers on the money trail. Gave him the dummy email address Gruber used to communicate with Frank "SevenBot" Abrams, and the payment history through Western Union. Figured it might take a few days, but they could probably count on a lead to Gruber eventually. Meanwhile, she and Stevens went right to The End.

It took a full day to get a warrant to search the suicide forum's servers. And it wasn't like the forum's owner was ready to play ball without one.

"Total invasion of my users' privacy," he told Windermere over the phone. He had a high-pitched, obnoxious voice that didn't blend well with his self-righteous tone. Clearly, he'd been waiting for a phone call like this.

"These people are consenting adults, American citizens," he continued. "They have a right to be protected against unreasonable search and seizure. If they want to die, who am I to try and stop them?"

"Only, they're not adults," Windermere said. "They're teenagers. Doesn't that bother you at all?"

But the guy had already hung up in her ear, leaving Windermere talking to an empty line. She put the phone down, told Stevens to start calling judges. Placed her next call to the FBI office in Bangor, Maine, where she'd traced the forum's servers, had the local field agents put together a team to raid the owner's house just as soon as the warrant came through.

"Be careful," Windermere told the Bangor agent. "This guy sounds like he fancies himself a real proponent of personal freedoms. If he's not deleting his forum records off those servers, he's probably cleaning his collection of assault rifles. So tread lightly."

The Bangor agent thanked her, assured her his team would move on the servers as soon as they had a warrant in hand.

Windermere ended the call. Turned to check on Stevens, found him rolling his eyes, explaining to the federal judge why Gruber's pursuit of those teenage victims should be considered a crime.

"State law says it's a felony to coerce or counsel someone into committing suicide," he was saying. "This guy is pretending to be a teenager and luring vulnerable kids to their deaths." He paused, listened. "Yes, I *know* it's a state law. But this guy's operating over interstate lines. He's clearly—"

He stopped abruptly. Listened. Caught Windermere's eye and grimaced. "Okay," he said. "Sure, I understand. We'll work on it."

He made to hang up the phone. Windermere had the handset out of his hands before she really knew what she was doing. Brought the phone to her ear. "Who am I talking to?"

A silence, and she was afraid the judge had hung up. But then: "This is Judge Waite," a woman said slowly. "To whom am *I* speaking?"

"Carla Windermere, FBI," Windermere told the judge. "You want to tell me why you're playing hardball on this warrant?"

The judge laughed a little, incredulous. "As I explained to your colleague, Agent Windermere, there's no federal law against encouraging people to commit suicide, even in situations like this. I told your partner I wasn't even sure why you're pursuing this case, when by my interpretation of the law, the target of your investigation is within his right to free speech to do what he's doing. I'm not even sure how you—"

"Oh, don't come at me with that free-speech bullshit," Windermere told the judge. "Soliciting someone to commit suicide is a felony in just about every state in the union. This is just another case of the law lagging behind criminals and their technology."

"Then it's a state issue," the judge replied. "I might suggest bringing your case to a judge at the state level."

"You're not listening," Windermere told her. She could see Stevens in the background, waving her off, wide-eyed. Ignored him. "We have a victim in Minnesota. Another in Texas, a third in Delaware. We have servers we need to access in Maine, and a suspect hiding God knows where. In which state, exactly, do you expect us to start?"

"Wherever you think you have the best shot," the judge replied. "You're a federal agent, Ms. Windermere. Surely you don't expect me to simply hand over a warrant without respect to the law."

"I am a federal agent," Windermere told her. "And you're a federal judge, *Ms. Waite*. These people my suspect is targeting, they're teenagers. *Kids.* You really want to go on record as the judge who prevented the FBI from chasing an online predator?"

The judge was silent.

"This isn't a free-speech situation," Windermere told her. "This is a case of impressionable young minds being preyed upon. You shut me down here, first place I'm calling is the Minnesota state courts. Second place I'm calling is the *New York Times*. You feel me?"

Waite still didn't answer. Finally, she sighed. "You have a fax machine over there, I assume?"

Windermere gave her the details. Ended the call and put down the phone. Stevens was staring at her. "That was a federal judge you were talking to, Carla," he said. "You kind of sounded like you thought she was a suspect."

"She *was* suspect, partner," Windermere said, standing. "Now, point me to the fax machine. And next time, leave the bad cop stuff to me."

< **68** >

Donovan paced the living room. Kicked an empty Funyuns bag across the carpet. *"Shit*, dude," he said. "Would it kill you to clean up a little?"

Gruber smirked up at him from the computer. "I like it this way. You want the place clean so bad, you do it. It's not like you're doing anything else."

The asshole had a point. Donovan had worn a track through the carpet already, burned a hole in his digestive tract eating White Castle and Taco Bell because this cornball Gruber really *was* flat fucking broke, not even a stick of butter in his fridge. Donovan had been here for, shit, a day and a half, felt longer than the six months he'd spent in juvie.

There was nothing to do but wait. Wait and eat shitty food, and listen to Gruber brag about the sick shit he was doing on the computer, the way he was luring his victims closer to death. Donovan had already sat through one lecture about how Gruber used Facebook, how he'd created accounts for both of his personas, filled them with stock pictures, built lives for these people.

"I found this kid on the Death Wish forums," Gruber told him. "He was from Kansas City, nineteen years old. Jumped in front of a train. Anyway, he left his Facebook page unlocked, so I stole his life. Copied all his pictures to my hard drive and created a new account." He grinned. "I call him Brandon."

Donovan didn't say anything. Figured it didn't matter what he said, Gruber wasn't going to shut up.

"I post the pictures every now and then, randomly, so it seems like they're just happening," Gruber continued. "And it's easy to make friends on Facebook. Teenagers are so obsessed with being popular, they'll add anybody just to pad their friend counts. It's self-perpetuating, too, because the more friends you have, the more people want to know you. Genius, right?"

Donovan had ignored him. Turned away and tried to stifle the urge to shoot the bastard in the back of the head right then and there.

He'd gone into the kitchen, called Rodney while Gruber was in the bathroom. "This dude is sick," he said. "This is kids we're talking about, man. This is innocent kids."

Rodney wasn't moved. "You got another way to come up with the money?" he asked. "The message must be sent, dude. Can't be backing down."

Outside, a train rumbled past, blew its horn, loud. The trains were always coming and going, shaking the whole house on its foundation. Donovan missed what Rodney was saying. Had to ask him to repeat it.

"I said, you don't think you can do it, I'll find someone else who can," Rodney told him. "So what's up, Curtis? You in, or you out?"

Gruber flushed the toilet. Came out of the bathroom, wiping his hands on his ragged T-shirt. Went back to the computer and sat down, opened up a chat window. Donovan watched him. Stifled his disgust.

"I'm in," he said. "I just wish this motherfucker wasn't such a god-damn piece of *work*."

< **69** >

Windermere faxed the warrant to Bangor. A half hour later, Bangor phoned back.

"Bingo," the agent told Windermere. "Got the servers in custody. No shots fired. Your guy talked a big game, but he caved pretty easily when the G-men showed up at his door."

"Sounds about right," Windermere said. "Can you get us those files, or do we need to fly out to Maine to see them?"

"We'll get them to you," the agent replied. "We snagged an admin log-in when we picked up the servers. I'll send it over and you can browse through your man's files from the comfort of your own home."

Windermere surveyed the Phoenix FBI office, the long row of work-stations in CID. "Or a cubicle farm in Arizona," she said. "Whichever's more convenient."

The suicide forum called The End had no users named Ashley Frey registered. And a search through the master archives brought back no hits for that name in either the chat logs or the thread histories.

"So what now?" Windermere asked. "We just spent a day leaping through epic hoops to get this data, Stevens. How do we use it to find Gruber?"

"Maybe Gruber's using a different alias," Stevens said. "He was always an angel on the Death Wish forum. How about searching biblical usernames?"

Windermere snapped her fingers. "Angels," she said. "I can dig it."

She searched through the forum's archives until she found a list of every user. Realized there was no way to pare down the search using biblical references, that she and Stevens were going to have to work through the whole list manually.

"Not exactly the most specific search criteria in the world," she said, settling into her seat. "I guess we'll do this the old-fashioned way."

Stevens rolled his chair over beside her. "Gruber's Frey accounts always had a number in the name," he said. "High nineties, probably supposed to be a year of birth. Any luck, he's doing the same thing here."

Windermere started to type something, stopped. "You want to find me a list of angels, partner?" she said. "I wasn't exactly the star pupil in Sunday school."

They worked down the list. Worked into the wee hours, alphabetically, through Abaddon, Arariel, Barachiel, Beelzebub. Found a handful of users for every angel they could think of, *A* through *F*, and discounted them all.

"Most of these guys are one-shot artists," Stevens said. "Came online, lurked for a while, maybe posted one thread, and vanished."

"Vanished?" Windermere said. On a suicide forum, the meaning wasn't good.

"Well, who knows? Maybe they all logged off, fell in love, and married the girl or boy of their dreams. Maybe they're all happy and well-adjusted insurance salesmen."

"Insurance salesmen? Happy?"

"Or, whatever," Stevens said. "I'm just trying to avoid the logical conclusion."

They kept looking. Hit the *G*s and the first user they came to was Gabriel98, some kid named Brandon in Council Bluffs, Iowa. A pretty boy, judging by his picture, undeniably handsome.

"Angel name," Stevens said. "Plus a nineties number."

"And a profile pic that looks too pretty to be real," Windermere said. "It's like he came from a spread in *GQ* or something, right?"

Stevens studied the picture. "This guy was online seven hours ago," he said, "chatting with someone named D4Death. Let's see what they had to say."

Windermere opened the chat window. Scrolled to the first message of the day and began to read.

‹ 70 ›

D4Death: *You there?*

Gabriel98: *Yup. How are you feeling?*

D: *I feel okay. You know. Just getting ready for school. So weird to think it's the last time I'll ever do this.*

G: *You saying that's a bad thing?*

D: *No. Just . . . weird. You don't feel that way?*

G: *What do you mean?*

D: *Like, aren't you scared at all? Nervous? This isn't exactly a minor procedure we're doing here. If we fuck up . . .*

G: *What? We could die?*

D: *LOL.*

G: *You're not going to fuck up.*

G: *Don't be nervous. Be excited. This is the last day of the rest of your life. Soon all your problems will be nothing, remember?*

D: *I know.*

D: *It's just a big step, is all. Like, it's hard to believe it's actually here.*

G: *You're going to be fine. I'll talk you through it. Just keep it together one more day, okay?*

D: *Okay.*

G: *You start to feel weird about things, come to me. Nobody else. We'll get through this together, right?*

D: *Okay.*

G: *Tomorrow, Dylan. It's all happening.*

D: *Yeah, man.*

G: *Tomorrow.*

D: *Tomorrow.* ☺

<<<

Windermere looked up from the screen. "We need to find this kid, Stevens," she said. "Like, now. Gruber's got him at the breaking point."

"It's definitely him, right?" Stevens said. "This is Gruber."

"Sure is. And he almost has this kid." Windermere scrolled down the chat log. "Damn it, he's been working him for months."

Stevens checked his watch. "And it all leads up to today."

"Exactly," Windermere said. "We need to find this kid *stat*."

< 71 >

Gruber didn't sleep. He never could, not the night before he watched. There was too much excitement, too many emotions. The anticipation mainly, imagining how the prospect would act in those final moments, trying to predict his mental state, his resolve.

This time, of course, was different. This time, Gruber had Donovan, a roommate and a prison guard all rolled into one. The guy was desperate for the money; Gruber had heard him talking on the phone, knew he was looking for a way out. Knew if Dylan Price didn't pan, Donovan would turn to that Smith & Wesson again.

Gruber tossed and turned beneath his flimsy sheet, his sleeping bag comforter. Listened to the trains shunting outside and tried to play out the next hours in his mind. Imagined watching Dylan in those final moments. Felt his heart race as he imagined the high drama of the act itself, then the glorious stillness.

Gruber thought about Sarah, too. He always did, the night before. Even during the act, he would catch himself picturing his stepsister, as if he were fifteen again, and watching not on a webcam but through that hole in the wall. He imagined that it was Sarah he was watching, Earl's daughter who was dying, over and over again.

Gruber kicked the sheets off. Slid out of bed just as dawn's first light appeared in the cracks between his dirty sheet curtains. It was Friday, Dylan's big day. Gruber walked out of the bedroom and into his little kitchen, cleared some space on the cluttered counter and rinsed a mug out with tap water. Started the water to boil for his instant coffee. Checked in on Donovan in the living room. The kid was sacked out on the couch, that big revolver dangling from his hand. He was snoring, his head tilted back to the ceiling. Unaware, defenseless.

Gruber knew he could kill the kid right now. There was a carving knife in a kitchen drawer that would do the job, easy. He could walk over there and cut Donovan's throat before the thug even woke up, before he figured out what was happening. Gruber watched Donovan for a while. Then he walked back into the kitchen and took out the knife, studied it, the way the blade caught the light.

You could do this. The thought sent electricity through his bloodstream. *You could really watch him die, up close and personal.*

But he would bleed all over the living room. Gruber would have to dispose of his body. And if Donovan woke up and started shooting, he could cause serious problems. Gruber didn't want problems. He wanted to watch Dylan Price die. He wanted Donovan to leave him in peace.

Still, it wouldn't hurt to build in a little insurance.

Gruber took the kitchen knife into the living room, quiet as he could. Slid open the bottom drawer of his computer desk, dropped the knife inside. Then he turned on his computer and opened his Internet browser, brought up The End forums. Logged in as Gabriel98, saw that

Dylan had sent him a message overnight. Pushed his glasses up his nose and read.

Dad fucking threw out my vintage comic book collection before he left for D.C. Nerdy and weird, he said. Thousands of dollars destroyed. You were right. It doesn't get better.

Let's do this.

Gruber grinned. Sipped his coffee. Checked his computer, his video recording software. Turned and called to Donovan.

"Hope you're ready, my friend," he told the thug. "The show's about to begin."

< 72 >

"**Pinned down** D4Death's IP address," Windermere told Stevens, clutching a printout. "Registered to one Douglas Price, lives in Baltimore. Has a wife and a son, Dylan."

"That's the kid," Stevens said. "Gruber called him Dylan in the chat log."

Windermere was already reaching for the phone. "You call Baltimore PD," she said. "I'm going to let Douglas Price know about his son's big plan for the day."

< **73** >

The phone wouldn't stop ringing.

Dylan Price rolled over in bed, tucked his head underneath the covers and tried to block out the noise. The light. He'd raided his dad's collection of single malts last night, the good stuff, figured if he drank himself into a stupor he'd probably feel better about the whole dying thing.

Now, though, Dylan had a serious headache. The sun was shining through his bedroom window and the phone kept ringing and ringing.

His parents were away—D.C., some conference for big-shot doctors, or whatever. They were gone, and he was home alone, and whoever was calling had never heard of voicemail. They must have phoned through the cycle like five times already.

"Freaking hell." Dylan crawled out from under the covers. Sat on the edge of the bed for a moment. Then he stood, swaying a little, lightheaded, and padded down the hall to his mom and dad's bedroom and that stupid bleating phone.

"What?"

A pause. Then a woman's voice. "Dylan?"

There was an urgency in her voice that set Dylan on edge. Made him suspicious, made his mind flash to that coil of yellow rope in the attic. "Yeah?"

"Dylan." Now the woman sounded relieved. "Dylan, uh, are your parents home?"

"They're gone," Dylan told her. "Out of town for the weekend."

"Out of town. Okay." The woman paused again. "Is there anybody else at home with you? Any adults or anything?"

"Uh . . ." Dylan frowned, thinking the woman must be pulling a scam or something, something shady. "Why? Who are you and why are you calling?"

Another pause. Muffled voices. "Dylan," the woman said, "my name is Carla Windermere. I'm a special agent with the FBI, and I need you to stay on the line with me, okay?"

> > >

Windermere held her breath, waiting for Dylan's reply. Beside her, Stevens was on his own phone, relaying instructions to the Baltimore Police Department, Dylan Price's address, an emergency, damn it.

They would have to find Douglas Price, too, Windermere was thinking. Get him home as soon as possible, get both parents involved.

But first, Windermere had to make sure she kept Dylan on the line. Knew if she screwed up and lost him, he was probably dead.

"FBI?" Dylan said slowly. "Like, the Federal Bureau of Investigation? What do you want with me? Is my dad in trouble?"

"Nobody's in any trouble," Windermere said. Choosing each word like it might make the difference. "I just need you to talk to me, okay? Let me know you're all right, and we'll get through this together."

Dylan didn't say anything. Windermere could picture him on the other end of the phone line, wavering a little, no doubt confused as hell.

"I still don't understand," Dylan said. "What is it you want?"

<<<

Dylan waited. The FBI agent didn't say anything, seemed to be calculating a response.

"Just stay on the line," she said at last, that note of urgency creeping back into her voice. "Can you do that for me, Dylan?"

The phone in Dylan's hand was a cordless. He carried it out of his parents' room and down the hall to his bedroom. Sat down in front of his computer, pressed a button, and the screen came to life. He logged in to the forum, typed a private message to Brandon. *You there?*

"Dylan?" the FBI agent said.

"I'm still here," Dylan told her. "But you still never told me why you're calling. Why should I even believe you're an FBI agent?"

"Just bear with me, honey. Everything will be straightened out in a minute."

On the computer, Brandon replied. *Morning, sunshine. Ready for our big day?*

Dylan read the message and relaxed a little. Everything was okay. Brandon was here. Whatever the FBI wanted, Dylan figured they could sort it out with his parents after the funeral.

"Sorry, but something's come up," he told the FBI agent. "I gotta let you go. I'm sure my dad can help you with whatever you need."

"Wait," the agent said. *"Dylan, no. Don't—"*

"Bye," Dylan told her. Ended the call.

On the computer screen, Brandon had written another message. *You still down to do this?*

Dylan surveyed his bedroom, savored the silence. His head was still pounding, that awful hangover. His comic books were mulch, and his dad was going to kill him for drinking all that scotch. FBI or no FBI, he couldn't think of a reason to stay alive any longer.

Totally, he wrote back. *Let's get started.*

‹ 74 ›

Windermere stared at her phone. "He hung up on me," she said, an abyssal silence on the other end of the line. "The kid just hung up, Stevens. *Shit.*"

Stevens was still on his phone, coordinating with the Baltimore PD. "Dispatcher's put out an all-unit call," he said. "Should have first responders at the kid's place within ten minutes, tops."

"Ten minutes?" Windermere checked the clock on the wall. "It's not fast enough, Stevens. They need to be faster."

"Gruber's not going to get him that easy," Stevens said. "They're getting there fast as they can."

"This kid's going to die, partner." She was up and pacing, tense, clutching at her arms. "Jesus, I killed him. I let him hang up the phone."

Stevens stood. Came to her, took her arms. "It's not over yet, Carla," he told her. "PD's on the way. There's still time."

Windermere said nothing. Wrenched free of Stevens's grip and kept pacing, watching the clock on the wall, helpless, wondering if she was watching the last minutes of Dylan Price's life tick away.

< **75** >

Dylan's attic.

A different view through the webcam portal, cardboard boxes and dusty furniture, heavy timber crossbeams running the length of the room. Darker than Dylan's bedroom, just hazy daylight coming in through a couple of low windows, the roof peaked and angled. And Dylan, bleary-eyed and hollow, his movements clumsy and unsure.

"Now loop the rope over the crossbeam," Gruber told him. "Make sure it's tied tight and secure. You don't want the knot to slip when you put your weight on it."

On-screen, Dylan did as he was instructed. He'd already formed the noose in the thick yellow rope, told Gruber he'd practiced last night until he got it right. Gruber was pleased to see the kid didn't seem scared.

"I'm sure glad you're here," Dylan said. "Even if you're not, like, *here*. I don't think I could do this without you."

"I'll be here," Gruber told him. "The whole time. We'll do it all together."

Dylan tied off the end of the rope. Surveyed his work, tested the knot, the strength of the line.

"Looks good," he said, turning back to the webcam. "I mean, I *think* it looks good. How does it look from there?"

Gruber stared through his screen at the noose. Behind him, Donovan muttered something, walked out of the room. Gruber watched him go. *Not everyone can do what I do,* he thought. *Not everyone can be an angel of death.*

Then he turned back to the screen. "It looks magnificent," he told Dylan. "You're doing great."

> > >

Dylan studied the rope. Wondered how he was supposed to feel.

He'd expected his heart to be pounding. Sweaty palms, nervous shakes, the whole gamut. He'd anticipated feeling terrified. Instead, he just felt numb.

It would hurt, probably. It would be unpleasant for three, four, maybe five minutes. Maybe longer. He would probably wish he hadn't done what he was doing. That was a pussy response, Brandon said. That was the reaction of a baby who couldn't take the pain, who wanted the easy way out.

There's no easy way out, Brandon had told him. *You'll suffer, one way or another. The only question is, do you want to suffer for years or for minutes.*

Dylan wanted to suffer for the least amount of time possible. He wanted his suffering to be over.

He would do this. Brandon would help.

He leaned down and picked up the noose end. Tested the knot one more time. It felt good.

<<<

"Three minutes," Stevens said, the phone to his ear. "First patrol unit took a wrong turn somewhere."

Windermere felt a numbness, an inevitability, like everything was playing out how it was supposed to play out. Like Dylan Price was already good as dead, and all that remained was to work out the details. She leaned against the wall, stared at her computer. Felt about a thousand pounds heavier.

"We got a webcam feed or anything?" Stevens asked. "Any way we can hack into Dylan's broadcast?"

Windermere shook her head. "No way to swing that now. We're just waiting and listening."

Stevens studied her, like he was waiting for her to do something. She didn't meet his eyes. Stared straight ahead until Stevens picked up his phone again.

"I need you at that house," he told the Baltimore PD dispatcher. "I need units at that boy's house *yesterday*."

< **76** >

This was it.

Dylan thought about his dad as he stepped onto the chair. Hoped the stupid prick would be the one to find him, wished he could see the look on his face. Would he be sad when he discovered the body? Angry? Would he see his son's suicide as just another failure, the final disappointment?

Fuck you, you miserable shithead, Dylan thought, tightening the rope around his neck. *I hope this ruins your life.*

He turned around on the chair, felt it teeter a little bit as he maneuvered to face the computer and the webcam.

"Okay, dude," he called out. "I hope you're ready for this."

Somewhere in the distance, a siren sounded.

> > >

Gruber felt his heart racing. This was it. This was the moment.

Donovan was in the bathroom. Gruber could hear the sink. He wanted to miss the show? So be it. Gruber regarded Earl's picture where it hung above the computer. *You'll be watching, won't you, Earl? You'll see how special I've become.*

"Ready," Gruber called through the microphone. "Do it for me, Dylan."

Dylan looked around the attic. Exhaled, his breath ragged. "Okay," he said. "I'm going to do it, I guess. Good luck, Brandon."

Gruber leaned closer, his heart racing. "See you on the other side."

"Yeah," Dylan said. He seemed to hesitate for one final moment, and Gruber wondered if this was it, if the kid had it in him, or if he would wuss out at the end like so many of the others.

Do it, he thought. *Do it, Dylan. For me.*

The moment didn't last. Dylan turned back to the webcam. He kicked the chair away. Then he dropped.

<<<

"PD's at the house," Stevens told Windermere. "They're pulling up outside."

Windermere grabbed the phone from his hands. *"Get those freaking cops inside,"* she told the dispatcher. *"Find the kid. Now."*

There was a silence. Then: "Ma'am, we're—"

"Now," Windermere repeated. *"You hear me? Now!"* She thrust the phone back into Stevens's hands. Kept pacing, seeing Dylan Price, the kid in the profile picture, gasping and choking for air, slowly dying.

"You heard her," Stevens was telling the dispatcher. "You tell your guys, *Move.*"

< **77** >

"Do you see, Earl? *Do you see what we've become?"*

Donovan came out of the bathroom, saw Gruber rocking back and forth in his chair, staring rapt at his computer. Couldn't see the image on the screen, but knew from the expression on Gruber's face that it wasn't good.

"I'm an angel of death, Earl, you twisted bastard. I turned this one like I turned your daughter, like I turned them all. Do you see what I've accomplished?"

Donovan felt his stomach turn. Sick, this was sick, and he was a part of this now. He reached for his uncle's Smith & Wesson, thinking, fuck's sake, he couldn't stand by and watch this.

Rodney would want his money, though. Rodney would want to know why Donovan had pussied out.

Think you can roll with this crew, but you can't take a little snuff film? Shit.

Donovan slid the revolver back into his waistband. Turned around, walked to the front door. Opened it and stood out on the stoop, the sky pissing rain above him, listened to the trains down the block and tried to drown out Gruber's maniac voice.

<<<

Dylan heard banging somewhere, footsteps. Distant, his mind foggy, choking, no air, the rope tight around his neck, cutting into his skin, the sounds like a dream from a thousand miles away.

The pain was worse than he'd imagined. He felt his hands at his throat, his feet swinging, none of it on purpose, his movements on autopilot. His body was fighting to live, he realized, not that it mattered. He'd be dead soon. His vision was going dark. He could feel his life slipping away.

Then something *CRACKED* near him, loud as a gunshot, and at first Dylan thought the attic crossbar had given way. But he was still hanging there, still slowly strangling. He was still dying.

It would all be over soon.

<<<

Gruber's breathing was heavy. He was panting. Hyperventilating. He closed his eyes and saw Sarah, dancing on the end of that rope. Felt his hand creep, unconsciously, to the front of his pants.

Then, on-screen, something *cracked*, loud. Gruber opened his eyes. *"No,"* he said, leaning forward. "No, no, oh *no.*"

<<<

The weight disappeared. The pressure on his neck vanished. Dylan opened his eyes just as a pair of strong hands grabbed hold of him. Hefted him up, bore his weight, released the strain on the rope and the noose and his neck and his windpipe.

A police officer, Dylan saw, big and strong and worried. More behind him, at the door to the attic, the little hatch in the floor. They'd broken it open to find him. Somehow, they'd saved him.

Dylan gasped for air, gulped it down, too relieved to be breathing again to feel anything but grateful.

< **78** >

"No!"

Gruber clawed at his hair, rocked forward violently, watched on the computer screen as the first police officer burst up through the hatch of the attic and dashed toward Dylan, lifting him up easily and slacking the tension in the rope on Dylan's neck.

"No, no, no, no, no." Gruber could hardly speak, the words blurring into one another, desperate and incoherent.

More cops appeared, crowding the room, filling it, cutting Dylan down from the rope and cradling him, carrying him to a mattress at the corner of Gruber's screen. Gruber rocked, clawed, watched through his hands as the cops loosened the noose around Dylan's neck, as they lifted it over his head, freeing him.

"What the hell are you *doing?*" Gruber screamed. *"Don't you understand? He* needed *to die. You're ruining everything!"*

A couple of cops glanced at the computer screen. Someone reached over, fiddled with the volume. Gruber could hear the police talking to one another, the boots on the stairs as the paramedics came up to tend to Dylan.

"No," Gruber repeated, slamming his hands on the keyboard. "No, no, no, no, *no!*"

Then it all dissolved, and he felt his vision go dark, felt his words slide together into one long, animal moan.

<<<

Gruber's sounds belonged to a wild being, some tortured, dying soul. Stevens shuddered as he listened through the speakerphone, a Baltimore PD officer's radio relaying the connection from Dylan Price's computer.

"My God," he said. "This guy's a monster, Carla."

Windermere didn't answer. Was barely listening. Still wasn't sure she believed Dylan Price was all right, figured she'd need to meet the kid in person before she could accept he was safe.

"Apparently, the parents are at a conference in Washington, D.C.," Stevens was saying. "Baltimore PD is getting ahold of them as we speak."

Windermere blinked. Felt her world come back into focus, little by little. "He timed it so they'd be away," she said. "No chance of being interrupted."

"Except he forgot about the FBI."

"Sure didn't make it easy." Windermere listened to the chatter through the speakerphone, the Baltimore cops, the paramedics. Gruber's disintegration fading off in the background. She couldn't hear Dylan, though.

What if they're wrong? What if they made a mistake and Dylan Price is dead?

Stevens caught her expression. "He's safe," he told her. "We saved him, Carla. It's over. He's fine."

Windermere didn't look at him. Kept her eyes on the phone, straining for some sound from Dylan, Some proof that he'd lived.

Stevens came over. Put his hand on her shoulder. "Come on," he said. "This guy is still out there. Let's figure out how we're going to find him."

< 79 >

Dylan Price's webcam was turned off when Gruber pulled himself from the floor.

Dylan was gone. The police and the paramedics had taken him away. They would monitor him and analyze him and keep him under guard. They wouldn't let him back on a computer. They would never let him come back to Gruber. Dylan wouldn't die for Gruber. And Gruber wouldn't get paid.

The front door slammed open. Gruber heard footsteps. The thug, Donovan, walked into the living room. Looked at the computer screen, looked at Gruber. Tilted his head.

"What the fuck's all the noise about, man?" he said. "Is it done, or what?"

Gruber wet his lips. Swallowed. Drew himself up and tried to put on a front. "It didn't work," he said. "Didn't go through. Not my fault. Bad luck."

Donovan relaxed, just for a moment. Then his face twisted, hard. "The hell do you mean, it didn't go through?" he said. "I thought you said this thing was a sure shot. What about my man's fucking money?"

"Never mind about the money," Gruber told him. "The fucking *police* were there. They knew what Dylan and I were planning, and they *ruined* it. They freaking *ruined* everything."

This was bad. This was worse than just a thug with a gun. Gruber had endured failure before, but never in such a spectacular fashion. The police bursting through the door like in an action movie, the drama and theatrics, the kid so damn close to the end. How had they known?

Gruber worked through the permutations in his head, the meaning. If the police had been watching, they were on to him. They knew his MO, his game, and they would come after him. They would find him. It was only a matter of time.

Donovan looked like he was working through some permutations of his own. "So the kid's alive," he said slowly. "You couldn't get him to do it. He's alive."

"Were you listening?" Gruber asked him. "The fucking *police*."

"He's alive." Donovan stood there for a moment, rolling the words around in his mind. Then he straightened and reached for that big revolver.

"Well, shit, man," he said. He was smiling a little. "If the kid's still alive, I guess we have to do this the other way, huh?"

< **80** >

Gruber stopped thinking about Dylan Price. About the police, and whether they could track him to this house. Stopped worrying about anything else besides surviving the next five minutes.

Donovan had the revolver out. There was no hesitation in his eyes, no willingness to negotiate. Not even any fear, not this time. He was too far from Gruber for the knife to be of any use. The room was too small for Gruber to escape.

If Donovan pulled the trigger, Gruber knew he was dead. The revolver was a beast. It would blow his head clean off.

But Donovan didn't shoot. He looked Gruber over like a hunter studies snared prey. His lip curled, disgusted. He advanced on Gruber.

"You're a psycho," he said. "You're a maniac, bro. I'm going to get in a lot of shit when I don't come back with that money, but, what the fuck, I'm doing the world a favor."

He raised the revolver to a firing stance. Gruber gauged the distance, watched Donovan's finger tense on the trigger, knew he was dead unless he found a way out—fast.

"You're not going to kill me," he said. Gathered all the bravado he could muster, and stared Donovan in the eye. "You're too much of a pussy for it."

Donovan's lip twitched. "Guess you're going to find out."

"I heard you talking to your boys on the phone," Gruber told him.

"You don't belong here, and they know it well as you. They made a mistake when they sent your punk ass up here."

Donovan didn't say anything. The gun stayed where it was.

"You're afraid," Gruber continued. Louder. Bolder. "You know you can't show up back home without their money. You fucked up, shit stain. Face it."

"Shut up." Donovan shook his head, sudden, and Gruber could see he'd struck a nerve. "Just shut the fuck up, dude, or I swear, I'll—"

"You'll *what*," Gruber said. "Blow my head off?" He laughed. "Do it, then. Pull the trigger. Then go home and tell your boys you couldn't get their money." He looked Donovan in the eye. "Do it, shit stain. Kill me. Show them what a fuckup you are."

Donovan's lip twitched again. He chewed on his frustration, the big revolver shaking, unsteady. Gruber forced himself to meet the kid's gaze. Challenge him, like he'd challenged Sarah. Like he would one day, God willing, challenge Earl.

"You know I'm right," Gruber told him. "You want to be a failure your whole life, asshole? Pull the trigger."

Donovan made a noise, a growl, strangled from somewhere in his throat. *"Shut the fuck up."* Raised the gun high and swung down at Gruber, the barrel arcing toward Gruber's head.

Gruber was ready for it. He dropped before the blow connected, hit the carpet, hard, and rolled for the computer table. Pulled the bottom drawer open and grabbed for the knife as, behind him, Donovan stumbled, his balance askew when the revolver didn't connect.

Gruber closed his fingers around the knife handle. Came out with it, just as Donovan regained his equilibrium. The kid was too late, though; the revolver pointed wild, toward the kitchen window. Gruber slashed forward with the knife, caught him in the midsection. Donovan dropped the revolver. Cried out. Gruber slashed him again, dropped him to the floor. Then he toed the revolver closer, reached down, picked it up. Trained it on Donovan and breathed heavy, got his wind back.

"I see I had you pegged right all along," he told the kid. "I *knew* you didn't have it in you."

< 81 >

Gruber found a roll of duct tape. Taped Donovan to the computer chair, wrists and ankles. The kid was bleeding where Gruber had slashed him, a couple deep cuts to the stomach. He'd soaked through his shirt, made a mess of the floor.

"Good thing I never liked that carpet," Gruber told him. "Shit, I think you might need an ambulance."

Donovan moaned, something unintelligible. Gruber laughed, patted the kid's head. Tested the tape, made sure his limbs were bound tight. Then he closed the curtains. Stood back and tried to work through his options.

The police had tracked Dylan. They would track him down next. He would need to come up with a plan.

Gruber knew he could disappear. He'd done it before, in Cleveland,

and he could do it again. Vanish from this place by tomorrow morning, find somewhere new, somewhere better. Montana, maybe. Colorado. Start over. Lie low. Fly under the radar, so the cops couldn't find him.

He could do it, but it would be difficult. He was still flat freaking broke. He didn't have enough money for food, let alone a bus ticket. Let alone a new stake at a better life. Anyway, something Donovan had said earlier was sticking with him. Something a little more important than just making an escape.

Gruber scanned the pictures on the wall, Sarah and Dylan and the others, scanned until he'd found Earl's mug shot. The thug had mentioned something about Rico Jordan paying Earl a visit.

Gruber set the revolver down on the computer table. Picked up the knife and stood over Donovan. Slapped him a couple times, hard, relished the way the kid flinched and drew back.

"Now listen to me," he said. Held the knife up so Donovan could see it. "We just proved this whole violence kick isn't really your game, so you play nice with me, and I'll go easy on you, understand?"

Donovan didn't speak, but he nodded a little. Gruber figured it was as good as he was going to get.

"You said your boss checked in on my stepfather," he said. "I need you to help me find him."

Donovan moaned again. Looked down at his stomach, his crimson-soaked T-shirt. "I don't know, man," he said. "I don't know anything about that dude."

Gruber rolled up the sleeve of the kid's T-shirt. Took the knife and drew a stripe down his arm, long and deep. Donovan screamed. Gruber slapped him again.

"My stepfather," he said. "Somebody in your crew knows where to find him. I want to know what they know."

Donovan panted. Gasped, tears in his eyes, snot and drool and whatever else. "Rodney," he said, low and desperate. "My boss. He knew a guy who did time with your old man. You call him."

Gruber patted the thug down. Found his phone in the front pocket of his jeans. Pulled it out, swiped it unlocked. "*You* call him," he said. Held up the knife again. "Don't say anything stupid."

< 82 >

Victor Rodney's phone was ringing. The call display read DONOVAN. He answered. "Took you long enough."

A long silence. A ragged breath. *"Rodney."* Donovan's voice was little more than a whisper. "Shit, man, I'm sorry."

Rodney snapped his fingers, and Marcus looked up from his magazine, his brow furrowed.

"What the fuck happened to you?" Rodney asked Donovan. "Where are you? What's going on?"

Donovan didn't get a chance to answer. Someone else had the phone, the same guy who'd called Rodney the first time around. Gruber. The whack job. This was bad news.

"I want to know about my stepfather," Gruber said, his voice January cold. "You tell me what I need to know, I'll go easy on this kid here."

Marcus was watching. Caught the expression on Rodney's face, shot one back, like, *What gives?* Rodney shook his head, said nothing.

"You're this kid's boss, aren't you?" Gruber asked. "He said someone in his crew looked up my stepfather. Earl Sanderson. You know someone who knows him?"

Rodney blinked back to the moment. Found his voice. "Yeah," he said. "Yeah, dude, that was me."

"So where the shit did you find him?"

Rodney hesitated again. Pictured Donovan in Gruber's hands, barely more than a kid. Supposed to be an easy job, hell, initiation to the crew. He swallowed.

"Louisville," he told Gruber. "Indiana side of the river. Town called New Albany, just across the bridge."

"I know New Albany," Gruber replied, as if Rodney should know that. "I grew up twenty miles from there. You got an address?"

"Hell no, I don't have an address," Rodney said. "Was a shitty little apartment building, real close to the bridge. Some bar on the first floor, something called the Rusty Nail."

"An apartment," Gruber said. "New Albany."

"Yeah," Rodney said. "Third floor, I remember. Last door on the left." He paused. "You going to give me back my boy, or what?"

"Yeah, you can have him," Gruber said. Then he laughed. "Come get him."

The line went dead.

>>>

Donovan was watching Gruber as he ended the call. He seemed a little more alert, a little more awake.

"You told them where you're going," the thug said. "They'll just send more guys down to meet you."

Gruber laughed. "Let them come. If they're all as hard as you, I shouldn't have a problem."

He picked up the knife again, relished the way Donovan's eyes went wide at the sight of it. Was about to try and coax another scream out of him when his own phone buzzed, loud, on the computer table.

A text message, from DarlingMadison. *Where r u? I'm worried. Let me know you're okay.*

Gruber's eyes found DarlingMadison's picture on the wall above the computer, sullen and shy, pretty and vulnerable, hiding herself from the camera. Had an idea, a two-birds, one-stone situation. Madison wanted to see him. She was worried. Maybe they could meet after all, after he looked in on Earl.

If the police had found Dylan, they could find Madison, too. Gruber would have to move quickly to keep the girl safe. She was special. He didn't want to lose her, not before they'd had their fun.

Gruber turned back to Donovan. Advanced on the kid, watching him struggle.

"I'm sorry," Gruber told him, though he wasn't, not really. "Anyway, you brought this on yourself."

He plunged the knife into Donovan's stomach once, then again. Put the knife to his throat and cut across, like in the movies. Stood over the chair, and watched Donovan die.

It was fun, he decided. The doing was fun. It was probably just as fun as the watching, maybe more.

‹ 83 ›

Madison was walking when her phone began to vibrate. She was tracing the banks of the Hillsborough River through Tampa, enjoying the sunset, about the only place she could find any peace and quiet and calm in her new hometown.

When she'd first started coming here, to the river's edge, she'd thought about jumping in, filling her pockets with stones like Virginia Woolf, drowning herself. She'd walked for hours, plotting her demise, until one day she realized she didn't actually want to die here at all, that she really just enjoyed being close to nature, the stillness of the water and the lush, quiet forest that lined the banks. She *liked* it here, she realized. It was a strange feeling to have.

She blamed her change in attitude on Brandon, whom she blamed for just about every positive change in her life. Madison didn't hate herself when she looked in the mirror anymore, found reasons to smile now, collected funny and weird stories to pass along to him when they talked, told him about her classmates, her mother and her sisters.

There's this guy in my class who I think has a crush on me, she'd told him. *Paul Dayton. He's always following me around, asking about you.*

What do you tell him? Brandon wondered.

Just that you're cooler than anyone here, Madison said. *And that I can't wait to meet you and run away with you.*

I can't wait, too, Brandon wrote. *But tell this Paul guy to mind his own business, k?*

Oh, I do, she wrote back. *I make sure he knows his place.*

Anyway, her phone was buzzing. Madison pulled it from her purse, checked the screen. A phone call, from Brandon. She smiled as she accepted the call. "Hey, you."

"Hi." There was an edge to Brandon's voice, a breathlessness, something off. "Are you alone? Can we talk?"

Madison found a clearing overlooking the river. Sat down. "Yeah," she said. "Yeah, of course. What's up?"

"I'm sorry I'm calling like this," Brandon said. "It's just . . . something happened." He paused. "My parents found out about us. What we're planning to do. They're trying to stop us."

Madison felt a sudden hollowness in her stomach, an empty sort of panic. Everything she'd hoped for, all the ways this crazy boy from Iowa had changed her life, had made her happy, and now he was going to tell her it was too good to be true.

Well, obviously. Madison fought the urge to cry, to kick something, to throw her phone in the river. "Okay . . ." she said.

"They found my account on the suicide forum," Brandon said. "They read all our messages and they know about our plan. They tried to call the doctors on me, the straitjacket people. They want to hospitalize me and drug me up so everything's numb and normal and awful. I don't want that."

"No," Madison said. "No, none of it, never. I'd rather die."

"Exactly," Brandon said. He exhaled. "Anyway, I got away. I'm calling from the road, but they know I'm coming for you, Madison. They're probably calling the Tampa Police Department right now. You have to get away."

Shit.

Madison looked around. The river barely moving, the trees hanging over the banks, dark shadows beneath, the last light of day disappearing fast. The muted noise of the city in the distance, the hum of traffic. A siren.

"They're coming for you, Madison," Brandon was saying. "Sooner or later, they'll show up at your house with a straitjacket and a suitcase full of pills, and they might as well be giving you a lobotomy. You'll be done.

"We have to run," Brandon continued. "Both of us. You have to meet me somewhere safe, okay?"

Madison felt like she was drunk, or high or something, suddenly weightless and drifting and floating off the ground. Couldn't parse what Brandon was trying to tell her.

"Meet you," she said. "Yeah, okay. But where?"

"Kentucky," Brandon said. "Louisville. I have a friend there who can hook us up with fake IDs, money, whatever we need. We meet there tomorrow night and then we drive off together. Disappear. Go out with a bang, okay?"

Tires squealed behind Madison. She flinched, spun, watched an old pickup truck lurch around a corner. Realized her palms were sweating. Louisville, Kentucky. Tomorrow night.

"You have to go now," Brandon said. "You can't go home again, do you understand? It's too risky."

She couldn't believe what she was hearing. Couldn't believe it was true. And at the same time, she figured she'd always known it would come down to something like this. Something crazy. Nothing about her relationship with Brandon was normal.

This, though, was bona fide bonkers.

"I need you, Madison," Brandon said, and she could hear it in his voice. "If you don't come with me, I don't know what I'll do."

Madison blinked back to the present. Barely hesitated. Skip town to save the boy of her dreams, or stay put and let him suffer alone?

"I'm in," she told him. "Don't do anything scary, okay? I'll see you tomorrow night."

< 84 >

Gruber ended the call. Pocketed his cell phone and walked out of his house. Came back an hour later with a jerry can full of gasoline, set it down beside him and composed a text message.

See you tomorrow, he told Madison. *Can't wait. ☺ P.S. Buy a burner cell phone at the drugstore and text me the number. Then ditch your real phone. Otherwise, they can follow you. They'll go crazy when they find out you're gone.*

He pressed send. Then he went into his living room and rifled through Donovan's pockets until he found the kid's wallet. A couple hundred bucks in cash, an Ohio driver's license, a buy-nine-get-one-free coupon to some Cleveland sandwich shop. Gruber took the cash, stuffed the rest back. Tore Earl's picture off the wall, stuffed it in his pocket with the cash. Deleted everything on his computer, wiped the hard drive as clean as he could, every chat log, screenshot, saved password and username. All of the evidence, gone.

Then he picked up the jerry can, unscrewed the lid, and poured gasoline all over the machine. All over the rug, the table, the living room couch, all over Donovan's body. Made a trail with the gasoline through the kitchen, into his bedroom, the fumes overpowering, wafting through the house, making him light-headed and dizzy.

When he'd doused the whole place in gasoline, he set down the empty can. Walked to the front door and surveyed the living room, Donovan in the computer chair, his arms and legs still taped tight, the blood everywhere on his clothes, his eyes still half open. And around him, the litter everywhere, old junk-food and candy bar wrappers, soda cans, the fumes from the gas making Gruber's eyes water. The house had been his prison for too many years. He wouldn't miss it.

He took a lighter from his pocket, a cheap gas station Bic. Flicked it until the flame appeared. Knelt down to the carpet and touched the flame to a wet spot, a puddle of gasoline, jumped back as the puddle ignited.

"Whoo." Laughing now, his eyebrows singed, the heat fast and intense,

the flames starting to grow. He stepped out onto the lawn, watched the place go up, black smoke and roaring flames, the cheap little house a firetrap to begin with, never mind the accelerant.

Satisfied that the house would burn to bare ash, he turned away and crossed the lawn to the sidewalk, where Donovan's old white Lincoln sat waiting by the curb, Gruber's suitcase beside it, stuffed with those few belongings he valued: some clothing, a picture of Madison, his voice disguiser, and the knife.

Whistling to himself, unable to contain his excitement, Gruber picked up his suitcase and chucked it into the passenger seat of the Lincoln. Turned the key in the ignition and idled away down the street, left the house burning behind him. He would find Earl tomorrow. By nightfall, he'd be with DarlingMadison. He couldn't wait to show her the real Brandon.

< 85 >

The burner phone more or less exhausted Madison's meager savings.

She unpacked the phone from its casing, powered it on. Spent twenty minutes stealing electricity from an outlet in a McDonald's, waiting for the phone to charge to full power. Texted Brandon the new number, and a few minutes later the burner phone buzzed.

This is me, the text message read. *Text me when you get on the bus. I'll be waiting in Louisville.*

Kk, Madison wrote. *See you soon.* She powered off the phone to save the battery and left the McDonald's.

She couldn't go home. If Brandon was right, the police in Iowa would have already called Tampa. They could be trying to find her. She wouldn't risk going back to her house, not with so much at stake, but she needed money; she was broke. She needed some way to buy a bus ticket to Louisville.

Madison stood in the parking lot outside the McDonald's and thought about it. Watched traffic stream by, headlights, cars pull in and park, people climb out of their cars and walk into the restaurant. Couples, families. Single men.

She could rob someone, she supposed. She would need some kind of weapon, and let's face it, she wasn't exactly the robbery type. Hell, the thought of riding a bus all the way to Kentucky by herself was scary enough. She didn't need to be committing any felonies.

So, no robberies. Madison walked away from the McDonald's, the new burner phone weighing heavy in her purse. She thought about texting Brandon back, asking if he could send her some money for the ticket, through Western Union or PayPal or whatever. But that would create a paper trail, wouldn't it? If people were really looking for them, they would figure out where Madison was headed pretty quick.

Anyway, she kind of wanted to show Brandon she could make it to Kentucky on her own. Prove she was someone he could count on, independent and resourceful, a good partner. That left only one option.

Madison pulled out her old phone and opened Facebook. Typed a name into the search box and found who she wanted.

Need to see u, she wrote in a private message. *Urgent. Can we meet?*

<　 **86** 　>

Dylan Price didn't know much that Stevens and Windermere hadn't already figured out.

They found him gathered with his family inside their handsome brownstone, an FBI special agent with them, a woman from the local office named Pickford. Stevens had been in touch with her from Phoenix, asked her to keep an eye on the situation before he and Windermere arrived.

Douglas Price stood by the window, looking like he'd paced a track in his expensive carpet. He was a large man, imposing, his wife and son much smaller. Dylan sat, sullen, on an easy chair, staring anywhere but at his father. Windermere could see the bruises on his neck from the noose.

"I'm sorry I hung up on you," he told Windermere, his voice flat. Hollow. "I know you were trying to help."

Windermere studied the kid, figured he was probably pretty pissed off at her, ruining his big plans and keeping him around on this earthly plane a little longer. "I'm just glad it worked out," she told him. "I know you don't feel it right now, but we're glad you're still with us."

Douglas Price snorted from the window. "He'll be paying for the doors your officers kicked down," he said. "He knows it, too. First thing tomorrow, he's finding himself a part-time job. What a mess."

"Forget about the doors," Stevens said. "I'm guessing you won't have a problem scaring up enough cash for replacements. What we're concerned about is that Dylan's all right, and that he understands what happened here today."

Douglas Price gave Stevens the once-over, a long, assessing stare. Then he turned back to the window.

"The police kind of gave me the basics," Dylan said, still staring at the coffee table. "They said Brandon wasn't, you know, actually Brandon. That he was some old guy, some freak who liked watching teenagers kill themselves."

"His name is Randall Gruber," Windermere said. "Comes from small-town Indiana, a rough upbringing. Abuse, violence, neglect. He watched his stepsister hang herself when he was fifteen."

"We're hoping you might have picked up on something that could lead us to where he's hiding," Stevens said. "Any kind of clue about his real identity."

Dylan's brow wrinkled in thought. "I don't know," he told Stevens and Windermere. "I always just figured he was Brandon, you know? I wasn't really looking for, like, clues."

"Did anything ever seem weird to you? Anything ever sound off?"

"His voice," Dylan said, "but I guess you already know that. It wasn't the voice of an old dude, that's for sure." He thought. "I remember he messed up his time zones once. Like, we were talking and it was night and he said something like, 'Crap, I have to go to bed, it's almost midnight here.' But he was supposed to be in Iowa, right? And that's a different time zone from Baltimore, but the thing was, it was almost midnight *here*."

"Could be he's still on the East Coast," Stevens said. "His last known location's still Cleveland."

"There were always these noises in the background, too, when we talked," Dylan said. "Like train whistles or whatever, locomotives. They were usually pretty constant. He told me he lived near a train yard."

"Train yard on the East Coast," Windermere said. "Anything else?"

Dylan thought for a minute. "I really just thought he was Brandon," he said, and he looked down from the ceiling and found Windermere, then shied away. "I thought he was, like, my *friend*."

Windermere felt a fresh wave of anger. Dylan Price looked small, vulnerable, a *child*. And Gruber had taken advantage of that vulnerability. It was brutal and unconscionable. And it pissed Windermere off.

"So, let me get this straight." Douglas Price turned from the window. "You're saying my son is a victim, is that right? He's not a head case; there's nothing actually wrong with him."

"We wouldn't be here if Dylan wasn't unhappy," Stevens said. "Randall Gruber found him on a website for suicidal teenagers. You're going to want to think about therapy."

"Wait a second," Douglas Price said. "You just said he wasn't a head case. Now you want to send him to a shrink?"

"Not just your boy," Windermere said. "We're talking about all of you. Because from what I can tell, sir, your boy isn't the only person in this room who has issues."

Douglas Price opened his mouth to reply. Couldn't. Closed his mouth and opened it again, stood there dumbfounded, his face going red, his muscles rigid.

Windermere felt her phone go off in her pocket. Ignored it. "You played a role in this, Dr. Price," she continued. "Your son didn't just wake up this morning and decide to off himself. I've read the logs from his chats with Gruber. You want to know what got him into this mess, it was you, sir."

Price turned on her. "I don't believe this," he said. "You come into my house and—"

"And save your kid's life?" she said. "Yeah, we did. You're welcome."

Now Stevens had her, was pulling her back, away from Price, toward the living room doors. "I think that's our cue," he told Pickford. "Keep an eye on them, would you? Anything comes up about Gruber, let us know." He tugged Windermere away. "Come on, Carla."

Windermere shook him off. Hit Douglas Price with the side eye one more time as she turned and walked out of the room, walking fast, blood pumping, feeling pretty good actually.

She walked through the Prices' empty, expensive house, Stevens hurrying to catch up. "What the heck was that?" he asked her. "You can't just—"

Windermere felt her phone buzz. Voicemail from Agent Schwartz in Phoenix. She held up a finger to Stevens, hit redial. "Talk to me, Schwartz."

"Oh, hey," Schwartz said. "Was just reviewing those chat logs for your Gabriel98 character."

"Yeah," Windermere said. Made the Prices' front door and burst out into the evening light. "And?"

"And it sounds like he was grooming another teenager," Schwartz said. "Someone named DarlingMadison, out of Tampa. Sounds like she and your subject have their own suicide thing going on."

< **87** >

"Wait," Paul said. "You want me to lend you money for *what?*"

"It's just two hundred bucks," Madison said. "Well, two hundred for the bus ticket and, I dunno, fifty for, like, food? Two hundred and fifty bucks?"

Paul's eyes goggled. He sipped his milkshake until the straw made a slurping noise. Then he sipped some more, maddening Madison both with the sound and the lack of a coherent answer. Time was wasting.

She'd found him on Facebook. They weren't friends, but that hadn't stopped her. She'd sent him a private message, asking if they could meet, and he'd pulled into the McDonald's parking lot twenty minutes later, driving some kind of beat-up brown Buick. She'd been working on him ever since.

"A bus ticket," he said. "What, so you can go meet your boyfriend somewhere? Why can't he just come to you?"

"His parents found out about us," Madison told him. "They probably called my mom already, so we have to sneak off together. We're meeting in Louisville tomorrow night."

"Assuming you can get the money for a bus ticket," Paul said, grinning.

"Duh. So are you helping me or not?"

Paul picked at his fries. He was taking a long time to come up with an answer, and Madison was using the time to compile a mental list of other people she could hit up for the cash. It was a short list.

"I don't really have very much money," Paul said. "I don't even know if I have two hundred bucks in my savings."

"I wouldn't ask if it wasn't an emergency," Madison said. "Paul, please?"

"How are you going to pay me back if you never come back to Florida? I'd have to be pretty crazy to lend money to a girl just so she could skip town. And to be with her *boyfriend*, no less."

"I'll get a job as soon as we figure out where we're going," Madison told him. "I'll wait tables or something. Work in a bookstore. I'll send you the money back, I promise. I just need it now, Paul, and fast."

She pulled out her phone, checked the time. Six-thirty in the evening. Forty-five minutes before the Greyhound left for Orlando. If she missed this bus, she'd be stuck until tomorrow. And what if Brandon showed up in Louisville and she wasn't there? What if he did something crazy?

"*Please*, Paul," she said. "I really need this. What do I need to do to convince you to help me?"

Paul looked across at her, a gleam in his eye, and she felt her stomach turn. Then he held up his hands.

"Never mind," he said. "I'll do it. Just, like, keep in touch or something, okay? Let me know you're all right when you get where you're going."

Madison leaned across the table and hugged him hard, scattering his empty milkshake cup and his tray to the floor.

"Thank you," she said, ignoring the stares from the tables around them. *"Thank you, thank you, thank you."*

Paul hugged her back. When she pulled away, he was smiling again.

"Come on," he told her, gathering his trash. "We gotta hurry if we want to get that money before your bus leaves."

< **88** >

Stevens and Windermere caught a cab back to the airport. Walked inside the terminal and stopped.

"So, Tampa?" Windermere said, eyeing the long line of check-in kiosks and ticket counters. "Debrief DarlingMadison, see if she knows anything more about Gruber?"

Stevens followed her gaze. "Assuming she knows anything new at all," he said. "Gruber was pretty careful with what he told Dylan Price, it sounds like."

"Train yard on the East Coast," Windermere said. "Yeah. And we can assume Gruber isn't coming back online, not after he watched half the Baltimore police force bust down Dylan's door. If he has any sense at all, he's gone to ground."

"In which case, we can put local agents on DarlingMadison, get back to the old-school," Stevens said. "Spell Mathers on the paper trail, the payments Frank Abrams sent Gruber for the snuff films."

Windermere thought about it. Figured they were on the right track, that DarlingMadison probably wouldn't give them much more than Dylan Price had. Still, something niggled in the back of Windermere's mind. According to Schwartz, Tampa PD was still trying to locate the girl.

"Girl went out for a walk, hasn't come home yet," he'd told Windermere on the phone. "Mom says it's not unusual, she does this all the time."

Would be nice to have this girl accounted for, Windermere thought. *Get her location locked in and make sure she's safe before we go chasing hunches again, what with all the crazy around.*

"Let's get our butts to Tampa anyway," she told Stevens. "I just have a feeling. We can pick up the paper trail from there."

She walked up to the Delta counter, was halfway through the purchase of two one-way tickets to Tampa International, departing immediately, when her cell phone started buzzing in her pocket again.

"One sec," she told the ticket agent. Pulled out her phone. Mathers. "Derek," she said. "What's up? Me and Stevens were just talking about you. Thinking about taking over that Western Union lead, giving you a break."

"Think again," Mathers said, not even trying to hide the glee in his voice. "I just heard back from Western Union themselves not five minutes ago. They said our man 'Earl Ashley' always picked up his payments at a check-cashing joint in Buffalo, New York, a suburb called Cheektowaga."

"Buffalo." Windermere held up one finger to the Delta agent. "You're sure about this?"

"Sounds like they had records of seven or eight payments going through that one location," Mathers said. "It seems clean to me, Carla."

The Delta agent was reaching for Windermere's MasterCard. She snatched it back. "Mathers," she said. "Your timing is impeccable. Remind me to do something nice for you when I get back to town."

"You?" Mathers laughed. "I'll believe it when I see it."

Windermere clicked off. "Change of plans," she told the Delta agent. "When's your next flight to Buffalo?"

< **89** >

Turned out Paul Dayton's savings account was a little short.

"One hundred and seventy-four dollars and eighty-nine cents," he said, counting out a pile of bills and a jumble of loose change. "Literally every last penny I have."

Madison took the money, counted it again, praying he'd skipped a couple twenties somewhere. Realized pretty quick that he hadn't.

"Crap," she said. "*Crap.* That bus ticket alone is two hundred bucks. Plus, I have to eat. What am I going to do?"

It was nearly seven o'clock, fifteen minutes before the Orlando bus pulled out. They were parked outside a Bank of America branch a couple blocks from the Greyhound station. Madison looked at the pile of money in her hands, and it might as well have been toilet paper. She needed another thirty bucks, minimum. Fifty would be better.

"I could, uh . . ." Paul said. He trailed off.

"Yeah?" Madison said. "What? Spit it out, dude."

Paul went red. "I could drive you," he said. "We could use that money for gas. You know, drive in shifts or whatever." He dared to look at her. "It might be fun."

"What," Madison asked, "you're just going to tag along while I go to meet my boyfriend? What are you going to do when you get there? How would you get home?"

"Your boyfriend could lend me the money to get back," Paul said. "Or something. Or I could, like, sell the car. I could even come with you guys. We could travel together. I wouldn't get in the way, I promise. I—"

"Shush." Madison held up one hand. She was thinking. "Start the car," she said. "Take me to the bus station."

Paul deflated. Stared at her a moment longer, like he'd been really pumped, like the whole road trip thing had sounded really good to him.

"Come on," Madison said. "Time's a-wasting. What are you waiting for?"

Paul just kind of sighed. Didn't answer. Turned the key in the ignition and pulled out into traffic.

"So, what?" he said when they were parked in front of the bus station. "It's five minutes past seven. What's your big idea?"

Madison opened the door. "Inside," she said. "Hurry."

Paul made a noise like he was just about at the end of his patience, but he followed her inside the terminal anyway. The place was crowded, people lining up for buses in every direction, the Orlando bus already boarding.

"Look around," Madison said.

"Okay," Paul said. "Why?"

Madison pulled out her old cell phone, the iPhone she'd been using until she bought the burner. "Look for someone who would want to buy a cell phone," she said. "Someone with cash."

Paul frowned. "Don't you need a cell phone?" he said. "How will you get ahold of your boyfriend?"

Madison flashed him her new phone. "Got a burner," she said. "Untraceable. Brandon's the only one with the number. So start looking."

Paul made like he was going to argue. She cut him off with a glare, and he sighed and scanned the bus station.

"There." He pointed to a man in a suit with a briefcase, a nice watch.

Madison shook her head. "Too legit," she said. "He'll want to know what the scam is. Plus, he might not have cash."

She checked the digital clock on the wall. Ten after seven. Five minutes.

"Keep looking," she said.

Paul kept looking. So did she. She didn't see anyone. But Paul nudged her. "How about him?"

Madison followed his eyes and could have kissed him. *"Perfect."*

He was a young guy, early twenties, white, but dressed up like a gangsta rapper: the flat-brimmed baseball cap, saggy jeans, a lot of gold jewelry. He was the kind of guy who would jump at a deal like this. Madison hurried over.

"Excuse me," she said. "I'm trying to get to Orlando and I'm, like, fifty bucks short."

The guy eyed her up and down. Pursed his lips. "Aw, honey," he said. "You need a loan?"

"Not on your life," Madison said. "I'm just wondering if you want to help me out by buying my phone. iPhone, only a year old. Fifty bucks cash. You in?"

She was already scanning the bus station for other possibilities, just in case this guy didn't want to play.

"Huh," the guy answered. "Fifty bucks, you said? I could maybe do twenty-five, you know, seeing as how it's the previous generation and all. The new one's coming out in a minute, you heard? I—"

"Fifty bucks," Madison said. "Yes or no. In or out. Right now. Go."

The guy looked at her. Looked at the phone. Looked at Paul watching in the background, fifteen feet away. He smiled a wide, toothy smile. Reached into his jeans for his wallet.

"Fifty bucks," he said. "Deal."

‹ 90 ›

Gruber took back roads. Drove Curtis Donovan's shitbox white Lincoln down Route 5 until he hit the state line, followed the lakeshore into Erie, Pennsylvania, the night closing in around his windows, the lake an empty void to the north.

He gassed up in Erie, paid with some of the cash he'd taken from Donovan's wallet. The news was playing on the TV above the clerk's head; Gruber lingered in the candy bar aisle, eavesdropping on the anchor. Left ten minutes later with a Milky Way bar and an optimistic outlook. There'd been nothing on the news about any murdered men in Buffalo, no house fires, no pictures of his face.

He followed Lake Erie into Ohio, then ducked south in Conneaut and zigzagged toward Akron. Avoided the interstates, any major highways, kept his eyes peeled for patrol cars, kept the radio turned to any major news channels.

He drummed his hands on the steering wheel as he drove. Couldn't help but feel excited, the way the game was playing out. Couldn't help but see Donovan's wide eyes, hear him sucking for air, feel the way the knife cut him deep. Imagined knocking on Earl's door holding that same knife, or maybe Donovan's big revolver. Showing Earl what a man he'd gone and raised, and then finding Madison Mackenzie when he was finished.

Gruber had big plans for Madison. She was his déjà vu. They would have so much fun together, just like he and Sarah had.

He made Akron around midnight. Took the Lincoln through a McDonald's drive-through, ate his dinner in the parking lot, and then drove around until he found a run-down warehouse on the east side of town, the parking lot dark and empty. Friday night, he figured he'd have the place to himself. He parked the Lincoln in the shadows and reclined Donovan's seat. Killed the engine and figured he should try to sleep awhile.

He was too jacked-up to sleep, especially at first, the way Donovan's death kept playing back through his memory, the way Earl's face kept showing up, too. In Gruber's mind, Earl hadn't grown older. He was the same age as he'd been in the trailer, around forty, maybe, still strong enough to kick the shit out of a little runt like Gruber.

Gruber had been fifteen then. In no shape to fight back. He was older now. He was nearly the same age as Earl had been. And Earl had grown older, too. He wouldn't put up much of a fight, Gruber figured. That was the part he was looking forward to best, the way he would show Earl how the situation had reversed, how Earl was the one who was powerless now. He would let Earl know how helplessness tasted, frustration. But he wouldn't let him know the feeling for long.

Gruber opened the Lincoln's door, blinked in the brightness as the dome light flickered on. Eased himself out of the driver's seat, stepped out onto the pavement. It was chilly out, cold, a raw wind blowing through the trees that ringed the lot. There was a moon somewhere up above, hiding in the clouds. It shone minimal light, no good for comfort, not that Gruber minded. He wasn't afraid of the dark anymore.

He pissed against the side of the warehouse. Shook off and zipped up and turned back to the Lincoln. The car was long, low and battered. It glowed white. Gruber studied the car, and got to thinking. Got to wondering whether Donovan had come up from Cleveland with anything more than a handful of extra bullets for that big-ass revolver.

The backseat of the Lincoln was empty; he'd checked. Ditto the glove box, save the registration papers. Nothing on the dash except a few coins for tolls and an aftermarket CD player. No cash. No spare ammunition. No cigarettes, and no drugs. Nothing worth pawning, smoking, or shooting. Gruber popped the trunk.

He circled around the rear of the car. Looked out to the road, strained his eyes for headlights. Saw nothing. Heard nothing. The night was quiet. He lifted the trunk lid, blinked again in the sudden light. Rubbed his eyes and stared down at the cargo compartment.

"Holy," he said, laughing a little bit, picturing Earl's face when he showed him. "Boy, you're in for a big surprise, shit stain."

< **91** >

Stevens called the Cheektowaga Police Department from the rental car lot at Buffalo Niagara International Airport.

"Honestly, I don't even know what we're looking for," he told the desk sergeant after he'd explained the situation. "Mostly, we're just fishing, hoping you guys might give us a shortcut before we start combing the neighborhood."

The desk sergeant kind of chuckled. "Near the CSX yard, you say? Funny you should ask. Got the Pine Hill, U-Crest, and Forks fire departments over that way right now. House fire. Could be arson, they're saying."

"Arson, huh?" Stevens said. "You got any details?"

"Some guy, lived alone, according to the neighbors," the sergeant replied. "Place is owned by some kind of slumlord, rented off the books, cash money. Flying under the radar, know what I mean?"

"Sure," Stevens said. "Anyone catch the tenant's name?"

"Not that I've heard. Sounds like the guy kept to himself, didn't come out to the neighborhood potlucks or pass out candy on Halloween. Kind of a hermit."

"I get it," Stevens said, thinking the guy sounded like he fit Gruber's profile. Thinking it was too late to drop in on the check-cashing joint Earl Ashley had used, thinking it would be a hell of a break if this arson made the case.

"Guess we might as well check it out," Stevens told the desk sergeant. "Got an address?"

The fire was dying out when they pulled up to the scene, the whole block smoke and ash and wet, fire trucks parked at odd angles, firefighters dragging hoses, dousing the ruins. Neighbors milling about, mingling with uniformed police officers, news crews. Windermere parked the rental car, and she and Stevens waded into the mix.

The blaze was pretty well put out at this point. A few flames licked up from the remains here and there, but Stevens figured the show was just about over. The house wasn't much to look at, what was left of it, mostly billowing smoke and charred aluminum siding, structural beams bent in crazy contortions.

Not that it had been a prize before the fire: a single story, probably, a handful of rooms. Old as Hades, too, judging by the rest of the block. As Stevens and Windermere walked closer, they could hear switch engines moving freight cars back and forth, the almost constant sounding of horns. "Sure sounds like the right place," Windermere said. She walked to a group of bystanders, flashed her badge. "Federal agents," she said. "Anyone want to tell me who lived in that place?"

The crowd drew back a little, muttered to themselves, looked past her shoulders, avoided eye contact. Stevens joined Windermere, pulled out a printout of Randall Gruber's last known photograph, and another copy where they'd run an aging simulation, fifteen-year-old Randall Gruber plus twenty years.

"Anyone recognize this man?" he asked, holding the photos aloft. "Anyone ever seen him before?"

More muttering. Stevens was about to give up, stow the pictures, find more gawkers to bug. Then someone pushed forward from the back of the crowd. A teenager, a boy, maybe fifteen or sixteen.

"That's Earl," he told Stevens. "That's who lived there."

Stevens and Windermere swapped glances. Stevens held out the photographs again. "Earl Ashley?" he said. "This guy?"

The boy took the pictures. Studied them. "I don't know," he said. "I just know that's Earl's place. I'm not supposed to go near there."

Windermere stepped forward. "Why not?"

The boy hesitated, conscious of the sudden attention. He backed away a little. "He's just weird, is all," he said. "Like, sometimes he'll come around me and my friends, try to talk to us. My dad says Earl's a creep. I'm not supposed to go over there."

Windermere looked at Stevens. "I guess that's our guy. But where the hell is he?"

Gone, Stevens thought. *Burned his house down and vanished.* But before he could get the words out, he heard voices behind him, urgent, excited, a murmur from the crowd. Turned back to the blaze just in time to see a group of firefighters emerge, animated, radios crackling.

Windermere hurried over, flagged down a fireman with a radio, Stevens right behind her. "What's going on here?" she asked the man.

The firefighter lifted his visor. Took off a glove and wiped sweat from his eyes. "We just found the body," he said. "Guess this poor dope didn't make it out after all."

He walked on. Stevens watched him go, his mind reeling, knowing he should be happy—hell, jubilant—knowing, if it was Gruber in there, that they'd caught a hell of a break.

But he didn't feel jubilant. He looked at the house, the cluster of firefighters again, knew there was more to the story. Knew, deep down, that what he was hoping for was a damn sight too neat, was bound to be too good to be true.

< **92** >

It was a long-ass bus ride.

Madison boarded the 7:15 to Orlando with negative time to spare. Convinced the ticket agent to hold the bus while she counted out the fare from Paul's savings and the fifty bucks she'd received for her phone. Boarded at seventeen minutes past the hour, the whole bus glaring at her, nobody moving their freaking backpacks and carry-ons to give her a seat. She wound up in the last row, the three-seater, wedged between two overweight sisters and the lavatory. Good times.

Paul had made a valiant attempt at a good-bye. Followed her as she hurried through the terminal to her bus, called out her name just as she handed her ticket to the driver. She turned around, impatient, feeling the driver and everyone in the bus staring at her.

Paul looked away, like he could feel the attention, too. "I guess I'll probably never see you again," he said.

"Probably not," Madison said. "But who knows? I'll get ahold of you somehow. I'll get your money back."

"Never mind that," Paul said. "Just be safe, okay?"

"Yeah," Madison said. "Okay."

"This guy, if he's creepy or whatever, don't be afraid to turn around and come home. You're not alone, you know?"

"I know." Madison shifted her weight, gave the driver an apologetic smile. "I really have to go, though."

"Take my number." Paul reached in his pocket, pulled out a crumpled piece of paper. Thrust it in her hand. "If anything happens, you can call me. Anything at all, okay?"

Madison unfolded the paper. He'd written his phone number on a baggage tag. His name. She folded it, put it in her purse. "I gotta go," she said.

"Yeah. I know."

She leaned forward and hugged him. "I'll be okay," she said. "Thanks again."

Paul hugged her back. Hugged her like he would keep on hugging her forever if she didn't make a move, so she did. She released him, stepped back, turned and climbed on the bus. Navigated down the aisle to the triple seat at the back, wedged herself in. When the bus pulled out, Paul was still standing there, watching it go.

The bus made it to Orlando at a quarter past nine. Madison peeled herself out of the seat, followed the rest of the passengers into the station, bought a prepackaged ham sandwich and a Diet Coke for seven dollars from the concession stand inside. Ate it while she waited in line for her next bus, the overnight to Nashville.

This time, at least, she got a window seat. The guy next to her was a Japanese tourist, a young guy, spent the first three hours reading his guidebook and leaning over her to snap blurry pictures of the darkness with a futuristic digital camera. He didn't try to talk to her, anyway, or even really look at her. He minded his own business, and she minded hers.

She was stultifyingly bored. Her old phone, the iPhone she'd hocked at the bus station in Tampa, held all of her music. Plus, it had Internet access, something her burner sorely lacked. She hadn't even had time to buy a magazine in Orlando, though she couldn't have afforded one anyway. She had about eighteen dollars left to get her to Louisville. She would have to budget wisely.

So she sat in her window seat and watched the cars pass by, head-lights on the highway. Thought about Brandon and how cool it would be to actually meet him, to hug him and kiss him and just, like, talk to him, person to person, face-to-face. She wondered if he would want to hook up the first night, felt a flutter in her stomach as she considered the idea. Hooking up with boys was not usually something on her radar; then again, neither was running away.

Madison wondered if her mother was freaking out yet. If she'd even noticed her daughter was missing. Of course she had—Brandon's parents had phoned the police. Probably all of Tampa was looking for her. She wondered if they would check the Greyhound terminal, if they would follow her to Louisville. She hoped not.

Somewhere around midnight, the bus pulled into a truck stop and Madison climbed down to the parking lot, stretched her legs, bought a candy bar inside the gas station and bummed a cigarette from a woman smoking by the bus door. Madison didn't smoke, but it seemed like the glamorous, nihilistic runaway thing to do. It made her feel cooler, anyway, standing under those harsh white gas station lights. It made her feel less alone.

The woman with the cigarettes had a book she was done with, some kind of romance novel, the kind Madison's mom liked to read.

"It's not bad," the woman told Madison. "Not enough sexy bits for me, but you take what you can get, hey?"

"Exactly," Madison said, and she took the novel gratefully, spent the next couple hours choking down the first ten chapters, some ditzy chambermaid and a handsome, rich lord. She fell asleep with the book in her lap, the Japanese guy snoring delicately beside her; slept a long, fitful night punctuated by gas stations and small towns, and a disorienting arrival in Atlanta around six in the morning.

She slept until the bus reached Chattanooga, Tennessee. Spent another three dollars on a stale gas station pastry, which brought her down to fourteen dollars and some change to get her to Louisville and Brandon.

By midday, the bus pulled into Nashville, and the tourist beside her was leaning over again, snapping pictures of the skyline and the Cumberland River as if he were afraid it was all going to disappear. She climbed off the bus and went straight to the bathroom, tried her best to do her hair in the scratched mirror above the sink, wished she'd brought her makeup, a toothbrush, clean underwear.

She was afraid. She'd pinned her hopes on this guy, and she would like to show up in clean clothes, a pretty dress maybe, her hair washed and brushed, her breath fresh, the rest of her not smelling like she'd spent a day on the road. Maybe Brandon would see her, *smell* her, and decide he was better off dead after all. Maybe he'd do it even if she was clean and pretty. Maybe he'd constructed a fantasy Madison that the real her could never equal.

Or maybe Paul was right and Brandon was nothing but a filthy sex pervert, and not really a cute boy at all.

Maybe, maybe, maybe. They were announcing her next bus, a four-hour haul that would take her to Louisville. Madison brushed her fingers through her hair one last time, splashed cold water on her face. Hurried out of the restroom and across to her bus, her stomach in knots, excited but worried, as she thought about what lay ahead.

< 93 >

The Erie County Medical Examiner's Office was located in a sprawling hospital complex in northeast Buffalo. Stevens and Windermere showed their badges at the door first thing the next morning, were buzzed in to a long, sterile hallway, low ceilings and plain walls. Their footsteps resonated, every other noise muted, the whole facility as solemn as the business conducted within.

The ME was a small, slender woman named Yoshida. She met them in the hallway, shook both their hands, a firm grip. Ushered them into an autopsy room with three examination tables and one body, badly burned.

"As you can see, the identification has not been straightforward," Yoshida told them, leading them to the center table. "The victim's skin is damaged well beyond the fingerprinting stage, so we're moving on to dental records and DNA, but both options take time."

Windermere studied the body, the extent of the damage. Knew any normal human being would be sickened by what she saw; hell, even Stevens was hanging back a step or two. Windermere wasn't sickened. She'd seen death before. And she needed to know if this corpse was Randall Gruber.

"We don't have time to wait on lab results," she told Yoshida. "I need to know if this here is my guy, today if possible. So what can you tell us?"

Yoshida frowned. "Very well," she said. "The first thing I noticed, beyond the obvious external burn damage, is that this man very probably did not die in the fire."

Windermere followed her eyes. "Well, he obviously died," she said. "You're saying he was dead before the fire started?"

Yoshida circled around the table so that she was facing Stevens and Windermere, gestured to the incisions she'd made on the victim's torso. "I've begun an internal examination," she said. "As you can see, the viscera are remarkably well preserved. The lungs, for instance, and the airways, are largely free of soot. This is abnormal with victims of fires, as you might imagine."

"He would have been breathing smoke," Stevens said. "If he was still alive."

"Exactly," Yoshida said. "That in itself is enough to raise questions, but there's something else, too."

She moved down to the victim's torso. "Abdominal lacerations," she said. "Deep cuts, and many of them, to the stomach, kidneys, and intestines, and even through the rib cage to the lungs and heart."

"Stab wounds," Windermere said. "This bastard got his with a knife."

"That would be my suspicion," Yoshida said. "Those wounds are consistent with serious violence."

Windermere looked down at the body. Figured she didn't necessarily feel bad for the guy. If it was Gruber—and who else would it be—he had the knife coming, and she could live with that kind of justice.

But who had stabbed him? And where had they gone?

Then Stevens spoke up. He was studying a chart at the end of the table, far away from the Y-incision and the victim's internal organs.

"This paperwork here," he asked Yoshida. "This is for the same guy?"

Yoshida followed his eyes. "Yes, that's correct," she said. "It's a slow day around here."

Stevens peered closer, squinted at the paperwork. "Says here you pin this guy at six foot, one sixty," he said. "Age, early twenties."

"Or younger," Yoshida said. "It's hard to be sure—"

Windermere hurried over. "Impossible," she said. "That doesn't make sense. Our man is thirty-five, easy."

"This man here isn't over thirty," Yoshida replied. "He's not even twenty-five. His bones haven't finished growing yet. Moreover, the vertebrae at the base of the spine haven't fully fused together. These are skeletal processes that take place in a young adult, not a grown man."

Windermere didn't reply. Didn't know what to say. Felt sick suddenly, and it wasn't because of the dead body beside her.

"How sure are you on the age thing?" Stevens asked Yoshida. "What's your margin for error?"

Yoshida shook her head. "Minimal. This man is barely out of his teens. I'm certain of it."

Which means this man isn't Gruber, Windermere thought, her stomach a roiling mess. *Which means he's still missing. Shit, shit, shit.*

Stevens cleared his throat. "You said Tampa PD were searching for the second victim. Did they ever find her?"

The second victim. DarlingMadison. Frank Abrams said Gruber had promised him two victims. Dylan Price was the first. DarlingMadison had to be the second. Now Gruber was missing—and Madison was missing, too.

"Not to my knowledge," Windermere said. She looked back at the body, whoever it was. Wished on her life it was Gruber, would have traded anything to make it that way. "We messed up, partner. We need to be in Tampa, like, yesterday."

< 94 >

Gruber left Akron as giddy as a kid on Christmas morning.

He'd known what he'd found in Donovan's trunk the moment he'd seen it, a canvas bag, long and slender, a satisfying weight when he held it. He'd savored the moment like that kid with his Christmas present, looked past the bag at the boxes of ammunition stacked up by the spare tire, and knew he was into something good.

There was more ammunition for Donovan's revolver, boxes of Winchester .44 Magnum rounds. And there were other boxes, too, boxes of spare ordnance for whatever waited inside that canvas bag.

It was a shotgun, Gruber discovered, a Harrington & Richardson twelve-gauge, the barrel rifled and fitted to fire a slug. The boxes were Brenneke Black Magic slugs for the shotgun, bear stoppers.

Gruber cradled the shotgun, looked skyward, the black night, the clouds racing past the moon. Muttered a silent thank-you, to Donovan and to God, knew Earl would shit his pants when he caught sight of Gruber and his boomstick.

He slept well past dawn. Woke up to the sun shining and cars on the road, figured he was lucky he wasn't staring down a cop.

He ate a cheap, greasy breakfast at a diner on the outskirts of town. Picked up a newspaper, scanned for anything relevant. Nothing. Maybe the police weren't on his trail after all. Or maybe the fine people at *USA Today* just weren't ready to spill about it yet.

He stopped at a shopping complex on the way out of Akron, found a Home Depot, bought a hammer and crowbar, a high-powered flashlight, a roll of duct tape for good measure. Used the crowbar to pry off the door handles inside the Lincoln, every one but on the driver's side. Used the claw end of the hammer to tear out the mechanics beneath.

Then he climbed in the Lincoln and kept driving. He stuck to the back channels again. State roads, two-lane blacktop, Route 42. Skirted Columbus and came down over the top of Cincinnati, crossed the Indiana state line on Route 50, nudged the Ohio River, with Kentucky on the other side, veered west where the river dipped south, took the long way.

He switched off the news radio, found music on the dial, a radio station playing classic rock, the hits of the seventies. Whistled along to that old Looking Glass song, the one about the barmaid in the harbor town, as he pulled into New Albany, the sun high in the sky. He felt good.

Earl and DarlingMadison. Two birds, and plenty of ammunition. Whatever tomorrow held in store, Gruber knew the night ahead would be epic.

< 95 >

Stevens and Windermere touched down in Tampa in the early afternoon. Got a rental car, drove out of the airport. Found themselves on a busy highway, eight or nine lanes wide, nearly flattened the rental car—and themselves—underneath a tractor trailer as they tried to cut across to their exit.

"Cripes," Stevens said, gripping the armrests in the passenger seat. "Careful, Carla. These guys are maniacs."

Windermere didn't answer. Wasn't listening. She'd spent the whole flight from Buffalo beating herself up about DarlingMadison, and she figured she still wasn't even half done yet. Might not ever be, if the girl didn't turn up.

You should have gone to Tampa the first time, she screamed at herself. *A missing girl, and you didn't think it was suspicious? You wasted yesterday and most of the morning in Buffalo, and that girl's long gone. She's probably dead.*

Stevens reached out, touched her arm. Jolted her out of her thoughts. "We'll find her, Carla," he told her. "It's not over yet."

She kept her eyes on the road. "Maybe not, partner," she said. "But it's close."

They found Madison Mackenzie's mom's house, found an army of city cops running around like the proverbial headless chickens, nobody quite sure which way was up.

"Who's running this show?" Windermere said, parking the rental car and buttonholing the nearest uniform.

"FBI's supposed to be on their way," the policeman told her. "But we haven't seen them yet."

"You're seeing them now," she told him. "Grab your five smartest pals and follow me."

She led them into Madison Mackenzie's house, where another couple uniforms stood guard over an exhausted-looking woman and a pair of crying girls. There was a wad of spent tissues on the kitchen table, an empty box beside them.

"She didn't tell me anything," Catherine Mackenzie informed Stevens and Windermere after the introductions had been made. She dabbed her eyes with a fresh tissue. "I don't have any idea where she could have gone at all."

Stevens sat down at the table opposite her. Windermere remained standing, every minute feeling like the girl was getting farther and farther away.

"Did Madison ever talk about meeting someone online?" Stevens asked. "A new friend or anything?"

"Nobody," Catherine said. "We hadn't talked very much at all recently. Between trying to work a couple jobs and taking care of the little ones"—she gestured to the two girls, who looked to be about six and eight—"I just thought she could handle herself, you know?"

"So you wouldn't have noticed if she seemed down," Stevens said. "Depressed or disengaged, anything like that."

"She was in her room a lot," Mackenzie said. "She was on her phone, the computer. I figured it was better she was at home than out screwing around, doing drugs, drinking."

"Sure." Stevens turned and met Windermere's eye, and his expression said pretty much the same thing she was thinking. *This woman doesn't have anything that will help us.*

Windermere turned to the nearest uniform, the guy she'd dragged in from the street. "I want an Amber Alert set up," she told him. "I want Madison's picture on the news, the Internet, in the freaking newspapers. I want people looking out for her, and I want it done now."

The uniform nodded. Turned and hurried off, radio to his lips, barking orders.

"And get me some capable cops who can help with my search," Windermere called after him. "*Move it.* There's a girl's life at stake."

The cop flashed the thumbs-up. Windermere watched him go, reached into her jacket and felt around for her cigarettes.

You're too late, she thought. *You should have locked that kid down before you took off for Buffalo. You chose wrong, Supercop.*

That girl's dead already.

< 96 >

Victor Rodney and Marcus Smart made New Albany early in the afternoon. Took Marcus's Malibu, some piece-of-shit blue rustbox, Marcus pulling off the interstate every twenty minutes to take a leak, buy a hamburger, shit, fix his mascara.

They'd driven up to Buffalo first. Punched in Randall Gruber's address on the maps in their phones, followed the directions. Knew they were too late from a block away, the whole street a mess of firefighters and police cars and ambulances, somebody wheeling a body bag out of a burned-down house.

Donovan. Rodney didn't know, but he *knew*, felt it deep inside like a sickness. Knew he would feel the same way for a long time, it gnawing at him, asking him why he'd sent the kid for the money. Asking him why he hadn't called the kid home.

Anyway, they were here now. They'd driven all night from Buffalo, found Sanderson's shithole apartment building with no problem, the same shady-ass bar on the ground floor. Marcus parked the Malibu across the street, other end of the block, and they settled in to wait, no idea if Sanderson even lived there anymore, but the way Rodney had it figured, it didn't really matter.

"You sure Gruber's going to be here?" Marcus asked him. "I mean, what the fuck's his beef with this guy?"

"I have no idea what his beef is," Rodney replied. "But he killed

Curtis to get ahold of the address. So we're going to wait here until he turns up."

At the mention of Donovan's name, Marcus went silent. Studied the building through the windshield. Rodney followed his gaze, saw the kid in his mind's eye again instead.

Too late now, he decided. And there was a fully loaded MAC-11 machine pistol waiting under Rodney's seat to make things right, or as right as he could make them, anyway.

Marcus didn't say anything for a while. Neither did Rodney; he figured he didn't mind the quiet, figured maybe he'd get a little peace for a change, at least until Gruber showed up.

But then Marcus's stomach growled and he shifted in his seat. "I'm starving," he said. "We gonna get lunch, or what? And I gotta take a piss, too."

Rodney looked out the window, looked up and down the street. Nothing moving but the goddamn interstate traffic on the bridge. Sooner or later, though, Gruber would be here. Rodney was sure of it.

"Piss in a bottle," he told Marcus. "And save your bitching. We eat when we put a hole through this dude."

97

Paul Dayton was watching TV in the family room, one of those high-stakes poker tournaments, when the local news anchor cut into the commercial break with an urgent announcement.

"An Amber Alert has been issued for Madison Mackenzie, a sixteen-year-old North Tampa girl who the FBI fear has been victimized by an online predator. Anyone with any information regarding Madison's whereabouts should contact the authorities immediately."

There was a picture of Madison on-screen, some artsy shot—her ducking away from the camera but twisting back to scowl at it, the typical Madison Mackenzie facial expression—but Paul was already reaching for his phone, wasn't really paying attention anymore.

"Hello?" he said when the 911 operator picked up. "I'm calling about that Amber Alert that just happened."

<<<

Stevens and Windermere were posted in Catherine Mackenzie's living room, having turned the house into a mini mobile command center, when the Tampa PD uniform came in with a teenage boy following close behind.

He was an unremarkable kid, brownish hair, could have used a haircut, but what struck Stevens about him was the expression on his face as he took in his surroundings. It was the look of a kid who'd just realized the game he was playing had higher stakes than he'd ever imagined.

"Paul Dayton," he told Stevens and Windermere after they'd found him a chair to sit in. "I go to school with Madison." He kind of laughed. "I would say we're friends, but she wouldn't."

"What we hear, she doesn't have any friends," Windermere said, glancing at Catherine Mackenzie, where she sat in the kitchen.

"That's valid," Paul said. "She keeps to herself, anyway. She—" He seemed primed to go into a long description of Madison Mackenzie as he saw her, checked himself, though not before Stevens caught a glimpse of just how Paul and Madison fit. He'd been a teenager himself once, had his own share of unrequited crushes. Figured he'd looked at one or two girls the way Paul was looking right now.

"Just tell us what you know, son," Stevens told him. "Can you help us find her?"

Paul scanned the living room—uniformed cops everywhere, plainclothesmen, some FBI agents from the local regional office. News crews outside, reporters doing their spiels. The house was chaos, and Stevens couldn't blame the kid for feeling daunted. But Paul squared his shoulders. Looked Stevens and Windermere direct, face-to-face.

"Yeah," he told them. "I can."

"She's head over heels for this guy from the Internet," Paul told them. "Brandon something, this dude from Iowa. She was always texting him in class or whatever, getting in trouble. One time, I got in trouble, too, just for helping—"

He stopped himself. "Anyway. This Brandon guy was going to come to meet her and they were going to run away together, like sometime pretty soon. But yesterday I get this message from Madison on Facebook, real desperate. She said plans had changed and she needed to get out of town. She was going to meet this guy in, like, Louisville, I think?"

Louisville. Sarah Gruber was from near Louisville. Louisville was not a good sign.

"She didn't have enough money for the Greyhound," Paul said. He glanced into the kitchen, hesitated. "I lent her the money for the ticket. I even offered to drive her. I should have stopped her, I guess. I should have realized."

"You couldn't have known," Stevens said, thinking the kid was probably so lovestruck he'd have jumped off the proverbial bridge had Madison given the order. "She left yesterday, you said?"

Paul nodded. "She took the afternoon bus to Orlando, then overnight from there. She said it was going to take her like twenty-two hours to get to where Brandon was."

"Twenty-two hours." Windermere had her notebook out. "And you put her on the bus when?"

"Seven-fifteen," Paul said. "Well, it was a couple minutes after, because she was so late, but they still let her board."

"Seven-fifteen," Windermere repeated, and Stevens knew what she was thinking. It was four-fifteen now. Twenty-one hours had passed since Madison Mackenzie boarded her Greyhound. Assuming she'd made her connections, she would arrive in Louisville in about an hour.

Stevens stood. "We need to get Agent Wheeler to that bus station," he told Windermere. "And then we need to get our asses to Louisville."

< **98** >

Gruber found Earl's building with no problem. Knew it was the right place from halfway down the block.

It was a grimy brick walk-up in the shadow of the Sherman Minton Bridge, a few blocks from the flood wall, a low, grassy hill that protected the town when the river overflowed. The building was three stories tall, run-down and old. The ghost of a bar on the first floor, all faded beer posters and boarded, blacked-out windows, the throb of some low-rent rock music wafting out from within. Above the bar were two floors of apartments, the windows narrow and greasy, bedsheet curtains and darkness behind.

It was a shithole. It was exactly the kind of place Gruber expected to find his stepfather, the kind of by-the-hour/by-the-week residence that housed only derelicts, ex-cons, the desperate, and the dying. It was hardly a step up from the Shady Acres Motor Court, probably wasn't a much better accommodation than the state pen. It was Earl's kind of place, Gruber figured, for sure.

It was late afternoon. The drive had taken eight hours—longer than Gruber had expected, but safer than the interstate. He'd made it to New Albany without any police trouble. Madison Mackenzie's bus would arrive in an hour. Gruber figured he'd left himself just enough time to deal with Earl before he met the girl, even factoring in how he wanted to take his time, do things right. Make Earl suffer a little bit.

Of course, that assumed the whole plan played out without a hitch.

And as Gruber slowed Curtis Donovan's big Lincoln to a stop down the street from Earl Sanderson's apartment building, he could see one big hitch standing directly in his way, in the form of a rusted-out Chevy Malibu parked across the street, those red, white, and blue Ohio plates standing out like a beacon, two men inside, just hanging out.

You told them where you're going, Donovan had said. *They'll just send more guys down to meet you.*

Gruber had laughed him off. Figured he could deal with whatever Rico Jordan's crew threw at him. And he could, but he hadn't really counted on the reinforcements showing up so soon.

Gruber turned the Lincoln down a cross street, drove up the block before the men in the Malibu could see him. Circled around to the back of the apartment building and parked, looking for another entrance. Found a rusted fire escape ladder and a back door for the bar, a heavy steel door by the dumpster that required a key. No luck. If he wanted into the building, he would have to go in through the front. And the men from Ohio had the front door covered.

Gruber walked back to the Lincoln. Popped the trunk and came out with the shotgun in its case, filled his pockets with ammunition. Slammed the trunk closed again. Then he stopped.

He'd been thinking he would just ambush the men, blast a couple new holes in that Malibu's bodywork, end the standoff, nice and easy, before he went in to find Earl. But that plan had some flaws in it. Most notably, what if Earl wasn't home? Second, someone was bound to notice a couple of dead mopes in a Malibu, midafternoon. They would call the police, and the police would investigate, and it would surely complicate matters if there were cops crawling around outside.

Gruber wanted to take his time with Earl. He wanted Earl to see just how grown-up he'd become, wanted to savor the fear in his stepfather's eyes. He didn't want to blow his shot because he had to clean up the trash outside first.

Shit.

Gruber went back to the Lincoln. Slid in behind the driver's seat, stared out at the apartment building. Sat there a long time until he'd figured out a plan. He turned the key in the ignition. Checked the time on the clock on the dash. Less than forty minutes before Madison's bus arrived. Well, she might have to wait a little while for old Brandon to show. Gruber knew he wouldn't get anything done until he shook the Malibu clear of Earl's apartment.

< **99** >

Rodney nudged Marcus as the Lincoln pulled out from the alley beside Earl Sanderson's building.

"*There,*" he said, pointing. "That's Curtis's Continental. That's the bastard right there."

Marcus watched the Lincoln pull out, make a right turn, drive away slow toward the Sherman Minton Bridge. "What's he doing leaving already?" he said. "You think he already got done what he came here to do?"

"The fuck does it matter?" Rodney replied. "Do we care about Earl Sanderson?" The Lincoln was beyond the bridge already, gaining ground, fast. "Well? What are you waiting for, B? *Follow him.*"

<<<

Gruber watched the Malibu in his rearview, the car and the apartment receding quickly—too quickly—behind him. The plan wouldn't work if the men from Ohio didn't see him. If they didn't take the bait.

Come on, he thought, easing off the gas. *Come on, here I am. Follow me.*

He was halfway down the main drag, closing in on the outskirts of town, before the Malibu moved behind him. Jerked to life and pulled out fast, like the men in the car had just realized what was happening. Gruber nudged the gas just enough to keep the big Lincoln moving, let the Malibu gain some distance. Wanted them close enough to see what he had planned, but hoped to keep enough space between them that they couldn't fire on him until he was ready.

It wasn't the best strategy in the world, what he was thinking about doing. It was risky, borderline stupid, and it would take up some time. And it assumed a hell of a lot about his own abilities with a shotgun. But it was the best he could come up with, the clock ticking down as it was, and anyway, it would keep the cops clear from Earl's place, and wasn't that all that mattered?

He would have to rework his plans, though. He would deal with these men. Then he would find Madison. Then he would come back for Earl. A few minor revisions, but no matter. It was good to be back in southern Indiana, good to be home. And Gruber realized he knew exactly where he would take Madison, just what kind of special game they could play.

But first, the men in the Malibu. Gruber made a right-hand turn at

253

the end of town, eased onto the Ohio River Scenic Byway, drove due west, the sun already settling toward the horizon between the thick stands of trees that lined the drive. He kept the Lincoln moving, the traffic thinning out, made sure to keep at least a couple of cars between Donovan's ride and the Malibu.

The men in the Malibu followed all the way to where the byway spit out near Maplewood, followed as he ducked under the interstate and onto the state road through Georgetown, still pointed west, the sun almost blinding ahead of the windshield.

His phone was buzzing in the center console. Madison. *I'm almost here,* she wrote. *Can't wait to see u.*

Gruber checked the rearview. Saw the men clearly, two of them, big men, and mean, watching the Lincoln like they knew he was prey. He typed a response to Madison one-handed. *Running a little late. Car trouble. I'll be there as soon as I can. XO.*

He kept driving. Glanced at the Smith & Wesson on the passenger seat and the shotgun in the back. Prayed the men in the Malibu held off until he had them where he wanted them.

>>>

Marcus shifted in the driver's seat. Rubbed his stomach. "God-damn, I'm hungry," he said. "This guy needs to hurry up and die so I can get something to eat."

In the passenger seat, Rodney squinted out the windshield, the sun catching every grease stain and bug spatter on the glass, the Lincoln barely visible up ahead, somebody's gleaming red Ford Super Duty the only thing in between.

Rodney reached for the MAC-11 beneath his seat, felt the familiar grip, the cold steel. In front of the Ford, the Lincoln was speeding up, opening some distance. The pickup truck lagged behind, in no hurry.

"I can pass this guy," Marcus said. "Give us a clear shot. I'll come up behind and you fill him with holes, cool?"

Rodney was about to tell Marcus, *Yeah, cool, step on the gas.* But then the Lincoln flashed its brake lights, a turn signal, right.

"Hold up," Rodney said as the Lincoln turned down a narrow dirt road. "Be easy. We'll nail him soon as you make this turn."

‹ 100 ›

Gruber hit the gas as soon as his tires hit dirt. Heard the Lincoln roar, felt the suspension bouncing, jarring, bottoming out. He kept his foot planted. Knew the men in the Malibu would aim to catch up here, this empty stretch of dirt. Knew they would see their opportunity.

He drove, bouncing in his seat, dodging potholes best he could, his eyes on the turn at the end of the road. This was a place he remembered only vaguely, from the occasional family drive out to the Hoosier National Forest, some twenty-odd miles farther west.

Bill Brothers Limestone, the place was called, and he'd always craned his neck as his mother drove past, peering in at the heavy machinery, the graders and the haulers, the deep pits in the earth. The place had closed down, just before his mother had taken up with Earl; Gruber could remember the last time they'd driven past the quarry, the trucks and equipment all gone, just a few boarded-up outbuildings and a couple big holes in the ground, slowly filling with water.

The place was deserted. Gruber reached the end of the road, made the turn, pointed the Lincoln west again, the sun a spotlight aimed square in his eyes, the Malibu hidden back there, somewhere in the dust cloud he'd kicked up as he drove.

There was a gate swinging loose off a rusted-out lock, signs of the odd party here and there—piles of discarded beer cans, old barbecue pits. Used condoms and cigarette butts, and beyond it all, the pits, brimming with water, deep blue and cold.

Gruber drove through the gate. Swung the Lincoln around an old storehouse weathered gray from the quarry dust, and near falling down from twenty years of neglect. He killed the engine with the car out of sight, stuffed the Smith & Wesson back in his waistband, and reached for the shotgun.

He heard the Malibu slow as he stepped from the Lincoln, the gravel crunch beneath the tires. Felt his heart start to pound, the adrenaline ramping up. Shouldered the shotgun and crept around the far side of the storehouse and back toward the gate, excited and terrified for what was to come.

>>>

Marcus stopped the Malibu. Fiddled with the sun visor, squinting in the glare. Rodney looked around, too. Couldn't see a thing, just the blinding sun up ahead and some ruins alongside, trash everywhere and detritus, the dust hanging in the air from how the cars kicked it up.

Marcus rolled down the window. Coughed. "The fuck did he go?"

Rodney noticed the storehouse off to the left and figured it was obvious, was about to point out to Marcus to follow, when something caught his eye in his peripheral vision, coming from beyond Marcus, behind him.

Gruber.

There was no time to warn Marcus. Rodney shouted something, wasn't even a word. Then Gruber was at the window with a big fucking shotgun, and Rodney was fumbling with the MAC-11, swinging around, and the shotgun roared once and blew a hole into Marcus, and Marcus jerked backward, into Rodney, knocked the MAC-11 from his hand. As Rodney bent down to grab the gun from the floor, he heard Gruber rack and reload with the shotgun and knew he'd never be fast enough.

He reached for the door handle instead. Wrenched it open and dove out to parched dirt and gravel just as Gruber put another slug through the windshield. Rodney scrambled away, the MAC-11 still in the Malibu, useless, heard Gruber behind him and pulled himself up and booked it, stumbling away from the car on uneven terrain as Gruber circled around from the driver's side.

Go. Move. Get the hell out of here.

But Gruber had the open gate behind him. There was nowhere to run but farther into the quarry, toward the pits, the water, skirt the edge to the far side and hope Gruber kept missing.

Rodney made it ten, fifteen feet before the shotgun roared again, and then he was flying, launched in the air from the force of the impact, and he knew he was hit, somewhere vital, too, because when he landed hard on the gravel and tried to scramble up again, he found he couldn't move his legs, couldn't make them cooperate.

Rodney clawed his way instead, pulled himself forward on his belly, legs trailing useless behind him. He heard Gruber's footsteps somewhere close, heard the freak breathing, laughing a little, taking his time.

There was nowhere to go, no escape but the pit itself, the lip three or four feet from Rodney's outstretched hands. He pulled himself toward it, heard Gruber load another slug into that shotgun, knew if he didn't find cover immediately, he was dead.

He lunged for the lip with the last of his strength. Reached it, looked down and saw black water and stone. Hesitated, just briefly, expecting another blast from behind him, another horse kick, then black. *Jump or die.*

Rodney jumped. Pulled himself over the edge, more like, tumbled down the jagged wall toward the water. Knew halfway down he was fucked anyhow. The water was deeper in the pit than he'd realized. There was no way back up the walls, not with that slug in him, not without his legs. He plummeted through open space, hit the water hard and felt the bite, cold, felt the slug hole in the small of his back for the first time, a terrible fire.

He plunged deep in the water, racking, twisting with pain, the shock of the impact. Got his head above water somehow, gasped for air, struggled to keep himself afloat with his arms, keep from blacking out, keep alive.

And then Gruber appeared at the lip of the pit, the shotgun in his hands, a little smile on his face. He stood there and watched Rodney struggle to stay afloat, trained the gun on him but didn't shoot, and Rodney gasped for more air, swallowed water, his strength waning, wished the bastard *would* shoot, get it over with, end the fucking game.

But Gruber didn't shoot. He just stood there at the lip in the twilight, watching Rodney fight the inevitable, smiling to himself like this bullshit was *fun*.

‹ 101 ›

They commandeered a Cessna Citation Mustang, took off from Tampa Executive Airport, ten miles east of Madison Mackenzie's house.

"This is a teenage girl in jeopardy," Windermere told Drew Harris when she called to request the jet. "We need whatever you can get us. Jets, tactical, helicopters. SEAL Team Six, too, if you happen to have the number."

Harris okayed the private plane. Told her he'd call Agent Wheeler in Louisville, set up a welcoming committee. Kick-start the search for Madison Mackenzie on the ground. Told her he'd do his utmost to help them, however he could.

Windermere thanked him. "I just hope we're not too late."

The flight was supposed to take two hours. Felt like seven or eight, the way the night sky never seemed to change through the Cessna's porthole windows, the way Windermere kept thinking about Madison Mackenzie out there, somewhere far below.

This would be a hell of a lot easier if we could call her, she thought. *Track her through GPS, or something.*

But they couldn't. They'd had the thought already, after Paul Dayton pointed them to Louisville.

"Like the last case, right?" Stevens had said. "Triangulate Madison's location through her phone, find her and Gruber both."

But Paul had overheard them, interrupted. "She sold her iPhone," he told them. "Even with my savings, she didn't have enough for the bus ticket. She sold that phone for fifty dollars to some dude at the Greyhound station."

"Sold her phone?" Windermere repeated. "How'd she expect to meet this Brandon character with no phone? He was just going to show up at the bus station?"

"She bought a burner," Paul said. "So they could be in touch. He's the only one with the number."

Windermere ran her hands through her hair. Let out a long, frustrated breath. *Come on, honey,* she thought. *You gotta be smarter.*

"I tried to get the number from her," Paul said. "She wouldn't give it. Said she was afraid I would sell her out. I gave her my number, though." He ducked his head a little, looked hopeful. "So, you know, maybe she'll call?"

Stevens was already turning for the door. "Forgive us if we don't wait around."

Now Windermere stared out the window as the plane shuddered its way toward Louisville. It was a cloudy night, visibility limited, and she couldn't see much outside, just condensation on the windowpanes, and an inky deep blue quickly turning black beyond.

They'd talked to Agent Wheeler in Louisville, sent him to the bus station. Told him to call the plane the moment he found Madison Mackenzie. But so far, Wheeler had been silent. Madison was still missing.

"Could be Gruber doesn't have the balls to do it in person," Stevens said from across the cabin. "Or maybe Madison freaks out when she sees it's him waiting for her, and not some pretty-boy teenager."

"And, what?" Windermere replied. "Gruber just lets her go? He has to know that she's going to flip out when she finds a thirty-something man waiting in the bus terminal where her dream boy is supposed to be. He has to have planned for this."

She rubbed the bridge of her nose with her thumb and forefinger. "No," she said, "he'll have her, partner. And he'll kill her, too. He didn't come all this way for a freaking tea party."

The plane shuddered again, dove into the clouds, night settling in, the day pretty much over, and Windermere could see nothing but her own reflection in the little porthole window.

Where are you, Madison? she wondered. *We're coming, honey. Just keep yourself alive a little while longer.*

< **102** >

The police were already there when the bus arrived in Louisville. There was a young cop in uniform waiting at the gate; Madison
watched him as the bus pulled in, felt a fear growing in her stomach as
he lingered by the door. The police were here, and that meant what,
exactly? Had Paul sold her out already?

What the hell, Paul? You had one job.

She sunk low in her seat as the bus stopped at the gate, tried not to
stare at the young cop. Pulled her hood over her face, tucked her hair
underneath, hid her face as best she could. Filed off the bus in a crowd,
her head down, stuck close to the people in front of her. They were a
young couple, in their twenties, tattoos and piercings and band logos
on their duffel bags. Madison shadowed them, close as she could,
nudged the girl ahead of her as they reached the step down.

"Excuse me," she said, pasting a smile on her face, like they were
all longtime friends and they'd traveled together. "Are you guys from
around here?"

The girl stepped down to the pavement, then glanced back at Madison, matched her smile. "Sure we are," she said. "Well, I am. He's from
down in Knoxville."

"Oh, cool," Madison said, eyeing the cop over the girl's shoulder as
she stepped off the bus. "That's awesome. Are you guys, like, together?"

"Four months," the girl replied. "I'm trying to talk him into moving here, but—" She reached ahead, hit her boyfriend's shoulder. "He keeps saying he likes Tennessee too much."

The cop was staring straight at them. Madison turned away quickly, laughed, loud, like she and this girl were all-time BFFs. Kept her face hidden from the young cop until she was past him and headed toward the terminal doors.

"You know anywhere good to eat around here?" Madison asked the girl.

The girl thought about it. "I mean, there's the big entertainment center on Fourth Street. There's, like, a Hard Rock Cafe and a bunch of other things, if that's what you're into."

There were more cops inside the terminal. Madison could see them from the door. Patrol cops in uniforms, and plainclothesmen, too. Madison could see their cruisers parked in front of the building. *Shit.*

"Awesome," she told the girl. "Thanks so much. Have a nice night!" Then she ducked away from the doorway, slipped between a baggage handler and a bus, hurried down the driveway toward the street, didn't dare to look back, imagined the young cop was right on her tail.

She made the end of the driveway. The cop hadn't followed, hadn't picked her out. Amazing. She turned, fast, away from the bus station, and started running toward the lights of the skyscrapers downtown, the traffic, searching for a place to meet Brandon, somewhere the police wouldn't find her.

She ran three or four blocks. Then she slowed, ducked into the shadows alongside a hotel. Pulled out her phone.

Good thing you're running late, she wrote to Brandon. *That bus station is swarming with cops.*

‹ 103 ›

The sun was gone when Gruber left the quarry, the last light of day all but slipped away. He kept the Lincoln roaring as soon as he hit open road, the gas pedal to the floor. Came in hot on Interstate 64, made New Albany and kept on driving, across the Sherman Minton into Louisville.

He'd wasted too much time on the mopes from Cleveland. The second one had died slow. Gruber had watched him struggle in the water, fighting to stay afloat, thought about shooting him, but decided against it. No sense wasting ammunition; it was a tough shot from the lip, and, anyway, Gruber had never watched a man drown before. He could still hear the mope's last strangled pleas before the water took him under.

The trip to the quarry had been exhilarating, a worthy digression. But there was no time to deal with Earl now. Madison's bus had arrived ninety minutes ago, and the girl would spook and bolt if he didn't get to her soon. He'd intended to take her with him, somewhere safe, when Earl was gone and dealt with. He would have to deal with Earl later. He decided that was fine. He had somewhere special in mind for Madison.

His cell phone buzzed as he came off the Sherman Minton and into downtown Louisville. Another text message from Madison.

I ducked the cops. I'm down the block now. Fourth Street, some crazy covered mall thingy. Are you almost here?

Fourth Street. The entertainment complex, bars and chain restaurants, spanning an entire city block. Gruber put the phone down. Steered the Lincoln down Liberty Street, the complex in the distance, lights and music, heavy traffic, a crowd. Madison would blend in there. Too many faces. Good girl. Good thinking.

Gruber parked the Lincoln as close as he could. Typed a response to Madison. *Car's still effed up. Sent my friend to pick you up. He shouldn't be too long. XO.*

He climbed out and started toward the canopy that spanned all of Fourth Street. Pictured DarlingMadison somewhere in the mix, knew she'd be waiting for him. Knew she'd be grateful for what he had planned.

Almost there, darling. I'll see you very soon.

< 104 >

Madison sensed the guy before she saw him.

She'd found the entertainment complex a few blocks east of the station. Gaudy neon lights, crowds, a million restaurants. An easy place to disappear. She found a bench by the restrooms, a secluded corner, wishing that Brandon would come faster, and dreading his arrival all the same.

She wondered if she should be worried. Maybe the police caught up to him, or his parents. Maybe they took his phone away and dragged him back to Iowa. Or maybe he'd gone and done something awful. Maybe he'd bailed and hurt himself before she could convince him he didn't have to.

She pulled out the burner phone and the bus tag with Paul Dayton's number on it. Typed the number into her phone and debated calling Paul, telling him he was right, that Brandon was a weirdo after all, that she'd come all this way for nothing. Thought about how pleased with himself Paul would be if she called, how cocky and insufferable he'd be about it. She was still trying to decide what to do when her phone buzzed, a text message from Brandon. Madison saved Paul's number and opened the message.

Car's still effed up, Brandon said. *Sent my friend to pick you up. He shouldn't be too long. XO.*

Madison felt her body relax a little. He was coming. He hadn't abandoned her. The car trouble thing was a bit worrisome, but at least he was close, right? This crazy scheme might work after all.

Then the guy appeared. Madison couldn't have explained why she noticed him; people had been walking in and out of the restrooms since she'd sat down. But this guy—it was like when the sun moves behind a cloud and all of a sudden there's a shadow, a chill. This guy was the sudden chill. She looked up and saw him and shivered.

He was a middle-aged guy, in his thirties, probably. A bad haircut, huge glasses, a tragic attempt at a mustache. Creepy eyes, and they were pointed her way. He'd caught her staring. Now he was coming over.

Madison studied her shoes, pretended like she hadn't noticed the dude. That her instincts weren't on high alert, that whole fight-or-flight thing, like she wasn't preparing to choose the "flight" option. She could feel him coming like they were the only two people in the whole place. He stopped a couple feet away. "Madison?"

Oh, *shit.*

She didn't know this guy. Figured he was a creeper, some kind of weirdo, another lonely old man who was going to try to hit on her. But he knew her name, and that meant, what?

"Madison Mackenzie, right? You're here to meet Brandon."

It meant this strange old guy was Brandon's friend, apparently. But why would Brandon be friends with this dude?

Madison wasn't dumb enough that this whole scenario wasn't setting off alarm bells in her head. But she was tired, too, and she'd come a long way. Hell, she'd *talked* to Brandon on the phone, and this guy sure didn't sound like him. She'd seen Brandon's profile on Facebook, all his friends. This was crazy, sure, but what about the entire situation wasn't?

"Where is he?" she asked.

The man smiled, and it was creepier than when he wasn't smiling. "He's nearby. He sent me to come get you. Didn't he tell you? He's . . ." Gruber paused. "Well, he's not in great shape, with what's going on in his life lately. He just really needs to see you, you know?"

Well, shit. "But he's here, right?" Madison said. "He's in Louisville?"

"Of course," Gruber said. "He's not far. I'll take you, but we have to hurry. I didn't feel great about leaving him alone, the way he was talking."

This was exactly the kind of situation people were always warning you about. Strange men. Internet friends. Shady scenarios. Madison knew she was gambling if she went with this man. Knew it wasn't the smartest play in the book. But what else was she going to do? She had no money, no way to get home. And anyway, if Brandon needed her and she walked away, well, hell, he might actually kill himself, and that was on her. She couldn't take that chance, she decided. She just couldn't.

She would go with the guy. Cautiously, though, like if he looked at her funny, or tried to put a hand on her, she'd run. Kick him in the balls first, so he knew who he was messing with. She would be smart. This creepy old man wouldn't get her.

He held out his hand. Stared down at her with hungry eyes, the kind of look Madison had been warding off since she'd hit puberty. She shivered, chased the scary thoughts away. Ignored Gruber's hand and pushed herself to her feet.

"Let's do this," she told him. "Take me to Brandon."

< **105** >

Gruber led Madison to where he'd parked the Lincoln down the street. The girl hesitated just a fraction of a second, when she saw the car, and Gruber knew she was worried. Knew this was the crucial moment, the girl's mind wavering between acceptance and fear. She could join him, or she could run, and he wouldn't know which until it was happening.

"I know how strange this must seem," Gruber said, pasting on his friendliest smile. "Brandon said you traveled a long way to get here. You must have been expecting to see him, not some weird friend of his."

Madison relaxed a little. "Yeah," she said. "I was. My bus ride was twenty-two hours long. I just want to see him, you know?"

"He wants to see you," Gruber said. "He really needs it. He'd be here, if it wasn't for the breakdown. His parents' car made it this far, but . . ."

He shrugged, mimed helplessness.

"He's fixing it now," he told her. "He'll have it running again soon, he said. Then you guys can be on your merry way. In the meantime"— he gestured to the Lincoln—"I'm afraid my old beater is the best I can offer."

He stood back and waited, let Madison take in the car and the street and the city around her. It was dark, getting cold. The car would be warm at least.

"I already said I would go," Madison said, reaching for the passenger door. "I just really want to see him."

"You will," Gruber told her. "Soon."

<<<

Madison climbed into the passenger seat of the big old white car. Buckled her seat belt as the old guy—Gruber—circled around to the driver's side. He got in behind the steering wheel, gave her another of those appraising looks, and then he turned the key in the ignition and shifted into gear, driving slowly away from the mall.

They drove in silence for a while, a classic rock radio station playing through intermittent static, the city passing by around them. Night was falling, and the city was all empty buildings and lonely shadows. They drove over a long freeway bridge across the river, got off on the other side, ducked under the freeway and followed the river. It was cold in the car, and Madison shivered, hoping Brandon's car had a better heater. Assuming there was a Brandon's car.

Assuming there was a Brandon.

The city sprawl gave way pretty quickly to houses and dirty little storefronts and deserted, vacant lots. There weren't very many people outside, not much light. The Lincoln passed a few cars headed in the other direction, but otherwise they were pretty much alone.

Gruber was eyeing her again from the driver's seat. "Brandon said you guys met on the Internet."

It wasn't a question, so Madison didn't reply. She stared straight ahead and listened to the music, the DJ, the static coming more frequently, the reception fading. The scenery outside was less civilization, more darkness. Farm fields and wasteland and dense, black forest.

This was a mistake, she realized. She should not have done this.

"A suicide website, wasn't it?" Gruber asked her. "People trying to kill themselves?"

Madison met his eyes, gave him a brief smile. Turned back to the window and still didn't answer.

"Suicide," Gruber said. "My stepsister did that. Hanged herself with a coil of cheap rope." He looked at her again. "You actually look a lot like Sarah, you know?"

He lisped when he talked. She'd missed it at first, but there it was. It was Brandon's lisp, only it wasn't Brandon talking. This was definitely a mistake. This was a very bad decision.

"I think I left something back at the mall," Madison said, keeping her voice calm, that friendly smile on her face. Innocent, nonthreatening. "My suitcase, actually. Can we go back and get it?"

Gruber didn't seem to hear her. He kept driving, kept talking. "She was sixteen when she did it. I was, well, I was fifteen."

"That's really sad," Madison said. "That's really tragic. I'm so sorry. Can we go back and get my suitcase, though?"

Gruber laughed, a terrifying sound, longer and louder than any sane person's laugh. "I watched her do it," he said. "There was this little hole in the wall between our bedrooms—you'll see it. I used to watch her all the time, and then I watched her die."

"I'm really, *really* sorry," Madison said. "You must miss her terribly. I can't even imagine—"

"My *stepfather*," Gruber said, interrupting her. "Earl, her father. He used to hit me so hard I thought my eyes would roll out of their sockets. He always treated Sarah better than me. I pushed her to it. I hated her. I *wanted* to watch her die."

Madison said nothing. What could she say? She was too busy trying to quell the panic that kept rising in her throat, pushing her to do something, anything, to get away from this guy. Grab at the door handle and pull the door open, leap out of the car at sixty miles an hour.

But the door handle was broken off, Madison realized. The door was locked and the handle was gone, and she was trapped inside this car with this creep. And wherever he was taking her, there was no way she was getting out until he got there.

"Please," she said. "Dude, please. Whatever you're trying to do, just please don't, okay? Please?"

"Twenty years." Gruber's eyes were distant. His voice the same, like he was seeing those years pass by outside the car, instead of the last rapidly dwindling traces of civilization. "Twenty years since I watched her."

His breath hitched, and he coughed, came back laughing again. "But I'll watch you tonight," he said. "I've waited so long for this. I'll watch you tonight, and it'll be just like before."

Madison shook her head. "I'm not your sister, dude. I'm not Sarah, I'm Madison. Do you understand? I'm a real, live human being. And what I need is for you to turn this car around and take me back to the city. Like, right now."

Gruber didn't answer. Madison wondered if she could kick out the passenger window and hurl herself through the gap without the creep grabbing on to her. Were there door handles in the backseat? Could she wriggle back there somehow?

"You want to die," Gruber said. "That's why you found that website. That's why you came all the way here. To die."

"No," Madison said. "No, really, it's not. I met Brandon . . . he and I were . . . I mean, at first, yeah, but not now, not anymore."

She *didn't* want to die, and never had she been more conscious of that fact than now, trapped inside a speeding car with this lunatic.

"It doesn't get better, you know," Gruber was saying. "My sister could have turned out a fuckup like me. I *saved* her by helping her die."

His eyes were jumpy and unfocused, Madison noticed, live wires. "Your mom, your sisters, your new school, none of it will matter anymore. The freaks in your classes, Lena Jane Poole, your runaway dad." He smiled. "I'll take you away from this messy life, Madison. Won't that be nice?"

"No." Madison spun and searched the backseat. A tire iron, something, anything. "I don't want to die, I swear to freaking God. Just take me back to the city, *please.*"

Brandon, she was screaming inside. *Paul. Someone, anyone. Help me!*

But there was no Brandon. She'd been stupid to ever believe there was. And nobody else was close enough to come save her. She was on her own with the madman. Trapped in his car. And like it or not, she would probably die.

What did you expect? Madison asked herself. *You found this guy on a freaking suicide forum, you moron.*

It was stupid. Maybe it was ironic. She would have laughed at herself if she wasn't so scared.

< 106 >

Gruber took the back road into the trailer park. Wasn't much of a road, mostly gravel and dirt and weeds, mud puddles, the trees hanging overtop like greedy fingers. The Lincoln's suspension lurched and jostled, bottomed out a few times. It was a slow, torturous drive.

He drove by memory mostly. Remembered hiking this road with Sarah to school sometimes, when they'd slept in and missed the bus. The road wound its way around back of a few farmers' fields, eventually dumped out in Elizabeth, a stone's throw from the high school. Not many people drove the back way, back then. Judging from the way the weeds grew, the road was just as neglected now. Nobody would notice the Lincoln.

This was a genius idea, he decided, and he muttered a silent thank-you to the mopes in the Malibu for messing up his plans. Nobody would find them here, Gruber and Madison, not while they played, not while Madison died.

Nobody would spoil their fun.

>>>

Gruber finally stopped the car on a stretch of dirt, no light for miles. He pulled over to the side, killed the engine. Removed the keys and slipped them in his shirt pocket. Then he turned to study Madison again, his face hidden in shadow.

"I don't normally do this," he said. Laughed a little bit, sheepish. "Usually, I'm just the person on the other end of the Internet connection, watching from a distance."

He pushed his glasses up on his nose. "But you're different, Madison. You're special."

"You don't have to do this," Madison told him. "Whatever you're planning, you don't have to do it. I don't want to die, I swear. Just leave me here and keep driving and, I swear to God, I'll forget I ever saw you."

Gruber didn't seem to hear her. "The moment I saw your picture on the forum, I knew you were the one. I *knew* you were special, Madison. That's why I brought you here."

He gestured beyond the car, through the black maze of trees, and Madison could see a gate to somewhere, crooked and pocked with bullet holes. There were shadows beyond, rectangular hulks, an impossible dark against the night sky. In the gloom, a NO TRESPASSING sign, rusty and faded, its message barely visible: SHADY ACRES MOTOR COURT, RESIDENTS ONLY. The place was a trailer park, Madison realized, long abandoned.

"I used to live here," Gruber told her. "Back before the accident. Mom moved us here when she took up with Earl. We didn't stay long, on account of Sarah dying." He laughed. "And neither did Earl, after the story came out. He went to jail, but he's out now. I was going to see him this afternoon, for old times' sake, but I ran out of time. So I guess I'll have to postpone our reunion for a bit."

There was no light but the moon. Madison couldn't remember the last time she'd seen a pair of headlights, even. The place was deserted. They were alone out here. No one would save her.

Gruber clucked his teeth. "I know you're scared," he said, and he actually sounded sympathetic. "Nobody reaches this point without feeling scared. But I know this is right for you. I know this is what you need."

He reached for the door handle, opened his door, and Madison blinked as the bulb in the ceiling sent a dim beam of light into the car. When she opened her eyes again, Gruber was out of the car, leaning back in, staring at her.

"You look so much like Sarah," he said. "That's how I know what I'm doing is right."

"You're crazy," Madison said. "You're certifiably nuts. You're not saving anyone, you're freaking killing them."

But Gruber wasn't swayed. "I know it doesn't seem like it now, but believe me, you'll see. If you could thank me when this is over, you would."

"Fat chance," Madison said.

Gruber just smiled. Dead-calm, serene, utterly at peace. As she watched him, he reached down between the driver's seat and the door, pulled out a long kitchen knife. The blade gleamed in the light, the sight of it sending cold spasms of fear through Madison's body.

"Don't worry," Gruber said. "This isn't for you. Not if you behave yourself."

He straightened. Slammed the door closed, plunging the car into darkness again. Madison heard Gruber walk to the back of the car, heard him open the trunk. Figured she didn't have much time left.

She spun in her seat, lifted her legs, and kicked at the passenger window. Kicked hard, her sneakers thudding against the glass, sending shock waves through her body, but doing no damage to the car whatsoever.

"Come on," she half shouted. *"Come freaking on!"*

But the window wouldn't give. She wasn't getting out until Gruber wanted her out. Madison sat still again. Felt the burner phone in her pocket and reached for it, pulled it out, scrolled to Paul's saved number. Gruber was slamming the trunk closed, and she could hear his footsteps on the gravel shoulder as he came around her side of the car. In a moment, he'd be on her again.

Madison dialed Paul's number. Slipped the phone into her pocket, prayed Paul picked up. And then the door was open and the light was on, and Gruber was smiling down at her, holding the knife and a coil of yellow rope in his hands.

"Don't be scared," he told her. "It'll be fun, I promise."

He reached in and took her shoulder, surprisingly strong. Pulled her from her seat, and she had no choice but to follow. He stood her up beside the car, studied her again in the dim light from inside, his fingers like shackles around her arm.

"She wasn't much younger than you when it happened," he said. "Not that much younger at all."

Then he closed the door, and it was darkness again. He turned her up the road, pushed her forward toward the gate.

"Come on," he told her. "This way."

< **107** >

Paul Dayton's phone was ringing.

He almost didn't catch it, almost missed the call. Was hunkered down in a corner of Madison Mackenzie's house, watching the cops come and go and trying to avoid the shade that Catherine, Madison's mom, kept throwing his way.

In hindsight, Paul knew he'd been stupid to help Madison. Some creepy Internet pervert was running a full-scale catfishing operation on her, and he'd pretty well wrapped her up with a bow and sent her to the guy. She'd be safe if he hadn't put her on that bus. She'd be unhappy, but she wouldn't be murdered.

He'd been beating himself up about it since he'd seen the Amber Alert. Figured there was probably a good chance he'd be beating himself up for the rest of his life.

But his phone was ringing, and for who knew how long? Paul reached for it, answered, caught it just before the half ring that meant it was going to voicemail. "Hello?"

There was nothing at first. Just ambient noise, the *swish-swish-swish* of wind or fabric rubbing together or something. Paul checked the number. A Tampa area code, but that's all he got. It wasn't a contact he'd saved in his phone.

Wrong number, he thought. *Pocket-dialed.*

"Hello?" he said. "*Hello?* I think you called me by accident. *Hello?*"

No answer. He was about to hang up, end the call, when he heard someone talking. A girl, her voice muffled. Paul strained to listen.

"So this is where you grew up?" the girl was saying. "Shady Acres Motor Court? Is that what they called it when you lived here?"

Someone else said something, a man, but Paul didn't catch it. Wondered who he was listening to, who he knew went exploring around trailer parks. Then the girl continued.

"Did you always live in Indiana?" she said, and Paul got it. Didn't wait for the answer, but stood, snapped his fingers at the nearest city cop, pointed at his phone, his heart suddenly pounding, his whole body a live wire.

"I got something," he told the cop. *"I got something here. I think this is her."*

< **108** >

Madison slammed her free hand over her pocket, like she was swatting a bug, prayed to every god and godlike deity she could think of that Gruber hadn't heard Paul's squawking coming out through her jeans.

But Gruber's pace didn't change; he pushed her through the gate and into the Shady Acres Motor Court—long rows of old, abandoned trailer homes, the roads patched and weed-choked, the trailers themselves empty and ruined. And beyond, just the forest, dense and tangled and dark.

This was the definition of nowhere, this place. But Paul had freaking answered his phone.

Slowly, cautiously, Madison moved her hand from her pocket. "So this is where you grew up?" she asked Gruber. Kept her voice loud, so Paul could hear. Kept her fingers crossed, too, that he was smart enough to know what to do with the information. "Shady Acres Motor Court? Is that what they called it when you lived here?"

Gruber grunted. Halfway to a laugh. "That's what they called it," he said. "'Motor Court.' Like anyone would be fooled that it wasn't just a crummy old trailer park."

"Did you always live in Indiana?" she said.

"Grew up in the city," Gruber replied. "Louisville. I never had any friends out here, not even Sarah." He paused, wheezed a little. "She was a bitch, if you want to know the truth. She never even gave me a chance."

He was pushing her down a long row of trailers, all of them empty windows and black, yawning doorways, their sides yellowed by age and the elements and marked up with graffiti.

"Which one's yours?" she asked him. "That's where you're taking me, right? Your old trailer?"

Gruber grunted again. Sounded like a yes. "Trailer eighteen," he said. "Eighteen Frey Lane. Sarah's room."

"Sarah's room." Madison felt her stomach turn.

"Yes," Gruber said. "A special place for your special night. It'll be just how it used to be, won't it?"

Not if I have anything to say about it, Madison thought. She touched the phone through her jeans, moved it a little higher.

"Eighteen Frey Lane," she said. "Okay, show me."

< **109** >

The plane surged forward. Banked left. The jet engines roared. Louisville's city lights pitched crazy outside the windows.

Then the pilot came on the loudspeaker. "Agent Wheeler just radioed up from the ground," he said. "Your girl called her friend in Tampa a few minutes ago. She's outside of town, the other side of the river. Someplace called the Shady Acres Motor Court. Indiana somewhere."

"Elizabeth." Windermere shouted it so they could hear her in the cockpit. *"He took her to Elizabeth, Indiana."*

A pause. Then the loudspeaker again. "There's a private airstrip north of town. We're rerouting now."

Windermere exhaled. Caught Stevens looking at her. "Back to the old stomping grounds," he said. "Guess he's trying to relive the past."

"You can't go home again, partner," she said. "Let's get down there and stop him."

They were landing in minutes. The plane came down hard, bounced and rattled along the short airstrip, came to a halt opposite a little sheet-metal hangar, a couple single-engine prop planes. No control tower, no terminal. Just a stretch of road and an Indiana State Police cruiser parked at the head of it, blue-and-reds flashing, a trooper waiting for them.

"Your Agent Wheeler called ahead," he told Stevens and Windermere. "Apparently the girl has the phone in her pocket, but he patched through the call and we can hear everything pretty good. Shady Acres Motor Court, Eighteen Frey Lane."

Windermere crossed the tarmac to the cruiser. "You a fast driver?" she asked the trooper.

The cop kind of waffled. "Uh . . ." he said. "Depends on the—"

Windermere showed him her badge. "Keys," she said. "Backseat. FBI is requisitioning this car."

Windermere drove. Stevens rode shotgun. The cop sat silent in the back.

Windermere had a heavy foot, but she'd only driven these roads once. Stevens was working Google Maps on his phone to try and pin down a route, Madison Mackenzie patched into the cruiser's radio, Wheeler and the rest of the cavalry somewhere in the way back, speeding toward them from Louisville.

"Trying to scare up a helicopter, too," the cop said from the backseat. "State police on both sides of the river, local cops, everything. People take it seriously when it's a little girl's life in danger."

Windermere muttered a silent thank-you to Drew Harris, knew if she'd asked for an army tank, her SAC would have found her a whole armored division. Knew she could have the army, navy, and air force on her side and it still might not be enough to save Madison Mackenzie, but at least they were still in business.

Smart girl, she thought as Madison's voice crackled through her phone again. *Amazing girl. Just hold on a little longer. We're coming for you.*

< **110** >

Even in the darkness, the place hadn't changed.

They'd left Shady Acres shortly after Sarah's death, moved back to Louisville, where his mother found a job and another boyfriend, and Randall stashed pictures of Sarah under his mattress, watched horror movies with death and violence and blood, captured insects on the street and pitted them against each other, watching to see the moment when one killed the other.

It was the watching that was important. He watched everything. Stayed in the background at school, out of sight, watching the girls as they fixed their makeup at their lockers, the boys in the change room. He set out food in the middle of the street and sat for hours by the living room window, hoping a squirrel or a stray cat or dog would venture out into traffic, get hit by a car.

He'd watched everything, but nothing compared to Sarah. Nothing ever had, even the prospects on their webcams, the suicide kids. Nothing brought Gruber that same high, until now. Until here, the trailer. DarlingMadison.

In this light, she could have been Sarah.

Gruber realized Madison was looking at him. Waiting for him. They were standing in front of the trailer, on the sagging old stoop, and he was zoning out, staring into the void beyond the empty doorframe.

He'd completely lost track of where he was, what he was doing. Why he'd brought DarlingMadison here.

He pushed her forward. Felt her buck against him, pushed harder, maneuvered her toward the yawning door.

"You think *you're* scared," he said. "I used to *live* here."

<<<

It was the scariest place Madison had ever seen in her life.

There was no door in the doorframe, just blackness beyond. Gruber pushed her toward the threshold, through a couple of dense, clinging cobwebs, his grip never loosening on her arm. The darkness was still and choking. The cobwebs hung from her hair, stuck to her face, making her skin crawl. She wanted to scream, knew it wouldn't do any good. Knew if she went into the trailer, she wouldn't come out alive.

Here it is, then. Here's where you make your stand.

Gruber continued pushing her toward the door. Madison resisted. Gathered all of her strength and wrenched her arm sideways, clawing with her free hand at Gruber's fingers, prying at him, digging her fingernails into his doughy skin. Heard the knife drop as he swung his left hand to grab her, felt the sudden release as Gruber's grip gave way, and then she was running, off balance, spinning away from the trailer and careening back toward Frey Lane, the darkness and the looming hulks beyond.

Madison ran. Stumbled over the gravel-patch yard, Gruber scrambling behind her, his feet kicking stones. He was old and heavy and slow, and she had the element of surprise. She was winning. She was getting away. She would live after all.

But then she reached the end of the lane, the lip where it met the larger crossroad, and the asphalt was cracked and broken up by years of neglect, cold winters, and overgrowth pushing up through the fringes. It was dark and the road was uneven, the lip a good three or four inches above the gravel in the yard, and Madison missed her step and stumbled, turned her ankle, staggered forward wildly, arms out and reaching for something, anything to keep her balance. She failed miserably. Fell flat on her face and skidded across the road, scraping her palms, knees, tearing her jeans.

She tried to stand, couldn't. She'd messed up her ankle. Gruber was coming, and she couldn't put weight on it, and she watched him approach like a horror-movie monster, lumbering, slow and steady. Tried to pull herself forward, crawl, anything. Wasn't fast enough, not by a mile. And then Gruber was on her.

Madison slapped at him, hit him, tried to gouge his eyes, do something, *anything* to be free of him. But he fought her off; he was angry now, ready for her fight and powerful enough to put her down.

He stood above her, pinned her down with his foot on her stomach, his face just a shadow, moonlight on his grimy glasses.

"Tsk, tsk," he said, breathing heavy. "What did I tell you about misbehaving? There's a way to do this that's decent, and a way that's unclean and foul, but it's going to get done either way. You *will* enjoy your surprise tonight."

She felt around for a weapon, a tree branch or a piece of scrap metal— hell, the knife—but there was nothing in arm's reach. The bastard had her again. And then he reached behind him, pulled something from his back pocket, and she watched him fiddle with it, heard the ripping sound, and she knew it was duct tape.

"Come on," he told her, flipping her onto her stomach, "It's getting late. And I really want you to see Sarah's room."

He brought her wrists together, and she heard the duct tape unspool again, felt it on her skin. And she screamed finally, loud and desperate and raw, though it was obvious no one was coming.

< **111** >

Madison screamed. It came through the cell connection staticky and muffled, rattled around the inside of Windermere's head and stayed there. Windermere grit her teeth, urged the cruiser to move faster. Saw the broken-down front gate of the Shady Acres Motor Court in her high beams, slammed down hard on the brakes.

"No sign of a car," she said, scanning the darkness. "We sure this is the right spot?"

Stevens was already out of his seat belt, reaching for his pistol, a tactical flashlight. "She said Shady Acres. Maybe they took the bus."

Windermere found her Glock, turned to the state trooper in back. "Guard the entrance," she told him. "Nobody gets out, understand?"

The cop nodded, pried his fingers from the panic bar above his head. "Got it."

"And tell Wheeler to set up a perimeter around the park once he gets here," she told him. "It's all forest back there. Gruber gets out into that, we might never find him."

Then she was out of the car and running, Maglite in her left hand, the Glock in her right. Hurdling the log at the front gate, Stevens beside her, huffing and puffing as she scanned the road signs, the empty trailers beyond, searching for Frey Lane and trailer eighteen and the girl.

Don't let him win, honey. Just a few minutes more.

< **112** >

Gruber finished binding her wrists with the duct tape. Flipped her back over, and the cell phone slipped out of her pocket. He cocked his head as it clattered to the ground, bent down to examine it.

"You *have* been misbehaving," Gruber said, and there was something to his voice now, a tremor that hadn't been there before, a knife's edge. "You just couldn't make this easy, could you?"

He stepped on the phone. Ground it beneath his heel, crushed plastic and metal. Kicked the wreckage away and then stopped, froze. Looked around, at the shadows, the empty husks. Madison tensed, too. She'd heard what he'd heard: low, faraway noises—voices, maybe, a car door. She opened her mouth to scream again.

Then Gruber was on top of her, his meaty hand pressing against her lips, smothering the scream before she could get a sound out. And then he had the duct tape again, a long strip of it, was wrapping it over her mouth and around the back of her head, ripping it roughly and pulling her to her feet, holding her upright when her ruined ankle buckled. She could hardly stand, let alone run. And no matter how hard she struggled, Madison knew he wasn't letting her go this time.

Gruber dragged her across the gravel yard again. Toward that open doorway. He stopped briefly to pick up the knife where he'd dropped it, the coil of yellow rope, showed her the blade. Like he was giving her a choice, and neither one of them good.

The cobwebs grabbed at her hair again. She was through them and into the trailer before she really noticed. They were in the remnants of a kitchen, litter everywhere. Dead leaves and dirt, years' worth of built-up grime. Nobody had been here in a long, long time, Madison knew. Still, there was a terrifying aura about the place. Bad things had happened here.

Then Gruber was pushing her forward, and she was staggering down a long narrow hallway, impossibly black, her shoulders bouncing off the cheap fake plastic-wood walls, her body moving faster than her feet, trying in vain to keep her weight off her ankle.

"This way," Gruber said, his voice higher pitched, tremulous, excited. "Sarah's room is down here."

There were doors in the walls, each side. Gruber paused at the first door, on the left. "This was my room," he told her. "I used to lie there and wait for Sarah to come home from her dates. I used to wait for her for hours."

Madison screamed through the duct tape. Struggled to break free. But Gruber's grip was firm. He wouldn't let go of her.

He shoved her forward again. Down the black hall to the next door on the left, sending more spasms of pain through her leg. Madison knew this had to be Sarah's room, where Gruber's sister had lived her life, unaware that her brother was watching her—and where, ultimately, she'd died. She knew Gruber wanted her in this room. Knew that however he planned to kill her, it would happen in here.

But the door was closed. And when Gruber reached around her, tried the doorknob, the door gave an inch, but no more. There was something behind it, something barring the way. A dresser or something, something solid. Something heavy.

"*Shit.*" Gruber grunted, shoved her out of the way. Pinned her between his body and the end of the hall as he threw himself at the door. Madison heard the flimsy wood crack. Heard Gruber draw back and try again.

He wasn't paying attention to her anymore. He'd wedged her in the little patch of hall between his body and the end wall of the trailer, left her to wait, confident that her ankle had her hobbled. He was breathing heavy, the door giving a little more each time. Madison waited, watched him through the shadows. Knew she'd only have one shot at escape.

Gruber drew back again. Hurled himself forward. Cannonballed the door off its hinges and fell over the threshold and into the dark room. Madison didn't wait to see if he was hurt. She leaned on the wall and forced herself to break for it, biting off another scream as she landed on her bad ankle.

She tried to ignore the pain. Focused on getting free. Limped down the dark, narrow hallway, fast as she was able. Reached the end of the hall just when Gruber realized she was missing, made the kitchen with its dirt and detritus, an expanse of dark and shadow between her and the trailer door.

She could hear him behind her, back on his feet and angry, chasing her, closing the distance. Knew she had to keep going, couldn't be sure her ankle would hold up long enough. Couldn't know for certain she wouldn't just collapse.

Only one way to find out.

Madison pushed herself off the wall. Stumbled forward, slipped on the old linoleum, her balance total crap with her arms taped behind her. Nearly fell, her ankle screaming, threatening to topple her.

She stayed upright. Aimed for the door. Gathered every ounce of her strength and threw herself at the night beyond.

‹ 113 ›

Stevens and Windermere hurried into the trailer park, crouched low, their pistols drawn, flashlights aimed down at the ragged road.

Stevens was a shadow. Windermere could hear him beside her, hear him breathing, his shoes shuffling across the pavement, a carpet of dead leaves covering Frey Lane. Watched the beam of his flashlight sweep along the trailers as they passed them, searching for number eighteen. Gruber's trailer.

This was creepy. The whole park was like a graveyard of bad juju, and it didn't help that Madison Mackenzie was at Gruber's mercy, somewhere inside. Windermere felt her heart pounding, heard Madison's scream echoing in her head. Pushed herself to move faster, find her before Gruber did what he'd come here to do.

Then she heard Stevens cough. Low, just loud enough to get her attention. He'd killed his flashlight, was gesturing across at a sagging double-wide. Windermere couldn't see the house number, but she knew they'd found the right spot. Could tell from the hammering noises coming from inside.

Muffled grunts and wood splintering; not exactly rhythmic. More like someone was battering something. Windermere raised her Glock, her flashlight, too. Spotted the trailer's open door and crept toward it.

A violent crash from inside. A heavy weight, falling hard. Windermere crossed the gravel front yard, her shoes kicking up stones as she went. Hurried toward the door, flashlight aimed inside, nothing beyond but dim shadows and the vague outline of old furniture, countertops, garbage and debris.

And then, a girl.

Madison Mackenzie, her mouth taped over, arms restrained, came *flying* out of the trailer. She made the front door at about the same time as Windermere, collided with her, knocking her back. The girl was screaming through the duct tape, her eyes wide and terrified. Windermere made a grab for her, missed, felt Madison squirm past her and tumble into the yard. Turned around to catch her, break her fall, a reflex, and when she turned back to the door, there was Gruber.

He was at once smaller and more menacing than she'd imagined. Five eight or five nine, hardly overpowering, thick around the middle, and those thick, greasy glasses. He was breathing heavy, his mouth contorted into a rictus of frustration, anger. He was holding a long carving knife.

The girl had distracted her. Windermere had lowered her gun when she reached for her, tried a bear hug and missed. Now she turned back to Gruber, raising her Glock as he lunged with the knife. Knew she wouldn't make it; Gruber was quicker. Forgot about shooting him and raised her left arm to ward off the blade, felt the knife cut her, hot and sharp. She fell onto the gravel, Gruber looming above her. Watched him raise the knife again, knew he aimed to kill her. Then Stevens's pistol roared, and Gruber staggered back, back through the doorway and into the dark trailer.

And then Stevens was beside her. *"Carla,"* he said. "Shit. Did he get you?"

Windermere put her other hand to her forearm, felt blood, the fabric of her favorite jacket in tatters. Didn't feel the pain yet, her adrenaline taking care of it for now, pushed Stevens away. "The girl."

Stevens turned, shined his flashlight down Frey Lane, caught Madison Mackenzie running into the arms of Agent Wheeler and an Indiana state cop three or four houses down.

"Safe," he told her. "She's okay, Carla."

Windermere released her wounded arm. Picked up her Glock. "Great," she told Stevens. "Then let's go get Gruber."

< 114 >

Gruber staggered back through the open doorway, more from the shock than the gunshots themselves. Saw the cops outside, two of them, and knew this game was over. Madison Mackenzie was gone.

More flashlights. The lady cop on the ground where she'd fallen, her partner with the pistol crouched above her, checking her wound. Gruber backed through the trailer, into the little kitchen. Knew he only had seconds to get free.

He backed into the kitchen counter. Knew the cops were coming, could hear more of them approaching. They would surround the trailer. They would wait for him to come out, or they would storm inside and shoot him dead.

Gruber dropped the knife. Pulled Curtis Donovan's revolver from his back pocket. Fired out through the front door, wild, didn't wait to see if he'd hit anything. He pushed himself off the counter, ran down the long hallway to his room, and Sarah's, Earl's on the back side. He was bleeding, he could tell, his left side starting to burn. The cop had shot him twice, shoulder and rib cage. Impossible to move without feeling it, his whole body screaming.

But he had to run. He did, passed his old bedroom, made it to Earl's room, halfway to Sarah's door. Heard the police behind him, crossing the threshold, their flashlights like laser sights. Knew he was dead if they caught him.

Gruber steamrolled through Earl's bedroom. A dingy old mattress in the middle of the floor; he slipped on it, nearly fell. Made the rear window and punched through the glass with the butt end of the gun. Cleared the shards away with the sleeve of his jacket and hefted himself over the sill.

He struggled, clawing at the outer wall of the double-wide, kicking his feet, until he'd pulled himself through the window and landed with a crash in the scraggy bushes beyond, his shoulder on fire, his midsection the same. Pulled himself to his feet and kept going.

Behind him, the cops had burst into Earl's bedroom. Gruber didn't look back. He ran.

< 115 >

Stevens and Windermere followed Gruber into the double-wide, the whole trailer shaking and crashing as he bulldozed his way through. Found themselves in an old kitchen, a narrow hallway to their left. Heard glass breaking somewhere in that direction, didn't slow down, kept moving.

Stevens took the lead. Windermere followed, her arm starting to ache, the blood really coming. Ignored the pain, but cursed herself anyway. *You could have taken him down, Supercop. But you blinked.*

Stevens passed a door on the left, an empty room. Made a right turn into somebody's bedroom and Windermere followed, the beam of her flashlight glancing down the hall as she went, a broken door hanging off its hinges, the remains of a wooden dresser behind. Then she was turning, chasing Stevens into the bedroom and toward the back, a broken window about waist high, Stevens shining his light through.

"He got out there," Stevens said, breathing heavy. Aimed his light at the backyard, more trailers beyond. "Bastard made the jump and I lost him."

Windermere reached for her radio. "We need this park surrounded," she said. "*Now.* If Gruber gets out to that forest, he's gone."

The radio crackled, affirmative responses. Windermere stared out the empty window. Touched her hand to her arm and drew back, wincing, eyes tearing.

"Damn it, partner," she said. "I think he really *got* me."

‹ 116 ›

Gruber heard voices as he ran from the trailer, men calling to each other, radios crackling. Engines rumbling. Knew there were more police out there, many of them. Knew they wouldn't stop searching until they found him.

None of them had ever lived in this trailer park, though, or spent time in the forest beyond. Nobody knew this place like he did.

Gruber ducked into the shadows of the next trailer over. Crept around to the rear of it, moving slow, cautious, careful not to step in any of the debris that lay scattered, pieces of scrap wood and siding, a hot-water tank, a plastic kiddie pool. He could hear the men in the distance, figured they were congregated at the park gate, fifty yards away or so. Could see light, intermittent, flashing against the trailers opposite him, the treetops, flashlights and red-and-blues from the police cars. Heard the crunch of boots on gravel.

Gruber ducked low and hurried through the yard behind the trailer as fast as he dared, weighing the odds he would stumble on something loud against the certainty that the police were coming behind him. He was still holding the revolver, knew he'd probably have to use it again if he wanted to escape the trailer park with his life.

The backyard ended in a low fence, most of the boards rotted away or torn out. Gruber hopped the fence, cut through the next backyard toward the trailer opposite, his lungs burning already, gasping for breath. He'd never been an athlete. Never taken care of his body. Never imagined he'd need to.

He reached the next trailer. More voices behind him, louder, doors slamming. He could feel his wounds, his shoulder and his side, burning like a hot fireplace poker jabbed into his insides. They were getting worse as the adrenaline wore off, hotter and hotter, the pain growing. He wasn't going to die, he didn't think, but he couldn't be sure. He just had to get out of there.

Gruber skulked around the side of the trailer. This one was almost collapsed, the walls hanging inward, the roof just a pair of steel rails and the night sky beyond. There was no light out this far, no movement. One row of trailers on the other side of the road, and then nothing but forest beyond. He was almost there. He could make it.

Gruber peered left and right, squinting in the darkness, saw no signs of life up or down the road. Gathered his breath and his courage and ran, crossed the road as fast and quiet as he could, heard no gunshots behind him, no voices. Reached the trailer on the other side, the shadows, and slowed down again. Caught his breath. Kept moving, toward the edge of the park. The fence, the back gate, the dirt road. Donovan's car.

He'd just reached the last trailer's backyard when he heard it. Was staring through the darkness, to the fence, could almost see the Lincoln in the clearing beyond, when the radio crackled somewhere ahead, across the yard and at the park boundary. A cop, somewhere out there, running down the fence line, moving fast. If he found the car, they would all come running.

Gruber crept across the yard to the gate. Heard the crunch of the cop's footsteps approaching, and crouched low against the fence, the revolver at the ready. Then he saw the cop. A little guy, short and stocky, ten feet away, and closing in quickly.

Gruber didn't have time to think. No time to do anything but attack. He launched himself from the fence, swung the butt end of the gun, and caught the cop in the temple. Knocked him down, saw the man reaching for his sidearm and fell on top of him, swinging down with the revolver again and again until the cop was quiet, the ground bloody.

It was over in seconds. The cop hadn't had time to call or cry out, reach for his radio. Gruber wiped the gun clean. Then he stood. Hurried out through the gate to the road beyond, the white Lincoln. Found the keys, started the engine. Drove away, fast as he dared, the park gate still dark in the rearview, no sign yet of any more cops.

< 117 >

Stevens left Windermere with a couple of Indiana state troopers, made them promise to get her to an ambulance. Helped her out of the trailer and then circled around back, pistol and flashlight raised, setting off in the direction he'd last seen Randall Gruber.

The night was all flashlight beams and distant voices, the hulks of dead trailers and overgrown lawns. He hurried across the Gruber back-yard, ducked alongside another dark trailer, fast as he dared, his whole body tensed and ready for Gruber to come at him from the gloom, swinging that knife.

But Gruber didn't come. Here and there, Wheeler's men searched other trailers, alongside the state troopers and the rest of the cavalry. Now and then, shouts would erupt in the darkness, triumphant, chase-is-on shouts, only to fall silent within the span of seconds, false alarms every-where, shadows playing tricks.

Stevens kept searching. Crossed another cracked roadway, another derelict trailer. Wondered if Gruber would try to hide out, if he'd run. Figured he'd shot Gruber once for certain, probably twice, figured a guy as unathletic as Gruber wouldn't have much taste for setting out on a chase. Figured he'd probably try and lay low, wait until the heat died.

Figured they'd be good if they locked the park down, established a perimeter, called in the canine unit, and waited for first light.

Still, he walked the park. Found his way to the back boundary, a low fence, a gate, some kind of clearing. And something else, too, some-thing that caused a glint when his light reached it.

He got on the radio. Told the cavalry, quiet as he could, that he was approaching the park fence. Told them not to shoot him, whatever they did. Then he crossed the yard to the fence.

He'd made it halfway there when he realized the glint in his flash-light beam had come from a pair of steel handcuffs. And that the hand-cuffs were attached to the belt of an Indiana state trooper.

A young guy, from the look of him, a rookie, or close. Stevens reached the body, saw the blood, lots of it. The man's face had been fairly bashed in, some kind of blunt object. He was dead.

"I got a man down," Stevens told the radio. "Back of the park. I need an ambulance, and I need backup, *now*."

He scanned his flashlight up from the body. Through the gate to the woods beyond, the clearing. It wasn't just a clearing, he saw, walking through the gate. It was a road, narrow, dirt and gravel and cavernous potholes.

Fresh tire tracks in the dirt.

He keyed his handset again. "I'm going to need motor units, too," he said, scanning the road, empty in both directions. "He found another way out of here, and he's on the move."

< 118 >

Gruber drove as fast as he dared, punishing the Lincoln's suspension on the uneven terrain. Kept the headlights off, navigated by memory, the road overgrown and neglected, but still there.

The road curled around the side of a low rise. Cut down into Elizabeth along the edge of a farmer's field, mud and loose gravel and irrigation runoff, the tires struggling to keep traction, the whole car bouncing and rattling forward. Gruber kept his foot down as far as he dared, prayed the car wouldn't get stuck. Knew it was the end if it did.

He was sweating, even in the chill October air. Shivering, his body cold and fire-hot at the same time, the adrenaline dumping off, the gunshot wounds taking over. He figured he might go into shock soon, knew he had to risk it.

The descent into town took a quarter of an hour. The mud path reached the county road just as it passed the old high school, enough light from the streetlights to make out the gymnasium, the football field. The parking lot where Todd McGee parked his pickup truck, the bleachers where Gruber had watched a game with Sarah and Todd, his mother's orders, Sarah and Todd barely putting up with him, their hands busy under the blanket they'd brought, both of them giggling and squirming and glancing over at him, making sure he wasn't paying attention.

He had been. He'd pretended to watch the game, but he'd been hanging on every bit lip and stifled laugh, every stolen kiss, consumed with envy and jealousy and hate. He remembered. And if he'd had more time, Gruber figured he might have paid Todd McGee a visit now, too.

But he didn't have time. He turned onto the county line, kept the Lincoln moving. Headed north, out of town, stuck to the back roads, more dirt and narrow one-lane pavement, skirted the lake and the dam and kept driving. Kept his headlights off, drove as fast as he dared. Knew the police would pick up the trail soon enough, knew he'd have to move fast if he wanted to see Earl before—

Gruber pushed the thought from his mind. There was nothing else but Earl, nothing that really mattered. He'd waited two decades to see his stepfather again. And nobody—no Cleveland thugs, no police, no FBI, and no teenage girl—was going to keep him from paying that visit.

He drove the Lincoln northbound on those back country roads, ignoring the pain in his shoulder, his side. Hit the Ohio River Scenic

Byway just outside of Lanesville, and turned east toward New Albany, toward Earl, just ten miles away.

The night had been a disaster so far. Madison Mackenzie was alive. The surprise was ruined.

But a few hours with Earl might just salvage the whole misadventure.

< **119** >

Windermere, at the park gate, sat in back of an ambulance as a medic tended to her arm. The wound throbbed where Gruber had slashed her, a long cut, but mercifully not so deep. Still, she winced as the medic cleaned the wound, applied gauze. Cursed herself for letting the scumbag get away.

Stevens figured the guy was driving for his life. Trying to buy himself time, put miles and minutes between his car and the trailer park.

"No way he'll get far," he'd told her. "A guy in his condition? Dunno if you got a good look at him, but he sure seemed like the type who spent his days sitting at a computer."

"Yeah," Windermere said, holding up her bum arm. "Beat me on the draw, though, didn't he?"

She didn't share Stevens's optimism. Knew her partner's theory made sense, but figured as long as Gruber was out there and not captured, she wouldn't feel particularly good about their position. Luckily, Madison Mackenzie was all right; Wheeler had her taken care of, medical attention, armed guard, the works. Gruber wouldn't get to her. She'd survived.

Still, a state patrolman was dead, some poor kid who just happened to be in the wrong place at the wrong time.

He could still be alive. Would be, if you'd taken Gruber out like you were supposed to, back at that shady-ass trailer. But you didn't.

"That road spits out in Elizabeth," Stevens was saying. "State patrol's looking out for him on all four points of the compass. He won't get far, Carla."

Windermere pushed herself to her feet. "So what the hell are we waiting for?" she said. "Let's track the bastard down."

"Sure," Stevens said. "You have a direction in mind?"

"Any direction," she told him. "Any which way at all. Just get me out of this ambulance and back on Gruber's trail before he puts another body in the ground, okay?"

Behind her, the medic made to pull her back down. "Ma'am, I really think . . ." he said. "This cut here, you're going to need stitches if you want it to heal right."

"You hear what I said?" Windermere replied. "We got a killer on the loose, pal. Bandage me up fast and let me do my job."

The medic stared at her. At Stevens and Windermere. Sighed, and reached for the gauze.

"Hurry," Windermere told him. "It's not even my shooting arm anyway."

< **120** >

They had Madison in an ambulance. The cops had insisted, even though she kept telling them she was fine, no injuries, nothing psychological. They'd piled her in and they were going to take her back to the city, to Louisville, "for observation," they said. *Bull crap*. Madison was hungry. All she really wanted was to eat. She'd figure out the rest later.

She knew she should be happy to be alive. She wasn't. She knew a night like tonight should come with some kind of epiphany, some realization about the worthiness of her life. It hadn't. All Madison could think about was going home to her mom, her sisters, Lena Jane Poole, and *Paul*, everybody knowing she'd fallen for some pervert on the Internet and nearly gotten herself killed. She figured she might choose death over having to walk back into her school again.

And Gruber was still missing. She'd overheard two cops talking outside the ambulance.

"Killed Stu Crowley," the one cop said. "Pistol-whipped him to death in the back of the park. Disappeared down that back road, got away clean."

"They put out an APB?" the second cop replied.

"Sure they did, but it's all four points of the compass. So many back roads and dirt tracks around here, could be days before they find him."

Madison knew this wasn't true. She knew the police would find Gruber soon, real soon, whether they wanted to or not. She gathered they hadn't heard about Earl. She figured she'd better tell them.

"Hey," she called out to the cops outside. *"Who's in charge out there? I need to talk to somebody."*

<<<

Stevens and Windermere commandeered an FBI Charger from the trailer park gate. Windermere was sliding behind the wheel, trying to figure out a way she could drive with her arm all bandaged up and hurting, when Agent Wheeler tapped on the driver's-side window.

"You guys have a second?" he said. "Got the girl over there—Madison? She said she wanted to talk to you before they take her to hospital."

"We don't have time for a visit," Windermere said. "Hop on board and patch her in through the radio." She reached for her seat belt, jarred her arm on the door handle instead. Winced and killed the ignition. "I think you'd better drive, partner," she told Stevens. "That creep really screwed me over back there."

<<<

She'd called for the police, and now here they were, a man's voice and a woman's voice on the other end of a radio—the FBI themselves.

"Stevens and Windermere," the man told her. "We tracked you to the trailer park. That phone call of yours was some smart work, let me tell you."

Madison looked at the cop next to her manning the radio. Felt stupid, this whole crazy night and everything was her fault. "Thanks, I guess."

303

Then the woman came on. "You have something you wanted to tell us?"

Madison nodded. Pushed her reluctance aside, forced the words out. "In the car," she said, "on the way here, Gruber kept talking about his sister."

"Sarah, yeah," the woman cop said. "We think he chose you for the resemblance."

"That's what he told me. I guess he was in love with her or something?"

"Obsessed," the woman said. "I don't think Gruber is capable of love."

"Whatever. He wouldn't shut up about her, anyway. And his step-father, too, Earl?" She paused. "I don't know if you guys know about him. The things he did to them, both of them."

"We know," Stevens said. "We have the backstory."

Ah, Madison thought. *So they know all of this. Waste of time, just like always.*

You suck.

"Okay, never mind, sorry," she said, unable to keep the disappointment from her voice. "You know everything about Earl, I guess."

Radio silence. Road noise. Then: "Try us," Windermere said. "What do you know?"

Madison looked down, looked away from the cop by the radio. Didn't want to keep talking. They knew all this, and she was wasting their time. *Useless, useless, useless.*

"I just think he might be going to see him," she said.

Another long pause, too long to be normal, and Madison wondered if they maybe didn't know everything after all.

"What makes you say that?" Stevens asked her.

"He kept talking about Earl, about . . . what he'd done to Sarah. What he'd done to him," Madison told them. "He said he tried to go see Earl today, but he couldn't for some reason. So when he was finished with me, he would go back and try again, have a reunion."

"A reunion," Stevens repeated.

"Sounds like revenge to me," the woman said. Madison heard an engine roar, urgent voices. Figured that was pretty much it for her involvement in the case. Was about to tell the cop to go ahead, turn it off, when the woman cop—Windermere—came on again. "Madison?"

"Yeah?"

"You've been a really big help tonight," Windermere told her. "Hang in there, honey, okay?"

Madison felt her face go red. "Whatever," she said, and didn't say anything else until she was sure Windermere was gone. Couldn't unhear her words, though.

You've been a really big help.

It was not an entirely unpleasant sensation.

< 121 >

Windermere's cell phone rang as Stevens drove. She checked the number: Mathers. Answered. "Kind of a bad time if you're hoping to talk, Derek."

Mathers coughed. "I could call back," he told her, "but I think you want to hear this."

Windermere looked out the window, trees flying past, Stevens with both hands on the wheel, at the ten and two, his mouth a thin line as he watched the road. "Shoot," she told Mathers. "But you start with the lovey-dovey crap and I'm out."

"Got a phone call from the Erie County Medical Examiner's Office," Mathers said, and Windermere forgot about the chase outside and zeroed in on his words. "Someone named Lily Yoshida, asking for you."

"Yeah, Yoshida," Windermere said. "Okay. What did she want?"

"She said she ID'd the body you and Stevens were asking about." He paused, and she could hear him flipping pages. "Somebody named, ah, Curtis Donovan, a young guy from Cleveland, nineteen years old. He did a six-month stint in juvie, happened to get a couple cavities, so they had his dental records."

"That's convenient," Windermere said. "She tell you anything else about the guy? Like why he wound up in Randall Gruber's house?"

"She didn't, but I called Cleveland PD, and they filled me in. Apparently this guy Donovan was on the come-up with Rico Jordan's old crew, currently operated by someone named Victor Rodney. I don't know who either of those guys are, but the Cleveland detective thought you would."

"I know Rico," Windermere said. "He and Gruber weren't friends. Guess they tracked him down after all."

"Guess so," Mathers said. "Cleveland thought this crew might have sent Donovan up to Buffalo to settle some debts. But it sounds like Gruber got the drop on him."

"Sounds like," Windermere said. "So, okay, there's the backstory. You know anything that can help me catch our bad guy?"

"Couple things," Mathers said. "First of all, Curtis Donovan drove a white '84 Lincoln Continental. So if you didn't find one back in Buffalo, you should maybe keep an eye out down wherever you are."

"A white '84 Continental," Windermere said. "Roger."

"That's not all you need to know, Carla," Mathers said. "Curtis Donovan wasn't much of a gangster, not according to what I found out. I guess he ransacked his uncle's gun cabinet before he left town, took every weapon and all the ammunition he could find." He paused just long enough to let the drama build. "And his uncle was loaded for bear. Like, literally. We're talking serious firepower."

Windermere felt the bottom drop out of her stomach. "Great," she said, looking at the night speeding by outside her window. "So now this fucker has an arsenal, too."

< 122 >

Gruber followed the Scenic Byway back into New Albany. Ducked under the Sherman Minton Bridge and pulled the Lincoln up outside Earl's apartment building. Opened his door and reached down to pop the trunk, figuring to pull the shotgun out again, prepare his assault. The pain stopped him.

It felt like all of a sudden, but it had been there all along. Burning hot and angry, the blood from the bullet wounds saturating his clothes. The pain was overwhelming, pounding, relentless. He closed his eyes, and when he opened them, five minutes had passed on the little clock on the dash, vanished like nothing, a time warp. He breathed in and out, ragged, wondered if he was dying, if this was where his life would end.

It wasn't. It couldn't be. Gruber urged himself out of the driver's seat, his vision spotty, his legs like limp spaghetti. Circled to the back of the Lincoln, found the shotgun where he'd left it after he'd dealt with the men from Ohio, the boxes of ammunition. Took two trips to get it all to the front seat, two long, painful trips, but he made it. Dumped the ammunition beside the shotgun, wriggled into his jacket, collapsed back into the driver's seat.

Minutes passed. Gruber caught his breath, summoned his strength. Heard a siren over the rush of traffic on the bridge, knew it wasn't a coincidence. They were coming for him. That was fine. So long as Earl suffered first.

He forced himself out of the car again. Grit his teeth and reached in for the shotgun, ignored the throbbing pain in his shoulder, his side, the way the blood blackened his clothes.

There was nothing after Earl. There was only tonight. Gruber would ensure he made the most of it.

< **123** >

Windermere and Wheeler worked the radios as Stevens sped them toward New Albany. They had the local PD en route to Sanderson's apartment, FBI backup coming out from Louisville. Took time to get these things sorted, however, and Gruber had a head start. Windermere figured she'd feel a hell of a lot better once she and Stevens were on scene.

Maybe Gruber's not even looking for his stepfather, she thought. *Maybe he's just trying to disappear.*

She knew this was wishful thinking. Knew the way this case had played out, they were heading for some new kind of violence before Gruber went away.

Any old time, she'd have relished the idea. The prospect of taking out a scumbag like Gruber, putting him down, letting him in on her own personal interpretation of justice. But this time was different.

This time, she was seeing Adrian Miller, R. J. Ramirez, Shelley Clark, and the rest of Gruber's victims. She was seeing Rene Duclair walking the hallways, hurt deep and betrayed. She was seeing Wanda Rose laughing, not giving a shit.

She was playing back all of Ashley Frey's chat logs, all the ways Gruber had preyed on his victims. All the insidious ways he'd turned them to his cause. The sick pleasure he'd derived from his watching.

Give me one more shot, she thought as the Charger devoured road. *Give me just one more shot at this scumbag. I'll make sure he pays for what he did to those kids.*

< **124** >

Earl's building wasn't much better-looking at night.

It was late, after midnight. Most of the windows were dark. There was a lighted doorway at street level, the other end of the building from the bar. A glass door scrawled over with graffiti, a broken buzzer.

Gruber's jacket had plenty of pockets to store ammunition. He emptied the boxes on the passenger seat, loaded up on .44 Magnum cartridges and Black Magic slugs, made sure to bring as many of each as he could carry.

He took the shotgun from the case and loaded it, slung it over his shoulder. Checked the revolver, stuffed it back in his waistband, prayed his wounded arm would hold out long enough that he could steady the bigger gun.

Gruber stepped back from the Lincoln and took off his glasses, cleaned the smudged glass with his grimy T-shirt. Replaced the glasses, shouldered the shotgun again. Slammed the Lincoln's door closed and limped across to the apartment.

The door was locked. The buzzer was broken. No matter. The Magnum rounds would shatter the glass. Gruber leveled the revolver, took aim, was about to fire when a figure appeared on the other side of the door. A man.

He was about Gruber's age, a Cardinals basketball hoodie and a brown, curly mullet. He was halfway out the door before he saw Gruber. Saw the revolver, the shotgun.

He blinked. Stared for a moment. The siren grew louder and the man glanced down the block and then back at Gruber, his thoughts coalescing.

"Oh, *shit*," he said, his hands up. "I didn't see nothing, man, don't worry. I won't tell them shit."

He looked back in through the doorway. Gruber shot him. The revolver kicked, hard, the gunshot echoing around the empty street, bouncing off walls as the man crumpled to the ground. Gruber skirted past him, ducked into the building.

So much for the element of surprise.

< **125** >

It took ten minutes on the deserted highway to get back to the lights of New Albany. Stevens piloted the Charger into the little town, Wheeler leaning forward between the two seats, passing directions.

"We're five minutes out," he told Stevens and Windermere as the Charger screamed toward the base of the bridge. "I snagged some Kevlar from my truck if you want to strap in."

Kevlar. Windermere wondered how much good body armor would do against ordnance designed to kill a black bear. Figured she might as well do the trial run. She let Wheeler pass her a couple of vests, set one aside for Stevens and slipped off her jacket, slid the other vest on herself. Felt her blood pumping, adrenaline and fear, as the Charger sped into the heart of New Albany, the Ohio River to their right, the whole town oblivious to what was about to transpire.

Stevens kept them rolling. Windermere checked her vest. Checked the action on her Glock, checked it again.

Five minutes. Nothing to do but wait.

< **126** >

Earl lived on the third floor. Gruber cursed the bastard for it.

He made the second floor with difficulty, his legs aching, his side burning, his clothing damp with sweat. Paused to catch his breath on the landing, then resumed the climb. Reached the third floor, the top of the building. Opened the fire door and peered down the hallway, listened for movement. Heard nothing, no sirens even. Just the low, maddening throb of the music from the bar, the whole building a subwoofer.

He drew the revolver again. Moved down the hall as quiet as he could, as quick as he dared. It wasn't easy. The shotgun jostled his shoulder. His side howled with every impact. He was out of breath, panting, dizzy from the pain and the exertion. He pressed on, knowing the cops were right outside. Hoped Earl would be somewhere ahead.

A door opened. A woman peered out. Saw Gruber and froze, her eyes wide, her skin gone bleach white. Gruber raised the revolver, fired a shot at her. Relished the way she cried out as the doorframe exploded above her.

She slammed the door closed. Locked it. He walked past, reaching into his pocket for more ammunition. Heard her crying through the door, knew he'd scared her straight. Knew she wouldn't poke her head out again.

The police would be here soon. He had moments to spare. The numbers on the doors counted down, 307, 306. Five units to go. Four. Then Earl. Then the end.

< **127** >

The radio crackled in the Charger. Stevens reached over to the dashboard, turned it up, caught the end of it.

". . . just pulled up to the building and there's a body out front, adult male, probable gunshot wound. The Lincoln's here, too."

"That'll be Gruber," Windermere said. She handed Wheeler the handset. "Make sure those investigating officers have backup. And plenty of firepower."

Wheeler relayed her instructions as Stevens stood on the gas pedal and wheeled the Charger out from behind a slow-moving Honda, steered into the oncoming lane, lights flashing and horn blaring, a blinding wall of headlights ahead.

Windermere braced herself for impact. It didn't come. The Charger swerved back out of danger, raced forward, the Honda wallowing behind.

Stevens let out a kind of laugh, a long ragged breath. Any other time, Windermere would have been impressed by his driving—hell, turned on, even. Right now, she was just wishing he could get them there even faster.

"End of the next block," Wheeler called from the backseat. "Lock and load."

‹ 128 ›

When Stevens pulled the Charger up to the apartment building, there was one cruiser parked out front, its red-and-blues flashing color on the dirty brick wall, a couple of uniforms on the sidewalk.

There was a body on the ground between them. Windermere felt it like a kick. Another poor bastard dead, at Gruber's doing. How many more to come?

"Dead when we got here," the nearest uniform was telling Stevens as they climbed from the Charger. "Whoever your guy is, he's got a hell of a big gun."

"At least two of them, actually," Stevens said. "No sign of him?"

The cop jerked a thumb in through the lobby. "We just got here," he said. "But I imagine he's inside somewhere."

Stevens studied the windows, the apartments above. "Third floor," he said. "That's where he's heading. Get on your bullhorn and tell everyone to stay in their rooms, on their floors, stay out of the halls. This guy is coming in hot."

The uniform hurried back to his cruiser. Stevens turned to Windermere. Gave her a look like *We've done this before.*

"Reinforcements are coming," he said. "What do you think? We lock this place down, get the building surrounded? Let the tactical guys earn their paychecks?"

Windermere knew he was laying out the smart play. They had Gruber contained; they could take their time. Establish a perimeter and sit back and wait. Hell, if he wanted to settle the score with his stepfather, Windermere figured that wasn't any skin off her back. They could both die in that building, easy-peasy.

But it wasn't just Gruber and Earl Sanderson in there. There'd been a woman in Sanderson's apartment the last time they were here. There were other occupants, too, other residents, who could get hurt in the cross fire while Gruber and Sanderson aired out their differences.

Anyway, Windermere wanted to see Gruber again, before it all played out. Wanted to make sure he got his, the right way.

"It's more than just Sanderson in there," she said, checking her Glock, turning to the door, trying to ignore the pain in her wounded arm. "We don't have time to wait."

< 129 >

As Gruber reached Earl's door, he heard voices on the stairs, far behind. Urgent voices, heavy boots, climbing fast. The police.

He wondered if the two cops who'd nearly killed him at the trailer park were here. Were they leading the charge? He felt the revolver in his hand, the shotgun on his shoulder. Felt his wounds aching and wondered if he'd get the chance to return the favor.

No matter. So long as you find Earl. Look him in the eye, just once, and show him what he made you. Show him who you are.

There was sound coming from inside Earl's unit. Cheesy music, a laugh track—the TV blaring. Like whoever was inside didn't know he was coming. Didn't realize there was an angel of death at the door.

Gruber tried the handle. It was locked. He pounded on the door, hard as he could. *"Earl,"* he called through the flimsy material. "I know you're in there, shit stain."

The TV volume diminished. Gruber listened, heard a man's voice, muffled. Angry. Then another voice, higher pitched, urgent. A woman.

Gruber tapped the revolver against the door. "I'm not here to hurt anyone," he called out. "I just want to see Earl. I just want to talk to my stepdad for a minute, okay?"

No answer. No one came to the door. Gruber heard movement, heard—*crying*. The woman was sobbing in there.

"Open up," Gruber said. *"Open up, and I won't shoot you, I swear it."*

Still no response. Gruber felt his frustration mounting. Glanced

316

THE WATCHER IN THE WALL

THE WATCHER IN THE WALL

back down the hall toward the stairway. The cops hadn't arrived yet, but they'd be here soon. He had to get through this door.

The woman was still crying on the other side. No one was letting him in. Time for a new tack. Gruber stepped away from the door. Swung the shotgun around on his shoulder, aimed it at the handle, the lock.

"I'm coming in there," he called out. "Whether you like it or not."

<<<

A mad dash through a trailer park. A high-octane car chase scenario. A standoff at an apartment building, an armed maniac at the top of a couple tall flights of stairs. Stevens was pretty well winded by the time he made the third floor.

Better than the good old days, anyway. Before I met Carla Windermere, I would have passed out from exhaustion back in Shady Acres.

Windermere was waiting for him on the third-floor landing. She looked down at him, impatient, like she was raring to jump into the hall and start shooting. Like she didn't give a damn if she got shot up or not, so long as she took Gruber down.

There was a door at the top of the stairs, heavy steel. A little window, wire-reinforced, a hallway beyond. Gruber at the end of it, holding a shotgun.

"That hallway's a kill zone," Stevens told Windermere. "If we run out there and Gruber comes around with that boomstick, we're both toast. We have to be careful."

But Windermere was already reaching for the door. "I'll take him," she said. "You hang back, give me cover. I'll neutralize him from here."

"With that wing of yours? Not a chance," Stevens said. "Anyway, it's too risky. It's a shooting gallery if he sees you."

"I'm not asking you, partner." Windermere inched the door open. "Hang back. Give me cover. Let me put this asshole to bed."

Stevens opened his mouth to tell her no, he didn't like it, she was too hurt for this cowboy stuff. Didn't get the words out before the world exploded down the hall.

< 130 >

The shotgun was a monster. It roared, kicked, nearly knocked Gruber flat on his ass. Screwed up his aim, too, not that it mattered much. He fired three slugs, point-blank, blew the flimsy door off its hinges.

Somewhere in the apartment, the woman was screaming. No sign of Earl. The door hung ragged and loose; Gruber kicked it aside. Stepped into the doorway just as the cops burst up from the stairwell behind him.

"Freeze, Randall!"

A woman called his name, and a high-powered flashlight searched the wall behind him, then another light. Gruber turned, saw the beams coming at him through the smoke from the shotgun, couldn't see anything past them. Didn't matter. He was here for Earl. He would find him.

He'd made it ten feet into a small living room—an ugly old couch and the TV playing a sitcom, the cops still shouting behind him—when he came across the woman. She was in her fifties or so, rail thin, a bruise under one eye. She stared up at Gruber from behind a flower-print easy chair, shivering, crying.

Gruber's shotgun was empty. He leveled the revolver in her direction. "Where's Earl?" he said.

The woman kept crying. Shook her head, her mouth working, but no sound came out. Gruber took a couple steps toward her. Jammed the barrel of the Smith & Wesson in close.

"I said, *Where the hell is my stepfather?*"

<<<

Windermere aimed her flashlight down the hall, searching for Gruber as the gun smoke dissipated.

Gruber had fired three slugs from the shotgun. Meant he could still swing out from that doorway and lay waste if he wanted. Stevens was right; the hallway was a shooting gallery. Still, she wasn't waiting around.

Haul ass. Save whoever you can.

Windermere dashed down the hall, fast as she could, sticking to the wall, the narrow doorways for cover. Could hear screaming from the doors she was passing, crying, shouting, all kinds of noise, the music from the bar below.

None of it mattered.

Gruber was through that smoke somewhere.

Stevens caught up to her two doors down from Sanderson's. "Careful," he said. "That shotgun's not empty, Carla. And he still has his handgun."

Windermere shook him off. "He won't be aiming that shotgun our way, not while he's still looking for Earl. Might as well gain some ground while we can."

"You'll get yourself killed running cowboy like this. Whatever you're dealing with here, just play it safe, okay?"

Another shot sounded from inside the apartment. Not the boom of the shotgun, something smaller. A strangled sound, and fresh screaming.

"No time for safe, partner," Windermere said as the shooting continued. "Either Gruber gets it, or Sanderson's poor girlfriend does. You going to let me do my job, or what?"

>>>

Gunshots. Loud, close, in rapid succession.

Not the police; they were still in the hall. These shots came from deeper inside the apartment. They blasted big holes in the wall above Gruber's head, sent him ducking down beside the screaming woman, behind the easy chair. She scrambled back, far as she could, wouldn't stop crying. Wouldn't shut up.

The crying. The laugh track from the TV. The cops' voices in the hall and the throb of the bass line from somewhere down below. Chaos.

Gruber peered over the top of the easy chair. Caught movement down a narrow hall. Someone's backside, someone running. Earl. It had to be Earl.

Gruber swung up with the revolver, fired, wild. Missed by a mile. The man turned a corner into a yellow kitchen, disappeared from sight. Gruber pushed himself to his feet, those gunshot wounds like hot pokers. Left the woman behind and started down the dark hall.

He made the kitchen doorway, stopped before the entrance. The apartment was tiny, barely half the size of the old double-wide. A dingy little bathroom at the end of the hall, little more than a toilet and sink. A crummy bedroom opposite the kitchen, a bare mattress on the floor, the covers messed and unkempt. A plastic carrying case for a pistol by the closet, a few scattered boxes of ammunition, American Eagle, .45 caliber.

The woman kept screaming. The cops kept approaching. Around the corner, Earl waited in the kitchen. No time for indecision. No time to waste. Gruber raised the revolver. Ducked low. Peeked around the corner and nearly got his head blown off, the shots coming back about chest level, if he'd been standing.

Gruber hung around just long enough to get a feel for the kitchen—linoleum, old appliances, peeling paint on the cabinetry. Caught a glimpse of Earl's face, too, by the window, his skin weathered and aged, those same hard, piercing eyes. Then Gruber was scrambling back again, self-preservation, his heart a drum machine, his whole body electric.

He crouched in the hall, the Smith & Wesson at the ready, that shotgun dangling from his shoulder, clattering against the wall. Was trying to figure his next move, some way to get to Earl without getting himself shot, when the cops showed up in the apartment's doorway.

Two of them, the man and the woman from the trailer park. Gruber swung around with the shotgun, pulled the trigger twice and fired off his last two slugs, his good shoulder feeling like a horse had kicked it. Couldn't be sure if he hit anything, but the cops disappeared.

They would come back with numbers. No time to waste. Gruber switched back to the revolver. Crawled down to the kitchen doorway, counted in his head, *One, two, three.* Then he was moving again, diving in through the doorway, bracing himself for more gunfire and squeezing off shots, his eyes closed, pointing the Smith & Wesson in Earl's general direction and praying he got Earl before Earl got him.

But Earl didn't get him. Gruber made the far side of the kitchen, the stove. Opened his eyes as the revolver clicked empty, realized he wasn't wearing any new bullet holes. Earl hadn't shot him. And Gruber could see why.

The kitchen was empty. The window was open, and Gruber could see the fire escape railing against the night sky beyond. Could hear Earl's boot steps pounding down the steel grating.

The coward was making a run for it.

< 131 >

BOOM.

Stevens threw himself to the floor as the slug tore a thumb-sized hole in the wall above his head. His flashlight clattered away, the beam making crazy patterns against the carpet, the ceiling, the wall. Stevens rolled away from Sanderson's doorway, ducked for cover, knew the slug would have killed him if he'd spotted Gruber a moment later.

He peered around the wreckage of Sanderson's door. Surveyed the living room, an overturned easy chair, a TV cranked loud, Sanderson's lady friend hunkered down in the corner—scared shitless, Stevens could see, but otherwise unharmed.

Windermere poked her head around, too. "You see him?"

"Down the hall," Stevens said. "Disappeared."

"So what are we waiting for?"

She was through the ruined doorway before Stevens could reply. Before he could tell her to slow down, be careful, watch her ass. Figured Gruber's shotgun was probably spent, couldn't speak for the handgun. Knew it'd be hard to miss a shot in the apartment's crowded confines, regardless of what weapon he chose.

But Windermere was off and running, her flashlight sweeping the living room, the hallway, her Glock following its lead. Stevens followed close behind, staggered himself so one of Gruber's slugs couldn't kill the both of them. Windermere swept through the living room, looked once at the woman in the corner and kept moving, making for the hall to the rest of the apartment. She hit the kitchen doorway and stopped.

Stevens crashed in behind her. "You see the fresh bruises on Sanderson's girlfriend?" Windermere asked him. "Guess old Earl hasn't changed his MO, huh?"

Then she was gone again, blitzing into the kitchen, her pistol raised, her injured arm by her side. Stevens tensed for more shooting, got silence instead. Found Windermere by an open window, peering out into the night.

She looked back at him. "Fire escape," she told him. "Call Wheeler. These boys are on the run."

<　132　>

Earl's boots pounded the stairs below. Gruber pushed himself to keep up.

The music from the bar was gone, replaced by sirens, getting loud and getting closer. Gruber made the second floor, landed hard. Hurried to the railing and spun over, pointed down with the Smith & Wesson, searching for Earl in the gloom.

Earl wore a mustard-yellow jacket. He was easy to find, but he was moving fast. Gruber fired until the revolver clicked empty. Fumbled in his pocket for more bullets, dropped more than he loaded. No matter. If he could catch up to Earl, he would only need one.

He kept going. Heard the cops above him, loud voices, radio chatter. More boots, these ones coming down toward him. Coming *for* him. He kept going.

There was a ladder between the second floor and the street. Gruber backed down it, quick as he could. Descended to the bottom and dropped to the ground, found himself in the alley, a dumpster, a couple parked cars. The police coming at him from above.

Earl was still running, out the far end of the alley, his mustard coat betraying him as he ran toward the bridge. Gruber could hear the rush of cars headed into Louisville, a train's horn. The sirens and the shouting and the pounding of his heart, his own urgent gasping for breath.

He hurried down the end of the alley. Pulled shotgun slugs from his pocket and tried to reload as he walked. Had two in, was working on the third when another cop rounded the corner in front of him, a man, mostly in shadows. He saw Gruber and reached for his pistol. Gruber brought up the shotgun and fired.

The cop took the slug in the midsection. Flew backward, doubled over, hit the ground hard. Gruber didn't slow down to admire the shot. He stepped over the cop and out of the alley. Found Earl running parallel to the bridge, down a wide, empty street, the train tracks and the low, grassy rise of the flood wall ahead of him.

Earl disappeared into shadow. His boot steps resonated. Gruber ignored the pain in his shoulder, his side. Gave chase.

<<<

The alley lit up. Another *boom* from the shotgun. Windermere peered over the side of the fire escape, caught nothing but silhouettes and darkness. Prayed Gruber had missed whoever he'd been shooting at—except Sanderson, *maybe*.

She hit the fire escape ladder. Dropped awkward, dropped hard, her cut arm bitching as she hit pavement. She ignored the pain. Looked up the alley in the direction of Gruber's boomstick, saw a dark mass at the entrance that could have been a body, booked it in that direction. Kicked brass as she walked, magnum cartridges, unspent—Gruber in a hurry to reload.

Stevens hit the ground behind her, puffing and wheezing. Somewhere in the distance more cops were arriving; she heard Stevens on the radio, calling in updates, hoped Wheeler was still out front to provide directions. Then she made the end of the alley, the dark mass on the ground. It was Wheeler, a shotgun slug through his belly.

325

Wheeler was ashen. He was holding the wound, teeth clenched, sweat on his forehead, blood everywhere else. Lots of blood. He saw her coming, tried to roll over, sit up, keep going. Gave that up pretty quickly, settled for nodding toward the bridge with his chin.

"Gruber got me," he said. Tried to laugh. "I guess that's obvious. He disappeared after Sanderson, over that way."

Windermere followed his gaze. A short stub-end street parallel to the bridge, train tracks at the end and a grassy hill beyond. She picked out both men, shadows on the move. Then she heard Stevens coming up behind her. Looked back down at Wheeler, gauging his chances.

"I'm going after Gruber," she told her partner. "I think Wheeler can make it, but he needs attention, fast. We leave him here alone, he dies here alone."

Stevens searched her face, got the gist pretty quick. "I can't just let you run off," he said. "They're both armed, Carla. You're hurt."

"You can and you will," she replied. "Call me some backup, and save Wheeler's life. We'll compare notes in an hour or so."

He started to complain. She was gone before he could get the words out.

< **133** >

Traffic roared, loud, over the Sherman Minton Bridge. Interstate cars and trucks into Louisville, eighteen-wheelers headed north, machine-gun engine brakes, rapid-fire, as they came down the grade.

Gruber chased Earl down toward the train tracks, the flood wall, the town opening up to empty lots and railroad outbuildings, no light but the moon and the streetlights on the bridge. A train was coming, long and slow, horn blaring. Gruber could see the headlights in the distance, feel the ground rumbling.

Earl was running, fifty yards ahead, aiming for the train tracks and beyond. Gruber stopped and took aim, middle of the road, fired and missed.

"I just want to talk to you," Gruber called. *"Just slow down for a minute and we can talk this thing through."*

Earl's response was a couple shots of his own, tossed over his shoulder and dangerous to nobody. He kept running—tottering, more like, an old man, decades of hard living catching up to him at the worst possible time. Still, he had distance. Was almost to the tracks. If that train rolled through before Gruber followed him across, the old man would get away clean.

And Gruber would die full of police bullet holes. No way. Not acceptable.

"I'm right behind you," Gruber called out. *"Catching up on you fast. You can't run forever."*

Earl looked like he aimed to try. He reached the end of the road, hit the train tracks. Stumbled up the roadbed, and Gruber slowed, timed his stepfather's climb. Fixed the Smith & Wesson at a point above the rails, knew Earl would be high and exposed when he reached the top of the ballast.

But his stepfather tripped as Gruber pulled the trigger. Fell into the rails, hands outstretched, and Gruber's shot missed high. He waited, aimed again, drew a bead on Earl's back. Earl caught his balance. Pulled himself to his feet. Gruber steadied the gun, exhaled, pulled the trigger.

Click.

The revolver was empty again. Earl disappeared down the other side of the roadbed. Gruber muttered a curse, hurried forward. The train was fifty yards away. Earl was on the other side. Gruber would make it, too. The cops wouldn't.

He would have Earl to himself, at last.

< 134 >

Windermere watched the train appear and urged her legs to move faster. Heard the horn blare as Gruber climbed to the top of the tracks, lit bright in the powerful headlights. Raised her Glock and aimed at him, thought about taking the shot.

Best of times, she'd have liked her chances at this distance. The guy was literally in a spotlight. He wasn't moving fast. She could have slowed, pulled up in a Weaver stance, leveled and fired. Put him down with one shot, let the train grind him to mincemeat.

Best of times, she'd have done it. But this was nowhere near the best. Her left arm was killing her, spasms of pain with every step. It would be exactly useless when it came to precision firing. She would have to slow to fire at him. She would probably miss. The train would roll through, a hundred cars long, and by the time she worked around it, Gruber would be gone.

Windermere didn't shoot. She let Gruber disappear down the other side of the embankment. She reached the end of the little street and crossed the dirt to the roadbed, didn't bother looking for the train at the top because she knew it was there, closing in, almost on top of her. Could feel the big locomotive like an earthquake, the headlight bright and blinding in her peripheral vision. She scrambled, the ballast rock giving way beneath her, her shoes scrabbling, getting nowhere, a quicksand nightmare scenario.

The train was upon her. Windermere was still climbing. Knew she was narrowing her options to a make or break, do or die. Knew if she hit the tracks a split second too slow, she was dead.

She climbed. Couldn't talk herself out of it. Knew she'd rather die than let Gruber get away, knew she couldn't live knowing she hadn't done everything in her power to bring him down.

The train was close, so close she could *feel* it, horn blaring, brakes squealing, the ground trembling like Armageddon. She reached the top of the roadbed. Heard someone shouting from the cab of the locomotive, ignored it. Dove across the tracks and practically took flight, the embankment dropping away beneath her, the train a wall of steel at her heels.

She had a moment to register what she'd done. Realize she'd made it, she was still alive. No time to celebrate, though; she was airborne. She braced herself, knew the impact would *destroy* her wounded arm. Landed on rock and it was worse than she'd imagined, hot fiery streaks of pain bursting up that arm, her hands scraped up and torn, something bashing her chin, knocking her head back, a concussion scenario.

She still had her Glock. And the train hadn't hit her. It was moving behind her, freight cars now, their brakes squealing. It would have to stop, she knew. Someone would call it in. But it would take time to back the train up, time she didn't want to waste.

With her good arm, Windermere pushed herself to her knees. Touched her lip, spat blood. Wiped rock fragments from her chin, the palms of her hands, her knees. She was on the other side, the bridge and the gentle rise of the flood wall, the river somewhere beyond.

She could see Gruber in the light from the bridge, climbing the grass. He was almost at the top. She raised her pistol again, her aim shaky, uneven. Knew she wouldn't make the shot, figured she'd rather he not know she was behind him.

She staggered to her feet. Started to the flood wall, the slick grass, started climbing.

< **135** >

All the night seemed to calm. Seemed to distill to just Earl. The cops, the noise, the light: it all faded into the background, and it was just Earl and Gruber, the flood wall and the bridge and the river beyond.

Earl was working his way down the river side of the wall. Gruber hit the summit, crested it, started after him. The grass was slick, muddy, a tricky descent. Gruber slipped, felt something tear, the wound in his side a lightning rod to a jagged, electric pain.

He regained his balance. Jogged down the hill as quick as he could, zagging, stumbling, watching Earl, watching the ground, trying to stay upright.

Then Earl fell.

He was almost at the bottom, a roadway and a little scenic rest area, a couple of benches and a copse of trees and the water. He'd nearly made pavement, solid ground, a chance to make up some distance. Then his legs gave out from under him, planted him flat on his ass, hard, a buffoon on a banana peel. His .45 clattered to the pavement. He tried to get up, failed, groaned and grabbed for his back.

You got old, asshole, Gruber thought, descending toward him. *Time caught up, and now you're fucked.*

He reached the bottom of the flood wall. The grass leveled out, ran about fifteen feet to the road. Earl was still down. Gruber ignored him. Crossed to the pavement, to Earl's .45. Picked it up, tucked it in his waistband. Turned back toward Earl, reaching in his pocket for fresh cartridges for the Smith & Wesson.

Earl was watching him, those hard eyes. Wasn't trying to escape, just watching Gruber approach. He wasn't armed anymore, but that didn't make him any less formidable. He'd aged plenty, too, but that didn't matter, either. He was still the man who'd brought Gruber to the double-wide, still the one who'd subjected him to his own brand of hell. Those eyes, the anger inside that raged like fire, that was still Earl. The contemptuous curl of his upper lip, that was Earl, too.

He took in Gruber's revolver, the shotgun swinging from his shoulder. Didn't seem afraid. Didn't seem to think the weapons hurt his chances any. Didn't seem to care that he was flat on his ass, at his stepson's mercy, the police still aeons away.

This was now. This was happening. Gruber had waited twenty years for this. He swung the shotgun around, pointed it at Earl's belly, one slug left loaded, one all he would need. But Earl just laughed.

"You want me to show you how to use that thing, peckerwood?" Earl said. "I'm not my daughter, mind. You can't just watch."

Gruber leveled the shotgun, was about to tell Earl it didn't matter, easy or hard, he'd be going regardless, when something caught his attention off to his peripheral. Movement up the flood wall, someone at the top, a woman, lit in silhouette by the light from the bridge.

The lady cop, the black woman he'd stabbed. The bitch just wouldn't take a hint.

Gruber spun with the shotgun, aimed it up the hill, pulled the trigger. The shotgun roared load. The woman disappeared. Gruber didn't have time to see where she'd gone, though, because a moment later, Earl was on him.

< **136** >

Windermere ducked the shot. Heard it *thud* into the grass a few feet away from her, not close enough to matter. The bastard was a terrible shot; that was a plus. He was a maniac, though, and still heavily armed. His poor shooting was cold comfort.

She looked up and saw Earl Sanderson take a leap at his stepson, catch him by surprise, send Gruber sprawling backward onto the road. Heard the shotgun hit the pavement, watched it skid away. One gun down. At least one more to go.

She scrambled down the hill as the men fought in shadow. Struggled for grip, her shoes slipping and sliding everywhere, the damn grass like a ski hill and Windermere without skis. The men kept fighting, didn't see her coming at them, and she toyed with the idea of shooting them both, right there, doing the world a big favor.

Thought better of it. There'd be paperwork. And besides, she was coming in too fast on the slippery grass. No way to get a clean shot; better the sneak approach.

She closed the distance. Kept her Glock level, kept her footing. The men were fighting like bears, rolling around on the ground, and she wondered how the hell she was supposed to separate them long enough to arrest the both of them.

Guess you're going to find out, she thought as the ground leveled out beneath her. *Guess you're going to find out real soon.*

>>>

Earl had been a strong man, twenty years back. He'd been able to kick the shit out of Gruber pretty easily, hardly ever broke a sweat doing it.

That was then.

As the older man tackled him, Gruber fell back, caught off guard by the force of the attack. Hit the ground hard, roadway grit digging into his back, his arms, his shoulder screaming, his side. Earl got in a few shots, climbed on top of Gruber. Rained punches down, hit him hard, like the old days.

Twenty years ago, he would have held the advantage. But things had changed.

Earl tired easy. His punches lacked weight. Gruber took a few, four or five, and then he reacted. Shoved Earl backward, freed his good arm. Ignored the pain in the rest of his body and focused on Earl's eyes, those hard, fiery eyes.

Focused on his left eye, in particular. Focused on clawing it from its socket.

Earl screamed. Drew back a shade, stopped with the punching. Gave Gruber enough ground that he could reach the revolver, scramble backward a little. Earl watched with his good eye. Laughed again from the ground. "You don't have the balls, shit stain."

Gruber laughed back. Pulled the trigger. Watched Earl spin backward and down.

Then the lady cop was there.

<<<

Windermere was nearly on them when Gruber shot his stepfather. The revolver roared, and Earl Sanderson torqued away, and then Gruber saw her. He spun, pulled the trigger too early. Missed by two feet, and then Windermere shot him.

Gruber fell back. Landed beside his stepfather. Windermere kept the Glock on him. Closed the distance. Heard sirens coming, lights in the distance down the narrow road.

Shit, she thought, looking down at Gruber and Sanderson, both of them shot, both of them still breathing. *I guess that's that, then.*

<<<

Gruber stared up at the cop. Barely felt the shot, just knew that it had knocked him on his ass. Felt Earl beside him, heard him breathing hard, wheezing, a sucking wound from his chest.

Gruber inched his way toward him. Reached for Earl's pistol where he'd stuck it in his waistband. The cop had her own piece trained on him, wasn't about to blink. Had a fire in her eyes like someone who'd been wronged, who'd been counting on a chance to be standing here.

"I don't want to hurt you," Gruber told her. "I don't care if I die. Just let me have this asshole, please. Let me kill him."

>>>

Windermere saw the way Gruber was fumbling behind his back. Knew there had to be another weapon back there, the way he was maneuvering.

Beside him, Sanderson's eyes were wide, watching her, pleading with her. He looked small and withered. He looked mostly pathetic. Windermere thought about the woman they'd found in his apartment, the bruise on her face. Figured the world wouldn't miss the degenerate prick.

"Please," Gruber told her. *"I've been waiting so long for this."*

Windermere knew the backup would be here soon, knew Sanderson would probably die anyway. Knew Gruber'd been aching for this; hell, he probably deserved it, the things Sanderson had put him through.

But she wasn't in the business of granting wishes to maniacs. And Gruber had done enough harm in the world already.

She shook her head. "I don't think so. Get your hands where I can see them. Whatever you're playing with back there, let it go."

Gruber didn't show his hands, though. And Windermere could see what he was thinking. Watched his eyes watch hers, calculating, like the kid raiding the cookie jar. She watched his body tense, knew he wasn't about to just give up the game.

And he didn't.

Windermere watched him reach back for the pistol, the last of his strength, that doughy face, those maniac eyes. Steadied her Glock and pulled the trigger, caught him in the chest, or maybe it was the shoulder, and his body went limp and his arm came back empty.

Game over.

Windermere shot him again anyway. She thought about Adrian Miller and pulled the trigger another time, watched his eyes go wide, and kept shooting, seeing Madison Mackenzie and Dylan Price, seeing R. J. Ramirez and Shelley Clark, Adam DeLong and the rest of Gruber's victims. Seeing Rene Duclair. She kept shooting until the Glock clicked empty, until Gruber lay back and she knew he was dead, until his breathing went still and his eyes went dark and lifeless, and Stevens and the New Albany cops were there pulling her from him, dragging her away from his body.

< 137 >

It was dawn when word filtered through the hospital, the doctors and the nurses and the law enforcement circus gathered outside: Agent Wheeler would survive the night.

Earl Sanderson wouldn't. And neither would Randall Gruber.

"Guess you shot him enough," Stevens said, handing Windermere a paper cup of coffee and easing into a plastic seat beside her in the lobby. "Said he was pretty well Swiss cheese by the time they got him into the operating room. Of course, they weren't exactly hauling ass."

Windermere held the coffee with her good hand, sipped it and stared at the floor. It was bad coffee, late-night hospital coffee. She drank it anyway.

She could feel the eyes on her, the Louisville city cops, Wheeler and the rest of the FBI guys. The hospital staff. They all knew she'd done it, emptied her clip into Gruber. Shot him in cold blood. Lost control.

"Not that anyone's blaming you for doing what you did," Stevens said. "The guy was a maniac, Carla. Everybody here has your back."

Windermere still didn't look up. Wondered what would have been better, Gruber dead, or him rotting his life away in some prison somewhere. Which would have been a more suitable punishment for the man who'd lured ten teenagers to their deaths?

She couldn't decide. She was in no mood to think about it. Honestly, she was in no shape to think, period, at this point. Exhausted.

But she could feel the eyes on her. Hear the whispers. Knew she should have stopped shooting Gruber when he dropped the pistol. Knew she should have listened to Stevens in the apartment, hung back and waited for tactical support, played it safe. Knew it was a sign of something irrational, something troubling, that she hadn't. That she'd been blinded by personal psychopathology, her hatred of Gruber and what he stood for. She knew she should feel ashamed.

She'd been taught to use sufficient force to neutralize a threat, no more. She'd given into her anger, an anger she didn't really want to think about. She'd never cared so much about the victims before. Not so much that she'd risk her career for them.

She drained her coffee. Grimaced. "So he's dead, Stevens. So what? Madison Mackenzie's still alive. Dylan Price is still alive."

Stevens met her eyes. "Wheeler's still alive, too."

"Yeah." Windermere stood. Started through the lobby toward the front doors, avoiding the stares from the cops and the hospital workers, the assorted looky-loos, wanting fresh air and maybe to bum a cigarette. "Exactly," she said. *"Exactly."*

< 138 >

Madison Mackenzie could feel the stares as soon as she walked onto school property. Kids stopped talking, stopped texting, stopped everything they were doing, just so they could watch her walk past them. Just so they could tell each other their story.

Girl meets boy on the Internet. Boy is a middle-aged predator. Girl falls for it hook, line, and sinker.

Girl must be a functioning retard.

She didn't even know what she was doing back here. She'd spent a couple days in the hospital in Louisville, trying to plan the rest of her life. Trying to decide what she was going to do with herself now that Brandon had turned out to be a big bust, and her face was in the newspaper, and there was that whole Amber Alert for her, and everyone in Tampa knew her name and how stupid she was.

She'd counted on Brandon to take her away from this mess. She'd pretty much fallen in love. And it was fake, all of it. What was she supposed to do now?

Madison didn't care. She just didn't want to go back to high school.

There would be teachers, the principal, guidance counselors, all of them watching her, asking questions. All of them concerned.

Really, though, it was the kids who were going to be the problem.

They cleared a path for her as she walked through the front doors and down the hall toward her locker. Madison could hear them whispering.

There she goes.

That's the girl who fell for that Internet weirdo.

That's Rudolph.

What a loser.

And at the end of the hall, like a pack of freaking hyenas, Lena Jane Poole and her little posse. They were watching her approach. Nudging one another. Whispering. Texting their friends.

Lena Jane's smile got wider the closer Madison came. She could already hear the punch line, some bullshit cutting remark that would have the whole school in stitches. She could already feel her face going flush, hot tears in her eyes, nothing to do but keep walking and pretend to ignore it, pretend the whole freaking school wasn't laughing.

Madison couldn't do it. She bailed before she reached her locker. Veered off down another hallway, blinking back those tears. Pushed her way through a crowd to the nearest doorway, crying for real now, heard people laughing in her wake.

She had to get out of here.

She pushed open the door and burst out into daylight. Took a couple deep breaths, and kept going. She was at the far side of the school, facing the football field. She could cut underneath the bleachers and out the other side, jump the fence and disappear. Hitch to the bus station, the train tracks or something. Hop a freight and ride it somewhere far away. Anywhere would be better than here.

She was halfway to the bleachers when someone called out behind her. *"Madison."*

Madison stopped. Recognized the voice, and considered ignoring it, knew Paul wouldn't let her go until she'd at least talked to him.

She wiped the tears from her face, best she could, and turned around. Saw him standing behind her, twenty feet away, that old cocky grin on his face.

Awesome. This is the last thing in the world I need right now.

She scowled at him. "If you're here to brag about how you saved my life, you can shove it," she told him. "And I *definitely* don't need to hear how you were right all along."

Paul had his hands in his pockets. Studied her, and she knew he could see where her tears had smeared her makeup. "I'm not here to brag."

"Bull. You've probably been waiting for this moment since you heard I got saved."

Paul took a couple steps toward her, slow, like she was a wild animal or something. "I heard they caught the guy. In, like, Louisville or something. I heard there was some big crazy shootout."

Madison hesitated. Then she nodded. "The FBI killed him." She remembered the two agents, the younger black woman and the older man.

"He sounded like a real freak," Paul said. "Like he was seriously off his meds or something. Totally insane."

"Yeah, and I fell for it," Madison said. "How freaking dumb do you have to be?"

"You helped the FBI stop this guy. Think about how many other kids he could have killed. You're pretty much a hero."

Madison scoffed. "Some hero."

"You are, you know."

"Yeah, *and*? What's the point? I went through all that crazy shit, nearly died, embarrassed the hell out of myself, and, wow, look at me, I'm right back here where I started."

"Better than being dead."

"You sure? Everyone hates me here. I have no freaking friends in the entire state."

"You have one friend," Paul said.

Madison glared at him. "You're just saying that because you want in my pants."

Paul held up his hands. "I'd settle for you not being dead. Rhodes's history class is a mausoleum without you."

Madison didn't say anything. She wished Paul would go away and leave her alone, and at the same time, she didn't.

"You called the police on me," she said. "You promised you wouldn't do it, but you told them where I went."

"They put out an Amber Alert for you," Paul said. "Nobody knew where you were. If I didn't speak up, that freak would have murdered you. And he'd probably still be on the loose."

"Still," Madison said.

"I had to make sure you stayed alive. You owe me a hundred and seventy-five bucks."

"Yeah, good luck with that. I don't think anyone's going to let me out of their sight long enough for me to change my clothing, much less let me get a job."

The bell rang. Resonated through the school yard.

"First period," Paul said. "I take it from your sudden and dramatic exit that you're thinking about skipping out."

"Not thinking about it, *doing* it. I was right in the middle of it when you interrupted."

"So where are you going?"

Madison looked across the football field. The city skyline in the distance. She didn't have enough money for another bus ticket. And who was she kidding? She wasn't going to be hopping any freight trains.

"I don't know," she said. She thought about turning around, walking back inside, into math class, showing her face as everyone stared. Felt fresh tears well up in her eyes, sniffed and turned away. "I just don't want to be here, is all."

Paul didn't say anything. She waited. Wondered if he was rethinking the whole following-her thing. If he'd turned and left her and gone back to class.

She turned around halfway—nope, Paul was still there. He wasn't smiling, not that cocky smile. "So let's not be here," he said. "Let's go somewhere else for a while."

She frowned. "Like where, exactly?"

"Dunno. There's a diner on Broad Street that does a pretty good breakfast. You ever had chicken and waffles?"

She shook her head.

"You hungry?"

"I mean," she said. "I guess so."

"So let's go. We can plan your great escape while we're eating."

He started across the school yard toward the football field, stopped and looked back at her. The cocky grin was still gone. And he was a heck of a lot cuter, she decided, without it.

"You're just doing this because you want to get laid," she said, walking to catch up.

"Nah. I just want my money back."

She punched him. He laughed. They kept walking, skirted the football field and left the school behind, the judgment, the staring, all that *Rudolph* crap.

Maybe I won't run away again, Madison thought. *Maybe not yet.*

< 139 >

"So you killed him."

Harris tented his fingers and leaned back in his chair, studied Windermere across his desk.

Windermere nodded. "Yes, sir," she said. Beside her, Stevens said nothing.

"Shot him eight times, the report said," Harris continued. "In the process of disarming him and attempting to save the life of one Earl Sanderson."

"Yes, sir," Windermere said.

A week had passed since Randall Gruber had died in that Louisville hospital. Since Stevens and Windermere had saved Louisville agent Bill

Wheeler, while failing to save Earl Sanderson, plus a neighbor from Sanderson's building, plus Curtis Donovan and an Indiana state trooper.

Plus Adrian Miller and the rest of Gruber's victims.

Stevens and Windermere had spent the week mired in paperwork, checking in on Wheeler in their free time, on Laura Dwyer, the woman in Sanderson's apartment. Dwyer didn't have much to say about Earl Sanderson. She didn't exactly seem overjoyed he was gone.

"Yeah, he was a bastard," she told Windermere. "He was a mean, rowdy old prick, and sometimes he got rough. But he paid his half of the rent, didn't he?"

She'd refused treatment for the bruise under her eye, told them all she wanted was to be left alone. Stevens and Windermere gave her space. Watched her walk out of the FBI office after giving her statement, and that was the last they saw of Laura Dwyer.

They ducked in on Rosemary McCarthy, too, Randall Gruber's old doctor. Figured she might as well hear from them how Gruber's life had played out. The doctor had listened, her face more sad than surprised, turned to stare out her window when they'd finished the story.

"Randall was just a boy when I treated him," she said. "He was traumatized, severely, but there was still a child inside. To the last day I saw him, I imagined there was something I could do to help him work through what had been done to him, what he'd done. I'd hoped there was a way he could, well, survive it."

Stevens and Windermere said nothing. There was nothing to say, no good response. Randall Gruber hadn't survived what he'd endured in that trailer. He might have done, Windermere knew, but she'd killed him, in cold blood. And she still wasn't sure how she felt about it.

. . .

"Every officer's report I've read says that the killing was justified, Agent Windermere," Harris said. "Says Randall Gruber would have shot you and escaped if you hadn't put him down. Is that true?"

He regarded her over the desk. Windermere hesitated. Knew the Louisville PD officers had sided with her in their reports. Knew Stevens had probably done the same. Knew it wouldn't matter a lick to anybody in the whole damn world that she'd gone overboard on Randall Gruber, let her feelings get the better of her. Knew Harris would be glad to sweep the whole thing aside, move on to another case.

But Windermere knew she didn't feel the same way.

She looked Harris in the eye. Let out her breath. "No, sir, those reports aren't true. I appreciate that my colleagues were trying to cover for me, but I didn't have to kill Randall Gruber. I shouldn't have done it."

"You're saying that you didn't need to use deadly force," Harris said. "That you could have subdued Gruber without him risking the lives of any other innocent bystanders."

"I let my personal feelings cloud my judgment, sir," Windermere told the SAC. "He was disarmed and immobilized, and I could have let up on him without endangering anyone, but I didn't."

She glanced at Stevens. Then back at Harris. "I lost control. I let my own feelings take over when I should have been impartial."

Harris didn't say anything. Pursed his lips and studied her across the desk. Flipped through the case file.

Finally, he sighed.

"This case would have been a whole lot more complicated if Gruber had lived," he said. "Teenagers or no, what Gruber was doing on those forums was still arguably protected by his First Amendment rights. We initiated our investigation on legally questionable ground, Agent Windermere. You could have brought him in from underneath that bridge, locked him up and put him on trial, and seen your whole case shot to pieces by some defense attorney with a bug up his ass."

"But I didn't," Windermere said. "I killed him without giving him the benefit of a trial. I overstepped my bounds as an FBI agent, sir. I—"

Harris held up his hand. "We both know what Gruber was doing was wrong, Carla," he said. "It was sick and it was twisted, and it goes against the spirit of every law on the books. Nobody in the world is going to fault you for what you did."

Windermere started to argue. Started to tell Harris how it didn't matter what Gruber did, that it mattered what *she'd* done, that she'd blacked out and emptied her clip into a bad guy instead of acting how she'd been trained.

But Harris cut her off.

"I'm not going to discipline you for what you did down there, Agent Windermere," he said. "You want some time off to talk to a shrink about what happened, that's fine by me. But you know and I know that that maniac had it coming. I'm not about to lose sleep over the fact that my best agent got a little overzealous on a man who'd just finished a killing spree."

Windermere said nothing. Knew there was nothing she could say that would sway her boss. What was she going to do, beg him to suspend her? She kept her mouth shut.

"Far as I'm concerned," Harris said, closing the case file and standing, "this case is closed. Good work to you both. Take a couple days off and then bring me another one."

Harris shook Stevens's hand. Nodded to Windermere. She hesitated another moment, her legs unsteady, feeling like she was walking through quicksand. She'd wondered how this meeting would go. Agonized. Knew she had to pay some kind of penance for what she'd done.

She hadn't expected Harris to brush off her concerns so readily. But he had. And that was pretty much that.

"Yes, sir," she said, turning and following Stevens to the door. "Thank you, sir."

< 140 >

Windermere walked back through CID to her own office. Felt Stevens beside her, but said nothing. Her partner said nothing, either.

Mathers was waiting at the door. Windermere ignored him, too. Unlocked the door and walked in, sat behind her desk, looked around, opened her filing cabinet and started to organize the case's paperwork, just for something to do. Knew both men were watching her, didn't want to meet their eyes. Figured she'd kill some time for a bit, duck out early. Grab a six-pack of beer and hide out somewhere and think for a while. Maybe pick up a carton of smokes, too.

Stevens sat down at his desk. Mathers hung around in the doorway, leaning against the wall. Watching her. She ignored both of them until she couldn't anymore.

"What?" she said. "What are you staring at?"

Mathers cleared his throat. "We're just worried, Carla," he said. "We want to know you're okay."

Like a goddamn intervention. Windermere gathered a stack of paper from her desktop and swiveled in her chair to file it away, her arm aching through the bandages where Gruber had slashed her. "I'm fine, Derek," she said. "Fine as I'm going to be, I guess."

"You know Harris was right," Stevens said. "There's no need to feel ashamed of what you did back there, Carla. That bastard had it coming a hundred times over."

"Yeah, but what if he didn't?" Windermere said. "What happens the next time, when it's not so cut-and-dried? What if I lose it on a guy who's just *probably* guilty?" She shook her head. "Heck, in the eyes of the law, Gruber wasn't even a criminal before we came along."

"He killed four people with his own two hands," Stevens replied. "He was a criminal, all right."

Windermere kept her head in her filing cabinet. Avoided his eyes, Mathers's, too. "Anyway, it's not about him," she said. "It's about me. I'm an FBI agent. I'm not supposed to be losing my cool like that. I'm sure not supposed to be emptying my clip into defenseless people, even if they are criminals."

Stevens didn't say anything. Neither did Mathers. They waited until she'd shuffled around enough paper to fill a Russian novel, waited until she'd run out of things to do and had to look up again.

"So, okay," Mathers said. "What are you going to do?"

Windermere exhaled. Tried to set her jaw, fake being hard, determined, confident. Knew she couldn't do it, knew she shouldn't even

349

try. Knew she should talk about her situation, about Wanda and Rene, about the way she heard their voices and hated herself every time she looked in the mirror.

She felt tired. She felt really damn tired.

"I just need to be alone," she said.

< 141 >

They left her alone.

Took some convincing, some raised voices, some threats. Took Windermere getting angry, pushing both men away. Finally, they left her. Mathers retreated to his cubicle, tossed a meaningful look and a raised eyebrow over his shoulder at Stevens as he left. Stevens backed away, too, to his desk on the other side of the room. Spent his time staring at his computer screen, clicking buttons, though she could feel his eyes on her whenever she looked away.

Just leave me alone, she thought. *Just let me handle this myself; is that really so hard?*

She knew this was wrong. She knew she was crazy for pushing them away, knew she'd never climb out of this funk on her own.

But she didn't know how to talk to them. Couldn't find the words without sounding like a victim, so she bolted. Shut down her computer and locked up her files, grabbed her coat and walked out of the office without a word to Stevens, cut behind Mathers's desk so he wouldn't see her. Hit the stairs and took them fast, figuring Stevens and Mathers would probably chase her, hurried through the security checkpoints in the lobby and out to her daddy's Chevelle.

She climbed inside. Turned the key in the ignition and fired up the big 396 and listened to the engine rumble and considered the possibilities. *Take a couple of days,* Harris had said. Well, she could do that. She could drive off somewhere, some small town with a motel and a bar and a liquor store, disappear and be self-destructive by herself for a while.

She put the car in gear. Backed out of her stall and revved and roared out of the lot. Caught Stevens and Mathers coming out through the front doors, scratching their heads, watching her go. Felt a perverse sense of satisfaction at how helpless they looked, how lost.

So long, boys. Supercop's gotta go.

She drove. Aimless, at first. Took the interstate southbound, I-94 down through Minneapolis, then I-35, a straight shot, until the city faded away to flat fields and farmland, the occasional lake. She'd lived here nearly four years, a transplant from Miami, still hadn't spent much time outside the Twin Cities. She was doing it now, though, driving, her foot heavy on the gas pedal, the sun arcing down toward the western horizon.

Her phone wouldn't stop blowing up, the first hour or so. Stevens and Mathers both, then Drew Harris, too. Voicemails and texts, everybody concerned. Windermere ignored them. Relished the silence every time the phone stopped buzzing. Figured, sooner or later, it would stop buzzing for good.

She was thinking she could make Memphis by morning. Eight hundred miles, give or take, down through Cedar Rapids, Iowa City,

Missouri. She'd reach St. Louis in the middle of the night, find a truck stop for gas and coffee, keep driving. Hit Memphis by breakfast, Southaven soon after.

She could find Wanda Rose, she knew that. The girl had married a dentist, probably stuck pretty close to home. She could dig up Wanda's address, pay her a visit. Catch up on old times, reminisce. They could talk about Rene, about how shitty Wanda'd been, back in the day. Windermere was pretty sure she could think up a couple ways to get Wanda to finally apologize, wipe the slate clean. Figured she could convince Wanda to regret what she'd done.

She hit the state line after about a hundred miles, figured she would drive until the sun had fully set before she grabbed a little dinner. Hell, another couple hours and she'd hit Des Moines. Find a cigarette machine, something cold to drink, something strong, something to keep her warm on the long drive ahead.

I'm a decorated FBI hero, she thought. *They want to arrest me for having a couple beers with my meal, they can damn well try.*

She was a half hour from Des Moines when the plan started to go stale. It wasn't the finding Wanda that bothered Windermere, it was the issue of why the hell bother? Even if Wanda broke down in her driveway, copped to a lifetime of guilt over what happened to Rene, it still wasn't going to bring the girl back. Wouldn't ease Windermere's conscience, either, for that matter. Wouldn't wipe the memory of Rene's hurt from her own mind.

Wanda was the ringleader. She deserves to be punished. You'd never have turned on Rene if it wasn't for her.

But that was pretty well bullshit. There was no justice waiting in Memphis, not for Rene Duclair. Not for Carla Windermere.

You can still go there. Visit Rene's grave. Find a motel and a six-pack and vanish for a while. Take some vacation time; get stinking drunk. Figure your shit out and come home.

Windermere knew she could run. Knew it would be easy. She could turn off her phone and keep driving, to Memphis, Miami, hell, all the way to Mexico. She had money saved up; she could disappear if she wanted. Try and forget Rene Duclair, try and forget Randall Gruber.

Try and forget Carla Windermere.

The highway was full dark, a steady stream of headlights in the oncoming lanes, red taillights up ahead. Windermere drummed on the steering wheel, stared straight ahead through the windshield. Tried to ignore the holes in her strategy, keep going. Keep running. Go the hell away.

But she would never be free of herself, she knew, no matter how far she ran. The scenery might change, but she would always wake up to the same face in the mirror, the same relentless voices spewing hate in her brain.

You're worthless.

Not good enough.

They'll never forgive you, once they know who you really are.

The answer wasn't in Memphis, no matter how tempted Windermere felt to run. It wasn't in Miami or Mexico, either.

She passed a road sign for Des Moines, fifteen miles distant. Felt something inside her break down, a dam burst, felt suddenly lost and adrift, a compass with no needle. She knew she wouldn't keep driving; knew she had to go home. Knew the only way she'd ever clear her head was by turning around.

She slowed the Chevelle, pulled off at the next off-ramp, pulled over.

Picked up her phone and dialed Stevens's number. Canceled out before the call went through, called Mathers instead. He answered on the first ring. "Carla," he said. "Holy crap, where are you? We're all worried sick."

"I'm in Iowa," she told him. "Just outside Des Moines."

He made to say something. Windermere cut him off.

"Listen, I'm sorry," she told him. "I'm coming home." She ended the call and turned the car around. Wondered if Mathers would be up when she got back to town, knew he would be. Knew she had some explaining to do.

ACKNOWLEDGMENTS

The Watcher in the Wall is inspired very loosely by real-life incidents, but it's also a fairly personal book for me. I've dealt with depression and suicidal thoughts since I was a teenager, and it's only now, two decades later, that I've started taking real steps to deal with it. In some ways, this book is a response to the dark stuff.

I hope you'll forgive me, then, if these acknowledgments go beyond the scope of this book. I might be breaking the rules here, but I couldn't have written *The Watcher in the Wall* without the people I'm about to thank.

Thanks to my family, first and foremost: my parents, Ethan Laukkanen and Ruth Sellers, and my two brothers, Andrew and Terry, and their partners, Phil Connell and Laura Mustard. You guys are my bedrock.

Thanks to my own partner, Shannon Kyla O'Brien, who supports me even when I don't deserve it, and who inspires me to be better.

I'm grateful to Raymond McConville for his empathy, and his humor.

Thanks to my friends, near and far, who celebrate my books more than if they'd written them themselves, and whose enduring generosity and kindness carries me through the worst of times, and sweetens the very best.

ACKNOWLEDGMENTS

My agent, Stacia Decker, is more than a business partner, at this point; she's a good friend, and I thank my lucky stars that I have her on my side.

As my career has progressed, I've only become more grateful to have found a home with my wonderful editor, Neil Nyren, and the fantastic team at Putnam. Ivan Held, Katie Grinch, Alexis Welby-Cassidy, Alexis Sattler, Sara Minnich, and Ashley Hewlett are all publishing rock stars, and the very best in the business.

I'd also like to give a shout-out to my copy editors, especially the very talented Rob Sternitzky, for their wit, wisdom, and above all, their patience. The copyediting department is truly the home of publishing's unsung heroes. Thanks to you all.

Finally, to the Madison Mackenzies, Dylan Prices, and Adrian Millers out there: Please, don't suffer in silence. This stuff gets easier when you talk about it, whether to a friend, a family member, a counselor, or someone on the other end of a hotline. There's no shame in speaking up, and I promise, you're not alone.

Heck, talk to *me* if you want. My contact info's on the back cover flap. I usually stay up late.

Just, you know, talk to somebody. We're in this together.